The Prince's Poisoned Vow

INFERNAL WAR SAGA I

HAILEY TURNER

Cover design by James T. Egan, www.bookflydesign.com
Map by Daniels Maps: www.danielsmaps.com

Professional Beta Reading by Leslie Copeland of LesCourt Author Services.
Developmental editing by Mackenzie Walton.
Edited by One Love Editing.
Proofing by Lori Parks: lp.nerdproblems@gmail.com
Proofing by M.A. Hinkle at LesCourt Author Services

To my dad.

You showed me the night sky as a child and always said dream big.

Six are the fallen, tempered into light
Grave is the wasteland riddled with blight
Breath is the poison with its roots in your bones
Never bury your memories in iron-sided tombs

Tithe for the borders to ward against the dead
Remember, remember, all the horrors that we fled
Send your prayers to the stars burning in the sky
We call this world a miracle, so build your walls up high

~ Constellation hymn from a Star Order prayer book

MARICOL

Northern Tundra

UROVA
MATRISKAV

DAIJAL
Haighmoor
Istal
NEW HAVEN

ASHION

Amari

Cosian

E'RIDIA
Sunrise Valley
GLENCOE

Eastern Basin

Foxborough

Celestine Lake

Northern Plains

GULF OF HELIA

Helia

Bellingham

Southern Plains

Karnak

CALHAMES

Seaville

CONSTELLATION SEA

TOVAN ISLES
PORT AVI

Oeiras

SOLARIA

Rixham

The Wastelands

Inferno

⁓

916 A.O.P.

One

BLAINE

Lord Blaine Westergard was ten years old when he carried the living heart of Ashion out of its capital city.

He didn't know it at the time, because the less people knew of such things, the better.

Warning sirens rang through Amari's air, the capital city awake when it should be sleeping, but it was difficult to sleep when smoke choked the streets. The sound of a scuffle past the pile of refuse Blaine knelt behind grew louder, and he chanced a look over the rancid mess that provided little in the way of cover.

The two men grappling with each other in the alleyway blocked the only way out, their movements quick and brutal. What light reached them from the gas lamps on the street was barely enough for Blaine to see his father's face. Mal Westergard, Duke of Westergard and captain of the Royal Guard, wasn't in uniform, while the other man was, and Blaine was too young to understand what betrayal meant.

Something skidded over the ground and came to a stop near Blaine. His father's pistol, with its brass gears painted military black, was within reach. He snatched it up with one hand, the pistol almost heavier than the infant he carried close to his chest.

As the son of a duke whose duty was defined by service, Blaine had been around weapons all his life. He knew how to chamber a bullet into the barrel of a pistol or load a rifle, listening as the gears clicked and locked into place for firing. He knew how to aim at a practice target or an animal while on the hunt and pull the trigger.

He did not learn how to kill a man until that night.

Blaine laid the swaddled infant on the dirty ground behind a broken crate, tucked safely out of sight, before facing where his father fought one of his own men in a losing battle. Blaine breathed in like his mother had taught him, gaze steady even as his heart beat wildly against his ribs, waiting to take the shot.

The soldier knocked his father against the alley wall, the glint of light on sharp metal all the prompting Blaine needed to pull the trigger with a hard press of his finger. He wasn't braced correctly, and the recoil almost toppled him over. Regaining his balance, Blaine stared wide-eyed at the body sprawled at his father's feet.

"Blaine," his father said hoarsely, limping toward him.

"Father," Blaine replied, his hands shaking, voice cracking with shock.

Mal gently pried the pistol from his hands, and Blaine screwed up his face, trying not to cry. Then his father pulled him into a tight hug, one big hand smoothing over the back of Blaine's head. "Hush, now. You're all right."

His father hugged him for a second longer before gently pushing him away. As much as he wanted the comfort, Blaine knew they still weren't safe. They hadn't been safe since fleeing the palace, a place he wouldn't have been if he hadn't stowed away in his father's motor carriage when Mal had been summoned by the queen's steward.

And if he hadn't done that, he would surely be dead.

"Where is she?" Mal asked.

Blaine sniffed hard before retrieving the baby, picking her up off the ground. She hadn't cried when the pistol went off, the drop of sleeping draught administered by the star priest enough to keep her under before they'd been put into a motor carriage. His father had abandoned the vehicle by Hollows Bridge on the western side of the

Serpentine River, the singular waterway that cut the capital in two. Blaine wondered if maybe they should've stayed in the vehicle after all.

"Hold her close for me. We're almost there," Mal said.

"Where are we going?" Blaine asked for what felt like the dozenth time that night.

His father didn't answer, merely steered him around the man Blaine had killed, his footsteps uneven. Warm fingers touched Blaine's jaw, keeping his face averted, and he tried not to think about what he left behind in that alleyway.

They weren't the only ones on the cobblestone street when they emerged, curiosity and fear driving people out of their beds. Despite the gunshot, they weren't looked at askance, because a limping man dressed in neat, dark clothing with two children in tow was less interesting than the ugly shine of fire that glowed against the sky.

Two turns later found them hurrying along the Western Promenade that followed the length of the Serpentine River. The crowd of people in their nightclothes was growing along the riverside, every face turned east and the horror unfolding there.

A deadly, bright orange glow haloed the night sky above where Amari's civic and royal centers were located. Windblown smoke made Blaine's eyes water, stinging his nose. When he glanced in the direction it came from, he saw several small, two-person ornithopters skimming low over burning buildings. The aeronauts aimed hoses attached to water tanks at the fire below in a desperate attempt to contain it.

The fire crews must have been called up, but Blaine hadn't seen any of their larger trucks with the water tanks pass them by. The only thing out in force, it seemed, were the peacekeepers who had followed them from the palace.

"This way!" a voice cried out.

His father's hand tightened on Blaine's thin shoulder, urging him on. "Hurry, Blaine."

He didn't know why the peacekeepers were after them when his father outranked them all as captain of the Royal Guard, a position that reported to the queen herself. The Westergard bloodline might not be royalty, but they *were* nobility and had dedicated generations to the preservation of the throne. It had been their singular duty ever since the civil war that had split Ashion in two, and an armistice kept the border in place.

Blaine was too numb to realize that fleeing through the dark like criminals while the city burned was how his bloodline kept their oath.

Pistols going off set the small crowd of observers shrieking and running away in a panic. Someone screamed in pain, and Blaine looked back, seeing the peacekeepers a block behind them and gaining through the panicking crowd.

"Don't look back," his father said, steering him around a corner with a steady hand.

The building that loomed before them was a grand thing at six stories tall, with a curved metal roof and a multitude of arched windows lining its walls. Situated alongside the waterfront, the airship hangar was one of a select group allowed within the city's borders.

Blaine knew where all the hangars designated for private and diplomatic use were in Amari, having been fascinated with airships since he was a small child after being gifted a windup toy of one by the queen herself. His governess used to take him on motor carriage rides to each location when he was younger, imparting history lessons with every trip. Which was how Blaine knew this hangar belonged to the E'ridian embassy and that the people inside had no obligation to allow them entry.

"Open up!" his father cried, pounding his fist against the smaller side door.

Blaine huddled close, staring back the way they'd come, knowing it wouldn't take but seconds more for the peacekeepers to arrive. Then the click of a lock being undone reached his ears, and the door opened.

Blaine let out a soft gasp when he saw the pistol held level with his father's face. The E'ridian's dark eyes never looked away. "Who calls?"

"I'm here by order of the North Star," Mal said, one hand gripping Blaine's shoulder tightly. "Please, there isn't much time."

"We were told to expect only you."

"I couldn't leave my son behind."

The pistol tilted up, and the safety was clicked back on. The E'ridian gestured for them to enter the hangar. The steel-lined brass door was yanked shut behind them and locked with a heavy dead bolt.

Footsteps pounded past the hangar's entrance moments later, muffled shouts reaching his ears. Blaine didn't realize he was holding his breath until he had to draw in air, lest he choke. He stared at the E'ridian who had saved them, the man dressed in the flight leathers and fur-lined jacket of a people who preferred the sky to the land, poisoned or otherwise, that everyone else walked on.

Dark eyes flicked from one to the other before coming to rest on the baby Blaine carried. "This way."

The hangar was half-lit and empty of people on the ground. They were led to the airship anchored to its dry dock by heavy ropes. The airship was on the small side, painted so dark a blue as to be almost black, with no other identifying marks on its hull. Its balloon was proportionate to the airship's size, the make of the entire thing having all the hallmarks of E'ridian engineers, for they were the most skilled when it came to the mechanics of flying.

The airship was mostly enclosed save for a small section of the deck at the prow, which was open to the elements. A pair of E'ridians stood at the railing, looking down at them. Blaine blinked, and when he opened his eyes again, they'd been joined by a woman whose tanned face and braided black hair were drawn on the pages of scripture.

"You there," the star god said.

Blaine knew his constellations, and he knew his prayers. He knew the Dusk Star watched over E'ridia the same way the North Star watched over Ashion. Nilsine was the goddess of the wind, carrying her blessing on the breeze to give her children flight. She was at once benevolent and wrathful, both the calm before the storm and the apex of it. She was a star fallen from the sky, but Blaine was too numb to make a wish.

As with all stories of the star gods, hers was an abstract tale Blaine had learned at the star temple during the Fourteen Month calendar's main holidays, his parents never one to attend the weekly congregations. For a boy of ten, raised in a cosmopolitan city where the Inventor's Guild held more clout than the Star Order, fun was had in science, not prayer.

Blaine didn't know it yet, but he'd learn how to pray anew after that night.

Someone tossed a rope ladder over the railing, its knotted ends hitting the floor with a soft thump. The star god descended with sure hands, jumping the last few feet to solid ground.

As she turned to look at them, Blaine noticed her leather trousers were open along both sides at her hips and thighs, closing nearer to her knees. The purposefully parted seams showed off the gold lines and starbursts of the Eagle constellation tattoo on her right thigh, one of six designs found on every Star Order prayer book Blaine had ever opened.

"You're late," Nilsine said.

Mal's voice cracked a little when he spoke, bowing deeply. "The queen is dead, my lady. We were pursued."

The star god tilted her head, gaze settling on Blaine and the baby that slept in his arms. "Her death changes nothing."

"It *should.*"

"Aaralyn told Ophelia what to expect if she raised import taxes on Daijal again and barred their debt slaves from her lands. Your queen sought to cripple that country and ended up crippling her own. You children never learn from your past mistakes."

"It is the children I think of now."

"As do I." The star god stepped toward Blaine, and he felt very much like a beetle about to be crushed under someone's heel just then. "Give her to me."

Blaine's father extended an arm between them, hand clenched into a fist. "This child is the only surviving Rourke. She is my duty."

"She is your failure, like the rest of her bloodline. Princess Eimarille lives, though not as Rourke for much longer, despite the name she carries. The prince survives but is to be grieved for as dead. No other mortal outside these walls knows about this child, so tell me, how can she be Rourke?"

Blaine's father bowed his head, eyes squeezed shut, before lowering his arm and stepping aside. As she passed him, the star god touched his shoulder with one gloved hand, the same way star priests did when they gave benedictions in festival crowds.

"Daijal's Blades were sent to all the cadet bloodlines back a dozen generations. You could not stand against them all, much less the ones who set upon the throne. You weren't meant to," she said quietly.

"I could have tried," Mal said.

"You would have died. You still might." Nilsine pulled her hand away, light glinting off the mirrored lenses of her goggles as she turned her head from him, gaze alighting on Blaine. "News of the queen's death will reach every country by way of telegraph wires before morning. The blood kin of Ashion royals no longer live, no matter what the rulers of Daijal or the Twilight Star will claim."

Nilsine reached for the baby Blaine carried, but he jerked away from her seeking hands.

"Father, this isn't right," Blaine said desperately. "We're Westergards. We're supposed to *protect* her."

Mal went to him, kneeling with a pained grimace, wavering there for a moment. He placed his hands on Blaine's shoulders and turned him around so they faced each other. "We *are* Westergards, and this is how we protect her. By letting the star gods guide her travels."

Nilsine hummed thoughtfully. "Yes, you are Westergards, are you not?"

His father's shoulders stiffened as he turned his head to stare at her. "My lady?"

"The babe is not Rourke. Her name was never written down in the royal genealogies. Has your son been with you since you fled the palace?"

"Yes."

"Then I will take him as witness."

The hands on his shoulders tightened to the point of pain, but Blaine bit back a whimper that tried to escape. He stared wide-eyed at the star god, not realizing what she meant until his father smoothed back his hair and pressed a firm kiss to his forehead with trembling lips.

"Guard her well, Blaine," Mal said in a ragged voice. He pulled the signet ring from his right index finger, tucking it into Blaine's front pocket for safekeeping. Blaine opened his mouth to protest, because his father *never* removed that ring, but Mal shook his head. "It would've been yours when you came of age."

Blaine blinked wetly, trying to steady his breathing. "Father."

Mal smiled, a cracked, ragged thing that didn't comfort Blaine at all. Then he stood and gently pushed Blaine toward the star god, who smiled in a way that made him flinch. He tightened his arms around the baby he carried, but this time, when Nilsine reached for the infant, he let the star god have her.

"Come, child. We must go," Nilsine said.

Blaine was ushered to the rope ladder, and the E'ridian standing beside it held it steady as he reached for the first rung. He climbed up slowly, losing his footing every now and then as he tried not to look down. One of the E'ridians on the deck extended a hand toward him when he was almost at the railing.

"It's all right," the woman said in the trade tongue that crossed all six countries of Maricol.

Blaine was hauled on board with a firm grip, going to his knees on the decking. He was urged to his feet and tucked out of the way against the railing. He peered over the edge, watching as the star god deftly climbed the rope ladder while carrying the baby.

"The peacekeepers will double back and attempt to breach the hangar once they see us launch. They've been demanding entry everywhere since the fire started. I will open the roof and stay behind to ensure your escape," the E'ridian on the ground said.

"Your sacrifice will be written in the stars," Nilsine replied before swinging herself over the railing.

Blaine stared at where his father stood on the ground, looking back with as much love as grief on his face. "Father?"

"Remember this night, my son. Remember it for those of us who are gone," Mal called out.

What happened next would come to Blaine in flashes when he was older: the sound of clockwork mechanisms grinding together as the roof cranked open; the rumble of the airship's engine as it prepared for flight; the shouts from peacekeepers looking for a way in and finding it with the help of a magician's clarion crystal–tipped wand.

The way Blaine's father looked when he died beneath a hail of bullets as the airship cut loose its anchor and rose into the smoky night sky.

Blaine didn't realize he was screaming until a hand clamped over his mouth and drew him back from the railing. Bullets peppered the air around them, pinging off the thin metal plating that shielded the belly of the airship's balloon. He was dragged through a narrow doorway into the flight deck as they cleared the hangar for the sky.

"Hush," Nilsine said as she knelt before him. She cradled the baby in one arm and raised her other hand to his eye level. Starfire shimmered at her fingertips, drawn from the aether, the same shade as the Eagle constellation tattoo branded into her skin. "This is your road now."

Everything went soft and hazy, his vision going dark at the edges. A calm swept through him, foreign and cold, tucking the panic away. The wind howled outside the flight deck door while the creeping cold of altitude bit past his thin clothing.

When Nilsine removed her hand, Blaine kept the star god's secret of a surviving bloodline behind closed white teeth.

13

Two

CALLISTO

The spyglass with its double lenses was cool against the bridge of Callisto's nose. Her keen eyes tracked an object through the night sky from her spot on top of a submersible, water from the Serpentine River lapping at the cold metal.

"Nilsine is heading east," Callisto said.

Farren's voice drifted up through the open hatch. "I can't see a bloody thing. Not that I care to, with the way the city is burning. Come on, woman. Get below already. We've a schedule to keep if you want to make it to the Warden's Island in time. The train won't wait for us if we dock late."

Callisto tucked the spyglass into the leather case attached to her belt, buttoning the flap. "I am reminded, almost hourly, of how much I detest traveling with you."

"You just hate going by water. Makes you seasick. That's all right, love. I've a bucket with your name on it if you would just *get below.*"

Callisto lifted one hand to her throat, fingers settling over the golden lines and starbursts of the Lion constellation inked into her black skin. It sat like an intricate shawl around her neck, drifting down over her collarbones. She swallowed, feeling the pressure against her fingers.

Even after thousands of years, some fears had yet to die with time. Her wariness of large bodies of water would always be an unwelcome companion of sorts. It had little to do with how poisonous the seas were and more about the vastness of the space between stars they'd come from.

"If we were to travel by land, you'd be in my same predicament," Callisto said.

"Land sickness is best handled with a good whiskey, but the earth has never bothered me as much as the waves bother you."

"You can keep them."

"Gladly. Now, I will push to dive, don't think I won't."

Her brethren's impatience was as fickle as the sea they were the dual god and goddess of. Farren had never cared for the limitations of land when there were oceans to sail, carried across waves by Tovanian ship-cities. But here in Ashion, they were as landlocked as they could be, despite the submersible smuggled out of Urova.

Callisto climbed down the hatch, taking one last moment to look at the fire still raging through Amari's streets. The glow looked almost like dawn, false light staining the horizon. It wouldn't be the first time the capital burned, but it *was* the first time they'd deliberately struck the match in this Age of Progress.

Callisto pulled the hatch shut behind her, twisting the metal wheel until it clicked and locked into place. With the submersible sealed, she descended the short ladder to the cramped quarters below.

Farren twisted in the captain's seat, long black hair falling loose down their back, hiding the Leviathan constellation tattoo that covered tanned skin stretched across spine and ribs. They blinked almond-shaped eyes at her, arching one eyebrow. "Done sightseeing?"

Callisto kept her gaze focused on their face and not on the highly filtered water flowing beyond the large glass panes of the front viewport. Traveling by water was never her ideal choice, but needs must during this difficult time.

"Get us moving."

Farren jerked their head in the direction of the tight space behind their seat. "Good luck getting that one to sleep."

15

They faced forward, feet pressing down on pedals and hands settling over the levers used for steering. The submersible jerked a little as the propellers churned in earnest, pushing the submersible below the surface and chugging forward through the Serpentine River. A single gas lamp jutted from the metal nose, their only light down here in the depths of the river.

Callisto knelt in the small space behind Farren's seat, staring at the five-year-old boy she had smuggled out of Amari on Aaralyn's orders. He looked back at her with gray eyes that held far too much fear in their depths beneath a thatch of unruly light brown hair. His night-clothes were stained from soot and smoke, and his feet were bare.

"I want my mama," the prince whimpered.

Callisto settled into a cross-legged position before him, propping her chin on her palm. Her fingers tapped out a rhythm against the edge of her jaw, slow and precise. "Your mother is dead."

He was old enough to know that meant his mother wasn't coming for him but not yet old enough to understand why or comprehend what he had borne witness to at the palace. He still cried for her through his lingering shock, great heaving sobs that turned his small face red and blotchy.

Farren gave a derisive snort. "Oh, nicely done. I'm pleased to see your way with children hasn't changed a bit since last century."

"You are here for transport purposes, not conversation. Close your mouth and steer."

"Be grateful I'm here at all. I could be hunting leviathans in the Gulf of Helia, not skimming over river bottom." Farren heaved out a sigh. "The things I do for you and Aaralyn."

Callisto ignored them, her eyes on the boy before her. She didn't understand his pain, had long since considered that not to be a problem. When one lived as long as she had, emotions were useless things.

Sighing, she lifted her left hand, calling forth the aether, the shine of it reflecting in his wet eyes. She extended her arm and pressed a fingertip to his forehead, letting the aether sink into his being, magic twining around his mind and soul.

"Close your eyes, and I will take your dreams."

Her words were honey-sweet, carrying with them a fog that shrouded his young mind. Like called to like, and she could feel the coiled burn of starfire in his soul. The aether lived in him, a thing all magicians, no matter their calling, learned to master. The connection to that otherworldly place filled with magic was more a knowing, a sensing, than parlor tricks in some spice lounge in Daijal.

She dragged her metaphysical touch through the shape of him, thinking about how easy it would be to remake him on her own, but that was not what she was here for. The soul wasn't something one mucked around with arbitrarily, and so the application of her magic was precise because it needed to be. You could change a person if you weren't careful. Destroy them, even, or end up owning them how Daijal owned debt slaves through banks.

Slavery was such a distasteful habit. That entire, deeply entrenched mess grown out of debt bondage was the reason Callisto and Farren were skulking through the river under cover of darkness, burying children.

Callisto used the aether to coax the prince's tired mind into sleep, fogging his memories. She pulled him into her arms, the boy dead-weight, and stared down at his face. She gently rubbed a smudge of soot off the underside of his small chin.

"Something tells me the prince will remember where he came from even if I try to make him forget," she murmured.

"He's young enough. He will succumb," Farren replied quietly.

"He is Rourke. They don't know how."

She slid a hand over the boy's chest, the skin of her palm catching on the soft fabric of his nightclothes. She could feel his heart beating with a steady rhythm that would be soothing in any place but this.

The voice of the Eclipse Star came to her, soft in the quiet but weighted like the anchors that held Tovanian ship-cities in place against storms. "It was either him or his sister. You had to choose."

"It wasn't a choice. Eimarille was already gone."

Farren shifted the steering levers with careful hands, the change in the engine vibrating through the decking. "Don't blame yourself for this mess."

"I don't. I never do. Believe that." Callisto held the prince tighter, bending her head to whisper into his ear with voice and aether alike. "Alasandair Rourke is dead. Let Soren rise in his place."

The Dawn Star built a wall around the prince's soul, one that would crumble over time but keep the starfire that burned there hidden until he could learn to live as someone else. Starfire was the mark of royalty in nearly every country on Maricol, and the Rourke bloodline had to be stricken from the genealogies if they were to survive.

In the morning, the broadsheets in all six countries would say Prince Alasandair Rourke died in the fire that razed nearly half of Amari.

He didn't.

He died in the river.

Three

PORTIA

Baroness Portia Dhemlan and her husband, Baron Emmitt Dhemlan, were the first of their bloodline to be written into the nobility genealogies. They'd been merchants and inventors before being granted their title and were still of that mindset, to the consternation of what passed for high society in the eastern provinces of Ashion.

It was their newness that spared them dying at the hands of the Blades, which ravaged the cadet branches of the royal family on the night of the Inferno.

Some days, Portia wished her husband hadn't accepted the title. Neither cared for politics. They much preferred making clarion crystals sing. But successful patents on water filtration inventions had ennobled them, and like any mother, Portia only wanted the best for her newborn daughter.

"At least you will live, my darling," Portia murmured as she stared at the sleeping infant in the crib. The nursery was lit only by the candle in her hand, the clock on the wall ticking toward the midnight hour.

At barely two days old, her daughter's naming ceremony in the star temple had been postponed once Portia had read the broadsheet that morning. Cosian was a small city nestled in the dry Eastern

Basin, far from the politicking of Ashion's royal court in Amari. But bloodlines crisscrossed the continent the same way railroads did, and everything was connected. Some families who once called Cosian home now danced amongst the stars, their bodies wrapped in funeral shrouds at the crematorium.

The coup upon Ashion orchestrated by Daijal was not the first one attempted between either country, but it was the only successful one since the civil war. The attempts at reunification between the two countries over the decades always ended in bloodshed, but never so devastating as this. The shock hadn't quite settled into the populace, but the horror of what had happened screamed forth from broadsheet headlines like sightings of revenants on cleansed land.

"Is she yet nameless?"

The unexpected voice of a stranger had Portia whirling around with a gasping cry, the candle shaking in her hand. She stared wide-eyed at the woman standing in her daughter's nursery, trying to find her voice for a scream and discovering it missing. She clutched her throat with frantic fingers, capable of breathing but not speaking.

"None of that, if you please. Let us not wake your household," the woman said.

"Too late. Let my wife go, magician," Emmitt said harshly.

Portia watched as her husband slipped through the connecting door that led from the nursery to their bedroom. The pistol in his hand glinted dully in the candlelight, the weapon pointed unerringly at the intruder.

The woman laughed softly, uncrossing one arm, and it was only then that Portia realized she cradled something against her chest. "I'm no magician, so save your bullets. They will not harm me, and I am not here to harm you."

"So you say."

Portia never left her daughter's side, so Emmitt came to stand by her, refusing to lower his pistol. The woman stepped closer, and Portia's gaze was drawn to the faint shimmer on her right thigh, candlelight reflecting on a golden constellation tattoo.

She gaped at the bright gold lines and starbursts visible through the open seam, the color of the Eagle constellation tattoo impossible to duplicate with modern ink. When Portia tried to speak again, she found her voice had returned to her.

"My lady," Portia said weakly.

The star god smiled at them, dark hair pushed back from her face by the brass goggles she wore. Portia took in her appearance, noticing the particular flight uniform favored by E'ridians. She was missing the fur-lined leather flight coat, which Portia distantly thought was a poor choice. Fourth Month on the calendar meant the season was just barely breaking free of winter.

Emmitt's hand holding the pistol remained steady, but Portia could feel her husband go stiff beside her. Carefully, telegraphing every move, Portia lifted her left hand and settled it on top of the pistol, pushing it down so the barrel aimed at the floor and not the star god gracing them with her presence. She set the candle down on the nearby dresser to free her other hand.

Emmitt drew in a sharp breath before clicking the safety back on, though he didn't relinquish his weapon. "My lady."

The Dusk Star smiled at them, but it never quite reached her eyes. "Have you heard the news?"

Portia tightened her fingers on Emmitt's wrist. "The queen and all her kin are dead."

"The named ones are."

It was only then that Portia realized the star god carried a baby in her arms, the infant swaddled tightly in a fur-lined blanket. The baby's face was tiny, hints of dark hair fluffed about the crown of their head. The baby was as new to this world as Portia's own daughter.

It was that thought that made her cover her mouth to hold in her cry.

Emmitt glanced worriedly at her. "Darling?"

Portia bit her lip, the taste of bile in the back of her throat an acidic burn. "Please, no."

"You pray to the stars, do you not?" Nilsine asked.

Portia swallowed thickly. "Always."

"Then trust in my guidance."

Portia felt rooted to the floor as the star god approached the crib to stare down at her daughter. One gloved hand reached out to stroke a finger down her daughter's cheek. Portia had the sudden urge to snatch her up and run.

"The queen's last wish was to name her daughter Caris," Nilsine said.

Portia mouthed the name silently, the syllables nothing like the ones she had expected to say for years and years to come.

They watched as the star god took their child from her crib and laid down the queen's nameless one in her place. Portia kept her eyes on the daughter she'd borne, her heart cracking the way clockwork gears broke under extreme pressure. Portia reached for her, but the star god took a single step back, the candlelight reflecting brightly in those ancient eyes.

"That's our daughter," Emmitt said hoarsely.

"Your daughter sleeps in her crib," Nilsine said, drawing no attention to the baby she now cradled in her arms.

"Can't we keep both?" Portia begged. "We would love them each as our own."

Nilsine's lips curved at the corners, the shadows on her face stretching deeper across her skin. "You have but one daughter, and you will raise her as such. It is decreed by the stars."

Portia covered her mouth once again, the nursery blurring through her tears. "*Please*. Let me say goodbye."

"There is no goodbye to be said here, for you have lost nothing."

Nilsine raised one arm to touch her thumb to each of their foreheads. The benediction coursed through Portia's mind, wrapping itself around her bones with a heat that burned like molten gold, like the tears she shed.

"You will not speak of this night to anyone," Nilsine said, voice echoing in Portia's ears like the storm sirens which pierced the air when the sky turned green and the winds howled ferociously.

Portia would never have betrayed a star god's divine decree, but the freedom to agree to it was taken from her. The way the nursery looked, her daughter's face in the candlelight, and the flicker of starfire was locked away in the back of Portia's mind, the edges of the memory already fading.

The memory was locked away, but the clarity of it wasn't hers to hold on to over the years. In the wake of that midnight visit, with a world-breaking secret sleeping quietly where her daughter once lay, Portia grieved through the smiles she offered well-wishers at the star temple days later.

And when the star priest asked for her daughter's name to record in Cosian's nobility genealogy, Portia's tongue shaped the sound of it with a hitch in her throat. "Caris Dhemlan."

It wasn't the name they had chosen, but it was the one they gave her.

In the end, Portia could do nothing but love her, as any mother would.

Four

EIMARILLE

"Would you care for some tea?"

Princess Eimarille Rourke ignored the question from the Daijalan ambassador and never looked away from the window of the private train carriage they traveled in, small gloved hands clasped tightly in her lap. The tips of her stained satin slippers barely touched the plush rug lining the floor.

The vast prairie fields of the Northern Plains stretched beyond the tracks they rode along as they headed west. The train had yet to make a stop, but Eimarille had overheard her captors discussing doing so that morning over a breakfast she hadn't partaken in. Apparently they were due to pick up passengers in Istal, and soon, if the way the Daijalan guards were becoming more active at the other end of the train carriage was anything to go by.

"My dear, you must eat something."

For all the ambassador's formidable rhetoric, he would never be able to convince a princess to do what he wanted. Eimarille was nothing if not stubborn when the need arose, and she had no reason to give in to people her mother had told her never to trust.

Thinking of her mother brought tears to her eyes, and she sniffled delicately, wishing for privacy. She hadn't been alone save the few minutes she was allowed to use the privy, and all the attention from the men around her made her uncomfortable.

"Give me a moment with her," another voice said. Eimarille clenched her hands tighter together at the sound of it, ten years too young to understand what she felt for him was hatred in that moment.

She watched the Daijalan ambassador's reflection in the glass, a ghostly shape that disappeared. The soft rustle of expensive clothes reached her ears as the man who had taken her from the palace sat across from her. The narrow table between them was set with delicate porcelain plates filled with all sorts of treats she had no desire to try. She knew it would taste like ash in her mouth, the way everything had since the fire.

"This is not how I thought we would meet, but you Rourkes have always been stubborn," the man said.

Eimarille turned her head to look at him. At some point during their travel west, he had changed out of the black clothing he'd worn in the palace when he'd stolen her from all that she knew.

Now, he was dressed in gray trousers, a pressed white button-down shirt, and a deep blue waistcoat that matched his eyes. He wore no hat but carried a slim black cane in his ungloved hands. A thin gold chain was hooked to his waistcoat, the end of it disappearing into a pocket.

"How should we have met?" Eimarille asked in as prim a voice as she could muster.

"It does not matter now." The man pulled a kerchief from his waistcoat pocket and offered it to her across the table with a coaxing smile. "You look like you need this."

"I want nothing from you."

"Everyone always wants something from me, my dear, but I give blessings how I see fit." He waved the kerchief at her, eyes never leaving her face. "Take it. I insist."

She didn't know what compelled her to take the kerchief, but Eimarille found herself reaching for the soft white square of fabric.

She used it to dab carefully at her eyes before crumpling it into a ball on her lap. "Who are you?"

He smiled, a faint quirk of his lips, but it never reached his eyes. "I've gone by many names over the years, but your generation would know me as Innes."

Eimarille's eyes widened fractionally, her gaze dropping briefly to the high collar of his shirt. "The Twilight Star?"

Innes leaned his cane against the wainscoting beneath the window. "Would you like proof?"

She hesitated only a moment before nodding. Innes undid the cravat around his throat, then the buttons on his waistcoat, and finally the top two of his shirt. The fabric was pulled aside, revealing the Viper constellation tattoo that stretched over the top of one pectoral, the glint of gold like the shine of starfire her mother used to command—like Eimarille was just beginning to master before everything exploded like an experiment gone wrong.

Innes pulled a slim device from his pocket and pressed a button on it. A blade snapped out, razor-sharp and thin. He pressed the edge to his skin and drew it down over the tattoo. What spilled out from the rapidly healing cut wasn't red like her own blood, but a molten gold liquid. No mortal would ever carry poison in their veins how the star gods did.

"My lord," Eimarille said faintly, half rising from her seat.

She might only be ten, but Eimarille had been drilled in etiquette since she knew how to walk. The Rourke bloodline bowed to no one but the star gods, and she wouldn't do her family's memory a disservice if she could help it.

Innes held up a hand to stop her. "Sit, child. There is no need for that."

Eimarille retook her seat slowly, chewing on the delicate skin on the inside of her bottom lip, a habit that turned her lips white. Her mother always told her it was a terrible facial tell, something she needed to stop doing. Except the queen was dead, and Eimarille still chewed on her lip, with no one to admonish her otherwise.

She thought she should feel something, anything other than the numbness that came with every breath she took, but she didn't. Innes might have struck the killing blow that took her mother's life, but she would still pray to the stars. It was the way of life on Maricol, habit turned into culture, and the star gods knew the roads everyone must walk. Perhaps this was meant to be, after all, if a fallen star was seated across from her.

Innes did up his clothes, the star god looking all too human to her eyes, despite the starfire she knew ran through his veins. Scripture was clear the six were blessed by the aether, that its magic manifested itself in their living forms. What burned inside her resonated in a way she was still too young to fully control, but she knew the truth of him, as all Rourkes did.

Innes pushed a plate of scones and honey butter closer to her. "Eat, my dear. I'm sure you have questions, but one must be well-nourished to hear the answers."

Eimarille obeyed him how she would never obey the Daijalan ambassador. She picked up the scone and broke off a piece, carefully dabbing some honey butter on it before popping it in her mouth. Innes nodded, pleased, so Eimarille ate another bite.

"Tell me, child. Are you good at keeping secrets?"

Eimarille raised her chin. "Of course."

Matters of state were to be spoken about only within the family or with their closest advisors, her mother always said. Eimarille had been groomed to rule since she was born. She'd been taking her mother's teaching to heart since she was old enough to understand what it meant to be a princess and an heir.

"Then you and I will keep one between us."

Eimarille glanced surreptitiously over her shoulder at the Daijalans at the other end of the train carriage. "Just us?"

"Look at me, my dear."

She faced forward again, setting down the butter knife, the taste of honey sweet on her tongue, washing away the hideousness of ash.

Innes didn't blink, his gaze never leaving hers. When he smiled, his teeth were unstained by whiskey, smoke, or spice. "There is magic in you, and it burns so very bright. You were made for so much more than a single country, Eimarille. I will watch you make history of a future I shall build across the continent, and you will be glorious."

For a moment, it felt as if she wasn't in her body but floating outside it. All that existed was Innes and the starfire that burned in them both, the mark of gods and royalty alike.

When Eimarille came back to herself, she discovered the train was idling on the tracks, the curtains drawn over all the windows. Innes still sat across from her, but the table had been cleared of food. The bustling sound of a crowd reached her ears, and she twitched aside the curtain just enough to peer out and see they were finally at a station.

The fashion of the people waiting on the platform was distinctly Daijalan, the jewel tones capable of standing out against the vast forest she knew covered the western half of the continent. Her attention drifted from the richly dressed citizens to the debt slaves that trailed after their masters, bank numbers tattooed in stark black ink on their necks. The clothes they wore were drab and functional as they tended to luggage and small children, gazes never drifting far from the ground.

Eimarille's stomach clenched at the sight, knowing it was her mother's attempt to keep debt bondage out of Ashion that had brought her here. She might be young, but she still knew it was wrong.

"Just the one?" a deep voice asked from the train carriage entrance, catching her attention.

"I only need the one," Innes replied.

Eimarille let the curtain go and straightened up, watching with wide eyes as a tall, broad-shouldered man dressed in dusty leathers with a gunslinger's belt around his waist approached their table. The Bear constellation tattoos inked across the back of the Midnight Star's hands were familiar from scripture books, even if his face behind the thick beard was not.

Behind the star god followed a girl who couldn't be more than a year or two older than Eimarille. She was thin, the features of her face lending themselves more to Urovan heritage than Daijalan or Ashionen. Her thick black hair was braided back in a single plait, and the gown she wore was functional for travel. The bottom of her skirt was embroidered with the six constellations of the star gods, while her shawl was pinned in place by a brooch only Star Order initiates were given.

"I hope you know what you're doing, brother," Xaxis said.

Innes smiled thinly. "Don't I always?"

Eimarille folded her hands together in her lap as she stared at the star gods. Xaxis studied her in silence for a long moment before finally turning toward the girl who had followed him onto the train. He placed a hand on her shoulder and pushed her forward.

"One Blade, as requested. She is no magician, and still requires continued training, but she will do."

"I asked for a Daijalan."

The smile Xaxis gave Innes made Eimarille want to shrink in her seat, but she didn't. "I will play this game with you only so far. If you wanted one of yours, then you should've done the job yourself."

Innes stood, and Eimarille watched him loom over the other girl, whose expression never changed as she dropped into a deep curtsy.

"My lord," the girl murmured, gaze downcast out of respect, not fear.

Innes touched her chin with two fingers, tilting her head up. He studied her, much how he had studied Eimarille, and in the end, he nodded a sharp approval.

"She'll do." He looked over at Eimarille, smiling slightly. "All good queens need a confidant when they make history."

Less a confidant and more a spy, Eimarille knew, as she watched the Urovan girl take a seat at the table. Her mother had always taught her to be wary of the friendship coveted by others. Very few wanted nothing in return for proximity to the throne. As her mother's heir, she had always been a target for two-faced children pushed into her orbit by power-seeking adults.

"Where do you go from here?" Xaxis asked.

Innes drew the pocket watch from his waistcoat, checking the time. "New Haven. King Bernard is expecting us."

"Aaralyn will never allow the girl to take the Ashion throne if you hand her over to Daijalans."

"A Rourke has always ruled our country, and one shall rule again, even if it takes a decade or two. Those in Ashion will want a queen to fill the absence that comes in the wake of a cleansing. I will give them and the rest of the world one of my own making."

Xaxis crossed his arms over his chest, the sleeves riding up a little, enough that Eimarille could see the lines of his tattoos crawling up his forearms. "I take it your assassins were thorough?"

Innes approached the table and reached for Eimarille, smoothing back her hair in a mockery of the way her own father used to comfort her in private. "Do you question my decisions?"

"I question your madness, brother. But we are all a little mad these days."

Xaxis turned and exited the train. Innes went to have a long conversation with the Daijalan ambassador. Left to themselves, the two girls kept quiet company together.

"What is your name?" Eimarille finally asked.

"Terilyn, my lady," the girl said, blinking dark eyes at her. "I am at your service."

Eimarille repeated the name softly, knowing that whatever waited for her at the end of the line, she wouldn't be alone. The Twilight Star had decreed it so, and despite the ache in her chest for the family he had destroyed, she was her mother's child. She would play this game of politics. She would become whatever she needed to be to survive.

Five

HONOVI

Glencoe was the thriving capital of E'ridia, nestled in the Sunrise Valley between the coastal hills and the jagged teeth of the Eastern Spine mountain range. Smaller towns were scattered throughout the range to support the mining operations, accessible only by airship and guarded by magicians year-round.

No one climbed the mountains on foot unless they were desperate. The Sunrise Valley was hard-fought for cleansed lands, and the native beasts who called the higher elevations home all had poisonous teeth. For all that the wardens had cleansed much of the continent for habitability purposes over the centuries, they'd left most of the mountains alone.

The airfield surrounding Glencoe was close to half the size of the city. Sectioned off by clan and commerce needs, the dry docks used for construction of new builds were separate from the ones inside hangars used to anchor active airships. The wooden piers stretching across the valley floor outside the city walls were lit by carefully tended gas lamps whose light only reached so far in the dark.

Honovi, *jarl* to Clan Storm, lengthened his stride to match his father's, his latest growth spurt at fifteen making it easier to keep up. He ducked his head against the cold night wind and shifted the shroud in his arms to a better position so the edges didn't drag. The linen was rough against his callused hands. Honovi wondered why his father had requested such an item from the clan's crematorium.

The moon above was half-hidden by the remnants of a storm that had petered out before sunset, the clouds drifting west. Fourth Month meant the Wolf constellation was rising in the sky, bringing with it the green of spring, and his eyes easily found the shape of it.

Like all E'ridians, Honovi learned to navigate by the stars from a young age. Trade was important, and the only safe way over the Eastern Spine was by airship. Night flying was a skill he'd only been learning for the last two years, but he knew enough that the airship landing tonight was captained by a skilled pilot.

He'd been curious about their identity ever since his father received the telegram during dinner. It wasn't every day someone was secretly greeted by the entirety of the *Comhairle nan Cinnidhean*, the ruling body that consisted of every *ceann-cinnidh* of E'ridia. The near dozen men and women who made up the apex of the country's government walked in silence behind Honovi. Every *ceann-cinnidh* and their *jarls* had arranged themselves in order of clan seniority, with Clan Storm at the front.

"Who lands tonight?" Honovi asked quietly, glancing at his father.

Alrickson, *ceann-cinnidh* of Clan Storm, never broke stride. "You'll see."

Honovi glanced over his shoulder to share a look with Frey, *jarl* to Clan Sun, who wrinkled her nose at him in silent aggravation. One hand curled around the end of her waist-length braid, a self-soothing gesture she'd yet to break as she learned the needs of her clan while standing in her father's shadow.

Frey had just turned fourteen and successfully completed her first solo captaincy. The twin braids all E'ridian children wore their hair in had been ritually braided into a single plait threaded through with beaded ribbons when she'd reached that milestone. It was the same ranking style Honovi wore, though he'd shaved the sides of his head, leaving the top untouched, as was tradition for the ruling bloodline of his clan.

The hulking shapes of airships inside their hangars on either side of the pier caused the air to smell of metal. The refineries at the outskirts of the city were idle and would not fire up until dawn. Repairs happened year-round, though new builds of airships of any size typically happened after the snow melted.

The pier they walked down led to a section of the airfield used to anchor foreign airships. Whoever was landing tonight wasn't E'ridian, or so Honovi thought. When he saw the dark-hulled airship of E'ridian make anchored in the dry dock, its keel hovering above the ground, he reassessed the situation at hand, as any good aeronaut would.

The group slowed to a stop, silently arranging themselves down the length of the pier to face the airship. Clan Storm was the oldest clan written down in E'ridia's royalty genealogies. As such, Honovi and his father stood in the center.

Honovi didn't see any ground crew present. He watched curiously as the gangplank was cranked out to connect to the pier, the scrape of metal on wood sounding loud in the night air.

The woman who appeared at the railing was of average height, but there was nothing average about the way his father and the other *cinn-chinnidh* knelt to her. Honovi hastily followed his father's lead, going to one knee as he watched the woman disembark. Gold glinted along her right thigh in the lamplight, and Honovi's eyes widened at the sight.

The Dusk Star was eerily beautiful in the dark, their goddess of the wind the one every clan prayed to as their guiding star. Nilsine planted one hand on her hip, the other curled over the hilt of the pistol she carried as she gazed at her children.

"Call for the shipbreakers in the morning. The dead you will deal with tonight, for there were spores on the storm wind," Nilsine said.

Honovi shivered at that warning, knowing the risk of revenants if the dead weren't burned to ash. No wonder his father had asked him to fetch the shroud before this meeting. For all that the wardens worked to keep the lands free of poison and revenants, the walking dead could not be completely eradicated. It was why every city and town, no matter the country, built their walls high against the blight.

Nilsine's gaze drifted from person to person before settling on Honovi's father. She stepped closer and placed her hand on his head, mindful of the gold metalwork woven into his braided hair as a symbol of his rank.

"Your clan will care for the boy on the airship. He is E'ridian now until I or my brethren say otherwise."

Honovi's curiosity piqued at that statement, but he knew better than to question a star god's order. Then the Dusk Star disappeared into the night, as if she had never set foot to ground in the first place. Honovi's father rose with a quiet sigh and headed up the gangplank with a sure-footedness that came from a lifetime spent boarding airships. Honovi was right behind him, gripping the shroud tightly, swallowing in shock at the sight that greeted them on the small forward deck.

The clan members had all died where they kneeled, hands free, a single bullet hole neatly placed in the center of their foreheads. Blood haloed their skulls, the shine of it black on the decking in the lamplight. But it was the smiles on their faces that would stay with Honovi, as if they had been thankful to die.

"Wrap them in prayers for the funeral rites," Alrickson said to his fellow *cinn-chinnidh*.

Every clan had a representative lying dead on the deck. The *jarls* and *cinn-chinnidh* separated to do their duty to the dead. Honovi worked alone while his father searched the airship for the boy Nilsine had given to their clan.

He was halfway done wrapping Clan Storm's dead, prayers falling from his lips, when his father came from belowdecks. Honovi watched him lean over the open hatch and extend his hand, gruff voice tempered with kindness.

"Up you go," Alrickson said in the trade tongue.

He pulled a blond-haired boy the rest of the way onto the deck, and Honovi paused in his shroud-wrapping. The boy was shorthaired and not dressed for a flight, wearing clothes that wouldn't be out of place in an Ashion city.

Alrickson waved at Honovi to approach, so he left the dead behind for his father and the boy who looked at them with haunted hazel eyes.

"This is Blaine. He is of our clan now. I want you to take him to your mother. Tell her tomorrow we will find a foster family for the lad," Alrickson said.

Honovi nodded. "Yes, Father."

"I will be home when I finish with the dead. Off you go now."

Honovi silently took Blaine's hand in his and led him to the gangplank. He took the way down slowly, keeping one eye on Blaine, who traversed the distance on shaky legs. When they reached the pier, Honovi shrugged off his leather jacket and placed it over Blaine's shoulders, cognizant of the chill in the boy's fingers. The cold night air bit at his skin, but he'd warm up enough on the walk home.

Honovi urged the boy forward. "Let's go."

Blaine stumbled into a walk, blinking rapidly. "They let her kill them."

Honovi glanced back at the airship, which would be torn apart for scraps beginning at dawn, the dead it had carried home set to burn in the crematoriums dedicated to every clan.

"It is always an honor to die for the star gods."

Blaine sniffed, lips trembling. He said nothing more, and Honovi let the silence settle between them as he led Blaine back to the city they both now called home.

Six

CALLISTO

Callisto remembered when the Poison Accords were signed, how fractious the world had been millennia ago. She supposed things hadn't changed much through three Ages. Countries had split yet again, betrayal ran rampant through the bloodlines, and revenants still roamed the land, necessitating the need for wardens and their alchemy.

For all that the borders had expanded mile by precious mile over the centuries, the natural state of Maricol didn't lend itself to human life. Living on the planet would always remain a fight, and every country paid its tithes in citizens sent to the island in the middle of the Celestine Lake to be made into wardens. To fight the dead in the poison fields required a resistance to such toxins, and tradition demanded a neutral party for that task.

Wardens had remade this world since the stars fell and would continue to do so in spite of the political games played by those who governed. Wardens, unlike everyone else Callisto and her brethren watched over, understood the real threat was Maricol itself, and there was no throne or council or senate in any country that could stand on poisoned land.

"Steady now," Farren said as they steered the skiff across the Celestine Lake's choppy waters. "Winter runoff will have tainted the lake water, so watch the boy. Make sure he doesn't breathe in the mist."

The low sound of the engine hummed in Callisto's ears as she checked to make sure the seal on the gas mask Soren wore was secured. It was sized for a child, a fit easy enough to come by the farther east they went. The scattered towns in Ashion's Eastern Basin and Solaria's northern hill country had laws about field gear requirements for their citizens. If one wanted to live in the borderlands, one needed to be prepared for what nature would throw at them.

The Eastern Spine was too vast to cleanse, so wardens had focused on other parts of the continent through every generation recorded in the genealogies, records that had weeded out the poison in people's families over time. The poison in the mountain soil always seeped into the water, drifted on the mist and wind, and rained like acid during the short-lived monsoon season that hit the region west of its peaks. The borders drawn by cartographers were clean and precise on maps, resembling nothing of the pockmarked reality of miles of constantly repoisoned land.

The Celestine Lake would always have high levels of alkaloids, no matter how many filters and purification machines were built into its shores. These days, such machines were looked at through a business lens rather than a survivalist one. Profit was more important to the owners of companies that retained the patents than the people who worked for them.

Competition amongst merchants meant putting up lives as collateral if one didn't have money for a new venture upfront. Debt slaves were how Daijal had become rich in the aftermath of the civil war between it and Ashion. Bartering lives was how banks did business these days, even in Ashion. Urova had long since thrown its lot in with Daijal, and if Ashion wanted clarion crystals mined from the northernmost country for its aether-powered machines that were overtaking steam-driven ones, then debt bondage–tainted trade with Daijal was unavoidable.

Queen Ophelia Rourke had sought to change that status quo. She'd lost her life and set her country to ruin because of her ideals. The power vacuum left behind would have to be filled, and soon. Callisto hoped Aaralyn realized that.

The Warden's Island loomed up from the fog sometime later. The fort which housed wardens, tithes, and the laboratories that altered lives was dimly lit along the walls.

The televox Callisto had stolen at a military-held way station on the train ride southeast chimed in her hand, the clarion crystal shard embedded in its steel casing pulsing softly. Televoxes were relatively new devices, portable, and capable of connecting people across great distances, but they were expensive to make and maintain. The general population of any country didn't have access to them, and the merchant class clamored for them like no other, but it was the military and nobility who had a stranglehold on the production.

Callisto thumbed the televox open, bringing it up to eye level so she could speak into it. "We're docking soon."

"I see you," a clipped, deep voice replied. "Anchor at the main pier."

Callisto closed the televox and tucked it into her pocket before looking over her shoulder at where Farren sat. "Did you hear?"

"It won't be a problem," Farren said.

Callisto couldn't see her brethren's eyes behind the heavy goggles they wore. Farren had been steering with the gas lamps cold, navigating the lake by way of spelled goggles capable of seeing in the dark, the sort favored by Tovanians when sailing Maricol's oceans and seas during storms. A lake with wind-driven waves was child's play in that regard.

Callisto picked out the shape of a shadowy figure holding a lantern at the end of an otherwise empty pier as they drew close. Tithes usually came during summer, when travel was easier and the waters were cleaner, which meant no boats were docked to impede their approach. Farren guided the skiff right against the pier with an ease that would make most sailors not of the Tovan Isles envious.

The Warden's Island's governor tossed them a thick rope to tie the boat to the pier. Callisto caught it and wrapped it around the metal cleat. The click of gears had Callisto eyeing the automaton that waddled up behind the governor. A small rapid-fire, multibarrel Zip gun was perched atop a boxy body held up by spiderlike mechanical legs. The sound of its tiny steam engine hummed through the air, giving life to its limbs.

"Expecting trouble, Governor?" Callisto asked.

The man shrugged and offered her his hand. "Revenants swim, my lady. We are always on guard."

Callisto was helped onto dry land, glad to be off the water. Farren lifted Soren from the bench and handed him to Callisto, who set the boy on the pier. The gas mask stayed in place as he looked up at her.

"Let's get inside."

Farren remained on the skiff. "I'll wait for you here."

Callisto took Soren's hand in hers and headed to the fort. The governor followed after them, the click of the automaton's clockwork gears loud in the air. He set it to guard the pier at the shoreline, Zip gun at the ready should Farren have need of it.

"Is anyone awake?" Callisto asked.

The governor shook his head. "No."

"Good. No one must know of my visit."

It was well past the midnight hour when they made their way into the fort. The governor guided them to his office, the lantern their only light save the occasional softly burning gas lamp on the wall. Once inside, he set the lantern on his desk before turning to face her.

He was an older warden, hair gone gray at the temples, with a scar cutting deep over his left jaw. It pulled at his mouth, making the line of his lips crooked. He was tanned, despite the months of winter they were shaking off, the natural darkness hinting at a Solarian ancestry he could never claim.

Wardens were nameless and stateless. The Poison Accords had seen to that. When tithed, who they were before coming to the island was stricken from the genealogies. Wardens were bound to the land, not to a country or its people. They used alchemy to cleanse the poison fields, fight revenants, and push the borders ever outward to keep everyone alive, regardless of politics. Wardens were supposed to be neutral, which meant they never took in those who could cast starfire.

Neutrality wasn't to be found in heads of state. Callisto knew she was breaking that long-held creed tonight, but she had no choice.

She gently removed the gas mask Soren wore, letting it dangle from one hand as she brushed the fingers of her other through his hair. He looked at her with dull gray eyes, the spark of who he'd been snuffed out by the walls she'd built to keep him alive and safe.

"I've brought you a tithe from Ashion for the poison fields. You will name him Soren," Callisto said, pushing the boy toward the governor.

Soren ducked his head, shoulders rising toward his ears. He didn't speak, and neither Callisto nor the governor offered him the comfort he so obviously yearned for.

"We'll make of him a warden for Maricol," the governor said, the ancient words ones she'd heard countless times.

It would involve years of brutal training to ensure his survival, years of building resistance to poison through the application of toxins. He would be changed by way of alchemy into someone who could walk the poison fields and face revenants without dying, but the making of a warden had never been kind, and not all tithes survived the process.

Neither did all wardens survive encounters with star gods. The governor was dead within the week of a heart attack, his body burned on a pyre and a new warden voted in to take his place. The secret he'd shared with Callisto was kept in his death.

Soren was but the first of many tithes that trickled in that year from Ashion, most of them children orphaned by the Inferno and sent as that country's payment per the Poison Accords.

And as was the way with all tithes, Callisto knew Soren would learn to forget where he came from.

Seven

MELERI

What remained of the city of Amari was draped in black ribbon, grief an almost tangible thing. From the gas lamps to the surviving buildings, to silken threads tied around the arms of every single person still loyal to the throne, it was impossible to escape.

Meleri Auclair, Duchess of Auclair, watched with dry eyes as what remained of the House of Lords argued amongst themselves in the old parliament building—turned into a museum long ago and now hastily reverted to the job of government—on the western side of the Serpentine River. The space was too small for how large the country had grown over the centuries, but the current parliament building had burned the same way the palace had during the Inferno.

The old chamber was cramped and smelled vaguely of smoke, as did most of Amari. The country's flag, that of a black wolf's head in side profile surrounded by red fire flowers on a white background, with the Wolf constellation picked out in gold thread at each corner, hung behind the empty Lord Speaker's seat. Other heraldic flags bearing bloodlines' coats of arms hung from the walls and ceiling. Meleri eyed them, cataloguing the ones that belonged to bloodlines who would have no new names added to any genealogies from here on out.

Despite the crowd of representatives below, Meleri knew there were more than a dozen empty seats to contend with, lost to Blades. She clenched her lace-gloved hand into a fist over the skirt of her gown, not for the first time bitterly glad no one in the Auclair bloodline had the ability to draw from the aether and cast magic. Theirs was a bloodline that had always chased after power of a different sort. It seemed that focus had saved them from eradication.

Too many bloodlines had come to an end on the night of the Inferno. Broadsheets were still reporting the names of families recorded as ended now. The one connecting thread amongst the dead, blatantly recorded over the decades, was the distant ties to the throne those families once had.

Genealogies served to keep a record of bloodlines, many of which had survived the poison of Maricol since the Age of Starfall. Meleri's was one of those, but they had long since lost the touch of starfire that had burned so brightly in the Rourke bloodline. As with the Wester- gard bloodline, the Auclair bloodline served the throne, even if Meleri knew they had failed in this, their most sacred duty.

She shifted on the hard wooden seat, the stiffness of her corset easily ignored beneath her blouse. Meleri prided herself on knowing the political makeup of parliament—who could be trusted, who could not, and who could be blackmailed with the right rumor—but the Inferno had changed everything. Whatever rose from the ashes, Meleri would have her work cut out for her when figuring out where the ruling class stood.

A pity she would have no queen to report her findings to.

Meleri came from a family of spymasters, heading up the Clock- work Brigade. Her network of cogs—from the lowest of scullery maids to the most gifted of inventors—passed along a sea of informa- tion that was distilled into warnings and threats for the throne to take action against. She should have *known* this attack upon her country was in the works. She should have known Daijal would not tolerate damage to their country's wealth, built on the backs of debt slaves as it was.

She had not, and that guilt would eat away at her bones like the fire in a crematorium for years to come.

"War will not bring back the Rourke bloodline," her husband argued from below, his voice rising over the others. "Daijal is most likely prepared to answer with the full force of their army at even a hint of troop buildup along our western border. We are not in a position to win that fight."

"They have broken the armistice. If that is not an act of war worthy of such a battle, then what is, Lord Auclair?" a woman snapped.

Meleri's gaze skimmed the crowd before settling on her husband. Julien had removed his top hat, holding it and his cane in one hand as he gestured with his other, the blond of his hair almost white beneath the light of gas lamps. The Auclair bloodline ran through Meleri, but like many spymasters before her, she had allowed her partner to take up the family's seat in the House of Lords while focusing on the intelligence that landed on her desk.

Politics was an omni-sided fight, and one person could not handle it all. She had delegated tasks at the beginning of their marriage twenty years ago when she was newly nineteen. It allowed Julien to learn the political ropes of parliament through her father while she remained by her mother's side. When her parents inevitably stepped down, she and Julien had taken over, partners in everything they did.

Except something had changed in the last year. He no longer touched her as he once had, and they slept in separate beds. He was polite in the way of a stranger, even to their children, and all attempts to reconcile had been for naught. At first, Meleri had suspected an affair, but no evidence was procured by her cogs.

The knowledge that he had, perhaps, simply fallen out of love with her was a grief of its own, nestled in her chest where her heart had once beaten. Perhaps if she had not been so focused on her own bloodline and more focused on the one sitting on the throne, none of this mess would have happened.

But what was burned was ash, and there was nothing she could do.

Nothing but bear witness.

The telegram she had received that morning, sent in code, was folded in her silk purse, as heavy as lead. The words would be meaningless if intercepted, but the news they carried had left her cold.

Princess Eimarille Rourke had survived the Inferno and been seen in the Daijal court.

The Iverson bloodline had been Rourke once, long ago. They'd broken off during the civil war and taken half the country with them at the time, the separation shielded by an armistice. Meleri's own bloodline had been severed, with distant relations in Daijal leaving the Auclair name behind in favor of Khaur. For all the years between then and now, the familial connection could still be found in the genealogies and the Clockwork Brigade.

Meleri knew King Bernard would claim kinship with Eimarille, distant as it was, and the law would see it as such in both countries. Eimarille, Meleri knew, was Bernard's way to the Ashion throne.

But if he thought reunification under Daijal rule would be easy to claim, his spies whom she knew were present for this gathering would disabuse him of that notion within hours.

"My lords and ladies of parliament," a woman's voice rang out in the air, cutting through the many arguments happening below. "Do you not trust the road I and my brethren guide you down?"

Meleri's breath caught in her throat as the crowd parted like water for the star god who walked amongst them toward the Lord Speaker's seat. The North Star's auburn hair fell down her back in thick curls, the blouse she wore sleeveless and overlaid with a fitted leather waistcoat. The style allowed the golden Wolf constellation tattoo covering her entire right arm to be seen by all and sundry.

Meleri rose to her feet, shock never something to keep her still, attention locked on her country's guiding star.

Aaralyn climbed the few steps to the dais, turning to look out across the crowd, exuding such a presence that it weighed heavily on Meleri's shoulders. The judgment in her gaze was searing, and everyone present went to their knees in fearful supplication. Meleri did not bow her head, peering instead through the wooden slats of the balcony's railing at the tableau below.

"Treachery burned the blood from the genealogies, as it burned our city. Those responsible are traitors to the throne, and my light shall never shine upon them," Aaralyn said.

No one spoke, the air vibrating with power so thick the dust motes danced in the dull spring sunlight shining through the high windows.

"If it was fire Daijal wanted, then it is fire they shall get. I have bled for our country, and the fire of my blood will not be put out so easily. The Ashion throne shall burn with starfire until one of true Rourke blood sits upon it once more. All others who try will become nothing more than ash."

Meleri could pick apart the twists in the decree better than most. She pressed her hand over her silk purse, listening to the soft crinkle of paper inside. She blinked and found herself pinned in place by the fierce attention of the North Star. Meleri could not look away, breath stuttering in her lungs.

"This is the decree of the star gods."

Hours later, after the House of Lords and the House of Commons had trekked across Hollows Bridge to the ruins of the royal grounds and borne witness to the burning starfire throne, Meleri found herself in her bloodline's surviving riverside estate. She took tea alone in her private office, absent of mortal company.

Aaralyn matched her sip for sip.

"Caris lives," the North Star said.

Meleri's teacup clattered heavily to its matching delicate plate. "Pardon?"

The star god, dressed now as a merchant's wife in a long-sleeved brocade gown that hid her tattoo, hair done up in a widow's twist and tangled with black ribbons, sipped at her tea. "Her name was never written into the royal genealogies."

Meleri swallowed dryly, trying to steady her breathing, thinking about the unborn child everyone had thought lost with their queen in the fire. "Who else knows?"

"A Westergard."

Meleri's sources had informed her the morning after the Inferno that the Westergard bloodline had been ended with bullets and poisoned knives. "I see."

Aaralyn set her teacup aside, staring at Meleri with hazel eyes that held nothing human in them. Meleri could not meet her gaze for long and didn't try to.

"Do you know why I am here?" Aaralyn asked.

"It is not my place to question the will of the star gods, my lady."

Aaralyn smiled, and it made her look like a dead thing. Like a revenant. "Of course not."

She picked up the telegram that lay on Meleri's desk between them, reading the innocuous message there. Starfire flickered around her fingers, burning the paper to ash that drifted down to the dark wood.

"Bernard seeks reunification on his terms. He has prayed for it repeatedly. I suppose he thought I wouldn't hear his prayers, as they were not directed to me, but I hear every whisper that falls from every mouth."

"That doesn't mean you are obligated to answer them for our sake," Meleri replied carefully, knowing how capricious the star gods could be.

"I answer the ones that have merit. I play favorites when it suits me."

"Is *that* why you are here?"

"A road has many paths. I am here to guide you down yours." Aaralyn stood and walked over to study the intricate metal and clockwork artwork that hung over the credenza. "Bernard seeks the throne through Eimarille. Parliament must stand firm against his interference."

Meleri winced, thinking of all the different factions and feuds that drove political discourse. "That will be a difficult task if we cannot put another bloodline on the throne. If it is left empty, then reunification is an argument that will not go away. Daijal will seek control, and they will gain it."

The burgeoning political give and take of who was best to rule in the wake of the Rourke bloodline's supposed eradication had been only momentarily defeated by Aaralyn's decree and the knowledge of Eimarille's whereabouts. Meleri knew the fight would continue in quieter spaces, for power abhorred a vacuum.

Aaralyn turned, hazel eyes burning gold in her face. "Oh, my child. That is what a revolution is for."

Meleri stared at the star god, hands gone cold and clammy. Aaralyn came back around the desk to stand beside her chair. Warm fingers touched her jaw, turning Meleri's head to face her.

"My lady?" Meleri whispered.

"You will put a Rourke on the throne. That is your road now."

Meleri could see the pitfalls in that private, personal decree, like a bad path that led straight to the bogs in the poison fields.

Aaralyn's fingers drifted up her cheek to press against her forehead, heat sliding through Meleri's skin, warming her from the inside out.

"I will always hear your prayers," Aaralyn said before leaving.

Meleri was well acquainted with how prayers could be answered. She'd seen the ruins of it mere hours ago.

It was no wonder, then, that it would be years before Meleri saw her guiding star again, years before she prayed.

Eight

VANYA

Blood feuds were the way of life for the Houses of Solaria. Loyalty was a commodity like anything else in the empire, easily bought and just as easily sold.

The Imperial throne was a prize all Houses coveted, and the House of Sa'Liandel had sat upon that apex of power for two centuries. Their continued rule had brought prosperity to the country against the backdrop of bloody politics at times. But as with any rising star in the night sky, there must come a fall.

Vanya Sa'Liandel of the House of Sa'Liandel had faced over a dozen assassination attempts by the time he turned eight and stood with his mother beyond the walls of Rixham, Solaria's most southern city. He would face more going forward now that he was his mother's heir.

This should not have been his road. Iosiv had been the Imperial crown prince for thirteen years before a poisoned blade finally found its mark. Assassins beholden to the House of Laxsom had succeeded where few others had over the decades.

The loss was still an ache Vanya carried, for he had loved his older brother. He remembered the way Iosiv's face had looked—still and cold and painted white in death—before the shroud was wrapped around his body by the star priests.

His mother had been as dry-eyed then as she was now, staring at a dying city, Rixham a grave of its ruling House's own making. The House of Laxsom had paid for his brother's life and the misuse of revenants against the living in a desperate attempt to secede with the eradication of their entire House. The city they called home, and all those who resided inside its walls, were collateral.

Empress Zakariya Sa'Liandel was nothing if not thorough, a trait that had enabled her House to remain on the Imperial throne for so long. A trait Vanya, even at the age of eight, knew he would have to adhere to if he ever wanted to rule as his mother did.

He shifted on the sparse brittle grass, the sun beating down on his thin shoulders. A light breeze tugged at the hem of his white robe, the fabric twisting around his thighs and the loose trousers he wore. A gold medallion hung from his neck on a thin, flat chain, the metal warm. Stamped on its face was his House's crest, the profile of a roaring lion.

Iosiv had worn the ranking medallion for as long as Vanya could remember. It was Vanya's now, and the symbol of his new rank felt heavy around his throat.

Movement down the line of legionnaires standing at their back had Vanya peering curiously around his mother. He watched as a tall woman walked toward them, her outfit close-fitting, made up of dark fabric and leather. No Solarian would wear such clothes in desert heat, but she appeared unbothered.

Hanging off both her hips were brass-lined pistols, of a different make than the ones issued to the Legion. The minute gears around the triggers matched the design in the hilt of the blade that jutted over one shoulder, a clarion crystal embedded in the pommel.

"Warden," his mother said coolly, never looking away from the smoke rising above Rixham.

"Your Imperial Majesty," the warden said, coming to a stop several feet away.

She rested her hands on her thick leather belt, close to her pistols.

Vanya noticed how nearby legionnaires belonging to the *praetoria* never took their eyes off her. The wariness on the faces of the men and women who guarded the Imperial throne and the House that controlled it made him curious about the warden.

"Your aid will not be needed here today."

"I find I must disagree. You've walled off an entire city and riddled it with spores."

"Have I?" his mother asked archly, the tone Vanya recognized right before she went in for the political kill.

The warden's lips pressed together in a hard, pale line. "Do you wish the Wastelands and its revenants to reclaim this area so badly? The swamps are enough of a breeding ground."

Zakariya reached for him then, settling her fingers against the back of his head in a gentle touch. "Rixham is a dead city. There is nothing living in Rixham."

The warden looked out at the ruin his mother had perpetuated and sighed. "We'll change the maps."

When they left the southern border of the empire a day later, the screams coming from Rixham lingered in Vanya's ears on the long train ride north back to Calhames.

News spread of the ruin his mother had enacted. Of course it did. There was no hiding a city of the dead, after all. She'd meant it as a warning to the other Houses who might think to attempt secession, and it landed the way the blade had in Iosiv's heart—deep and cutting. When the Senate next convened, there were no representatives from the House of Laxsom on the floor and never would be again.

The blood feud, such as it was, had been ended with extreme prejudice.

The Daijal ambassador appeared unconcerned with the backdrop of shifting power amongst the Houses as he stood before the Imperial throne. Vanya sat where Iosiv once had, the seat smaller than the Imperial throne, watching sweat slide down the ambassador's face. The finery he wore was too thick of a fabric for southern heat, but appearances were everything in the Imperial court, even for outsiders.

"There has been upheaval in the north," the aide assigned to him by his mother whispered into Vanya's ear as he watched the proceedings with keen eyes.

He tilted his head how he had seen Iosiv do many times before and said nothing. It wasn't his place to speak, not when his mother commanded everyone's attention.

"My king requests you acknowledge his claim to the Ashion throne," the ambassador said.

"I've heard the Ashion throne burns with starfire by the will of the North Star," Zakariya said.

The ambassador's smile became tacked on. "It is a meaningless decree."

"Is it? You need a Rourke."

"We have one."

"That does not mean you have the Ashion throne. Solaria will not align itself with a puppet or its master. Our border will remain open for trade, but your politics are not ours."

The ambassador inclined his head. "Of course, Your Imperial Majesty. Daijal will remember your stance."

That did not mean Daijal would abide by it. Countries were like Houses, but on a larger scale, as Vanya would come to learn. And as with Houses, loyalty could be bought, and it could be sold.

It would be many years before Vanya discovered the cracks in his House's hold on the Imperial throne. But when he did, the deepest ones could be traced back to Rixham, where revenants clawed at the city walls, waiting to leave the grave his mother had put them in.

Nine

AARALYN

Helia was a Daijalan coastal city, carved into the white seaside cliffs facing west. A playground for the rich, it was a place where decadence was preferred, and the risks of attempting to climb the social ladder could be found in the bank numbers tattooed on the necks of debt slaves.

The railroads leading to Helia came from all over. Its port was as thriving as the capital city of the Tovan Isles, located far out in the Gulf of Helia. Tovanian ships came and went in all seasons, watched over by the Daijal navy, who could never hope to keep up with the other country's ship-cities.

The lower tiers of the cliffside city catered to the poor and working-class, a place where the riffraff weren't looked at twice and a gunslinger hailing from across the eastern border was ignored save for what their coin could buy. A person could find a drink just as easily as they could find a body in their search for a good time. For all its decadent notoriety, Helia was one of Aaralyn's favorite places to relax.

Prayers tasted as good as the alcohol on her tongue where she sat drinking whiskey at a corner booth, the brim of her leather cap pulled low over her face. Her hard eyes and expression said she wasn't there for any sort of company save the barmaid who kept refilling her glass with every auron handed to her.

Innes slid into the bench across from her anyway. He rested his elbows on the table and leaned forward, giving Aaralyn an icy smile over the cracked wood that had seen the points of far too many knives.

"I thought you were tired of playing the melodramatic god. Wasn't it Farren's turn to take on that ridiculous role this century?" Innes asked.

Aaralyn finished her whiskey with one long swallow, eyeing Innes over the rim of the chipped glass. After a moment, she licked her lips and set the now empty glass aside. "How long has it been since we last met? Five decades? Six? You're still as arrogant as ever."

Innes shrugged and stretched out one leg beneath the table, knocking his boot against hers. "I learned from the best."

"And I have regretted immensely that you were such a good student."

Innes' smile tempered itself into something that was almost human. "I love you, too, my darling wife."

"Husband." Aaralyn offered her own smile, just a small twist of her lips, but it was the secrets in her eyes that she knew always stoked Innes' anger. Her next question only served to sharpen his temper. "How fares the Daijal court?"

She knew all about his actions and his sins, the dirt on his boots that came from the forests of Daijal and the ashes he'd carried with him from the damage done in Ashion. They had the grit of the world ground into their skin like the poison in their veins that wouldn't let them die.

"Eimarille is mine," Innes said after a moment, the noise of the pub intruding between them.

"I let you take her out of Amari. Of course she is yours."

They'd birthed that bloodline long ago, in the space between stars, and had equal claim to the children that came after. They'd shared so much and lost so much and become so much more than the memory of what they once were.

But despite all that, she would always love him, in some way.

Aaralyn leaned across the table, reaching out to curl her fingers around the silk cravat he wore. Innes followed the pull of her hand willingly, let her press her mouth against his. Like all the times before, he was familiar to her.

"Did you think I was not prepared to play this game of yours?" Aaralyn whispered against his lips, tongue snaking out to trace the edges of his teeth.

"Our children hunger after progress. They have a right to it."

"And they are enslaved when they cannot pay the cost of dreams." She pulled back far enough to look him in the eye. "If you go down this road, there will be war."

Innes pressed his thumb to her full bottom lip; she could feel the crescent moon marks his fingernails cut into her jaw. "Aaralyn, love of my never-ending life. What makes you think there isn't war already?"

Innes pried her fingers off him with a gentle hand, and she let him. He pressed a kiss to the back of her knuckles before rising to his feet. They stared at each other through a space that echoed with history before he turned his back on her and walked away.

Aaralyn watched Innes go but did not follow after him.

The North Star never had.

Roads

❧

931 A.O.P.

One

SOREN

Soren kicked dirt over the smoldering embers of the pyre he'd been monitoring for the last few hours. Revenants took forever to burn, and he couldn't move on until the dead were ashes, but stars, he was hungry. He hated eating around burning bodies.

"Damned bogs," Soren muttered, squinting at the murky pool of water that had filled a fissure in the land some ways past the pyre.

He'd thought the *vasilyet* ruled over by the House of Kimathi in the northwest of Solaria had been cleared of bogs the other year, but apparently not. Either the maps were wrong—which he doubted, because no warden worth their pistols or blades would falsify the borders—or, if this couldn't be attributed to a spring thunderstorm, parts of the water table had breached the surface within the last year.

Either way, it was a headache. Fens and bogs, found in the plains that stretched halfway across the continent, were spore incubators. Soren wasn't equipped to drain one alone, and he clicked his tongue against his teeth in frustration.

He'd been assigned a western border this year, one that should've been easy enough to map. Like any warden, he traveled with only what could fit on his velocycle. Filtration and purification machines were too large and bulky to haul around the Southern Plains alone.

Which meant he had nothing to fix the problem spread out before him.

Soren wiped sweat off his brow, getting back to the business of burying the pyre. He didn't fancy trying to outride a grass-fed wild-fire. That was a death sentence, and even that sort of heat wouldn't burn off bog water. Once he finished covering the embers and stomping down the dirt, Soren retreated to his velocycle.

He preferred the streamlined frame of his velocycle, with its heavy-tread wheels, compact engine, and durability, over a motor carriage or truck. Considering the terrain he needed to reach in his travels, it was easier to ride a velocycle. His was made with dark metal, with none of the chrome and ridiculous accessories found on city vehicles owned by members of high society.

Soren dug through the storage compartment located behind the second seat, set above the back wheel, until he came up with the map book and a pen. Soren settled on the ground and uncapped the pen with his teeth, flipping through pages until he located the section he needed.

He was a two-day ride from Bellingham, closer to that border city than Solaria's capital. The field markers he'd passed matched up with what was on the map well enough as he pinpointed his position, muttering under his breath as he did the calculations in his head. He tapped a finger against the gridded paper and hummed thoughtfully.

Ensuring cities were free of contamination and setting up a resupply station was one of the easier assignments a warden could get. Soren wouldn't know. Those kinds of assignments were given to older wardens who had earned something of a break after years mapping the borders. At twenty, Soren had a couple more decades, if he was lucky and survived, before he got a plum job like that. This was only his third year traveling the borders and poison fields alone, and the wardens' governor had sent him into Solaria each time.

Soren didn't mind the pollen that hung in the breeze blowing across the Southern Plains so much as he minded traveling through the heat in his field leathers. The plains were hot and muggy, even in Sixth Month at the height of spring, and sweat made his skin itch beneath his clothes. But comfort wasn't a part of a warden's life, so he made do.

Soren marked the spot on the map of cleansed land to indicate where the poison fields had returned. He'd have to send a telegram to the Warden's Island at the next town large enough to have a relay station to ensure there'd be enough time to send a team to drain the bog and cleanse the land. The winter snows never reached this far south, but summer storms did. If the bog overflowed, the poisoned water would spread, and they'd never hear the end of it from the Solarian Senate.

Soren used his finger to trace the black line that ran close to the spot he'd just marked for the poison fields. He raised his head and stared at the remains of the dead. Revenants were always drawn to the living, and while there weren't any way stations or villages nearby according to the map, there was a railroad.

He sighed tiredly. "I'll need to check that out."

The bog was out of the way, but not out of the way enough that debt slaves, probably fleeing Daijal, had found it and died there. The water was too poisonous to drink directly from the land like this without filters and purifiers, portable or otherwise, but people desperate for hydration wouldn't care. So they'd died, and the spores had taken over to send the revenants searching for the living.

If there were more than just the three revenants he'd killed and burned, if they made it to the railroads, that would be a problem. City walls could keep out the dead, but spores were contaminants no one wanted to unintentionally bring inside any abode, and those didn't need bodies if they hitched a ride on a steam train.

Soren stood and tucked the map book away before retrieving a small, cloth-lined and padded box from the compartment. Inside were glass vials that would hold the water and soil samples he needed from the area as undisputed proof of poisoned land. The level of toxicity would help guide the neutralization plans. He gathered his samples and labeled each one thoroughly before putting everything away and locking the compartment again.

After double-checking that the embers were contained and that he wouldn't accidentally start a wildfire during his third year as a full warden, Soren threw a leg over his velocycle and settled into the seat. He rolled his shoulders, adjusting the weight of the blade strapped to his back before reaching for his helmet. The thin metal plates were leather lined, and the strap that kept it in place fit snug beneath his chin.

The helmet, like his short sword, was standard-issued to wardens, along with his pistols and short-barreled rifle. Guns were good for distance, but one could run out of bullets, and close quarters needed something a little sharper to keep revenants at bay. He reached up and touched the pommel, gloved fingers tracing the beveled edge of the clarion crystal there, catching on the tiny lock on the side.

The central space inside the hilt was used to store different vials of poison, each one capable of being dispensed out of holes in the cross guards to coat the blade. The poison incapacitated revenants long enough to keep the dead from walking any farther than where they dropped. It was also a good weapon against any of the dangerous wild fauna that roamed the land.

Domesticated animals were carefully guarded, always tested for contamination, and were never allowed to graze unattended. Their wild counterparts were vicious and dangerous, and Soren had more than one scar from encountering them on his travels. Smaller animals tended to ignore humans for the most part.

Soren remembered when he was younger and had gone through the exposure needed to become mostly immune to the poison in the land that seeped into everything. Years of agony back then with alchemist intervention meant what would kill almost anyone else barely bothered him these days.

No one traveling the railroads would have that immunity, though, and revenants never cared about machines. He kicked the stand up and twisted the knob to start the engine. The grinding sound of pistons and gears startled some small animals that went darting away through the grass.

Soren pulled his goggles down over his eyes and pointed his front wheel west. The heavy tread of the velocycle's tires ate up ground as he rode toward the railroad tracks that were several miles away.

The whistling of the wind was a loud, familiar sound, the only company Soren kept when he traveled the poison lands to map the borders. Being a warden was lonely, dirty work, but it kept the world safe. It was an honor, every wardens' governor always said, to be tithed. Mostly, Soren thought it was a slow way to die, and maybe that was why he'd been taken to them all those years ago.

The memory was a distant thing in his mind, fifteen years buried, and the time before that was nothing of note in his head. It had to be.

As Soren approached the railroad tracks, he kept an eye on the surrounding area, searching for the distinct movement of revenants. He saw nothing but a thin plume of smoke licking at the sky in the south, the dark spot growing larger as it drew closer.

He veered south, riding parallel to the railroad tracks. He'd check the rails for a few miles after the train passed before looping back north. If he didn't see any hint of revenants, he'd move on, add it to his report. No use chasing a ghost that wasn't there.

Except there was nothing ghostlike about the dead.

Soren smelled the revenants before he saw them, the rancid sweetness on the breeze making his nose twitch. The train had lost momentum and had smoke pouring from its frame, not all of which came from the smokestack. Even from a distance, Soren could see flames licking at the smoke.

"Aw, hell."

If it derailed, he'd have to deal with the bodies. This close to the bog, he couldn't risk the dead rising to hunt across the Southern Plains for the living. Soren revved the velocycle into a higher gear, tires churning against the prairie dirt. He narrowed his eyes as he realized the shadows lining the edge of the slowing train weren't smoke but the revenants he'd smelled on the wind.

They moved with unnatural speed, spore-driven, mindless in every way save their desire to kill and spread what animated them. Soren hadn't seen any of the dangerous flowering death vines around the bog that would account for the number of revenants he could pick out, but maybe they hadn't come from *that* bog.

Someone hit the train's brakes, and the sound ripped through the air with a ferocity that set his teeth on edge. The pitch made the revenants shriek as they raced alongside the train, which wasn't going as fast as it could but still fast enough. Some got caught beneath the massive wheels, dragged under and torn to bits. Less for him to worry about, then.

Still a mess he'd have to clean up.

Soren lifted one hand off the steering handlebars of his velocycle and unholstered the pistol on his left hip. If he could lead the revenants away, then perhaps it would give whoever rode the train time to set up a defense, pull the steel shutters down to lock in place, and climb to the carriage roofs to fire on the dead. Train workers knew what to do during a revenant attack.

At least, they should have.

The explosion that sent the engine rising off the rails, flipping back end over front, was edged in the white-gold shine of starfire—the mark of royalty and star gods. Soren's eyes widened behind his goggles, something sharp hooking into his chest at that display of magic, behind his ribs, the memory a fleeting thing.

More explosions had him shifting the grip on his pistol so that he could squeeze the brake lever. The back wheel skidded out, dust rising all around him as he came to a hard stop. Ahead of him, the train carriage behind the engine jumped the track and dug a deep furrow in the dirt, sending a wave of dust and grass into the air.

The cascade effect pitched most of the train carriages behind it off the tracks in a tumble of broken metal. Several other carriages remained on the track as forward momentum was lost, but the train wasn't going anywhere after this.

Neither would any survivors if Soren didn't reach the revenants first.

Half the dead had been caught in the starfire and the crash, but those that didn't burn converged on the more intact train carriages. Revenants that had lost legs in the derailment dragged themselves over the ground, clawing their way to the living like moths to a flame.

Soren revved the velocycle's engine and drove toward the train wreck, taking a wide turn around the burning engine still going through mini explosions. He couldn't afford shrapnel in his tires or his own flesh, not with a horde to deal with. Driving past it, he saw the way the grass crackled and burned, and a chill settled in his skin, momentarily driving out the heat.

He did not particularly care to outrun a wildfire.

Soren steered the velocycle toward the rails and the damage there, putting a poison bullet into the head of a revenant that launched itself at him from the ground on stumps that passed for legs. The body shuddered and dropped, and Soren chambered another round.

Wardens were masters of alchemy and poisons. They'd built their immunity on generations of trial and error. What they'd found over the centuries for weaponry use was a mix of alchemy that could neutralize revenants, toxins that ate away at spore-filled rotting flesh. The death vines—all their various kinds—that spawned the spores were notoriously difficult to eradicate, mutating over time from the mix of poison that could still, always, be found on Maricol.

Soren's poison-coated and poison-filled bullets were issued yearly, the chemical makeup of the toxins changing as needed depending on his assignment. They were enough, here, to put down the revenants so they *stayed* down, long enough that he'd have time to burn them.

But there weren't enough bullets in the chamber for all the revenants clawing at the wreckage, and he wasn't about to throw a grenade into the mess, not if there were survivors. Although, looking at the twisted metal and broken train carriages he sped by, his hopes of finding anyone alive slipped a little.

Twisting the handlebars, Soren skidded around as he braked again, coming to a hard stop some distance from the wreckage and the rapidly growing fire. He flung himself off the velocycle, hearing it fall to the earth, not having time to kick down the stand. He put the rest of his bullets in between the eyes of revenants before shoving his pistol in its holster and reaching for the poison sword on his back.

His fingers curled around the hilt and unsheathed it, thumb sliding close to the cross guards, feeling for the controls blind and finding them. He toggled the small switch there, releasing poison down the center channel of the blade, the general concoction that would hopefully stop the revenants in their tracks. And if the poison didn't, if the spores had changed too much already this year, chopping off their heads worked well enough.

He'd burn them later. Right now, Soren needed to incapacitate the damned things.

He kept his footing as he threw himself into the middle of the horde, sword gripped tight in his hand as he used it to clear a path. He chopped off arms and hands, cut off heads, and kicked the bodies aside in his race to the wreckage. Dodging a pair of revenants that lunged at him, Soren spun on his feet, getting a fleeting glimpse of the crest painted on the train carriage he'd reached.

The roaring lion's profile, painted in gold and surrounded by the Dusk Star's constellation, was only used by the House sitting on the Imperial throne.

Definitely royalty, then.

"*Fuck*," Soren growled, taking off another revenant's head, adrenaline spiking.

He could not leave without helping whoever was in that train carriage. If they were dead, he'd have to bring the body, and not ashes, back to Calhames as proof.

"Please be alive," he panted under his breath as he skewered a revenant and kicked it off his sword.

The sound of gunfire from the train carriage made his head jerk around in surprise, instinctively ducking. He brought his sword up, cutting through a revenant's rib cage. Bullets didn't pepper the air above his head, so he kept moving, aware now, though, of the threat that waited for him inside the wreckage.

He put down what remained of the revenants, needing to recoat his sword with poison only once. Coughing against the smoke billowing in the air, Soren walked over bodies on his way to the train carriage entrance, the metal stairs there crumpled from a near decoupling. He sheathed his sword and drew the pistol holstered on his right hip, chambering a round. The click of gears was comforting, and he blew out a breath before stepping into the charred space where the train carriage door had been.

Soren let his pistol lead the way into chaos and hoped to survive it.

Two

VANYA

Vanya Sa'Liandel, crown prince and heir to the Imperial throne held by the House of Sa'Liandel, recognized betrayal when he tasted it on his tongue.

He finished the sip of spiced red chai anyway, knowing that to spit it out would be meaningless and draw attention to his predicament too early. The poison had already crossed his lips. He had perhaps ten minutes, no more, before the toxin worked its way through his veins, stealing the ability to move and breathe.

The quiet killer, he thought, setting the glass cup on the table.

Usually odorless and tasteless in small quantities when ground into powder, it was most often placed in a drink taken before bed, to incapacitate slowly during sleep. The victims never knew they died after they closed their eyes. There was a fine line, though, when too much of it meant *flavor* in a drink, and the tartness that bloomed in the back of his throat tasted the same way the mourning berries smelled on the vine.

Vanya blinked, continuing to stare at the documents spread out on the table as if nothing were amiss. The rumble of the train as it moved over the tracks was a noise easily tuned out, as was the bustle of servants and *praetoria* attending him in the private royal train carriage. They had all been sworn to his House, but it seemed that loyalty was no more. None of them could be trusted.

Vanya smoothed his fingers over the words of the marriage contract he'd been reviewing. The barrister who represented his House in such negotiations had sworn there was nothing out of place in his betrothal to the granddaughter and heir to the *vezir* of the House of Kimathi. The contract was in his House's favor. The attack on him today was a strong indicator someone did not want this marriage to happen. Someone with enough money and clout to infiltrate his closest circles of servants and guards.

So, perhaps no Blade contracted out of Daijal's Star Order kept him two-faced company in the train carriage. They knew their poisons better than anyone but the wardens. No Blade, then, only a House.

That left, oh, every major and minor House in existence.

Vanya closed his eyes, wishing briefly that he could have traveled by airship to Bellingham, but his mother had claimed that transport. Queen and heir did not travel together. In case of an attack, one would hopefully be alive in the aftermath to ensure their House remained on the Imperial throne.

Apparently, his House's enemies had found their mark this time. It only took them twenty-three years.

Vanya's personal store of antidotes was in one of his smaller luggage, the set brought with him into the carriage—which was stored in the wooden cabinet at the other end. He could not be sure it hadn't been tainted, but not taking it would be foolhardy. Standing between him and possible life was everyone he couldn't trust.

All five train carriages and the engine of the royal train were manned by people whose loyalty was now in doubt. Vanya needed to find a way to stop the train, but that was a task better done after he'd swallowed the antidote.

He stood, trying not to move as if he were desperate, despite the tingle he could feel starting in his fingertips. One of his servants rose to their feet from the bench on the opposite side of where he'd been working. The interior of the train carriage was done up in dark wood, deep reds, and the shine of accented gold. The gas lamps were cold in their sconces, and Vanya eyed the discreet bases that contained the gas needed for light.

A possibility of distraction, if he played things right.

And he was very good at playing this assassination game ever since becoming the Imperial crown prince.

"Your Imperial Highness," the servant said with a deep bow. "How may I serve you?"

Vanya thought about dissembling, but he was down to nine minutes according to the clock ticking away on the wall. He smiled at her, knowing she hadn't been the one to prepare the chai, but proximity bred guilt in a situation like this.

"You can start by telling me who poisoned my drink," Vanya said, keeping his voice calm, attention on everyone else.

They all froze, but denial wasn't forthcoming. The sentence for betrayal against a House was death. The gold ranking medallion that hung around Vanya's neck over his white robes was a negligible weight he refused to let them take from him. But he wanted answers and was down to eight and a half minutes.

The click of a pistol's safety being undone was loud in his ears. He had no guns of his own nearby, though he could shoot them well enough. Only Vanya didn't need a pistol when he could command starfire.

The genealogies had recorded the ebb and flow of starfire in the Houses since the founding of Solaria. Vanya had studied those records enough to know where the Houses stood when it came to magicians in the family. But starfire existed in the House of Sa'Liandel like no other, and Vanya reminded the traitors on the train carriage of just how terribly it burned.

Starfire exploded from his hand without need for a clarion crystal–tipped wand to direct its power. Vanya's stubborn will was enough, and he set the servants nearest him aflame before they could go for a weapon. Their cracking screams were choked off in seconds as starfire consumed their flesh down to bone. The smell of burning bodies was suffocating, but Vanya kept moving. If he could make it to his personal effects, to the antidote there, then he stood a chance of surviving this latest attempt on his life so long as it wasn't contaminated.

Poison made him slow, though, and Vanya was forced to duck behind a silk-draped chaise as one of the *praetoria* legionnaires opened fire where he'd stood. He drew on the aether to power the starfire in his hand, the heat something that had never bothered him.

He aimed the starfire at the gas lamps, shattering the casings and igniting the gas. A ball of red fire, lacking the gold tint of starfire, exploded outward. It caught the soldiers by surprise, forcing them back, buying Vanya time for a more direct attack.

He twisted around on one knee and tossed starfire at the *praetoria* legionnaires, their shouts turning into screams. Vanya moved even as his attack fell amongst them, catching sight of a soldier farther back speaking into a televox.

"Blow the engine!" the legionnaire barked.

Vanya cast starfire at the soldier before he could issue any other orders. The man jerked back, screaming through the flames. Smoke made Vanya wheeze, or perhaps it was the poison creeping through his veins.

The remaining soldiers stumbled away from the starfire, unable to shoot at their target. Vanya couldn't be sure they were truly *praetoria* legionnaires or imposters, and he had no time to find out otherwise. He was distantly aware of the shouts coming from the carriages on either side of the one he stood in. Reinforcements, but for whom, he couldn't be sure.

"Who sent you?" Vanya ground out, forcing his tongue to curl around the words as he stared at the soldiers.

The woman bared her teeth at Vanya, the look in her eyes that of a fanatic. "The dead will have you."

"I think not."

He let starfire fall on the three to consume them. Vanya was running out of time—five minutes, the clock on the wall said—but even as he took a step toward the storage racks, the train carriage shuddered on the rails, its speed slowing. Vanya managed to keep his footing, lunging for the only thing that could save him, but he didn't make it in time.

The forward door to the train carriage was shoved open, and soldiers pushed their way inside, having crossed the narrow bridge connecting the two carriages over the couplings. They had pistols in hand, aiming for him, even as Vanya caught sight of something outside the windows that made his blood go cold in a way he couldn't blame on the poison.

Revenants clawed at the exterior on both sides, rotten hands scratching at the metal as the train lost its momentum.

Vanya was not dying here, not like this.

He thrust his arm forward, starfire exploding from his hand, the heat of it less than what he was normally capable of. Already he could feel a slowness afflicting his body, a sluggish, creeping numbness he couldn't fight.

Starfire slammed against the front of the train carriage, burning through the soldiers there and cascading farther outward. Vanya let it burn without limits, let it crawl over the two train carriages coupled between his and the engine. But he couldn't keep it up, the clock ticking down the breaths his body could take.

An explosion ripped through the air from the direction of the engine, the deep sound of a grenade going off. The world lurched in a way Vanya felt in his stomach, teeth rattling in his skull. He lost his balance and fell, crashing against the table one of the servants had used to prepare his midday meal.

He slid to the floor, one hand grappling for the bolted-down table leg. Most of the furniture was secured in place, but not all. Vanya gritted his teeth as he struggled to curl up under the questionable safety of the table as the train carriage juddered in a frightening way.

The screech of breaking metal filled the air, the train carriage lurching off the track as the entire train derailed. Vanya tried to brace himself for the impact, but his body wasn't cooperating. His breath came in sharp little gasps, lungs working overtime as he tried to hold on to the table leg, feet braced weakly against the wall.

Everything in the luggage racks spilled over, pitching to the floor around him. Everything not bolted down went tumbling through the train carriage. Vanya lost his grip on the table leg as the poison in his body dug deeper. He slid across the floor, slamming into a charred body as something hard knocked against the side of his head.

Colored spots erupted across his vision, dizziness making the world spin. Then the train carriage jerked to a hard halt, the sudden stoppage sending him sprawling. His hands slid over scorch marks in the rug as he came face-to-face with the burned visage of someone who was once loyal to him.

His starfire had disappeared, but the fire from the gas lamps had taken root in a chaise. Smoke clogged the train carriage, and Vanya tried to cough, but he couldn't take a deep enough breath. He attempted to sit up, but his arms didn't want to work.

"Move," Vanya told himself, the word coming out slurred.

His heart wasn't pounding quickly anymore, the poison slowing everything down. He managed to raise his head only a little, blurred vision taking in the jumbled mess of everything. Vanya didn't know where the luggage with his carefully packed antidotes was, and something cold settled in his gut.

How many minutes did he have left? If he couldn't move, he'd die here by fire, which would be a blessing considering what waited for him outside in the plains. Vanya had no desire to be torn to pieces by revenants while still alive, or worse, get bitten and become infected by the spores. He'd much rather burn than have his body wander on after his soul had fled for the stars.

Vanya closed his eyes, and when he managed to open them next, someone stood in the train carriage doorway. He tried to call upon starfire, but his fingers wouldn't move, and the heat of the aether felt so very far away.

The person was all shadows to his eyes, coming closer. A hand touched his shoulder, rolling him to his back. Vanya blinked, unable to make out who knelt over him.

"Shit," the person muttered in the trade tongue, voice distinctly male. "What happened?"

Something bright glinted over the man's shoulder, catching

Vanya's fading attention. The pull of a clarion crystal tugged at his soul, but the shape of the thing wasn't a wand. His thoughts forced themselves into a desperate sort of order as he struggled to answer the question.

"Quiet killer," Vanya mumbled.

The man swore. Vanya didn't feel the hands on him, just knew he was moving when the world tilted. He was yanked to a sitting position and hauled across the man's shoulders. Everything was upside-down, black spots eating away at the edge of his vision. The smoky darkness of the train carriage abruptly disappeared as he was carried into sunlight.

The metal of the train was replaced by dirt and dry prairie grass. Vanya stared at the pieces of revenants the man walked through without worry. Some distant thought snagged his attention, because there was only one kind of people who lacked the crippling fear of the dead that everyone grew up with, no matter the country.

The world went right side up seconds later, and he found himself sitting up, head lolling on his neck. It was getting harder and harder to breathe, and Vanya couldn't shove down the panic suffusing his thoughts, sluggish as they were.

Fingers touched his face, but he barely felt them as his head was pushed up and back. Something was shoved between his lips, and cool liquid trickled over his tongue, a blooming sort of warmth following in its wake. And perhaps, by the grace of Callisto herself, he still had seconds on the clock, because Vanya could still move his throat, and he swallowed the chance given to him.

Three

SOREN

When Soren walked into the damaged train carriage, he hadn't expected to come across any survivors, much less the Imperial crown prince. Neither did he expect to need to administer an antidote to mourning berries, but at least he had the chemicals available to hastily mix it up. Wardens carried cure packs for others, not themselves, and this wasn't the first time Soren had to reverse a poisoning for some unfortunate person.

The prince was breathing, shallowly, but his lungs were working. Which meant the antidote *should* reverse the damage, if they were lucky and the stars shined on them.

Soren removed the vial from the prince's lips, keeping hold of his face with bare fingers. He'd removed his gloves before touching skin, not wanting to transfer any poison from his fight with the revenants to a man he was trying to save.

His fingers were pale against the prince's darker skin as he kept the prince's head up so he could swallow without choking. Soren studied him with a critical eye, counting his breaths. Dark lashes fluttered as his eyelids twitched, expression frozen from the poison that afflicted him. His black hair was cut short, but not short enough that

Soren couldn't see the tight curls in the strands and the cut along the side of his head that still bled.

His white robes with their brilliant gold-and-crimson embroidery across the shoulders and chest were stained from ash and blood and smelled of smoke. His loose trousers weren't much better. The gold ranking medallion with its roaring lion head hung askew from his throat, rising and falling at deeper intervals as his chest began to expand with more ease.

Soren sighed in relief, watching the prince come back to life in slow increments. Quiet killer was a gradually attacking poison, but the reversal was always quicker. Soren never looked away from the prince's face until dark brown eyes stared back at him.

"You with me?" Soren asked.

"Hmm," the prince mumbled, mouth twisting into a grimace. "I'm going to be sick."

His voice was deep, and he spoke with a clarity not usually found after a poisoning, but Soren figured this probably wasn't the first time the prince had suffered through something of the sort.

Gripping the prince's shoulders, Soren hauled him away from the velocycle. He braced the other man with an arm curled around his chest, letting him expel whatever was in his stomach onto the ground beside them. It wasn't much, and when he finished, Soren carefully eased him back up against the velocycle.

The prince wiped a shaky hand across his mouth, blinking rapidly as he stared at Soren. His pupils weren't quite right, but his focus was better than Soren thought it would be, given the circumstances. "Warden."

"Yes," Soren said as he set the empty vial on the ground. "I go by Soren."

"Vanya," the prince said. "Vanya Sa'Liandel."

"I know who you are."

Wardens might not have any presence in the governments of Maricol, but they all knew who was in charge of the countries whose borders they monitored. The prince hummed tiredly, eyes falling shut. Soren studied him for a moment longer before glancing over his shoulder at the wreckage, the bodies of the dead, and the growing fire. He grimaced, turning back around to find the prince's piercing attention on him.

"What's wrong?" Vanya asked.

"The derailment caused a fire. It's spreading. We need to go."

Soren had half a tank of fuel left, enough to hopefully outrun the start of a wildfire that was growing behind him. At least the wildfire would take care of the bodies.

Vanya's head tipped to the side, gaze focusing beyond Soren. He lifted a hand, fingers twitching, and Soren watched starfire pool in Vanya's palm, the aether tugging at his awareness in a way he'd long been told to ignore.

He shoved the old, aching want deep, watching as Vanya curled his fingers inward to make a fist. Fire gutted out behind them with a burst of sound, like hundreds of candles going out at once. When Soren looked back, the fire threatening to lick at his velocycle's wheels as they rode off had disappeared. Only smoke remained, acrid in the air, and the breeze was quick to pull it into the sky.

Vanya's arm dropped to the ground, breathing ragged. "The fire won't be a problem."

Soren studied the sweat beaded on his brow, mingling with the blood there, and sighed. "I need to check you over."

Vanya's fingers twitched, but he made no move to stop him. Soren took that as permission and set about patting the prince down with firm hands, checking for broken bones and other hurts. Aside from the cut to the head and growing bump there, Vanya only hissed when Soren's hands pressed too hard on his ribs.

"They don't feel broken," Soren said, listening to him breathe.

"Bruised."

Considering the state of the train carriage Soren had found him in, that was to be expected. He was lucky, actually, that the wounds sustained weren't so terrible. A possible concussion, bruised ribs, and a wrenched ankle discovered when Soren got him standing were the only physical ailments aside from the poisoning.

Vanya swayed on his feet once he was vertical, and Soren gripped his broad shoulders firmly to keep him from keeling over. They weren't of height—Soren's eyes were level with Vanya's mouth—but the prince didn't have the look of one leading a soft life. There was muscle beneath his expensive clothes, and the calluses on his fingers and palms didn't lend themselves to a life spent without a weapon in hand.

"Since you took care of the fire, I need to see if anyone else survived," Soren said.

"If any did, they die here."

Soren stared up at him. "Why?"

Vanya managed a smile that was more grimace than anything else. "Because they all conspired to murder me."

"I'm not killing them."

Vanya heaved out a tired sigh. "Then I will."

It wasn't a warden's place to interfere with matters of state. Wardens were neutral amidst all the politics twisting through every country on Maricol. Soren had no say in who lived and who died when royalty gave an order like that, even if his preference wasn't murder. He was a warden, after all. Their underlying duty was to save lives in the poison fields, not take them.

Soren guided Vanya backward until he sat on the velocycle. "Stay here. I'll scout around."

He straightened up and hesitated a moment before unholstering one of his pistols. He pressed it into Vanya's hand, not letting go until the prince had a good grip.

"Don't shoot me when I return," Soren said.

Vanya raised one eyebrow. "That would be poor repayment of what I owe you."

"You don't owe me anything, princeling."

Soren left before Vanya could argue further, unholstering his other pistol. He worked his way through the smoldering wreckage one train carriage at a time, finding mostly bodies. He dragged them out one at a time, piling them on the ground with the scattered remains of the revenants. He was sweating by the time he finished, shoulders aching from hauling dead weight around.

All total, there were over forty dead to deal with, some having died from the crash, while others had died by the starfire that had enveloped the train before the engine blew. Two died of bullets fired from the pistol Soren had given Vanya, a mercy if there ever was one, because the wounds they'd sustained from the crash were a slow, agonizing way to die.

"I need to burn the bodies," Soren said.

Vanya nodded, passing back the pistol. "Let me handle that."

Before Soren could protest, Vanya gestured at the pile of dead. Starfire flickered at his fingertips before igniting on the corpses. The heat made Soren turn his head to the side as starfire consumed the dead with a controlled quickness. He studied Vanya's profile, noticing the tension in the prince's jaw, the stiff way he held himself as he concentrated on the task at hand.

He was, Soren could admit, very nice to look at.

Soren attributed that stray thought to weeks spent alone in the poison fields and let it drift away, much like the smoke rising from the massive funeral pyre. The starfire burned everything quicker than normal fire, cutting down what would've taken hours to perhaps thirty minutes judging by his sturdy pocket watch.

Only ash remained once Vanya let the starfire gutter out. Soren eyed the blackened ground before nodding in the direction of where his velocycle was parked. "Come on. Let's get out of here. I'll take you wherever you need to go."

"Bellingham. Don't stop anywhere else until we reach that city."

Soren leveled him a flat look. "I'll need to refuel at way stations along the way for a ride that long. You can deal with that, otherwise we're walking when I run out of fuel."

"I won't be safe in public. Someone tried to murder me and managed to get my household to turn against me. I am without any support of the Legion or others I can trust, and have no way to contact my House."

"You have me."

Vanya turned his head to stare at Soren, looking more clear-eyed than he had before. The weight of his attention made Soren want to shift on his feet, but he held his ground.

"I suppose I do," Vanya said after a moment.

Soren led the way back to his velocycle, getting seated first. The prince settled in the space behind him without complaint, body bracketing Soren's. It couldn't be comfortable, not with the weapons Soren carried on his person, but Vanya didn't complain. He merely wrapped his arms around Soren's waist and lifted his booted feet to brace them on the studs sticking away from the frame.

"Let me know if you need to stop," Soren said as he kicked the stand up.

"I will be fine."

Soren rolled his eyes as he started the engine. "I mean it. It'd be a waste of my effort to save you from this mess only to have you pass out and tumble off and crack your skull the rest of the way open."

Vanya hooked his chin over Soren's shoulder, his voice a counterpoint to the engine, even through the helmet he still wore. Soren tried not to shiver at the sound of it. "You won't let that happen."

Soren revved the engine, pointing his front wheel toward the northern horizon. "You better hope I won't."

Four

BLAINE

Blaine loved flying almost as much as he loved his husband, though truly, it was a close call most days. Honovi had given him a home, but flying had given him the sky, and Blaine had found something like peace up in the clouds years ago on the deck of the *Skyborne*.

The thrum of the airship's engine was as familiar as his own heartbeat and always would be. The engine room was hot and stuffy, causing Blaine to sweat beneath his fur-lined leather flight jacket. The discomfort was easily ignored as he did a final check on the gauges, part of his job as chief engineer. He logged the numbers in his little leather notebook before weaving back through the cargo bay and heading abovedeck.

Blaine climbed up the narrow, twisting metal staircase, leaving the cramped quarters below for the forward open deck. A cool breeze smacked him in the face, and he breathed in deep. His lungs didn't need to work so hard at the lower altitudes, and it was a nice change from the last leg of the flight.

Crew shouted amongst each other as they prepared for landing. Straight ahead off the prow, a burst of violet-colored smoke erupted in the air at their balloon level. The aerial marker indicated their docking location, the color different for every berth in the many numbered sections of the airfield below.

"We're marked!" someone shouted.

"I'll tell the captain," Blaine called out. He headed for the flight deck and pushed open the door, leaning inside. "Engines are good, and the marker just went off."

"We're in position. Ground crew said we have clearance to descend. I'm deploying the anchor in thirty seconds," Honovi replied from his spot at the airship's helm in the flight deck, radio in hand, brass goggles shoved up over his flight cap.

It was a familiar sight to Blaine after all these years. The chinstrap drew attention to Honovi's strong jaw, the features of his face sharp and handsome. Tall and broad-shouldered, he made an excellent aeronaut captain on top of his duties as *jarl* to Clan Storm. He made an even better husband, in Blaine's opinion.

They'd married five years ago but been together long before that. The *jarl* was thirty now. He spent more time captaining airships than on the ground, crossing borders for trade and to assist ambassadors under guidance of the *Comhairle nan Cinnidhean*.

Blaine had seen Honovi's skill at negotiating up close and personal, having accompanied him on every flight since he'd earned the right to stand as crew. Being married to Honovi and traveling with him meant Blaine was privy to a level of politics most E'ridians never encountered.

Blaine gave a lazy salute to his husband. "I'll notify the crew." He ducked back out onto the open-air decking, raising a fist in the air and making a circle with his arm. "We're descending!"

The crew around him shouted back acknowledgment as the creak of gears rumbled through the air. It came from the outside hull panel as Honovi remotely deployed the anchor.

Colored smoke dissipated above them as Honovi maneuvered the airship with deft skill. The engines changed pitch as the airship descended, the oblong balloon casting the deck in shadow.

Blaine rested a hand on the railing, peering over the side through his goggles as the ground came up to meet them, Glencoe spread out like a glittering maze behind its walls. Clan Storm laid claim to a northern airfield, and the sky tower tasked with keeping air traffic organized had assigned them a berth closer to the city than the fields of the Sunrise Valley. The sun was directly overhead, and they'd made good time coming up over the Constellation Sea from their trip to Solaria.

Shouts from other crew members passed back and forth through the air as they descended. Blaine could feel the change in the air temperature, the chill from the higher altitude bleeding away the closer they got to the ground. His fur-lined leather jacket was always too warm during summer once they reached the earth, but spring tended to be cooler.

The engines changed pitch, and Blaine automatically noted the sound. Nothing sounded off, and if it had, he'd have gone belowdecks in an instant to deal with the problem. Blaine had triple-checked the engines while they were docked at Seaville, though, not wanting to risk overlooking anything before the long flight back home over open seas.

Their cargo hold was filled with merchandise belonging to the Eastern Winds Trading Company. Honovi's bloodline owned the lucrative trading company, and the family was very hands-on with it. They were returning home with another set of signed contracts regarding spices and tea, which would aid the company's bottom line.

Blaine knew Honovi was a good aeronaut captain, but he'd grown into his role as *jarl*, an unofficial diplomat, and a cutthroat merchant over the years. Trade negotiations required a delicate touch, the same way an airship sometimes needed a light hand, and Honovi excelled at getting what the clans needed.

The engines worked to reverse the airflow running through the ballonets. The balloon provided buoyancy in the sky, but the engines did the steering. Honovi brought them down lightly into the dry dock inside a hangar, the anchor caught by ground crew and connected to the very large magnet that would help keep the airship in place.

Secondary rope anchors were tossed up from the dock, and Blaine wasn't the only one to catch one. He yanked it over the side of the railing with a firm tug, gloved hands sliding over the rope. He knotted it deftly around the metal cleats interspaced along the railing before signaling it was in place.

Someone cranked open the gangplank, and then it was all hands on deck as the airship was swarmed by ground crew and clerks employed by the Eastern Winds Trading Company. They were easy to make out, dressed in sturdy coveralls or kilts rather than flight leathers.

Blaine removed his flight cap and goggles, dragging his braid out from beneath his flight jacket. Some loose hair caught on the gold marriage torc he wore, but he tugged the strands free. The plait reached midback and was twisted through with a colorful beaded leather strand indicating his association with Clan Storm.

It wasn't anywhere close to the elaborate version Honovi wore as *jarl*. Neither was it the style Blaine had worn as a boy in Ashion, but he'd spent fifteen years in E'ridia, and this country was home now more than the one he only barely remembered.

He returned to the flight deck to log the energy levels of the clarion crystals that powered their airship. Steam engines had run the clans' airships for centuries, but the risk of explosions with those models had always been higher.

Clarion crystals used to be reserved solely for magicians and priests of the Star Order. Then some promising engineers centuries back had discovered that, when cut into different shapes, they could conduct and amplify energy. These days, clarion crystals were a hot commodity, their commercial use gaining traction in everyday life.

E'ridians had always focused on the mechanics of flight over everything else. Airships were what enabled them to traverse the Eastern Spine, mine the mountain range, and settle the Sunrise Valley and hills along the east coast of the continent. Without that form of transportation, their people would've remained in Ashion at the end of the Age of Starfall. These days, Maricol's skies were filled with the clans' airships, and they had ambassadors in every country.

Blaine dumped his goggles and flight cap on the navigation table amidst the maps and discarded astrolabe and sextant strewn about there. He picked up the logbook and entered the needed information before signing off on it with his initials.

"We're logged," Blaine said, flipping the logbook closed. He'd pass it off to the maintenance crew in a bit.

Honovi nodded, continuing with the shutdown procedure. The airship shuddered as it settled more heavily into its berth, staying upright through wooden supports and the air balloon floating overhead.

Someone cleared their throat from the doorway, and Blaine looked over his shoulder at the reed-thin man in a kilt who stood there. The plaid draped over the left shoulder was pinned in place by a ranking brooch that depicted his place in government. It wasn't overly large, which spoke of him probably being a clerk of some sort. The length of plaid fell to his waist, though, and that spoke of a higher rank held than frontline government worker.

"Welcome home to captain and crew," the man said.

Honovi nodded absently at the traditional greeting as he went about his own lockdown procedures. "Any reason why the *Comhairle nan Cinnidhean* has need of me right now? My father knows I need to offload my airship first."

"I'm not here for you, *jarl*. I've been sent by the Seneschal's Office for your chief engineer."

As the second-highest level of government, the Seneschal's office was in charge of implementing all decisions made by the *Comhairle nan Cinnidhean*. A clerk sent by the seneschal was of an importance that left a knot in Blaine's stomach. He straightened up and turned away from the navigation table. Honovi's hands paused over the control board, and he looked back at Blaine with a frown on his face.

"What need do you have for my *husband*?" Honovi asked, brown eyes narrowing.

The clerk drew himself up straighter at the pointed demand. "It's not your business, *jarl*."

Which was the wrong thing to tell Honovi. Blaine shared a look with the airship's navigator before clearing his throat, hoping to head off an argument. "I'm at the *Comhairle nan Cinnidhean*'s disposal."

Honovi's lips curled. "We both are."

The clerk frowned before realizing this was a fight he'd lose. "I have a motor carriage waiting at the wall."

Blaine pushed away from the navigation table and headed for the doorway, patting Honovi on the arm as he passed by. "It'll be fine."

Honovi removed his goggles and flight cap, handing them off to his navigator. He pulled his long black braid from beneath his fur-lined leather jacket, the plait free of ranking adornments other than the beaded clan ribbon. The sides of his head were shaved, a style Honovi had favored since they were young, though new hair was beginning to grow out.

Blaine's fingers twitched with the memory of carefully trimming and shaving Honovi's hair before landing in Seaville all those weeks ago. Generally, only family or partners were allowed to tend to each other's hair, and the ritual was one Blaine performed every few weeks.

He waited while Honovi signed off on arrival paperwork and handed over the bill of lading to a representative of the Eastern Winds Trading Company. Then Honovi gestured for Blaine to precede him off the airship where the clerk waited impatiently for them on the pier.

The walk to the outer wall didn't take nearly as long as it would have if they'd docked farther out. Honovi overtook the clerk, and Blaine kept pace with him, dodging past ground crew and cargo being moved about with the aid of mechanical carts and lifts. Spring was always a busy time with airships arriving and departing as the trade routes opened up after heavy winter storms across the Eastern Spine.

True to the clerk's word, a motor carriage waited for them inside the city walls, the seneschal's seal painted over the door. The engine popped and sputtered at rest, making Blaine want to get under the hood and fix the noise. They climbed into the rear seat of the motor carriage and got settled, belting themselves in.

The frame of the motor carriage was enclosed, with windows all around them, and Blaine spent the drive into the center of Glencoe watching the bustle of people and vehicles they passed. The city was so very different from the confined space of an airship with a limit on crew. Even in the sky, Blaine could find space to be alone. Here, Glencoe was a raucous city filled with color, and it always took a day or so for him to acclimate to the crowds.

Boulevards from the airfields led to the center of the city through inner defensive walls. The park and gardens that surrounded the heart of government were all in bloom as they reached the civic area. The vibrant ascadia trees were of particular note, the pale pink blossoms a welcome sight after a long winter abroad.

E'ridia's capitol building in Glencoe was built from stone carved from a quarry in the eastern hills outside the Sunrise Valley. During the last Age, the pale gray stone had been turned into an imposing building where the *Comhairle nan Cinnidhean* now ruled from. The older buildings of Glencoe had stood the test of time and poison runoff better than the newer ones. Their underlying construction was different, and Blaine had always been fascinated by that lost history.

In the grand scheme of things, history was politics, and Blaine had never been particularly keen on getting mixed up in them, despite who he had married. Receiving a summons from the *Comhairle nan Cinnidhean* wasn't something he could ignore, though, even if he couldn't figure out what he might have done to gain their attention. Between the two of them, Honovi was the one most often called upon.

Blaine flexed his clammy fingers before discreetly wiping his palms on his trousers. He hadn't felt this nervous since his first time crewing an airship at sixteen, well past the age most E'ridians hit that milestone.

"It'll be fine," Honovi said as the motor carriage braked to a shuddery halt. Really, someone needed to check on the mechanics of the vehicle.

"Easy for you to say. You aren't the one who got issued the summons," Blaine muttered.

Honovi slanted him a faintly amused smile as he opened the motor carriage door. He'd undone the top buttons on his flight jacket, and the matching marriage torc he wore caught the sunlight. "You've stood before them plenty of times before."

"No, *you* stood before them giving reports while I waited in the balcony for you to finish. Being in the same room as them doesn't count."

Honovi laughed as Blaine followed him out of the motor carriage, humor softening the sternness of his mouth. Blaine let his attention linger there for a second before flicking his gaze up to meet warm brown eyes. Honovi leaned down and kissed him gently, ignoring the sound of the clerk impatiently clearing his throat.

"We'll stand before them together," Honovi promised, taking Blaine's hand in his.

They followed the clerk across the large plaza, the grand fountain bubbling away in its center. In the middle of the fountain was an airship built to scale out of clockwork gears that rotated on a pillar. Water poured from the prow in a spray that drifted a little on the breeze.

Directly ahead of them was the capitol building, surrounded by a grand promenade that wrapped around the massive circular heart of government. People scurried here and there, the job of government never ceasing.

"Do you know what they want from me?" Blaine asked, raising his voice a little.

The clerk never looked back at him. "It will be discussed behind closed doors."

Blaine winced at that, sharing a concerned look with Honovi. He'd never been privy to a closed-door meeting before, and the knot in his stomach grew heavier.

The crowd in the plaza was typical of midweek. Blaine and Honovi were some of the few wearing flight leathers, their clan association hinted at in the plaid shoulder panels. Everyone else wore kilts, suits, or gowns, with clan adornments in everyone's braids a prominent accessory. Blaine could pick out clan association by the different patterned kilts, intricate embroidery, or plaid everyone wore.

They climbed the grand steps to the promenade, the pillars holding up the roof carved with the constellations of the star gods at the top. The gold leaf there glinted in the sunlight, catching the eye.

The heavy wooden doors leading into the building were propped open. A pair of peacekeepers manned the entrance, directing visitors to the information desk in the grand lobby. The clerk guiding them was waved through, as were they. Blaine stayed by Honovi's side as they walked a familiar path to the center chamber the building's foundations had been laid around.

Three concentric circles filled with offices surrounded the central chambers and were bisected by six main halls, one for each clan. Between each circular structure were gardens encased in glass, filled with plants fed by filtered streams and shallow ponds. All hallways led to the *Comhairle nan Cinnidhean* chambers with its stained glass windows, tributes to the star gods painted on its vaulted ceiling, and a mechanical astrolabe hanging from the ceiling that moved by way of clockwork gears.

The two-story chamber was ringed by a balcony allowing for public viewing of the *cinn-chinnidh* as they debated into governance the laws brought by clan representatives through the Seneschal's Office. Blaine rarely stepped foot onto the chamber floor, and he tried not to hunch his shoulders as they entered the hushed space. The clerk closed the door behind them, the sound of it locking loud in his ears.

The entire *Comhairle nan Cinnidhean* was present at the circular table situated beneath the astrolabe, the center area hollowed out into open space. Only the *cinn-chinnidh*, though, and not their *jarls*, which made Honovi's presence an outlier. Blaine was surprised to see a trio of Ashionens standing in the center space rather than seated at the adjacent table reserved for ambassadors.

Maybe they weren't ambassadors, Blaine decided as they drew closer and he got a better look at the foreigners' clothing. Practical and drab, with none of the whimsical finery his memory teased him with. E'ridians held pride in their embroidery, plaid, and embellished cuts of cloth if they weren't wearing leather flying gear. Upon first glance, the people standing before the *Comhairle nan Cinnidhean* looked to be no one of note, but then, they wouldn't be there if that were the case.

"*Jarl* Honovi, you were not summoned," Leena, *ceann-cinnidh* of Clan Lightning, said in a firm voice.

"You summoned a member of my clan and my personal airship crew, who happens to be my husband," Honovi said lightly, but Blaine could hear a thread of steel running through his voice. "I think it only right to have escorted him."

"And now you may leave."

Honovi planted his feet and tucked his thumbs around the hard leather of his belt. He looked as if he stood on a swaying airship, prepared to guide it through a storm, rather than on solid ground before the rulers of their country. "I would prefer to stay. You bring Ashionens into our speaking space, and they do not have the look of ambassadors. What need do they have with one of ours?"

Blaine squared his shoulders and lifted his chin. While he hadn't forgotten where he had come from, he was E'ridian now, down to his bones. It had taken little time to assimilate into his adopted country's culture as a child. Honovi had helped with that ever since escorting him off that long-destroyed airship, easing the way by virtue of his status as *jarl*.

Blaine hadn't been adopted into the *ceann-cinnidh*'s family within the clan, but his and Honovi's friendship had grown into a love they hadn't thought about denying. When he'd married Honovi, Blaine knew whatever loyalty he'd once had to his birth country would forever be severed. Once unraveled, he could not reweave those ties.

Or so he liked to tell himself.

"The summons was for Blaine. Abide by the *Comhairle nan Cinnidhean*'s orders, *jarl* Honovi," Leena said.

Honovi blinked at her before turning his head to look at Blaine. The kindness in his eyes rooted Blaine where he stood. "Do you wish me to leave?"

Blaine never hesitated when he shook his head. As if he would ever say no to such a thing. "I would hear the *Comhairle nan Cinnidhean*'s words with you here."

Honovi nodded, and a stubborn tightness came to his jaw, a

tension Blaine knew well when Honovi was set to get his way during trade talks.

"I have a right as *jarl* to hear what the *Comhairle nan Cinnidhean* has to say regarding one of my clan. I have a right as his husband to the same. I will stay," Honovi said, a challenge in his words that made not a few of the *cinn-chinnidh* bristle around the table.

Before anyone else could protest, Honovi's father raised his hand in a gesture asking for silence. Alrickson kept his eyes on his son and no one else. *"Jarls* were present the night Blaine came to us. This is not a secret we break confidence on if *jarl* Honovi stays. And he is right. Blaine is of our clan."

Something like ice trickled down Blaine's spine, catching his breath the way a sudden drop in the atmosphere sometimes did. He wrenched his attention to the Ashionens, finding the three staring right at him.

"I am at the *Comhairle nan Cinnidhean*'s disposal," Blaine said around a tightness in his throat.

Honovi gestured for Blaine to follow him to the only empty spot at the table, one with a small riser for someone to place notes on. The spot was used by those who'd come to argue their cases before law and country. They took up the space with clear intent, standing side by side. The Ashionens shifted on their feet to face where Blaine and Honovi now stood.

"An Ashionen arrived during the winter snows, carrying a message on their tongue from someone of particular note in their country. It was received in secret, and we debated its merit over the course of many weeks. Ultimately, the request could not be ignored. We sent word back that we would hear their concerns. These representatives arrived in the wake of that request," Alrickson said.

Every eye was on Blaine, and he refused to react. He kept his face expressionless despite the churning in his gut, the clamminess of his hands, and the distant voice of a star god echoing through the valleys of his mind.

This is your road now.

The icy uncertainty faded when Honovi gently gripped Blaine's hand, reminding him that he wasn't alone.

"What do they want?" Blaine asked, forcing his voice to remain steady.

The lone Ashionen woman stepped forward, dipping into a smooth, deep curtsy with a skill that did not match the station of her clothes. As she straightened, she picked at the clasp of the choker around her throat.

Her face shimmered, magic peeling away along with the thin gossamer veil she removed. The face she'd had before was gone, replaced by sharper, more beautiful features. Even her eye color had changed, gone from an unassuming brown to a pale hazel, while her ashy hair lightened to a brighter blonde.

Blaine sucked in a surprised breath, as did Honovi, though they were the only ones to do so. The *Comhairle nan Cinnidhean* didn't appear shocked at the use of magic before them. The woman clasped her hands together in front of her, carefully holding on to the veil. When she spoke, it was with an accent that jolted him, the crispness of nobility falling from her lips. He wondered if it was true, or merely an affectation.

"You may call me Mainspring. I am here on behalf of the Clockwork Brigade," the woman said in the trade tongue. "We are a group who stands against the encroachment of Daijal rule in Ashion."

"You are a rebellion," Aslaung, *ceann-cinnidh* of Clan Mountain, said in a voice as dry as thin mountain air. "Rebellions outside our borders should not concern us."

"Perhaps, my lady. Perhaps not. But Daijal cares naught for borders, and that country cares even less about the dead. Revenants walk where they shouldn't, and have since the Inferno, as you well know."

"Ask for aid from the wardens, not from E'ridia."

"We have. It has not been enough." The woman drew in a breath, her hazel eyes never looking away from Blaine. "That warning is not the only reason I am here. We have sought answers in the ashes of the Inferno over the last many years. What we have gleaned could be of great help to our country. A child was delivered to your care fifteen years ago, were they not? A babe graced by the protection of the star gods themselves?"

Whoever this Ashionen was, they were used to standing before people of power and giving nothing away. Mainspring posed the question without any inflection in her voice, but it didn't matter. Blaine still froze where he stood, mind tossed back into a past he'd tried so hard to forget.

He had been the only mortal to walk off the airship in Glencoe. He'd carried no babe in his arms when he left all that he'd been behind. The child had been relegated to Nilsine's care for that long flight east until she wasn't. That was a secret he hadn't given voice to back then, and he certainly couldn't now.

Blaine had spent the last month or so speaking the trade tongue, and it was easy to work his lips around the sound of it. The languages of Maricol were similar, drawn from the same origin, but the accents and dialects differed, carving out space inside borders. The trade tongue stole from all of them to form a bastardized language that most people involved in trade or who lived in major cities and border towns spoke.

"I was the only one brought to Glencoe. There was no babe aboard for that trip," Blaine said. It wasn't the whole truth, but it was truth enough, and he would hold to it.

The woman's shoulders dipped ever so slightly, the only hint of her disappointment. "I see."

"Why are you here?"

"King Bernard has betrothed Princess Eimarille to his son. He seeks the Ashion throne through her bloodline. Rumor has it his wedding gift will consist of oversight of Amari and its surrounding provinces. Preparation, if you will, of her puppet position beside the crown prince."

"You hope for a different queen with this missing babe?" Honovi asked into the silence that followed her words.

"Fire kills many things, but it cannot kill hope," Mainspring said with a conviction in her voice that made Blaine bite his tongue. She stared at him, gaze steady, chin held high at a challenging angle. "Am I wrong, Your Grace?"

Honovi frowned. "Blaine is not of your nobility."

"He is a Westergard."

It was a guess on her part, and a good one. Blaine curled the fingers of his free hand against his palms, the leather gloves he wore preventing him from slicing open his skin. He was E'ridian now, but he'd been Ashionen before fire burned away all that he had known.

In the forests, it was known that some trees needed fire to thrive, their seeds incapable of growth without it. Perhaps this was what Nilsine had made of him when she'd carried him east. A seed planted to grow in the ashes of the past.

Honovi stared at him with a frank, questioning gaze, tension holding him still. "Westergard?"

Blaine unstuck his tongue from the roof of his mouth. "That is not my name."

Because it wasn't, not anymore. E'ridians did not carry surnames, only clan affiliation, and Blaine had given up his bloodline in an airship hangar as a child. He'd never spoken of his past to Honovi, and his husband had never demanded it, not in the wake of a star god's decree.

What's more, Blaine had no idea if the babe they'd left Amari with had survived, or what Nilsine had done with her in that border city he knew not to speak of, but it did not matter. For him, there was no Rourke left to guard, and without that duty, he had no right to a name that had existed in the genealogies since the Age of Starfall.

Mainspring spread her hands, palms up, asking for help or forgiveness, it was difficult to say. One could never trust a spy, after all. "The North Star guided me here with orders to bring a Westergard home. I would like to believe she did not guide me wrong."

Blaine glanced up at the constellations painted across the ceiling of the chamber, mapping out the night sky. The stars led them home, always, even now.

He wondered what they looked like above the Northern Plains, without the teeth of mountains biting into them. He used to know, once.

"Blaine?" Honovi asked into the quiet.

He drew in a breath and steadied himself against the inevitable. "I will hear the North Star's decree."

And he knew he would obey it, even in the face of Honovi's quiet despair that radiated off him like starfire.

Five

HONOVI

"Why was I never informed?" Honovi demanded.

He kept his voice level, but anger gave it a depth that rang through the air of his father's office in the capitol building. The space was decorated with artwork created by Clan Storm artisans as well as tintype photographs of their immediate family. Honovi had spent many a day with his father in this space, learning how to govern. At the moment, the space did not give him the comfort it once had.

Alrickson sat behind a wide desk overflowing with files and paper, a jar of fountain pens in danger of falling off the edge. The connecting door that led to a larger office housing his aides and the telegraph machine there was closed and locked. Honovi couldn't make out any sound of people working beyond, which made him wonder if his father had sent them away so as to not overhear this private meeting.

His father let out a heavy sigh, and Honovi took a moment to study him. Alrickson's dark hair was threaded through with copious amounts of gray, the jeweled metal hair adornments he wore far more elaborate than even Honovi's finest set. The wrinkles bracketing his mouth and eyes appeared deeper than they had even a year ago. Honovi was uncomfortably aware of his father's age, though it hadn't slowed him down.

As with the other *cinn-chinnidh*, Honovi's father wore a kilt and a long-sleeved button-up shirt, neatly ironed and embroidered on the front. The jacket over that was a deep gray, and the draped plaid that fell over his left shoulder was pinned in place by an eagle brooch. The fall of the fabric would reach the ground when he stood, a length only *cinn-chinnidh* were allowed to have.

"For the same reason none of the other *jarls* were informed. Secrets don't live long in silence when many people hear them," Alrickson replied.

Honovi unclenched his jaw with effort. "This concerns my husband, Father."

"It concerns where he came from, and that was information we could not simply ignore, my son."

Honovi reached up to touch the torc hanging around his throat. "Blaine is E'ridian. I was there that night when the Dusk Star commanded him to be, remember? As were the other *jarls*."

"His clan status will not change, but my job as *ceann-cinnidh* and your job as *jarl* is to weigh the requests that come before the *Comhairle nan Cinnidhean* with respect, an open mind, and keen ears. The winter messenger made clear they had come at the behest of Ashion, not Daijal. The star priest who judged his truth was in agreement. They believed the same of Mainspring."

"The cogs she brought with her are magicians. She may be as well. What's to say their magic is different than that of our star priests? Different enough to lie through?"

The two guards who had stood silently behind Mainspring during her argument before the *Comhairle nan Cinnidhean* had said nothing. Honovi had not missed the empty ties on their belts that would carry a clarion crystal–tipped wand. The focus weapons were banned for outsiders in the chamber, and the astrolabe held a dampening spell that made casting magic with or without a wand difficult.

"Do you doubt the strength of your mother's belief?" Alrickson asked mildly.

Honovi flushed and shook his head, feeling like a child in that moment and not a man of thirty years. His mother, Isla, was the high priestess of the Star Order in E'ridia, one gifted with tremendous magic—magic which Honovi had not received, though his younger sister had. He'd felt lacking as a child because of its absence in his blood. Perhaps that was why he'd thrown all that he was into piloting airships. Flying was something he could be good at, a skill where magic wasn't required to succeed.

"No, of course not. But I doubt these Ashionens have our country's best interests at heart."

It went unsaid he thought they didn't have his husband's best interest at heart.

"The *Comhairle nan Cinnidhean* agrees. That is why we allowed the winter messenger to return to the Ashion spymaster and send us a representative."

"The Clockwork Brigade does not have the backing of their government."

Alrickson nodded in agreement. "Not publicly. It can't."

Rebellions were messy, and the one that had risen from the ashes of the Inferno in Ashion was a stubborn thing. Honovi had been privy to the *Comhairle nan Cinnidhean*'s spy reports on the actions the Clockwork Brigade took against the Daijal court over the years. He hadn't paid much attention to it all, because Ashion wasn't E'ridia, but he realized perhaps he should have.

"The Daijal court has spent several hundred years attempting to remake their sister country in its image through subterfuge. The *Comhairle nan Cinnidhean* does not believe that hunger for power will die after they absorb Ashion," Alrickson said.

Honovi stared at his father, a coldness settling in his chest. With a sigh, he kicked out the nearest chair so he could sit, leaning forward to rest his elbows on his knees. "I doubt they could cross the Eastern Spine to become a threat. The eastern provinces of Ashion are against everything Daijal stands for. I've heard that rhetoric enough when we trade with them. The Clockwork Brigade is embedded deep along those borders."

"Expansion is not off the table."

"They'd try for Urova first, or Solaria." Honovi smiled thinly. "I wish them well with attempting to take the southern empire and its Legion."

It was well-known the Solarian Houses murdered each other out of tradition, and yet, their empire still stood. If anything could unite the Houses, though, Honovi rather thought encroachment on their right to rule would be it. And that was *if* Daijal could muster an army capable of taking on the Solarian Legion. A ground fight would be a bloodbath, as much as an aerial battle against E'ridia's airships and aeroplanes would be.

The countries of Maricol weren't meant to be united as one. The Age of Starfall was proof of that. The Great Separation during that Age had been inevitable back then, and they thrived now because of it. But Honovi couldn't ignore the pinprick of unease his father's words brought him, if only because the star gods rarely interfered with their children so blatantly. Whenever they did, history made note of it.

"Daijal is building an alliance with Urova and has done so since before the Inferno. They'll find support, not a fight, in the north," Alrickson said.

Urova lived in winter more than spring, its people scattered about thick snowy forests and icy tundra. They traded with E'ridia in the eastern coastal towns, traveling by submersibles through the ice floes and ocean rather than by air over the mountains. That country had held up its side of trade treaties, but Honovi wondered about the future.

"All of this is why you set the closed-door meeting today, isn't it?"

His father nodded slowly. "Gathering at night is too indicative of wanting to hide something. The *Comhairle nan Cinnidhean* has a history of holding closed-door meetings. It's not out of the ordinary, and we had Mainspring arrive early to wait in a private office. They weren't seen by anyone."

"The other *jarls* will need to be told," Honovi warned.

Alrickson shifted on his seat, adjusting the plaid that fell across his left arm. "They will be notified when necessary. You would have been as well."

The pointed reminder that he should not have stayed for the

meeting made Honovi straighten up. "I was not going to let Blaine face this alone."

"You will need to."

The words were said pragmatically, but they hit like a blow to the head. Honovi curled his hands into fists, having nothing to say to that because his father was right. Mainspring had come for Blaine and no one else.

It didn't matter that the *Comhairle nan Cinnidhean* was seemingly interfering in another country's sovereignty by giving tacit aid to a rebellion. He could see how that could be explained away—by sending Blaine away with no support, despite the marriage vows between them. Honovi's position as *jarl* meant any decision, any travels he embarked on, carried the weight of the *Comhairle nan Cinnidhean* with his presence.

E'ridia could not be seen as supporting rebels in another country.

Which meant Honovi could not follow Blaine down this road as he was.

It left a fiercely sour taste in his mouth, like unripened cloudberries high on the peaks, the knowledge that he might have to give Blaine up. That Honovi's next flight might have a new chief engineer manning the engines and standing beside him on the decking.

"He is my husband."

Alrickson's gaze held a kindness that skirted too close to pity for Honovi's comfort. "He belongs to the star gods. You knew that when you married him."

Honovi clenched his teeth together so hard his jaw popped at the hinge. "Blaine gave his vows to *me*, not the star gods."

"And the *Comhairle nan Cinnidhean* cannot ignore the threat Mainspring hints at. Blaine is clan, that will not change, but he must walk this road without you." Honovi wanted to argue, but Alrickson raised a hand, cutting off his words. "Blaine will keep us informed of what happens in Ashion. I do not trust the Clockwork Brigade to be truthful if that truth aids us more than them. Blaine knows his duty, the same as you know yours."

In this instance, Honovi's duty was to stay, and Blaine's was to go, and he didn't know when their roads would cross again. Part of being *jarl*, of being *ceann-cinnidh*, of one day sitting where his father did, was to know that clan and country came first over everything else. It had to. They wouldn't have survived the poisoned land or revenants if the clans hadn't banded together all those centuries ago.

But he'd given vows; he wore a torc; he shared a bed with someone he'd promised forever with. Loneliness was a terrible gift for doing one's duty, and his heart hurt at the thought of letting Blaine go.

"How will you explain Blaine's absence from my side?"

"Mainspring has her story for him to follow. Ours will be we have sent him to join the diplomatic corps in another country while you remain here. Think of it as additional training he needs so as to aid you when you take up the mantle of *ceann-cinnidh.*"

"The stars will guide us," Honovi said, the prayer rote on his tongue after years of flying beneath the night sky.

Alrickson nodded assent, and Honovi stood, flexing his fingers wide. He left the office, finding Blaine waiting for him on the wooden bench outside, flicking the lid of his pocket watch open and shut.

"Honovi?" Blaine asked, rising to his feet.

Honovi drew him in for a fierce kiss, holding him close. "It'll be all right."

They had precious few hours left to them. Honovi had paperwork still to file and a meeting with the Eastern Winds Trading Company representative, but he left it all by the wayside to take Blaine home one more time.

Six

HONOVI

"I wish you wouldn't go," Honovi said.

He leaned against the doorframe that separated their bedroom from the living area, the suite of rooms in the four-story clan home having belonged to them since their wedding day. Three generations lived inside the large building, typical of E'ridian families, but few were home at the moment.

"You know I have to," Blaine said from where he stood before the large bedroom closet, sifting through storage boxes on one of the shelves.

"You always said Ashion had no claim to you. Not anymore."

Blaine sighed softly but kept on with his search. "It doesn't."

"Then why are you choosing to leave?"

"Because the star gods ordered me to."

His voice was quiet amidst the mess he'd made. Clothes were strewn on the floor, and bits of mechanical parts were scattered around his boots, boxes upended, as if he were searching for something.

Porters had delivered their travel trunks from the airship while they'd been in the meeting all afternoon. Blaine had emptied his onto the bed and was steadily filling it up again. Honovi had to stop himself from tipping everything back out.

"The winter messenger came from the Ashion spymaster herself. They can't be trusted," Honovi said.

"The Ashion spymaster is against all that Daijal stands for. The clans' own spies have said as much. Your father and the other *cinn-chinnidh* confirmed that winter messenger did not hail from Daijal, and Mainspring confirmed she represents Ashion."

"And that makes all the difference, does it?"

Honovi couldn't help the sharpness of his voice. When Blaine glanced over his shoulder at Honovi, there was a tiredness to his gaze that was new. "It does."

Honovi frowned, staring at Blaine, the thick blond braid having fallen over one shoulder. Honovi's gaze traced the line of his jaw, the freckles across his cheeks that were coming up darker now that the sun was out more. Blaine had always drawn Honovi's eye, always caught his attention, ever since he walked off that airship captained by the Dusk Star. He'd never questioned that pull, though a traitorous thought slipped through his mind as he wondered if Blaine ever had, if he did now.

"They are not your clan."

Blaine dropped his gaze, turning to face the closet again. "They are not, but they are where I came from. I can't ignore that."

"You have for every day you've lived here."

Blaine hunched his shoulders. "I know. But there's a truth I've ignored for too long. I can't keep ignoring it when it stands in front of me asking for help."

Because they both remembered the night he'd arrived in E'ridia and the halting hints of his past he'd shared over the years. Not enough for Honovi to ever paint a full picture, but enough to know Blaine would always keep some secrets. And Honovi had let him, because a star god had told them to.

Honovi stayed where he was, watching in silence as Blaine dug through items they'd accumulated together and separately over the years. It was a few minutes later when he found whatever it was he'd been looking for. The tin box he came away with was small and fit in the palm of his hand.

Blaine approached Honovi, opening the box as he did so, tipping out a tarnished ring into the palm of his hand. Blaine held it with care, a distant look in his hazel eyes that Honovi desperately wanted to ease.

"What is that?" Honovi asked.

"The only thing I brought with me to Glencoe."

He handed the ring to Honovi without a word. Honovi held it between his thumb and forefinger, staring at the flat top of it and the crest skillfully etched into the metal.

"She called you Westergard."

Blaine hooked a finger through one of Honovi's belt loops. "The Westergard bloodline was stricken from the nobility genealogies."

"Was it?"

Honovi couldn't help the sharpness to his voice, fingers curling around a ring no clan member would ever wear. Their bloodlines were not so rigid as some of the other countries. The clans did not try to kill each other like the Solarians did in pursuit of a throne, nor did they cleave themselves apart as Ashion and Daijal had done. The clans worked together because there was no survival to be found alone.

It was why they had a *Comhairle nan Cinnidhean*, not a king or queen. It was why starfire was not an indicator of singular rulership but dedication to their people was. Honovi had no magic, no starfire running through his veins, but that did not make him any less a *jarl*.

But he was a *jarl*, not a *ceann-cinnidh*, and he could not order Blaine to stay, despite how very badly he wanted to. And he knew, with a certainty that made his bones ache, that their vows would not be enough to keep Blaine in E'ridia.

Blaine leaned forward to rest his forehead against Honovi's shoulder, sucking in a sharp breath. He held it for the longest time before finally letting it out on a slow sigh.

"I was Westergard once," Blaine said in a voice barely louder than a whisper, as if he couldn't bear to part with the words.

Honovi closed his eyes and pocketed the ring before wrapping both arms around his husband. He could hear it in Blaine's voice—the regret for leaving, for being called to a road Honovi wasn't sure he could follow. Because Mainspring had offered Blaine something Honovi never could—recognition of a past lost.

Honovi was vaguely familiar with the Westergard bloodline only because it had always shadowed the Rourkes. He knew it had been eradicated during the Inferno, or so history and their own spies said. But Westergard was simply another name for *duty*, and Honovi understood the lengths one would go to uphold such a thing. Being smuggled away by a star god wouldn't be enough to keep him from protecting the clans if it were he who'd lost a homeland.

And it wasn't as if Blaine was risking himself alone. The Clockwork Brigade had a plan. Spies were useful that way, and the cogs that were all the people who made up the Ashionen rebellion had spun their way past the Eastern Spine to Glencoe. Politics was ever tangled, and not even borders could keep it out.

Mainspring promised forged papers and a meticulously built background for a bright Ashionen engineer who had traveled far to attend the Aeronautical Institute, E'ridia's premier university. A man who had assimilated into the culture deep enough that no one would question the accent he'd carry back to Amari. An offer of employment lecturing about engine development waited for him at Amari's Aether School of Engineering, despite Blaine having never taught a class in his life.

But he knew engines, and Honovi wondered how Mainspring had come to discover that fact, or if she just assumed every E'ridian would know how to fly and have a love for the mechanics of it all.

Honovi turned his head to press a kiss to his husband's temple, lips ghosting over soft skin. "I wish you would have told me this. I would have kept your secret."

Blaine nodded jerkily before lifting his head, lips finding Honovi's for a kiss that almost hurt before he pulled away. "It wasn't mine to tell."

"You're Clan Storm now, no matter what anyone says. I want you to remember that." Honovi ran his hand over Blaine's head, fingers catching at the start of the braid at the nape of his neck. He pressed their foreheads together and swallowed tightly. "What do you need?"

"Mainspring said we leave tonight with her cogs. There's an Ashionen airship set to depart for Foxborough before the sun sets. She said we'll take a train from that city to Amari after we land. I can get in contact with you through the embassy there once we arrive and I get settled wherever Mainspring puts me."

"All right."

Blaine chewed on his bottom lip. "And I need you to cut my hair."

Honovi jerked, a full-body shudder that wrenched him back a step. Blaine refused to let him go, finger still hooked tightly through his belt loop.

"No," Honovi ground out.

"I will always be E'ridian, but I can't look it where I'm going. Please, Honovi. Do this for me."

Blaine's entreaty felt like a betrayal, even as he understood the safety passing as Ashionen would provide him. That still didn't make it easy to hear Blaine asking for Honovi to strip him of his culture.

In the end, he could not say no. In the end, Honovi refused to let anyone else carve his husband into a stranger. He reached up and touched his fingers to Blaine's jaw, staring into familiar hazel eyes. Hidden in their depths was an old grief Honovi couldn't ignore. "Is this what you truly want?"

"It's not about what I want. It's about what is needed from me. I'd hoped the star gods would not call me back." Blaine swallowed thickly, blinking rapidly. "But I can no more walk away from this than you can from being *jarl*."

"Did you expect a summons like this?"

"Not like this."

"But you expected *something*. And you never told me."

Blaine wrapped his fingers around Honovi's wrist. "Did you forget who brought me to E'ridia?"

Honovi flexed his fingers, mouth twisting into a grimace. He'd not seen the Dusk Star since that long-ago night, and some days, Honovi thought he'd dreamed her. But the reality of her visit had grown up beside Honovi for the last fifteen years, held safe behind the Eastern Spine and chasing the wind into distant lands on airships.

Perhaps that was her intention all along.

They all knew of the Inferno, knew of the coup that had gutted Ashion's royal bloodline. E'ridia had recalled all their ambassadors for the years following the political upheaval. Only when things had settled, when the Ashion parliament defiantly continued, albeit monarchless and fighting a losing battle against the Daijal court, did the *Comhairle nan Cinnidhean* send their airships back to that country.

Honovi had cut his teeth on trade talks beside ambassadors there and with the Houses of Solaria amidst their Senate and Imperial court. He wondered what placement he could find in the west, on the upper part of the continent, because he did not want Blaine to go alone. But his father's words still rang in his ears, and duty was like an airship anchor, heavy and unyielding to the winds.

Honovi twisted his hand so he could tangle their fingers together. "I don't know Ashionen style."

Blaine lifted his hand to brush two fingers over the space where his collarbone would be beneath his shirt. "Mainspring said to crop it short, but up to here is fine."

It wasn't, but it would need to be.

Honovi dug up a pair of scissors from the writing desk sharp enough for the job at hand while Blaine sat backward on the desk chair. The thick length of his braid fell down his back, the color lighter than Honovi's, always tucked beneath a leather flight jacket and cap when on an airship.

Blaine had never been one for hair adornments, even during festivals, preferring the simple beaded clan ribbon twined through the plait over anything else. Honovi was used to the catch of metal in his own hair, the weight of his rank twisted through the mohawk and braid he'd worn for years. It was easier to undo Blaine's plait than his own, removing the tie at the end to separate the three sections.

Honovi gently tugged the clans ribbon free of the thick strands, the intricate beadwork cool against his palm. He tucked it away in his pocket before fetching a comb from the washroom across the hall to work the teeth of it through the blond waves of Blaine's hair. It might have been easier to chop it all off when it was still braided, but Honovi had wanted Blaine to keep the clans ribbon the way he'd kept that ring.

The snip of the scissors cutting through hair sounded overloud in the room. Blaine's breath caught in his throat, the sound barely audible, but Honovi heard it anyway. He kept cutting, blond hair falling to the floor in chunks, and he tried not to feel ill. When it was done, and the trim was as even as it could be, Honovi combed Blaine's hair back into a loose queue, using the clans ribbon to tie it into place.

"There," he said in a rough voice. "It's done."

He stepped back, watching as Blaine lifted a hand to touch what remained, fingers carding through the loose strands. "It feels strange."

Honovi didn't think he was only talking about his hair.

But it was over now, the years he'd grown up as clan scattered on the floor. Honovi stepped over the shorn locks, catching Blaine up in a kiss that turned into another and another, until they were gasping into each other's mouths.

It was easy, then, to guide Blaine back into the bedroom. Easy to shove everything off the bed and push his husband down onto the mattress, to strip them both of their clothes the way he'd done to Blaine's history here.

Honovi didn't temper his hands or his mouth, didn't soften the blow of being left behind by being gentle or slow. He sucked bruises into Blaine's skin, bit at his collarbone, and stroked him to hardness with dry fingers until Blaine squirmed in his arms from the rough handling.

"Please," Blaine whispered against his mouth when Honovi reached for the jar of oil ever present in their nightstand drawer.

He was too impatient to go slow and pushed two fingers inside Blaine without stopping. The sound his husband made had Honovi hiding his face against Blaine's neck, licking at the skin there.

"*Please,*" Blaine begged again, and Honovi couldn't deny either of them this memory.

He worked Blaine open with skill born from years of touching each other this way. When Honovi finally sank into him, Blaine tipped his head back with a choked-off cry, eyes squeezed shut, the short strands of his hair twisted against the pillow.

Honovi hated the sight of Blaine like that but loved him all the same, and it was easy, so easy, to pull out and thrust back in, to chase a pleasure neither knew when they'd get again. Honovi held Blaine down and fucked him until it almost hurt, until Blaine came with a sob, holding Honovi close and kissing an apology to his lips.

Honovi came moments after Blaine, too keyed up to make it last, grinding in deep as his climax punched through his body. Blaine cradled him close in the aftermath, both of them a sticky mess, in no hurry just yet to move.

Blaine stroked a hand over Honovi's back, fingers ghosting over his braid, tracing what he'd given up. His embrace lacked the joy of a long-haul flight well done, of negotiations won, grip tinged with a desperate uncertainty Honovi could almost taste.

"I need to finish packing," Blaine said in the quiet that had settled around them.

Honovi closed his eyes, holding Blaine tight for as long as he could. "I'll help."

Because he always had. Because that was his duty as *jarl* and Blaine's husband.

Seven

BLAINE

The motor carriage drove through the streets of Glencoe, the sound of its engine taking up space where words should be. Blaine glanced at where Honovi sat in the driver's seat, both hands on the steering wheel and staring straight ahead. They'd passed through the last inner defensive wall, the buildings in this area of Glencoe of newer architecture. Even in the gas lamp-lit streets, Blaine could see that.

He could also see how much Honovi wanted to turn the motor carriage around and drive them both away from the inevitable.

"You didn't have to come," Blaine said quietly. They'd already said their goodbyes in private, pressed the words into skin.

Honovi slanted him an unreadable look. "What sort of husband would that make me if I didn't see you off?"

Blaine reached across the bench and settled his hand on Honovi's thigh, needing the contact. "I'd rather leave you surrounded by clan than by yourself on the docks."

Honovi looked back at the street as he maneuvered the motor carriage through the evening bustle of dockworkers heading home for the night. However deep his anger ran, it didn't stop him from covering Blaine's hand with his own. Blaine was glad for his touch.

"The Dusk Star decreed you were clan until she said otherwise, and she hasn't. You're following the North Star's order here, but I want you to remember you'll always be clan."

Blaine swallowed tightly at those words and turned his hand upside down so he could slide his fingers between Honovi's. He lifted his husband's hand to his mouth to brush a kiss over warm knuckles. "I'll always be yours."

He'd left his marriage torc behind, and the absence of its weight around his throat left him feeling off-kilter, which was no way to be when meeting with Mainspring. Blaine had a feeling he'd need all his wits around him to match words with that woman.

The airfield's main gate came into view up ahead. Blaine caught sight of Mainspring by the gate, and Honovi pulled the motor carriage to the side of the street. He braked to a stop and locked the wheels in place before turning off the engine.

Mainspring and her cogs approached, the woman giving Blaine a nod when he finally climbed out of the motor carriage, the trade tongue slipping free of her lips. "You're cutting it close. I thought you'd changed your mind."

Blaine tilted his head, meeting her gaze through the veil she wore and replying in the same language. "If I had, you would have been informed."

Honovi came around the motor carriage to stand beside Blaine, catching his attention. "I'll hand off your trunk to the porters."

He spoke in E'ridian, and Blaine switched to the language he considered his native tongue these days. "This isn't a permanent goodbye."

Honovi raised his hand to run his fingers through Blaine's shorn hair, the absence of his braid almost as jarring as the emptiness around his throat. "I'll find a way to follow you."

It wasn't what the *Comhairle nan Cinnidhean* would have preferred, but Blaine had no doubt his husband would somehow build a road back to him. Blaine forced a smile before pulling Honovi into a kiss that was as desperate as all the ones from earlier. He wanted to remember the way Honovi felt in his arms; the way he tasted; the timbre of his voice. Blaine packed away the memories in a tight little ball he hoped to never forget.

"I know you will," Blaine said when they parted. Honovi managed a rictus of a smile that looked ghastly in the shadows cast by the nearby lamppost. Then he stepped away, out of reach, and Blaine's fingers curled on air. The ache in his chest didn't fade. "I'll write you."

"No, you won't," Mainspring said.

Blaine turned his head to look at her, irritated by her eavesdropping and wondering just how much E'ridian she knew. "You seem to think you get a say in this."

"You risk too much on our end if you remain in contact with anyone here in E'ridia." She kept her voice low, a quiet murmur within their close conversation circle, not wanting to be overheard.

"The clans will require updates, and I promised to provide such to my husband and my *ceann-cinnidh*. You can call me whatever you like for this shadow game of yours, but I am clan, and that will not change."

"He'll send such communication through our embassy in Amari," Honovi said, staring at Mainspring.

A flash of annoyance flickered across her eyes before she imperiously held out her hand. "I'll see that ring you spoke of during the meeting."

Blaine slipped his hand into his flight jacket pocket, retrieving what she wanted to look at. He held it up for her perusal but refused to relinquish it. In the glow from the nearby lamppost, he could just make out the shadowy grooves of a crest he hadn't claimed for years.

Mainspring nodded after a moment. "Very well. Now, let's be off."

She turned and headed for the gate that would lead to the airfield and the launch docks, her cogs following dutifully at her heels. She seemed to have every expectation that Blaine would follow—and she would be right.

Honovi snagged him by the elbow, reeling him in for one last kiss. "Safe travels and strong winds."

Blaine nodded and forced himself to walk away from the man he loved, refusing to look back.

For I am starshine lest you guide me wrong.

The song prayer whispered through his mind, and Blaine let the memory of drum beats and chanting and eerie pipes in a Star Order temple drown out the desire to stay by Honovi's side. Duty was never an easy thing to keep.

The sun was dipping below the horizon at the edge of the Sunrise Valley, casting the airfield in long shadows and turning the mountains on the horizon aglow in burnt oranges. The sky above was darkening, with the first stars shining in the east. Despite the hour, the docks still bustled with workers loading and off-loading cargo from airships.

It was a long walk to the far edge of the airfield, where a large Ashionen airship was anchored, its design nowhere near as sleek as one of E'ridian make. Mainspring presented their travel tickets to the attendant on the dock with a little flourish. The attendant took them after glancing at the pocket watch in his other hand before putting it away. "You almost missed the gangplank closure."

"It's a good thing we didn't," Mainspring said lightly. "We had a bit of trouble with lost luggage, but it was thankfully found."

The attendant checked the tickets beneath the glow of the gas lamp bolted to a post and punched a hole in the corner of each one, indicating they were cleared for boarding. The porters had made it to the assigned dock and were already halfway up the secondary gangplank that provided access to the cargo bay of the airship. Blaine's party went up the main gangplank for the decking.

An attendant on the open-air deck directed them toward the interior. The enclosed space was the first-class dining room, the shutters over the interlocking glass panels folded back for the evening flight.

They took a narrow, twisted set of stairs belowdecks, where another attendant checked their tickets and directed them to their berths: two interior rooms, with no windows and no beds, only two benches facing each other, with shelves bolted overhead for carry-on luggage, and a single gas lamp turned low giving off light.

Mainspring's two cogs went into the room across the narrow hall from theirs. Mainspring only carried with her a satchel, which she tucked out of the way on the shelf over one bench. A blanket was folded on each thinly cushioned bench, with a pillow stuffed into rough linen cases perched on top. It was a far cry from the captain's quarters Blaine had always shared with Honovi.

"We'll land in Foxborough before sunrise to catch the steam train. I'd rather our transfer happen under the relative anonymity of darkness," Mainspring said.

Blaine took a seat on one of the benches, watching as she sat opposite him. She grimaced at the accommodations before dragging the blanket over her lap. Curiously, she didn't remove the veil.

"Who are you really?" Blaine asked in the trade tongue now that they were alone.

She did him a kindness by responding in the same language. "Secrets aren't kept if they're told, and the Daijal court has eyes and ears everywhere."

"We're still docked. I can leave right now."

Mainspring pressed her lips together before she let out a heavy sigh. When she spoke, her voice was barely louder than a whisper. "I'm Lady Lore Auclair, of the Auclair bloodline. I was the only one my mother could send when our desperate inquiry over winter bore fruit."

"Auclair bloodline," Blaine echoed just as quietly, dredging up what he knew of the remaining bloodlines in Ashion. "Yours is the oldest in Ashion."

"Because the Rourkes are gone."

"There's Eimarille."

"The North Star considers her Daijalan, and we follow the will of our guiding star." Lore smoothed the blanket over her lap, lifting her chin. "You'll need to change before we land. Marcus has a spare outfit for you in his carry-on satchel. You're of his build. It should mostly fit."

The corner of Blaine's mouth tugged downward. "Very well."

"And you'll need to speak Ashionen."

Blaine frowned. "Why?"

"We've built a new identity for you, one you must live as while in

Ashion. You're Tristan Arquette now, and you must speak ours, not E'ridian. How much of it do you remember?"

He picked out the words in careful Ashionen, stumbling over the pronunciation here and there, for it was no longer the language he knew fluently. "I was ten when I left. I didn't lose it completely, if that's what you're asking. We trade enough with Ashion it comes in handy."

"But you're no longer fluent."

Blaine shook his head. "No. I'm not."

"We can work with your lack of fluency. We'll need to immerse you in Ashionen culture over the coming weeks to make you even passable before the end of summer."

The idea of attending what was, for all intents and purposes, etiquette classes made him want to groan. She didn't press the issue, which he was thankful for. It was difficult enough to leave his home and not know when he would return. But to know he'd have to become that which he'd given up at a star god's urging left him uneasy.

Lore let the conversation lapse until after the attendant had been by to check that they were settled and warn them the launch was imminent and to remain seated. Lore locked the cabin door after the attendant left. The sound of the engines grew distantly louder, and the airship juddered after being unmoored from its dock. The pop in his ears as they rose in altitude was a familiar pressure.

"Will you sleep like that?" Blaine asked.

Lore blinked at him. "Pardon?"

He lifted a hand and gestured at his own face, not giving voice to what he meant but clearly indicating the veil she wore. "It can't be comfortable."

"I do not take it off when I'm in the field unless there is no other choice."

The Clockwork Brigade was made up of secrets, and Blaine would have to live one where he was going. It left a sour taste in his mouth, but there was no backing out now. They were already in the air, heading west, back to a country that could never be home for him.

Eight

SOREN

"You should walk around. Stretch your legs," Soren said as the fueling hose clicked off, indicating the gas tank was full.

"You should hurry up and finish so we can leave," Vanya countered from where he sat on the velocycle. He still wore the helmet, though it did little to hide his face. Soren hoped he wasn't getting sunburned from riding beneath a cloudless sky.

Soren rolled his eyes, glad his goggles probably made the motion difficult to see. The last thing he needed was another argument with his royal pain the ass. "In a minute."

The way station was an outpost that couldn't even be called a village. Government owned and operated like every way station in Solaria, it was nothing more than a travel stop some distance from the railroad tracks, not even large enough to merit an actual train station. A single clerk operated the way station, and he hadn't been much for conversation when Soren had gone inside to pay.

The single, drab building sat adjacent to the fueling tank stand, its roof arched like a barrel and all gutters leading to a water reclamation tank. The filters and purifiers looked to be mostly up-to-date, which had prompted Soren to buy a travel bottle of water for Vanya after paying for the fuel. Soren could drink off the land and survive the impurities. Unfiltered water would sicken or kill pretty much anyone else, and they'd come too far for him to let Vanya die because he was thirsty.

Soren removed the nozzle from the velocycle's gas tank and twisted the cap over it until it made a satisfying *click* noise and locked in place. He shoved the pump back into its cradle before turning to face his charge.

Vanya looked better, but that wasn't saying much. His trousers were stained and dirty, though he'd removed his outer robe with its stark embroidery and tied it over the travel compartment. The gold ranking medallion was tucked beneath one of Soren's undershirts that Vanya now wore, the gray fabric stretched obscenely tight across the other man's chest and shoulders. It clearly did not fit. Soren tried not to dwell on how that wasn't necessarily a terrible thing.

Bruises had come up on Vanya's dark skin as they rode, and he moved with a stiffness that not even Soren's bruise balm could fix. His stride, when he walked, had a faint hitch to it as he tried to hide the limp from his wrenched ankle. A magician who could mend bone would be of far better help than Soren's meager offerings, but they wouldn't get that until they reached Bellingham.

They were less than a day's ride from that city, but the sun was dropping lower in the sky, far past its zenith. If they continued, it would be another night ride, and Soren was tired enough to know that wouldn't be a smart move. His eyes burned from exhaustion, the dry grittiness on every eyeblink a warning that he needed sleep.

He'd never thought twice about camping out in the open, but it had been a headache to do so ever since he'd picked up Vanya from the wreck. Vanya could sleep; Soren had to stand watch. The stimulants he'd taken to stay awake for the last few days were beginning to wear off. He needed to rest in a place that was marginally defensible, at least for Vanya's safety.

Soren looked back at the way station building, knowing it had one or two guest rooms available for travelers to rent. He also knew Vanya was opposed to staying anywhere public. Soren didn't see how a single clerk was *public*, not when they could hide away in a room, but arguing with Vanya only produced a headache.

It seemed Soren didn't mind the pain.

"We should stay here for the night," Soren said.

"Absolutely not. You said we were close to Bellingham," Vanya said, frowning at him.

"Half a day isn't exactly close. It'd be a night ride if we continue."

"So we continue."

Soren scoffed tiredly. "You're not the one driving. I am, and it's getting to the point my eyes are crossing."

"Then I'll drive."

"Have you ever even driven yourself before? Don't you have servants for that?"

He couldn't keep the sarcasm out of his voice. Vanya didn't seem exceptionally pleased about his tone, judging by the icy look he shot at Soren.

"I was trained alongside Legion officers growing up when it came to my military education. That included learning how to drive," Vanya bit out.

Soren flicked his fingers at the velocycle Vanya sat on. "That is not a steam tank."

"Of course not. It lacks the weaponry that would be found on one of ours."

The scorn in his voice made Soren scowl. "That's my velocycle you're disparaging."

Vanya waved off his words. "I'd add a mini-Zip gun to it if I thought you'd let me. We could consider it payment for your actions."

"I didn't save your damn life because I wanted *payment*."

Something like surprise flickered across Vanya's eyes before it disappeared. Soren couldn't even be sure that was the emotion he'd seen. Vanya was ever the politician, with an expressionless mask for a face. It hadn't cracked much, if at all, since they'd started north.

"I could see if they have a telegraph machine inside. You could contact your House in Bellingham," Soren said, unbending enough to offer up a possible compromise. They were too remote to hope for access to a telephone, as those devices were generally accessible only by the ruling class, merchants, politicians, or the military.

Vanya's mouth settled into a hard line. "No."

"Do you even know how to use a telegraph machine?"

The look Vanya shot him was incendiary, shoulders stiffening. "Bellingham is under the governorship of the House of Kimathi. I wouldn't trust their clerks to receive a private message meant for the empress."

Soren never understood the power plays between the Houses and had no desire to. "Then why are you going there if you don't trust them?"

"There's a marriage contract in play."

Soren knew enough about the politics between the Houses to understand the headache that was. "In that case, don't you think it's important the Houses know you're alive?"

Vanya arched an eyebrow. "Not if the House of Kimathi was the one who poisoned me."

Soren rubbed at his forehead above the leather edge of his brass goggles. He wanted to be nowhere near that political headache, but he was already committed. "I don't trust my reflexes to keep you alive on the plains for a night ride after days of no sleep. If you won't contact anyone, then we're staying here for the night."

"I'm capable of looking after myself."

Soren bit his tongue so he wouldn't say something exceedingly rude. The wardens' governor would be thoroughly displeased if the House of Sa'Liandel sent a complaint about his attitude after this whole mess.

"Against revenants?" Soren asked.

"There's been none on the road."

"That's not to say they aren't out there. I found a bog where one shouldn't be, remember?"

His samples were still carefully stored away, along with his map. Vanya had seemed interested in them during the time they'd camped out for a few hours during daylight hours yesterday so the prince could get some rest. Soren had stood guard, passing time by going through his logbook.

"The wardens will be well compensated for your actions. I'll ensure my mother provides aid for whoever is sent to cleanse that section of land." Vanya shifted on the velocycle, mouth twitching as if he wanted to grimace but was forcing himself not to. "That still doesn't absolve me of the debt I owe you."

"Wardens don't hold debts. We guard the borders. We keep the edges. No country owes us anything but tithes for that," Soren reminded him.

"When we reach Bellingham, we'll settle this." He pointed at the seat in front of him, staring at Soren. "Let's go."

Vanya spoke with an arrogant authority that told Soren the prince was not used to being disobeyed. His people might be forced to follow his orders, but Soren was a warden. He did as he liked, when he liked, bound by nothing but the Poison Accords.

"The way station sells jerky. I'm getting some."

Soren turned on his heels, heading back to the small shop inside the way station, feeling Vanya's gaze boring into his back with every step he took. His store of jerky and hard brown crackers was low, since it was really the only safe food he was willing to let Vanya eat on the road.

The middle-aged clerk looked up from the book he was reading at the counter that doubled as an administrative desk. "Back already, warden?"

Soren picked up a couple of parchment-wrapped packages of jerky from a basket on the shelf and set them on the counter. "Forgot these."

"That'll be a fiver."

Soren dug out the aurons, passing over a crumpled note and taking the jerky with him. "How's business been?"

The clerk snorted, lifting his mug of chai to his mouth. The brimless, rounded cap he wore was neatly embroidered around the edge with plain black thread depicting the six star god constellations. Perhaps it was the drink that made him more amenable to conversation this time. "You missed all the excitement by a few days. Apparently a train got derailed south of here. A convoy of Legion engineers passed by on their way to clear the tracks. Didn't stop for any fuel, though."

"Shame."

They'd missed that convoy. He wondered if the group had passed by when they'd been camped out away from the road during the day. He didn't know how long it would take to clear the tracks, but he hadn't seen or heard any trains since the derailment.

Soren gathered his jerky and waved goodbye to the clerk, heading back outside where Vanya waited.

"I got you dinner," Soren said once he was within earshot.

Vanya sighed. "Your idea of food leaves something to be desired."

Soren shoved the jerky into the compartment behind Vanya and locked the lid in place. "You're not in any position to be picky."

"When we get to Bellingham, I'm going to have a feast thrown in your honor so you know exactly what you've been missing all these years."

"Rude."

Vanya cracked a smile. "I don't think I've ever been called that to my face before."

"First time for everything."

Soren did a cursory check of his velocycle's tires before straightening up. He was about to sling his leg over the seat when movement down the road caught his attention. The road they'd been driving down that passed the way station had been empty all the way to the horizon when they arrived. Now, two shadowy figures were making their way toward the way station, stumbling in a manner that made the hair on the back of Soren's neck stand on end.

He yanked open the travel compartment again and removed his double-lensed spyglass. Tipping it out of the case, Soren pushed his goggles up and placed the spyglass over his nose, adjusting the lenses with one hand. The figures came into magnified view, blurry at first, before sharpening into the rotten bodies of revenants.

Soren dropped the spyglass back into the case, dumped it into the travel compartment, then hauled Vanya off the velocycle. "Get inside the way station."

"What are you—" Vanya began, annoyance bleeding through his tone.

"Revenants," Soren cut in, shoving Vanya toward the building. "Get inside and tell the clerk to close the storm shutters and bar the door. Don't open it again until you hear from me."

Vanya stared at him for a couple of seconds before wrenching his gaze toward the road and the threat coming their way. "I can burn them if you let me."

Soren raised an eyebrow. "This close to a way station and all its fuel? I thought you wanted to hide, princeling? Starfire won't help you with that."

Vanya glared at him. "What will you do, then?"

"My job."

He stared the Imperial crown prince down until Vanya turned on his heels and walked into the way station. Seconds after the door shut behind Vanya, he could see the clerk in the window, frantically cranking a lever. Metal screeched as the storm shutters unfolded on the outside of the window and lowered over the glass. They locked from the inside, because no one in their right mind stepped beyond solid walls amidst the threat of revenants.

Wardens weren't generally regarded as sane by the general population in any country, but that had never stopped Soren from meeting a threat head-on. He climbed onto his velocycle and left a trail of exhaust and dust behind when he pulled out of the way station and onto the road.

Soren scanned the immediate area, not seeing anything in the fields on either side of the road, but that wasn't to say more revenants weren't out there, waiting. A pity the way station lacked a warden resupply station. He'd have to watch his bullets.

Soren slowed his velocycle to a crawl before finally braking to a stop. He locked the brakes and kicked the stand down but kept the engine running. Then he reached for the shotgun where it was mounted on the frame and pulled it free.

Undoing the slide lock on the short barrel, Soren checked the cartridge count. The gears turned and locked when he slid the cover back into place. Leaving his velocycle behind, Soren walked down the center of the road, keeping the revenants in sight, short-barreled shotgun heavy in his hands. When he was a good few meters from his ride, Soren stopped and planted his feet, allowing the revenants to come to him.

They moved with the slowness of the newly risen, which made them easier to put down. What remained of their flesh was bloated in places. One revenant was missing most of its arms, the limbs most likely scavenged by a wild animal. Their robes were messy, bloody things, but even beneath the filth, Soren could see the clothing wasn't as well-made as Vanya's.

They'd been no one of note, though he knew they were probably missed by someone. Their names would never be carved onto a memory wall in a columbarium, but at least Soren could put them to rest.

Soren braced the stock against his shoulder and sighted down the barrel at the walking dead. He pulled the handguard back, and the first round found its home in the smaller revenant's head, entering through the chewed-off nose and out the back in a spray of sludgy brain matter. The revenant went down and didn't get back up.

The empty cartridge was ejected and a new one chambered as Soren pushed the handguard forward along the barrel. The lingering revenant screamed in that hideous way they had—like a wild thing caught in a trap, incapable of freeing itself. Soren aimed at the second one and fired, slug finding its home in the revenant's neck. The head flopped forward as the body collapsed.

Soren lowered his shotgun and scanned the area, on high alert for any hint of movement. Nothing in the immediate area appeared to be a threat anymore, not with the revenants taken down by poisoned shotgun slugs. He retreated to his velocycle, retrieving his spyglass so he could confirm the plains around the way station were empty of revenants. No movement met his eyes, and after a few minutes, Soren put the spyglass away.

This was *supposed* to be cleansed land, according to his map. He'd been taking the back roads—which weren't so much roads as open ground—with Vanya because they should have been safe. But the revenants from before at the train wreck and the ones today had to come from somewhere, and that bog was not where it should have been.

What Soren wanted to do was a grid search, figure out if another bog or fen had cropped up in this area of the plains. But he had an Imperial crown prince who he was responsible for at the moment that took priority. Soren knew if he left Vanya alone, the prince wouldn't send a telegram for help; he'd probably walk to Bellingham on his own.

The mere idea of that was enough to make Soren's stomach twist.

He put his shotgun away in its holster on the velocycle and went to drag the bodies of the revenants off the road. He took them far enough into the prairie grass that no one could see them from the road. He unsheathed his short sword, not bothering with activating the poison, and chopped off the revenants' heads. He'd burn the bodies in a bit, but first he needed to let Vanya know they were in the clear.

For now.

Soren rode back to the way station and parked his velocycle beneath the canopy. When he made it to the door, he banged his fist on it. "It's me. Open up."

The sound of a dead bolt unlocking reached his ears, and then the heavy door was pulled open by Vanya, the clerk behind him pointing a long-barreled shotgun at the entrance. Soren arched an eyebrow, taking in the clerk's steady hands.

"Revenants are down and off the road. I need to burn them." Soren looked at Vanya. "We're staying here tonight."

Before the prince could protest, the clerk thumbed the safety on his shotgun and let the barrel rest against his shoulder. "I won't charge you for a room."

Soren nodded his thanks. "How long has it been since you saw revenants around here?"

"I wasn't assigned to this way station during winter, but the record books don't have any entries about that. This is the first appearance since I started here during Fourth Month."

Soren filed that information away. Perhaps the revenants were typical stragglers, incapable of surviving in the wilderness and dying because of it. But the horde that had run after the train had numbered almost two dozen, and that was more than was typically found in cleansed land these days.

"I'll be back later. Keep the door locked just in case."

"I'm coming with you," Vanya said.

Soren shook his head. "It'll be safer for you here."

"You already took care of the threat."

Vanya stepped outside before Soren could protest, squinting against the sunlight. The clerk was more than happy to follow Soren's order, and the heavy door was shut and locked again in seconds.

"This isn't your job," Soren reminded him as they trudged back to his velocycle.

"Solaria is my country."

"Wardens keep the borders, not you."

The borders were ever changing and didn't necessarily mean the defined country lines on maps. It was wherever the poison fields existed—the bogs, the fens, the dead. Wardens might have pushed the boundaries of every country ever outward over the Ages, but pockets of poison were inevitable. Alchemy could only change so much for so long, and they were always one mistake away from another Dying Time, or so the wardens taught.

In the three years since Soren had been promoted to a warden in the field, he could see the truth in that history, for Maricol was not an easy mother to love.

"The borders of Solaria are still mine," Vanya said as he sat in his usual spot on the velocycle.

"I'd say you're greedy for a prince, but you're the first one I've had the unfortunate luck to meet."

Vanya looked at him, gaze raking up and down Soren's body with a casual assessment he didn't know what to do with. "Oh, but I am greedy. I wouldn't have survived this long if I wasn't."

Soren shook his head and got on the velocycle. "That's not greed. That's stubbornness."

Vanya's hands settled on his waist, his grip familiar after so long traveling together. He leaned against Soren's back, uncaring about the weapons in the way, lips brushing over Soren's ear when he spoke.

"You should know we Solarians are an entirely stubborn people."

Soren swallowed, blaming stimulant-driven exhaustion for the shiver that snaked its way down his spine. "Clearly."

He ignored the prince behind him in favor of the task at hand, because the dead couldn't rest until they were ash.

Nine

VANYA

Bellingham was a dot on the horizon that grew larger as the sun neared its zenith. Soren remained a steady, warm presence in front of Vanya on the velocycle as they rode toward the city. Vanya had changed back into his robes an hour ago, ranking medallion hanging prominently around his neck. The stained white fabric of his clothing whipped against his body from the wind blowing past them as Soren kept a steady speed.

They'd left the way station at dawn, when there was enough light in the sky to see the land and any threats that walked it. The clerk had kept the way station locked down throughout the night, the gas lamps burning bright inside and outside the building. Soren had kept watch for half the night on the roof, and not even the chai the clerk had brewed for them before they left had eased the tired line of his mouth in the morning.

Vanya had wanted to smooth the worry from Soren's brow, wipe the exhaustion from his gray eyes in that moment, but they'd still had miles to go. So Vanya had said nothing when Soren chugged the chai and answered Vanya's questions about the day ahead with curt, one-word answers.

The complete lack of deference directed toward Vanya was startling and new, almost amusing. He'd spent his life catered to and expected to be listened to, not ignored. Any anger he could have had about the situation was buried under the knowledge that Vanya was alive only because of the warden.

He'd have died for certain if Soren hadn't walked through the wreckage of the train carriage to find him. If he hadn't had the antidote to the poison Vanya thought he could still taste in the back of his throat. Vanya was viscerally aware he still breathed because Soren belonged to no House that would see him dead.

We keep debts; we do not owe them, his mother always said.

Vanya knew well the danger of becoming indebted to someone of the Houses, but Soren was a warden—nameless, stateless, holding loyalty to no one, only his duty. There was little threat in owing Soren his life, not when the wardens were bound by the Poison Accords and stood outside the laws of every country. The debt could be safely paid, no one the wiser, and his House would be in the clear. The tricky part was getting Soren to accept such a payment.

Vanya tightened his arms around Soren's waist, mindful of the poison sword sheathed across the warden's back and the pistols holstered on both hips. Without a helmet, his light brown hair tangled in the wind. The fair skin on the back of Soren's neck, normally covered by the helmet Vanya now wore, was sunburned from their travels. He had to quash the desire to brush his lips over the reddened skin, curious about the heat to be found there.

Soren was different and dangerous in a way that Vanya could not ignore and did not want to. The handful of days spent under Soren's watchful eye as they headed north had left Vanya wanting in a way he always dealt with by *taking*. Vanya wasn't shy about letting his interest be known, but Soren was either oblivious or ignoring him.

Vanya hated to be ignored.

He licked his lips, probing at the cracks there, and swallowed a sigh. The Southern Plains that made up the northwest area of Solaria weren't nearly as hot as the desert-edged hill country he called home. The western rainforest and eastern swamps clung to the edge of the continent, but the Wastelands crept ever northward over the years.

The road became more crowded with vehicles and travelers the closer they got to Bellingham, the offshoot roads bringing farmers and merchants from the outlying towns and villages in the *vasilyet*.

The walls of the city towered higher than any building save the tallest Star Order temple, the spire there lit at the top with a fire that never burned out. Vanya could see it winking brightly against the blue sky. So, too, could he see the Imperial flag flying above the main gate next to the House of Kimathi flag.

Good. His mother was still in residence.

The black tapestries that hung from the wall on either side of the main gate were cause for concern. The Dawn Star's constellation was painted in gold at the top of each tapestry, while a prayer for the dead took up the rest of the space. Such a tapestry was only ever raised for the House that controlled the Imperial throne.

"Someone thinks you're dead," Soren called over his shoulder against the wind as he weaved around several motor carriages pulling into the line to get inside the city.

Vanya raked his gaze over the mourning of his name on the tapestries and grimaced. Perhaps he should have attempted a telegram or found a place that had a telephone. It was too late now to regret his silence, not when they had finally reached Bellingham.

Peacekeepers manned the checkpoint into Bellingham alongside several legionnaires, taking record of citizens and foreigners who had come to visit. Bellingham was a major trade city, with most of its commerce running across the Daijal border. The House of Kimathi oversaw the day-to-day business of trade for the Imperial throne, and that House's wealth and status was bested by none save the House of Sa'Liandel and the House of Vikander in the northeast.

It was why the marriage contract had been initiated to begin with. The House of Vikander was already loyal to the Imperial throne—as loyal as a House might be. His bloodline had spent several generations and an untold amount of political and societal clout to gain that House's support. They'd then turned their sights on the House of Kimathi, whose disdain for Vanya's family was well known and ran deep.

But disdain was not enough for them to say no to a marriage between one of their own and the Imperial crown prince when his mother had first put forth the offer. Vanya had thought the House of Kimathi had approved of the match after a year of negotiation. The wreckage he'd left on the railroad tracks in the south spoke otherwise.

He had no proof of treachery, though, only history.

Soren ignored the tidy line of travelers waiting to pass through the pillared main entrance and drove to the gate. He braked to a halt when ordered to by a couple of legionnaires who weren't shy about pointing their service pistols at them.

"State your business," one called out as the soldiers approached. The tan of their uniforms was broken up by the crimson-and-white *effiyeh* they wore on their heads, held in place by a black band.

Soren's status as a warden should have given him right of passage, but Vanya supposed the false news of his death had put everyone on edge. He removed the helmet and slid off the velocycle.

"Is this any way to greet your prince?" Vanya asked, holding himself up tall despite the ache in his ribs and ankle. Soren's bruise balm had eased some of the sharpest pain, but it couldn't heal him completely.

His robes were a mess, but the ranking medallion was in full view, and there was no denying who he was. The soldiers' eyes all went wide, faces washing out pale in shock. The woman who had spoken took a step forward, the ranking stripes on her uniform jacket's upper arms indicating she was in charge.

She went to one knee, fist over her heart and head bowed, her fellow soldiers half a second behind her in their show of respect. "Your Imperial Highness."

Her voice shook, but there was a brightness in her blue eyes that he read as relief. Around them, the line of travelers was erupting in a raucous chorus of disbelieving cheers to welcome him back from the dead in a way that was not a horror. The lieutenant got to her feet, slipping her pistol into its holster before giving him a sharp salute.

"The empress is in residence at the Imperial estate. I will send a legionnaire on ahead to inform Her Imperial Majesty of your return. The rest of us will escort you," she said.

Vanya nodded, agreeable to her quick decision-making. "I will ride with the warden."

"I'm fairly certain they have a motor carriage you can use," Soren said as Vanya retook his seat.

"I have a feeling if I let you go, I would not see you again. We still have unfinished business between us."

Soren revved the engine, guiding his velocycle forward at a speed slow enough for the soldiers to keep up at until they could make it to their own vehicles. "You owe me nothing."

Vanya let the argument lie in favor of the winding ride through Bellingham to the Imperial estate, flanked by more and more legionnaires as the crowds gathered to cheer his arrival. Every major city in Solaria had an estate house that belonged to the Imperial throne, a place of residence they stayed in when visiting the far-flung corners of the empire.

He supposed arriving home in a more discreet manner might have been the safer alternative, but Vanya didn't particularly care to hide the fact he wasn't dead. If anyone within the House of Kimathi had ordered his murder, then he wanted them to know they had failed.

When Soren finally drove through the gates leading to the Imperial estate, his mother and father were waiting for him, standing on the grand pillared porch, dressed all in mourning black despite the heat. Every household servant lined the front drive, bowing as they drove past. The legionnaires on duty all saluted, and the cheering from the streets didn't abate at all.

Soren braked to a halt at the bottom of the steps leading to the estate's front entrance. Vanya slid off the velocycle and ignored the pain in his ankle to climb the steps to his parents, heart beating fast.

When he reached the porch, Vanya bowed, despite the ache in his ribs. "Rumors of my demise have been greatly exaggerated, my Lady Mother. I apologize for any grief it may have caused you, but I am not dead."

Empress Zakariya Sa'Liandel stepped forward and folded him into her embrace, hands clutching at him tightly. She didn't cry, but the redness to her eyes and hitch to her breath was evidence enough of the grief she'd borne for the last several days.

"My darling prince," Zakariya said, pulling back so she could frame his face with both her hands, her gold rings cool against his skin. "It is so *good* to see you returned to us."

Zakariya had foregone her crown and instead wore chains of gold over her long, tightly twisted hair. The golden links were interspersed with diamonds that glittered like stars, the stones matching the ones embedded in the rings she wore and the wide array of necklaces that draped over her shoulders. The gold stood out against the black of her fitted robe, the long sleeves made of sheer, airy voile and caught at the wrists with gold bracelets.

She stepped aside only far enough to allow his father to greet him. Emperor Consort Taye of the House of Sa'Liandel was taller than his mother, hair a dark blond going gray throughout, with light brown eyes and skin that had tanned over the years beneath the desert sun. Vanya had gotten his height and broadness from his father, and he was able to look his father in the eye after they embraced.

"Let us go inside to discuss your return," Taye said.

Vanya nodded before half turning to look down at the courtyard where Soren still sat upon the velocycle. "I would bring the warden with me."

Zakariya made a soft noise in the back of her throat. "As you say. We have much to discuss."

Vanya gestured at Soren to join them. It took a few seconds before Soren deigned to get off his velocycle, taking the steps up to the porch at an unhurried pace. He inclined his head awkwardly to Vanya's parents, brass goggles shoved on top of his head, face streaked with dirt from the wind of their ride. He didn't appear nervous, though there was a hint of exasperation in his gray eyes when Soren finally looked at Vanya.

"I was going to head over to the warden resupply station here in Bellingham. I need to report back to the governor about the revenants," Soren said.

"We have telegraph machines here for you to use, and any supplies you need we will obtain for you," Vanya said.

Soren arched an eyebrow. "Is that so?"

Vanya smiled slightly at the faintly irritated tone in the warden's voice. "Come inside and out of the heat. We'll discuss what happened with my mother, and then I will take you to the bathhouse. We could both use a soak."

Vanya desperately wanted to scrub off the grime of their time on the road. Public bathing houses outnumbered the drinking houses in almost every city of Solaria. Even small villages had at least one inside their defensive walls. It was only polite to wash away the potential threat of poison from their bodies before moving about society.

"You could use a magician who excels in healing," Soren shot back.

"How badly are you hurt?" Zakariya asked sharply before Vanya could respond.

Vanya bit back a sigh and gestured at the open front doors to the estate. "This is a story better told inside."

Zakariya pressed her full lips together. "We were given photographs of the wreck."

Vanya remembered the vicious tumble about the royal train carriage as the train derailed. The bruises on his body had not all faded away, some too deep for the bruise balm to fully penetrate. And he *ached*, for traveling by velocycle and sleeping on the hard ground wasn't conducive to healing. He wanted to be seen by a magician skilled in healing magic, wanted a long, hot soak in a bathhouse. He wanted to show Soren what the warden had been missing on the road.

"I survived," Vanya said gently. "And I owe that survival to Soren. Now, come. Let us go inside."

Zakariya pulled him into another embrace, her hands clutching at him in a way that spoke of grief deferred. Then she put him at arm's length, and they turned to face the servants, *praetoria* legionnaires, and the citizens crowded in front of the gate at the end of the drive.

"The star gods have shined on us this day, for they have returned my son, your prince, to us. We mourn no longer what might have been. Tonight, Solaria shall celebrate his return," Zakariya called out.

The cheering that went up was expected, even if Vanya doubted everyone in Bellingham was thrilled with his return. Such was the way of the Houses and all the distant, wavering bloodlines who aligned themselves with ever-changing promises.

Amidst the noise of celebration, Vanya was ushered inside, the thick walls of the estate allowing for a cooler temperature inside. Some of their household servants had remained inside, quick to set up the table in the foyer with a plethora of cold juices and flavored water.

Vanya hesitated as they approached it, thirsty in a way not easily ignored now, but the memory of the quiet killer on his tongue would not disappear. He was surprised when Soren grabbed a glass of citrus juice, took a quick sip, swished it about his mouth before swallowing it, then offered the glass to Vanya.

"It's fine. You can drink it," Soren said.

Vanya took the glass from him, fingers slipping slightly on the condensation. "Resorted to becoming my own personal poison tester now?"

Soren grabbed his own glass. "Hardly. I need to use your telegraph machine and was promised a bath. I can't do that if you set fire to this mansion like you did to the steam train."

"Then you shall have one." Vanya curled his fingers at a nearby servant. The young woman dutifully stepped forward and bowed, hands clasped together in front of her. "Take Soren to the bathhouse here and provide him anything he needs. He has my full authority to use our telegraph machine for any warden business he requires."

"Yes, Your Imperial Highness," the servant murmured.

"I'll join you when my meeting is finished," Vanya told Soren.

Soren arched an eyebrow before downing his juice in one go and leaving the glass on the table. Then he allowed himself to be led from the hallway, booted feet making no noise on the mosaic-tiled floor.

"I think that conversation you promised us cannot wait," Taye said in the wake of the warden's absence.

Vanya let himself be led through the cool hallways of the estate to his mother's private office that overlooked the rear garden. Spring meant the flowering bushes were in bloom, while the cluster of white-barked trees native to the plains provided enough shade to cool the area when the sun was high overhead.

Vanya sank onto a chaise, the soft cushions taking his weight easily, and let out a tired sigh. He closed his eyes, listening to the bustle of people around him in the room and the firm orders his mother gave out, one after the other. Then her hand settled on top of his head, and he was reminded of the way she'd touched him as a child like this, always guiding as he stood beside her when she faced down heartbreak.

"I thought I had lost you," Zakariya murmured.

"I pride myself on being difficult to kill," Vanya said, finally opening his eyes.

His father had taken a seat across the way from him, watching them. Servants darted in and out of the office to set up a luncheon on the low table between them. Platters of meats and cheeses, bean dip, herbed rice, and the thin flatbread his people ate with everything. It was enough to feed a squad of legionnaires, and really, Vanya could've eaten the whole thing.

Zakariya pulled her hand away. "The magician comes. Let him see to you."

The servants left. Vanya discarded his dirty robe and succumbed to the exam provided by their House's private magician who excelled in healing magic. The touch of the aether on his body as he ate his weight in food didn't leave him nauseous, though he winced when something *popped* in his chest, ribs realigning themselves.

"A crack, but not a break," Basri murmured as his wand traced the grooves of Vanya's rib cage, aether-drawn magic spilling out of the clarion crystal. "If this is all you came away with from that crash, you were very lucky indeed, Your Imperial Highness."

"I was poisoned."

"With what?"

"Quiet killer."

The sound of a glass shattering had Vanya looking over at where his mother sat, wine dripping from her fingers like blood onto the tiled floor. She slowly flicked shards of glass off her finger, staring at him with equal parts horror and rage.

"I would know who was on that train," she said through clenched teeth.

"We'll pull the records and excise the bloodlines from our employ," Taye said calmly.

"Soren had the antidote. He administered it to me in time. Breathe easy, my Lady Mother. I yet live," Vanya said.

Zakariya accepted the napkin Taye handed her and cleaned off her hand. "We'll finish this conversation in private."

Basri lingered only long enough to finish his healing, prescribe some medicine from his apothecary that Vanya would take with his next meal, and then took his leave.

"Quiet killer," Zakariya said flatly once they were alone.

Vanya nodded, settling deeper onto the chaise, enjoying the absence of the ache in his bones. "In my chai."

"Tell us."

Vanya did, leaving nothing out. He was meticulous in his recollection, and Soren loomed large over the past few days of memories.

Zakariya studied him across the food and cold wine between them, expression impossible to read. "Wardens are outside our laws. This debt you owe can be forgotten."

"*I* will remember, and I will not owe him," Vanya said sharply. "He deserves more than my thanks. I would be dead without Soren's help."

And he knew that Soren should not have technically interfered at all, but the warden hadn't known at the time it was Vanya in that train carriage. The revenants had been enough to draw his attention and keep him there, giving aid and unknowingly indebting Vanya to him.

"Your life is priceless to me. If it was a House who had aided you, it would cripple ours."

"Then we are lucky it was only a House that tried to murder me."

Zakariya sighed before reaching for a glass of the cold red wine. "The marriage contract was void upon your death. We will need to inform the barristers they must revive it."

"We cannot be certain the House of Kimathi had no hand in this travesty," Taye warned.

"The train and all evidence was burned with starfire. A pity, that, but I would have made the same decision if quiet killer was on my tongue." His mother's gaze cut his way. "But an heir must be secured, and this will allow us some measure of control over that gods-forsaken House."

Vanya inclined his head at his parents. "I will abide by your will."

Zakariya set her wineglass down and stood. She came around the low table, and Vanya stood to receive the hug she offered. The comfort in the wake of near-certain death made him hold her tighter than he normally would.

"We celebrate your return tonight with a feast. Your betrothed and her House will join us, as will the warden. For now, go rest," she murmured.

Vanya pressed a gentle kiss to his mother's temple and took his leave, ever the diligent son.

Ten

SOREN

Soren had been in his share of bathhouses over the last couple of years when traveling through Solaria. Some of them had consisted of nothing more than a tiled room with a single tub, while others found in public squares were capable of tending to dozens of people at a time. He had never been lucky enough to visit one whose sole purpose was built for luxury until now.

The bathhouse the servant led him to was connected to the main building by a pathway covered by a pergola draped in enough vines to provide some amount of shade. The outside of the bathhouse was built with cream-colored stone, and a golden domed roof had round, stained glass windows embedded in it. The entrance was doorless and braced on either side by two pillars holding up a multifoil arch.

Inside, the bathhouse was exquisitely decorated, with pale sand-stone tiles underfoot and gleaming white-and-gold tiles covering every inch of the walls and bathing pools. Lounging benches for drying off and socializing circled the edge of the space against the walls, separated by expertly carved stone tables.

In the center were two bathing pools filled with water, with large and small grooves carved into the floor around the pools. Steam rose from one of the pools, and the thought of soaking the stiffness out of his muscles in hot water had Soren hurriedly stripping out of his clothes and weapons in the antechamber. He deposited everything on one of the free-floating storage shelves connected to the wall.

"Leave my things alone," Soren told the attendant on duty.

He wasn't sure she understood him, despite the trade tongue he used, but his gear could be dangerous to those who weren't wardens. Normally, he carried nothing of it with him to a bathhouse, but he doubted it would be stolen here by those serving the House of Sa'Liandel.

Soren entered the bathing room, quietly pleased to find it all to himself. He climbed into the smaller hot water pool, ignoring the attendant who came in carrying a silver tray filled with jars of oil, small blocks of soap, and various bathing tools. She set it on the tiled floor near the edge of the pool before leaving.

The water was hot enough to make him hiss, but Soren dunked himself all the way under anyway. The heat seeped past his skin down to his bones, easing the ache of the long ride and the fights and the work he'd put into keeping Vanya safe off the main road.

Soren let himself sit there for a long moment, eyes closed and head resting on the dip in the edge of the pool for such purpose. He roused after a while, loose-limbed in a way he rarely got, and reached for the soap tray. He scrubbed himself clean with a bar of pale blue soap that smelled of the ocean, getting rid of the grime of travel.

Getting clean on the road was a haphazard affair. One got used to the grit of dirt and dried sweat that water from streams couldn't completely wash away. Soren was glad for the respite here and wondered how long he could stay before someone summoned him. In the end, a summons never arrived, but Vanya did.

Soren was still relaxing in the hot pool when he heard footsteps on the tile. He cracked open one eye before blinking both open at the sight of the Imperial crown prince walking into the bathhouse, wearing no clothes or robe, all the bruises he'd carried on him from before gone from his dark skin.

A servant trailed in his wake, carrying a tray laden down with food and a pitcher of what looked like the cold red wine favored by Solarians year-round. The servant set the tray near the edge of the cool water pool before bowing in Vanya's direction and exiting the bathhouse.

"I can tell by your face you've been in there awhile," Vanya noted in amusement.

Soren lifted a hand from the water and pressed the back of it to his cheek, feeling the heat in his skin. "Yeah."

He let his gaze drift from Vanya's face to his well-muscled chest, lower still before he remembered where he was and who this was. Soren blinked hard and refocused his eyes on Vanya's face, noting the half-lidded, assessing gaze offered him.

Vanya smirked. "Join me in the other pool."

It was less a question and more a demand as the prince stepped into the larger, cooler pool of water. Soren absently noted that he moved better now, that Vanya no longer held himself with a stiffness attributed to sore muscles and bruised bone.

Soren rubbed at his nose and stayed where he was for the time being, watching from a distance as Vanya washed himself clean in the other pool. Only when the prince gave him a pointed look did Soren finally drag himself out of one pool and make his way to the other. The shock of the cooler water made him shiver, and he quickly went neck-deep to acclimate.

Vanya watched him from where he stood in the middle, the water level up to his hips, clear enough it hid nothing, all the grime from being on the road washed away now. Nudity was an accepted social aspect in Solarian bathhouses, and Soren normally didn't mind, but Vanya's attention made his skin prickle in a way that made him wish for privacy.

It had been months since he'd last shared a bed with anyone. The last time had been during winter on the island with a fellow warden. Soren hadn't been blind to Vanya's attention over the last few days, but he had rather thought it might have come from hitting his head too hard during the train wreck. Clearly, even after being healed, that wasn't the case.

"The feast I promised you will happen tonight, but I had the servants make up a platter for you. Eat something," Vanya said.

Soren closed his eyes and tipped his head against the edge of the pool. "In a moment."

He could hear the faint splash of water as Vanya moved through the pool. Soren thought nothing of it until something touched his lips and the smell of fruit filled his nose. He opened his eyes, finding Vanya seated beside him on the pool bench, a berry held to his mouth with steady fingers.

Vanya arched an eyebrow. "Eat."

"I can feed myself," Soren said, lips catching on the fruit.

"I know you can, but allow me this."

They'd traveled together long enough for Soren to know Vanya was prone to demands rather than asking for permission. He supposed it came with being a prince.

Soren wouldn't know.

Couldn't know.

And there was a choice here, Soren knew. He should abide by his duty as a warden and not get mixed up with matters of state. But if that were the case, then he should have left Vanya by the wayside days ago.

Soren didn't blink as he parted his lips and allowed Vanya to feed him the berry. Vanya's fingers lingered against his lips for a second as he chewed before the prince pulled them away. Soren had barely finished swallowing before a different fruit was brought to his mouth, and he allowed himself to eat that one, too.

There were vegetables dipped in hummus, sweet dates, and small pieces of spiced meat. Toasted flatbread dipped in yogurt, fried balls of grain, and a flaky pastry layered with honey and nuts rounded out the rest of the offering. The last one had Soren chasing after Vanya's fingers, unable to stop himself from licking traces of honey off the prince's skin, forgetting his place.

Soren froze, staring up into Vanya's eyes, aware of the ache in his cock that had crept up on him through the intimate gesture of being fed by hand. Before he could jerk back, Vanya curled his fingers beneath Soren's chin, thumb pressing down over his bottom lip. When Soren flicked his tongue out, he could still taste honey.

Vanya's gaze darkened, and it was, perhaps, unsurprising when he said, "I would have you like this."

Soren let his head fall back against the edge of the pool, staring up at the prince. "You're getting married."

"I'm not marrying for love. It's a contract for an heir. I expect my future wife to indulge in courtesans the same way I do."

He said it casually, as if sex was less politically fraught than it was in the north. Perhaps it was, Soren could concede. The southern empire was far less sexually constrained than some countries.

"That's probably not the best way to learn to trust her in your marriage bed."

"Nicca is the granddaughter to the *vezir* of the House of Kimathi. She is heir after her mother. If you know Solarian history, you know there is little trust between our Houses."

"And you think you'll build any by fucking other people?"

Vanya's mouth quirked at the corners, as if he thought Soren's words humorous. "I think you shouldn't concern yourself with matters of state."

Soren arched an eyebrow and gestured at the space between them that had grown smaller. "It's a little late for that."

Vanya trailed his fingers over Soren's jaw, down his throat, to settle on the hard line of his collarbone. His touch was warm, and Soren went still. "Then tell me what you wish as payment, and we shall consider our business concluded."

It wasn't that easily decided and cast aside. Wardens weren't paid in such a way. The Poison Accords didn't allow it.

"I can't," Soren confessed. "It's not my place. I keep telling you that you owe me nothing."

Vanya hummed thoughtfully before leaning down, lips brushing against Soren's in a touch that made his gut tighten in anticipation he had no right to feel. "I'll decide what I owe, not you."

Soren should have turned his head aside, should have slid away across the smooth stone bench he sat on in the water. He should have done whatever it took to put Vanya and all the prince represented out of arm's reach.

But Soren stayed where he was and allowed himself to be kissed because it wasn't often he was *wanted*. Wardens were never wanted, they were needed, and need wasn't always kind. Vanya kissed him with a focused intensity that left Soren gasping for air when he wasn't even close to drowning.

Vanya's hands were warm even beneath the water, and Soren allowed himself to be pulled to his feet there in the pool. A strong arm wrapped around his waist, and he found himself pressed up against Vanya's chest, still being kissed. Soren slid his hand up Vanya's arm to the back of his neck, holding him in place like he had the right to when he didn't.

Vanya nipped at his bottom lip, and Soren didn't bother suppressing a shiver when Vanya's hand trailed over his ass. He leaned into the next kiss and groaned at the feel of Vanya's hard cock against his stomach. The obviousness of his desire wasn't something Soren shied away from. He was twenty, after all, and this was meaningless in all the ways that mattered except pleasure.

Soren let himself be tugged across the pool to the shallower end, let himself be pushed down into a slanted groove along the pool edge that was carved wide enough to cradle him. The tiles lining it were smooth and cool against his back, sunlight shining down from the stained glass windows above. He could feel through the tiles the faint thrum of the filtration and pump machinery buried beneath the floor of the bathhouse as it worked to cycle the pool water.

Vanya stepped between his legs, bold in the way only royalty could be, his hands warm on Soren's thighs. His brown eyes were half-lidded and dark with lust, though Soren knew he wasn't much to look at compared to the nobles and courtesans Vanya had to choose from. He carried scars on his body, evidence of the job he'd been tithed to do, and there was nothing soft about him.

Vanya didn't seem to mind nor care as his hands mapped Soren's body with a sureness that made him shiver beneath the firm touch. The prince didn't seem to be in any rush, which was maddening after a time, and left Soren squirming against cool tile and the water he couldn't completely submerge into at this angle.

It was only after the dozenth time of Vanya's hand brushing across his hard cock without *doing* anything that he finally snapped, pressing the heel of one foot against the small of Vanya's back in a pointed manner.

"Either fuck me or don't," Soren growled, hands gripping Vanya's forearms.

"I'll have you however I like" was Vanya's mild reply, amusement in his voice, in his eyes. The arrogance in that statement should've turned Soren off, but it left him feeling hot beneath Vanya's gaze, as if the pool they were in was filled with warm water, not cold.

Vanya's touch, though, that continued with intent, and it made Soren's nerves burn, made him gasp and arch into the teasing pressure. When Vanya reached for the soap tray and dipped his fingers into a jar of viscous oil, Soren couldn't suppress a shiver of anticipation.

Vanya pressed a hand to one of his thighs, pulling his leg up and outward. Water lapped low around him, but Soren barely noticed as fingers stroked down the sensitive skin behind his balls to his hole. Vanya circled his finger there before slowly pushing in. Soren tipped his head back against the tile, mouth dropping open on a groan at the intrusion.

"Has anyone taken you like this before?" Vanya asked, sounding absently curious as he moved his finger within Soren's body, those dark eyes pinning Soren where he lay better than anything else could at the moment.

Soren swallowed around his tongue, trying to remember how to think. "I grew up in barracks."

Vanya pushed a second finger into him, sooner than he would've preferred, the burn from the stretch making Soren hiss a little. "That wasn't an answer."

Soren squirmed on Vanya's fingers, glaring up at him. "Yes."

He was no virgin, if that was what Vanya had hoped for. Soren found comfort in the arms of his fellow wardens sometimes, and he found release in brothels when he needed to. Being a warden was lonely business, and companionship was typically bought for a night when on the road. Soren knew what he liked and what he didn't.

Vanya seemed to want to find out, his touch sure and demanding as he opened up Soren on his fingers and then his cock. When he first pushed inside, Soren let out a strangled moan, fingers scrabbling at slippery tile. Vanya's hands on his hips gripped him like a vise, firm and unyielding as he took Soren, sliding in and filling him up like that's where the prince belonged.

It was a fleeting thought that was immediately driven out of his head when Vanya rolled his hips, grinding in deeper before pulling out only to thrust back inside him with *intent*. Soren's teeth clacked together with the force of Vanya's next thrust, water splashing against both of them as Vanya set about fucking him hard enough Soren couldn't string a single word together in any language he knew.

All he knew was the hot drag of Vanya's thick cock inside him, the heat snaking up his spine, his own hand on his cock, stroking in time to Vanya's thrusts. All of it anchored him in his body, forcing him to ride a wave of pleasure that he had no desire to fight. When he came, his shout echoed overloud against the walls of the bathhouse, and Vanya leaned down to steal the rest of his voice with a hard kiss.

He was still hard inside Soren, and Soren slid his hand between them, fingers parting around where they were joined. He lifted his head up, ignoring the water sliding down his neck as he chased after Vanya's mouth.

"Put your back into it, princeling," Soren murmured, looking up at Vanya through his lashes, the hazy aftermath of release settling in his skin.

Vanya's laughter at his words was low and thick, without any artifice that would have come with an audience. It was just the two of them here, the worlds they came from momentarily set aside. "If that's what you want, warden."

And *oh*, for a prince, Vanya followed that order *well*. He pushed Soren's legs up toward his chest, and Soren gripped his shoulders, holding on, as Vanya fucked him hard and deep, chasing his own release. Soren had already come once, oversensitive in a way he couldn't quite ignore. He dragged his fingernails over Vanya's warm skin, holding on tight as Vanya did as Soren wanted, and put his back into it.

He choked on a cry as Vanya somehow got deeper, unable to jerk away from the teeth-shivering feel of being held down and fucked by someone who no longer cared about Soren's pleasure, only their own. When Vanya came with a shout, buried deep in Soren's body, Soren held him close as they both shuddered through his release.

Soren closed his eyes, breathing shallowly, skin hot and buzzing. His cock was half-hard again from Vanya's ministrations, but he was in no hurry to find release again. Vanya pressed a kiss to the corner of his mouth, and Soren turned his head into it.

They kissed softly, the ache of what they'd done finally starting to settle into Soren's body. He became aware of a tiredness edging everything, a slow, languid feel to his body and thoughts that came from sex as much as a comedown from the stimulants he'd taken to stay awake over the last few days.

Vanya pulled out with a sigh, hands stroking Soren's hips and stomach. "Let me wash you."

Soren closed his eyes against the sunlit glow of the stained glass windows high above, the taste of honey long since gone from his lips, but something sweeter remained. Something he knew he couldn't keep, shouldn't have tasted in the first place, but it was too late for that.

"Whatever pleases you, princeling."

Soren could feel the ghost of Vanya's touch long after their time spent in the bathhouse.

Eleven

SOREN

"So, you are the warden who rescued our prince."

The trade tongue was spoken with a light Solarian accent. Soren turned his head to stare at the young woman walking toward him on the garden path. She was beautiful, with long brown hair held back from her face by a glittering net of gold threaded through with diamonds and pearls. The jeweled strands swayed against the loose waves of her styled hair that cascaded over one shoulder.

Her gown was similar in fashion to all the others Soren had seen throughout the celebration: layers of voile that flowed from a high waist, colorful and intricate embroidery tracing the neckline, and sheer sleeves caught at the wrists by dozens of golden bracelets. She wore more jewelry than many of the other nobles who had been paraded past him to submit their thanks for his actions.

Soren was keen enough to know most of the people expressing themselves as relieved most likely weren't. The Imperial family seemed not to care, and he hadn't spoken to Vanya since he'd been officially introduced at the start of the feast. They'd parted ways shortly after, with Vanya leaving Soren for the necessity of mingling to prove he was alive with the political and social elite of Bellingham.

Of which the young woman most certainly was a part of, if Soren was to go by the expensive jewels weighing her down.

"I am," Soren finally said, inclining his head in her direction. Wardens bowed to no one, but polite acknowledgment was allowed.

She hummed thoughtfully, clasping her hands in front of her, studying him with hazel eyes that appeared more green than brown beneath the shine of gas lamps illuminating the garden.

"I am Nicca Kimathi of the House of Kimathi. I am betrothed to His Imperial Highness."

"Still?" Soren couldn't help but ask, because the politeness required for political pitfalls was beyond him as a warden active in the field.

Nicca arched one painted eyebrow. "The barristers are dealing with the paperwork."

"Lucky them."

Nicca's gaze flicked up and down, taking Soren in, though she let nothing cross her expression to show how she felt about his presence at this invitation-only feast. For something that had been thrown together in less than half a day, the Imperial servants had outdone themselves. At least, Soren thought so.

The gardens had been hastily but extravagantly decorated. Pillows and soft rugs lay beneath canopies set out between the garden pathways. The night sky above was littered with stars, the sun having set an hour ago. It hadn't taken all the heat yet, and Soren could feel sweat sliding down his spine beneath his field leathers.

The firepit being tended to by a pair of cooks on the other side of the festivities probably didn't help with the heat. The mechanical fans blowing the smoke high into the air rather than letting it drift into the well-dressed crowd was a nice touch. Servants slid through the crowd, offering up small dishes to snack on before the main meal. Drinks in colored crystal glasses with flowers and wedges of fruit floating in each one were passed out on silver trays.

Soren had tried one of the drinks, found it cloyingly, almost sickeningly sweet, and discreetly poured it into a potted plant when no one was looking. He'd managed to get a glass of plain water after asking three servants. He wasn't one for heavy drinking, because a drunk warden was a dead warden, and he knew enough about how the Houses passed the time to trust no one here.

No one but Vanya.

"You seem not to be enjoying the festivities," Nicca said after a moment.

Soren chose his next words carefully. "I'm a warden. We don't get invited to things like this."

He'd have much preferred finding a curry house for dinner and catching up with any warden passing through the resupply station in Bellingham. Instead, he was stuck at a party where he couldn't be certain anyone wouldn't try to poison each other.

At least the alchemy that made him a warden would save him from that headache if that came to pass.

Nicca smiled at him, her lip rouge a pale pink to match the embroidery on her gown. "You are the guest of honor. Saving the life of an Imperial is always cause for celebration."

Soren hid his grimace behind his water glass. "I did my duty as a warden."

"There are few in Solaria who would do as you did. I find myself thankful for your presence."

Few others within the Houses would, Soren knew. But he kept his peace on that, and Nicca smoothly filled the silence that followed her words by extolling the virtues of her home city. Soren listened with half an ear, trying not to look like he was hunting for an escape, when they were interrupted by Vanya.

He stood out in stark white robes with a gold cloak that hung off his shoulders by heavy-looking jeweled pauldrons. A single gold circlet sat upon his brow, less intricate than the crown the empress wore, while the ranking necklace hung around his neck. But for all the subtleties of Vanya's dress, the expense of them clearly showed his position.

"There you are, Soren," Vanya said with a wide smile. "I wanted to introduce you to the Tovan Isles ambassador. I was telling her about your velocycle, and she says they apparently have something similar they use for fun on the waves near Port Avi."

Nicca bowed to him, her gown fluttering gracefully around her body with the motion. "Your Imperial Highness."

Vanya's expression remained polite as he held out his hand and let Nicca slip hers into his grip so he could draw her upright. "Lady Nicca. I'm pleased to see you are well."

"And I am pleased you have returned to us."

"As everyone here tonight has so kindly stated."

They made small talk while Soren stood awkwardly beside them, everyone around their little group watching their interaction like hawks. Soren tried not to let his shoulders stiffen beneath the attention. He was relieved when Vanya finally extracted himself from Nicca's presence and guided Soren along with him back to the center of the party.

"Is this water?" Vanya asked, taking the glass from Soren and frowning down at its contents. "Let's find you a better drink."

"You don't need to," Soren said. If Vanya got him another of those sweet alcoholic drinks, he'd feed it to the nearest flower bush.

"Tonight is as much about you as it is about me. You should enjoy it."

"You can enjoy it for the both of us."

Vanya smirked at him before taking a sip of the drink in his hand, a flower falling off the rim. He didn't seem to notice. When he spoke, his voice came out low, the words meant for Soren alone. "I'll enjoy you tonight once the feast is over, if you like."

Soren kept his face impassive, even if he couldn't stop the way his breath caught in his throat, remembering their time in the bathhouse. Pleasure was part of Solarian society, grown out of a refusal to apologize for enjoying life in a world where the dead walked if they weren't burned and where the Houses killed for power.

The promise in Vanya's eyes meant nothing more than that—a seductive way to pass time together before the prince married Nicca to bring a House to heel and Soren left for the poison fields.

In the end, it was simple. Soren was twenty and young and not bound by the games the Houses played. His status as an outsider could, perhaps, ensure the House of Kimathi didn't try to strike him down before he left Bellingham. Soren remembered well what happened when bloodlines went to war amongst each other.

"If you like," Soren echoed before taking a sip of water.

He'd take today, and he'd take tonight, and wouldn't feel guilty for standing in a world long since denied him. Soren knew how to be a warden, even if he had no idea what it was like to be a prince, but here he was the guest of honor. It was only fair to let Vanya see to his comforts.

Twelve

JOELLE

Vezir Joelle Kimathi of the House of Kimathi was born in Seventh Month, under the Lion constellation, and she was as fierce as the animal the stars represented. In her sixth decade, she'd escaped the ravages of the sun that shined on Solaria by virtue of her position as *vezir* for the House of Kimathi. Her rank meant she could not escape the politics that dictated the games the Houses played.

Being *vezir* meant she had absolute control over the members of her House, and it was her duty to see them survive. Her word was law, her demands were orders, and her life was lived in pursuit of the Imperial throne.

As such, she bowed to the only person she would ever owe a debt to, but it was no mortal she gave gratitude to that evening after the celebration of the Imperial crown prince's return had ended.

"Your guidance was ever true, my lord," Joelle said, ignoring the fiery ache in her joints as she held the deep bow.

Warm fingers that held the heat of the summer sun in them touched her jaw, guiding her back to a standing position. Joelle raised her gaze from the intricately mosaiced floor of the House of Kimathi's personal star temple on its ancestral grounds to meet the eyes of a star god.

The Twilight Star was not a star god Joelle had thought she'd ever find herself worshipping, but his promises had held true over the years, unlike Solaria's guiding star. Giving Innes her loyalty for his attention over the silence offered by the Dawn Star was merely good prayer.

"Unlike my sister, I do listen to the prayers of our children, and I do grant them as I see fit," Innes said.

He wore the robe and trousers of a Solarian noble, the fabric a rich blue in color to match his eyes, but the clasps down the center were undone. It put on display the golden Viper constellation tattoo across his chest, the lines glowing as if made from starfire. The Twilight Star spoke Solarian with a flawless accent, the sound of his voice soothing in the deepest hours of the night. No one else was present in the small star temple lit only by the endless flame that burned at the feet of the statue carved in Callisto's likeness.

"My House is forever indebted to you."

Joelle would be bitter about that truth if she didn't know what was promised. Having her granddaughter betrothed to the Imperial crown prince put her House within grasp of the power they'd sought to claw back for centuries.

Innes had promised her what seemed impossible when she'd been younger, her own children not yet old enough for the secrets she continued to keep, but she'd bartered their lives anyway. That he'd kept his promise meant he would always have her loyalty and her House.

Innes settled both too-warm hands on her shoulders. "I know. But you made the right choice, my child. Your people will thank you for it in the future."

Joelle could only hope. She'd given him her granddaughter and what had once been the cleansed lands of her *vasilyet*. She'd done so for the future of her House, of her country, because the House of Sa'Liandel had dictated the direction of Solaria for too long.

"If that is a blessing you will impart, I will carry it with me."

Innes smiled as he stepped past her. "You will carry whatever I ask of you. You will sacrifice what I require for the Imperial throne you wish your House to regain."

When she turned to watch him leave, the only thing her eyes met was the empty space of the star temple. Joelle would have wondered if he had even been present if she didn't have the lingering warmth of his touch pressed into her shoulders.

She sighed and glanced back at the depiction of the Dawn Star, Callisto's granite-carved face a mask of flickering shadows cast by the candlelight. One of the smaller candles that encircled the endless flame had burned out, the wick curled down.

Joelle walked over and touched a finger to the burned wick, calling forth starfire from the aether. Heat sparked at her fingertip, igniting the wick with a flash of white-gold fire. Her House still carried starfire in their souls, but it was lessened in the generations that came after her. But they had it, and it was still enough of a spark to stake a claim on the Imperial throne.

"If you had ever heard my prayers, perhaps I would not have turned from the road you were supposed to guide me down," Joelle felt compelled to say into the quiet, heavy darkness.

As with all the nights before in her life spent in prayer, Callisto did not answer.

Joelle left the star temple behind, cognizant of the stars spinning through the night sky above, the Viper constellation brighter than all the rest to her weathered eye.

Thirteen

VANYA

Vanya woke the night after the feast in his bed in the wing of the Imperial estate, white sheets tangled around his waist, half the space taken up by someone else. Servants had drawn the curtains at some point to keep out the sunlight for as long as possible, but it was clearly midday judging by the brightness that bit at the edges of the hidden windows and the heat creeping inside.

Soren lay beside him, sprawled out on his stomach, breathing deep and even as he slept. He looked younger like that, without the hardness that settled onto his face when awake. But Soren had known what he had wanted when Vanya had guided him away from the gardens after the feast was over and to this bed.

Faint bruises shadowed Soren's hips, and Vanya knew if he fit his hands there, they would match his fingertips. It pleased him, even though Vanya knew he couldn't keep the warden. An offer to stay and be his courtesan for a time would be soundly rejected, of that he was certain. Wardens had their duty, and that was something Vanya could respect.

Sighing softly, Vanya sat up and left the bed for the attached washroom. He went through his morning ablutions with a lazy attention to detail, mindful of the faint throb in his head from too much chilled

153

wine last night. It wasn't bad enough to keep him from returning to bed and the man sleeping there, but Vanya had his own duties to attend to.

When he entered the bedroom again, a body servant waited for him. The young man bowed and proceeded to help Vanya into a set of light robes and trousers for the day, attending to him in a way he'd missed on the road.

"The kitchen sent a light spread, Your Imperial Highness. It's set up in the living area," the servant said in a quiet voice before bowing himself out.

Vanya turned to study himself in the mirror, catching sight of Soren's gray eyes watching him in the burnished glass.

"Join me?" Vanya asked him.

"I need to get on the road," Soren said, not moving.

Vanya tried not to feel displeased about that. "You can leave after."

Soren let out a quiet sigh. "After, then."

Vanya nodded and gestured at the low dresser against the far wall where the servants had, at some point that morning while they slept, deposited Soren's gear. "Take your time."

Vanya was seated at the table in the living area by the time Soren showed up, plate filled and headache powder sprinkled into his juice to hide the bitter taste of it. Fruit, cheese, spiced nuts, boiled eggs, and flatbread had been neatly placed on a platter. The heat wasn't nearly as oppressive as it had been on the road, and the breeze coming from the open windows was nice.

Soren was dressed in his field leathers, but he'd left his weapons behind. He took the seat across the table from Vanya and didn't hesitate in filling his plate with food. They ate in silence for a time, with Vanya flipping through the broadsheet a servant had left on the table with the food, perusing the news articles.

"Anything interesting?" Soren eventually asked.

"Only my miraculous rise from the dead," Vanya replied.

"Truly a newsworthy event."

The dryness of his tone had Vanya looking over at him, seeing the faintly teasing smile on the younger man's face. "You seemed pleased enough last night with my presence."

Soren shrugged, but the faint flush to his cheeks couldn't be explained away by sunburn. "You asked me to join you."

"You could have said no."

Soren reached for a bunch of grapes and proceeded to pick them off the vine one at a time. "I didn't want to."

Vanya remembered the way Soren had sounded in his bed when Vanya had pinned him down and had him, taking pleasure before giving it. He remembered the way Soren had looked beneath him, while riding him, warm and wanting and Vanya's to take apart. It was a memory he could keep, even if he couldn't keep the man who made them.

"So you'll sleep in my bed, and yet, you will not tell me what I can give you to make even our debt," Vanya said.

"I told you that you owe me nothing. I'm a warden, princeling. Debts are meaningless to us."

"And I told you they are not so easily wiped away."

Soren let out a quiet, disbelieving laugh. "You belong to the House of Sa'Liandel. You're the Imperial crown prince and Solaria's heir. You have everything and anything at your fingertips to clear a debt. You can make it law, if you so choose."

"And yet, you will accept nothing that I have to offer."

Vanya stared at him, watching the way the smile faded from Soren's face. He was too well trained to fidget beneath Vanya's attention, meeting his gaze without looking away, without any sense of deference to it. His frank assessment was so different from all the courtiers and military officers Vanya was used to facing.

"I did my duty, as any warden would. Can't that be enough?"

Perhaps it could be, if Vanya was anyone else but who he was. Except he knew if any of the Houses discovered that he had not paid Soren accordingly for the life debt owed, they would use that information against him and his House. That was leverage Vanya could ill afford anyone to have over him. His return from the dead was already making the negotiations with the House of Kimathi a fraught affair.

Nicca was a good match to procure an heir, though he wouldn't put it past her House to entice her to murder him in their marriage bed once she was with child. It was a game his mother had played, though she'd lucked out with his father, whose loyalty had been bought, eventually turning into a love some Houses called a lie.

Vanya knew otherwise. He knew what his mother had negotiated for, what she ultimately gained, and he would not be her son if he didn't try for the same. Whether or not Nicca could be that for him remained to be seen. And even if he didn't have her, there was Soren.

Vanya stood from the table and went to the credenza where a small marble box sat, delivered that morning at his request. He picked it up and carried it with him back to the table, setting it beside Soren's water glass.

Vanya tapped his finger on top of the gold-speckled lid. "Open it."

Soren glanced at him curiously before reaching for the box. He undid the latch and opened it. Inside, nestled against dark velvet, was a gold medallion imprinted with the House of Sa'Liandel crest, hanging from a slender golden chain. The side profile of a roaring lion showed up in intricate lines. When Soren pressed the tiny button at the top, the face of the medallion opened like a locket, revealing only a tiny, sharp protrusion on the smooth, inside face.

"What is this?" Soren asked.

Vanya took the medallion from him and cradled it in his palm. He settled his thumb over the needle-sharp protrusion and pressed down. The pinprick drew blood, and Vanya smeared it over the gold backing there before closing the medallion up again.

"You cannot tell me what you want for payment, and I cannot leave a debt unpaid. Consider this a promise of future payment for whatever help you need, whenever that might be," Vanya said as he deposited the medallion back into Soren's care.

Soren stared at him. "I don't want a blood vow."

"Then tell me what you *do* want." Soren's silence made Vanya sigh. "I will pay my debt when you ask me to, but you need to *ask*."

"This vow you're offering comes with no boundaries."

"You're a nameless, stateless warden. What do you think you could ask for that would be impossible for me to give within the confines of the duty you adhere to?"

Vanya had thought about it all through the feast last night when Soren had tried to deflect all the goodwill directed his way and come to the conclusion this was the only road he could take. Soren was stubborn, but Vanya knew, eventually, he could pay the warden what was owed.

Soren curled his fingers over the medallion, staring at Vanya with an unreadable look in his gray eyes. "And if I never return and ask for anything?"

Vanya waved off his words. "You'll return."

"What makes you so sure about that?"

"Because you will come to Calhames bearing the biannual border updates from the wardens and report directly to me."

Soren narrowed his eyes. "That's not my place. A senior warden always handles that duty."

"It will be your place now. I will make the wardens' governor aware of it today after you leave."

Vanya had already told his mother, who hadn't been pleased about his decision to offer a vow like this, but it was—legally speaking—an acceptable stopgap. To ensure the debt could one day be paid, Soren had to visit him. Eventually, he might come bearing a request that Vanya would be well within his right to answer.

"I said I would take you home to your House, and I did. That should be enough," Soren said.

"You know it can't be."

Soren didn't move to put the medallion on, so Vanya did it for him, prying it out of his grip to hook it around his throat. The medallion was bright against his dark brown leather vest and shirt, glinting in the light. Soren lifted one hand to touch it, never taking his eyes off Vanya.

Vanya stroked his knuckles down Soren's cheek, thumb grazing the corner of his mouth. "Where will you go when you leave? Back into the poison fields? Home?"

"I have no home to go back to," Soren said quietly.

"You'll come back to me," Vanya said with a surety that made Soren flinch, but there was no denial that came to the warden's lips. "I will see you again before winter when you bring me the border reports. Perhaps by then you'll have thought of something I can give you."

"And if I don't?"

"Then I will see you next spring."

After a moment, Soren nodded. "Fine."

"Good."

Vanya kissed him, and it felt less like a goodbye than he thought it would.

Embers

❧

932 A.O.P.

One

EIMARILLE

First Month was guided by the Twilight Star, winter a cold blanket of snow that had settled upon Daijal well before the new year began. The forest surrounding New Haven was a winter wonderland that Princess Eimarille Rourke could barely see from her rooms in the palace through the frost-edged windows. The teacup in her hands was warm, though, and while the hour was early, the fur-lined dressing gown she'd slipped on kept away the chill.

The fire in the hearth had been urged to a full burn by a servant, its light adding to the gas lamps that illuminated her bedroom. Eimarille could hear a bustle of movement in her personal parlor beyond the door but made no move yet to leave the well-cushioned window bench.

She took another sip of her flowering tea, the dried blossom in the glass teapot on the nearby tray having unfurled when hot water was poured over it. The color of the tea was pale gold and the taste reminded her of the palace gardens in full bloom.

Eimarille ran her thumb along the delicate rim of the teacup, tracing the gold design there. She'd enjoyed a different tea as a child, but that wasn't a flavor to be found in the Daijal court's kitchens. If anything had been popular in Ashion, it was sneered at in her adopted country. She had made it a point over the last sixteen years to always smile politely during those arguments with courtiers. She did, after all, come from that unfortunate country, as they liked to gently remind her.

The insults through the years had always been subtle, but she'd allowed them and remembered who spoke them. Eimarille had kept her blood name rather than accept Iverson when the Daijal king had taken her in as his ward, claiming a distant kinship the country's highest court of law had signed off on. Eimarille had learned to hate the man less over the years, if only because Innes had asked it of her.

One must make alliances of enemies, or one must dig their graves.

Eimarille sipped at her tea, thinking about the lessons the star god had imparted to her since she came to Daijal. Innes had been the breakwater all of King Bernard's demands had crashed against as Eimarille grew up in the Daijal court, learning new customs, new politics, new beliefs, new ways to pray. Even as a child, Eimarille knew how to shape herself into who she needed to be to survive.

She'd traversed the road Innes had laid down before her, walked her way to this moment of early winter morning, a dusting of snow like a blessing on her wedding day. The streets would be cleared of snow from the palace to the star temple, where she would wed Prince Wesley Iverson under the only constellation that mattered to her.

They'd grown up together in the Daijal court, orbiting each other through the years. She'd immersed herself in her studies and then in politics while he'd earned an officer's commission in the Daijal army that he rarely tended to. A prince had no need to command an army when he would be king one day and have generals to do that for him, Wesley always said. Such a retort was usually given right before he went off to join his friends in what fun the capital could provide such a rowdy group.

Eimarille thought it foolish not to build up those relationships and had made it a point to know the name and rank of every officer who passed through the Daijal court. She sent letters of congratulations whenever one was promoted, keeping a finger on the pulse of the military leaders and their needs. She did so not simply because Innes had told her to but because she could see their use if she could shift their loyalty to *her*.

Wesley might be their contemporary, but she would be their queen, and the crown outranked everyone.

Small steps down a long road, she remembered being told. Sound advice from a dead woman, Eimarille surmised with a faint twist of her lips. Queen Ophelia Rourke had made serious mistakes in the long run, and Eimarille had no desire to emulate her birth mother in that fashion, but some choices made were worth studying. In hindsight, Ashion hadn't been a terrible learning foundation, but she could see the cracks that had brought its ruin—cracks she was determined to mend in her own way.

But to fix something, sometimes you had to break it first.

Her bedroom door was pushed open on hinges that squeaked softly, an annoyance she'd learned to ignore growing up, but a precaution Terilyn had refused to allow to be altered. Her lady-in-waiting was ever cognizant of Eimarille's safety, and for good reason. She wouldn't be the Blade that Eimarille cherished if Terilyn ignored her teachings.

"The servants have readied your bath," Terilyn said.

Eimarille looked over at the woman who had been given to her on that long-ago train ride west and smiled. "Is it to your liking, darling?"

"It is to yours, and that is all I care about."

Terilyn crossed the room on silent feet, the silk dressing gown she wore cinched tight around her slender waist. Her thick black hair tumbled loose around her shoulders down to her waist. Eimarille had undone the plait before bed last night, mindful of the sharp spikes that doubled as accessories, the design meant to harm if anyone grabbed her hair in a fight.

Terilyn had been in many fights over the years, ever Eimarille's dangerous shadow. She bore scars on her body that belonged to Eimarille, acquired out of duty and love. Blades were notorious, after all, of being singularly dedicated to their cause. Bernard had sought to banish Terilyn only once. He'd lost a finger to Innes for that hubris, a wound blamed on a hunting accident. He was lucky it hadn't been his head.

The tray was pushed aside, and Terilyn sat beside her. Eimarille slid her bare feet outward, tucking her cold toes beneath the other woman's thigh. Terilyn hooked one hand around Eimarille's ankle, callused thumb stroking over the dip in the bone there.

"Are you pleased with this choice?" Terilyn asked, her almond-shaped brown eyes trained unerringly on Eimarille. She was beautiful by Urovan standards, merely pretty by Daijal's. Eimarille thought her fellow countrymen and women blind in that regard.

"Well enough."

The Daijal court had been a prison as a child, but Eimarille had learned how to make it a home. Choices, no matter how inconsequential, were a type of freedom, and she'd made plenty over the years to claw back some semblance of control.

She'd been given no choice in marrying Wesley, but Eimarille had allowed herself to accept the inevitable to gain what she wanted. Better to work with what one had than to mourn a different road she'd never get to walk down. She'd chosen to appreciate the opportunities marriage to the Daijal crown prince provided, but she would never love him.

Her heart belonged to her Blade, after all.

Terilyn took the teacup from her, setting it on the tray, before gently nudging Eimarille's legs apart. She slid between them, hands gliding up Eimarille's legs, catching the hems of her sleeping and dressing gowns, rucking them up toward her hips. Eimarille leaned back against the plush cushions piled on the bench. She bent one knee, let her other leg hang off the side of the bench, toes brushing against the rug there.

Eimarille settled her hands on Terilyn's shoulders, sighing softly as those familiar, talented fingers stroked up her inner thighs, hidden by the soft fabric between them. But there was no hiding from the hungry intent in her lover's eyes, and she never wanted to.

"He'll take you like this tonight," Terilyn murmured as she stroked her fingers over the soft folds there between Eimarille's legs before sliding them in deep. "But he won't please you."

Eimarille let her head fall back, arching into the steady movement of those knowing fingers. "Of course he won't. He's not you."

Terilyn kissed a delicate line down Eimarille's throat as she undid the belt of her dressing gown. The fabric shifted, falling open, and Eimarille tugged it off one shoulder. She curled her fingers over the loose neckline of her sleeping gown, pulling it down, able to because she hadn't bothered with the ribbon that held it in place in the back.

Her nipples hardened once her breasts were bared, the chill coming off the window stronger than the heated air of her bedroom. Terilyn bent her head and drew one into her mouth, tongue flicking at the tight nub. Eimarille moaned softly, eyes falling shut as she tangled her fingers through Terilyn's thick hair.

Pleasure crept up on her in a soft build, Terilyn drawing it out of her from years of knowing how. Eimarille came with a soundless cry she buried in Terilyn's hair, cradling her lover close, shivering through the aftermath.

And it was true, she knew, hours later when Eimarille stood at the altar in the star temple, dressed in a white wedding gown and delicate veil that sparkled like the stars from thousands of diamonds, new crown heavy on her head as she stared at the man she was to marry. Wesley would not love her how Terilyn did, but Eimarille still meant the vows she gave to him before the high priestess of the Star Order in Daijal, the sweet voices of the children's choir singing a prayer different from the one she'd known in Ashion.

She would do right by crown and duty, as she always had, but only Eimarille knew the subtle distinctions in the promises she gave.

And that was her choice, one not even the star gods could take from her.

Two

EIMARILLE

"I could kill her, if you like," Terilyn offered.

Eimarille never took her eyes off the broadsheet spread out beside the breakfast plate she'd hardly touched. The opinion piece on the newly passed banking laws—gifts of the Daijal parliament to Eimarille as a wedding present—by one Meleri Auclair, Duchess of Auclair, printed out on the front page was benign enough, if one didn't read between the lines.

The surviving noble bloodlines in Ashion who retained allegiance to a dead queen numbered less than they had these days. Some of that was due to deaths; mostly, it was due to Eimarille's politicking, but even her skill with words couldn't bring the Auclair bloodline to heel. Eimarille was honestly surprised the duchess hadn't touched upon Bernard's decree that Amari, Ashion's capital, was now hers to oversee. Perhaps the citizens of Ashion could see the lie in those words as well as she did.

"And make of her a martyr? That isn't useful to me," Eimarille said.

"It would please you."

"Yes, but some pleasures are worth waiting for, dearest."

The affectionate endearment slipped easily from her lips when it was just the two of them in a room. The servants knew her habits and had set out the food before leaving. Terilyn always took it upon herself to serve them both during those times.

Wesley's plate was left empty, her husband still abed, though not for much longer. The last couple of weeks since the wedding had found her getting to know his habits on an intimate level. The way they each lived wasn't quite complementary, but they were adjusting. Eimarille had always been an early riser, and she missed lying beside Terilyn. Their mornings together with no one else around were precious, but the separation was ever jarring to her.

Eimarille lifted her teacup to her mouth, then grimaced, the smell making her stomach twist unpleasantly. She set it back down and picked up her toast instead, butter smeared thick on it. Eimarille took a small bite, chewing slowly as she continued to read the broadsheet.

"What would be of use to you, then?" Terilyn asked.

Eimarille glanced at where Terilyn sat to her right at the table in the private dining room that had come with the suite of rooms Eimarille and Wesley had moved into after the wedding. The space, like most areas of the palace, was ostentatiously decorated, and Terilyn had been working relentlessly with the chamberlain to make it less gauche and more to Eimarille's taste.

That meant replacing all the furniture, putting up new wallpaper, and updating the sconces and chandeliers for the gas lamps. Terilyn had overseen the transition of one drawing room into Eimarille's personal office since Wesley had claimed the actual allotted office, a space he hardly ever used. No matter. Eimarille was adept at making a home in a place that didn't initially belong to her.

"Decimation of the Clockwork Brigade, but we're still working on that."

Terilyn wrinkled her nose in distaste at the mention of the rebellion. The Clockwork Brigade had grown out of the resistance to the banks, their debt slaves, and the stranglehold support the Collector's Guild had on the financial industry.

Smugglers had been taking debt slaves out of Daijal to find safe harbor in other countries since before the civil war. Their efforts had culminated in what was now the Clockwork Brigade, a wide-ranging network of spies, activists, and outright anarchists that the Iverson bloodline had failed to root out and expunge.

They still didn't know who ran the Clockwork Brigade, but Eimarille had her suspicions. She hadn't been privy to the identity of her birth mother's spymaster before leaving Ashion, but she had her own spies these days. Blades were useful that way. They might be forged in Daijal, but they secreted themselves in every country.

Eimarille took another bite of her toast, grimacing at the taste of it. She swallowed and then abruptly stood as the toast tried to come up her throat. Eimarille covered her mouth with one hand before darting over to the side table, where the servants had left the breakfast spread. She grabbed the half-filled pitcher of water and promptly emptied her stomach of what little she'd had so far into it.

Terilyn was by her side in an instant, smoothing back her hair as Eimarille braced herself against the side table. "That's the third morning this week."

Eimarille drew in a sour breath and pressed a hand over her stomach, the corset she wore beneath her blouse something she wished she could do without. It was easy to lace up at the moment, but she knew that would eventually change. At some point, she wouldn't be able to hide the truth.

"I know."

She knew what her sickness meant but had yet to inform her husband or the king. For a while longer, she wanted to keep the secret as hers and Terilyn's alone.

Terilyn handed her a linen napkin to wipe her mouth. "Perhaps we should postpone our visit to Evergreen."

"No. I won't miss our appointment with the high general."

Evergreen was the officer's commissioning school for the Daijal army. Eimarille always made a point to visit, even in the midst of winter. Besides, the high general wasn't the only one expecting her today.

She stepped back from the side table and retreated to her seat, pushing her plate aside in favor of her tea. Terilyn covered the water pitcher with a towel. She'd take it with her when they left, hiding the evidence of Eimarille's morning sickness. The servants had long since stopped looking askance at the strange tasks Terilyn conducted that most other ladies-in-waiting would never dare to do.

Then again, most ladies-in-waiting weren't a Blade honed by the Star Order.

"You'll need to see a doctor eventually," Terilyn said once she retook her seat.

Eimarille curled her hand around her teacup. "I know."

Terilyn frowned at her, worry creasing her brow. She blinked it all away when the door to the dining room opened up, calmly rising to her feet as Wesley entered, servants trailing in his wake. It was less out of respect and more to discreetly pick up the tainted water pitcher and slip out to discard it after curtsying to the crown prince.

"Good morning," Eimarille said, not getting up from her seat.

Wesley was dressed for a day of winter hunting rather than a day abroad in the city. His cream trousers and crimson woolen coat were offset by black knee-high boots. His blond hair was brushed back, though some strands fell forward around his blue eyes. He was handsome, with a square jaw and straight nose.

He'd been considered quite the catch by every noblewoman who danced their way through the Daijal court over the years. Eimarille had made no friends and only enemies with the female courtiers since her arrival sixteen years ago. They'd all known, even then, what her presence meant in regard to the Daijal throne.

None of them would ever sit upon it, but they'd still tried to seduce Wesley. Many were successful in finding themselves in his bed, and Eimarille knew he still saw several of his mistresses. She knew them by their smug smiles when in court, knew their names, though it hardly mattered. She allowed Wesley his indiscretions because it kept him occupied.

"Good morning," Wesley replied, finally taking his seat at the dining table. "You always rise so early."

Eimarille smiled. "I enjoy the early hours of the morning."

Lying beside him was so different than lying with Terilyn. They never slept the same hours. More often than not, Eimarille was late to bed and early to rise when she was home at all. She hadn't stopped work on her patronages or traveling to make herself known to the politicians as the crown princess rather than a hostage turned willing ward. There was something satisfying about watching people bite their tongues when before they were happy to deliver any barbed insult, veiled or otherwise. Rank had its uses.

Despite their discordant evenings, Wesley always found time for sex, which Eimarille provided not because she loved him, but because he was the only one capable of giving her a legitimate child with a direct claim to the Daijal throne.

Wesley's empty plate was soon filled with food dished out by servants. Terilyn swept back in after a time, hands empty, and retook her seat beside Eimarille. Wesley eyed her the way he'd eyed her for years—wary and annoyed by her presence in equal parts.

"I see you're ready for a hunt. Did you forget our appointment today?" Eimarille asked.

"I had my secretary adjust my schedule. I have better things to do than waste my time at Evergreen when the sky is clear of snow for once," Wesley said.

Eimarille held her tongue, considering drunken revelry a waste of time over gaining political ground. She supposed Wesley thought he had nothing to worry about, being the crown prince of Daijal and all. But hubris was a downfall many had experienced, and Eimarille had no desire to slip down that slope.

Eimarille carefully sipped at her tea, her stomach slightly more settled after being emptied. "Very well."

She was secretly relieved for his absence. It would make what she had to accomplish far easier on her own than with him by her side. Eimarille had been more assertive about making her presence known in all the circles of the Daijal court since their wedding a few weeks ago. At thirty-one, Wesley was five years her senior and still acted as if he had no duties to attend to despite the crown he wore.

He'd been much the same when they were younger, cruel in a way that never touched her by order of Innes, but she'd seen the devastation he could command with a single word. Wesley indulged in the societal ruin of others like a game, and Eimarille knew few called her husband friend. But he had power people coveted, and she'd tied herself to him, for better or for worse, to gain her own foothold in Daijal.

The royal genealogies gave her a very thin claim to this country's throne. Marriage, on the other hand, provided a different, but no less valid, road.

"We'll leave you to it. Good hunting," Eimarille said as she rose to her feet.

Terilyn silently followed her lead, the pair of them leaving the dining room for the royal family's private wing. On the way, Terilyn sent a servant to the garage to notify a chauffeur to ready a motor carriage.

Eimarille sat at the vanity in her bedroom while Terilyn touched up her rouge before removing the thin gold circlet from its velvet-lined storage box that had been delivered from the vault while they ate. She carefully secured it in Eimarille's hair, adjusting it so the fine gold point was centered on her forehead. Then she went into the closet and came back with a fur-lined, fitted woolen coat the color of a stormy sky, gray-blue like Eimarille's eyes.

Terilyn wore a cape, which provided her more freedom of movement, allowing her access to the blades and derringer secreted on her body. The weapons were easily reached through discreet slits in the fabric of her gown's skirt.

Eimarille pulled on a pair of fine leather gloves before taking the muff Terilyn handed her to help keep her hands warm on the ride to Evergreen. After a final glance in the mirror, Eimarille left the bedroom, Terilyn at her usual spot to the right of her and half a step behind.

The covered patio that linked to the garage where the fleet of motor carriages was housed bustled with servants. The motor carriage chosen for today was enclosed in deference to the winter weather. The driver waited by the motor carriage with the door open. He bowed at their arrival and offered his hand to help Eimarille and Terilyn into the back of the vehicle.

Two other motor carriages, one in front and one in the rear, rounded out their escort. The guards seated in those vehicles were well armed for Eimarille's protection. She'd grown out of thinking of herself as a prisoner, but there'd been a time she had chafed at the entourage always given her whenever she left the confines of the palace.

Settling into the motor carriage, she buckled the lap belt and slipped her hands into the muff again. The motor carriage was surprisingly warm despite the cold weather, courtesy of the heat spell applied by the Daijal court's retained magician. It made for a comfortable ride to Evergreen at the outskirts of the city, the military school tucked between two defensive inner walls.

Snow dusted the sidewalks, the streets themselves cleared of it from the snow shoveling machines. Eimarille saw one in passing at an intersection, the bulky machine belching steam every now and then as the operator maneuvered the large shovel in the front to move snow aside.

People stopped on the street to watch her motor carriage pass, seeking a glimpse of Eimarille inside. Occasionally, she removed her hand from the muff to wave. The general goodwill followed her to Evergreen, and they were greeted in the wide courtyard of the military school by a rank of cadets standing at rigid attention.

High General Kote Akina met her on the courtyard, opening the door of the motor carriage and offering his hand to her. She took it with a light touch, his fingers curled around hers as she alighted from the vehicle. Kote offered the same support to Terilyn, then bowed deeply to them.

"Welcome, Your Royal Highness," Kote said as he straightened up. "It is always a pleasure to have you here."

"You're too kind, High General," Eimarille said.

Kote was a tall man fifteen years her senior, taking after his Tovanian father with his brown skin and dark hair, but his startling green eyes came from the Daijalan mother of a noble bloodline, who had given him up at birth after quite a scandal.

Kote's official place of residence was located in the cluster of buildings making up the Department of Military Affairs at the governing heart of New Haven. Meeting him there would draw too much attention, but meeting him at Evergreen, where Eimarille got to know up-and-coming officers, had never been looked askance at.

Her visits had always been seen as quaint by the king, and he'd allowed her them without reproach, believing all she did was inspect the cadets before taking her leave. And she did inspect the cadets, a duty Kote proudly walked her through, extolling the virtues of the newest class of officers-in-training.

"You admitted more for the class this year than last," Eimarille said.

Kote kept his pace to hers, hands clasped behind his back as he escorted her through the halls of the administration building to the office assigned to him when he was in residency. "It seemed prudent. When the Defense Council approved the extra scholarships, we had an uptick in interest from men and women with a commerce background."

"I take it the nobility weren't as keen?"

"I've trained nobles. The military way of life is not for all of them."

Eimarille smiled slightly. "An accurate assessment if ever there was one."

Wesley's absence was a pointed reminder of that truth. It was tradition for some noblemen and even some noblewomen to attend Evergreen. They did so not out of an expectation they would continue their military career in any useful way, but because the uniform was a status symbol.

The Daijal court was built on status, while Evergreen was built for functionality, not beauty, a detail Eimarille never failed to note as she walked its halls. Its walls and rooms lacked decorations that weren't historical maps of past battles, portraits or busts of dead officers who'd made their mark upon Daijal history, and clockwork replications of the army's war machines.

Kote's working office here showcased the accomplishments of his career, from a dedicated lieutenant getting his hands dirty in the field to a skilled captain who'd kept their eastern border whole in the face of Ashion skirmishes. He'd risen in the ranks at a fast pace, earning the rank of high general at a shockingly young age, partially due to his experience on the ground that not even Eimarille's husband could claim.

It was the star god who stood by the window staring at the courtyard below who had engineered Kote's road. Skill could only take one so far whose bloodline wasn't written out in any worthwhile genealogy. That's what came of a child born out of wedlock, whose noble family refused to acknowledge his existence.

But Innes had seen something useful in him, and Eimarille could concede the Twilight Star had been correct in that assessment. Kote was useful, and Eimarille could do so much with *useful*.

She dipped into a deep curtsy, as did Terilyn, while Kote came to strict attention and saluted. Innes turned away from the window and acknowledged them with a nod and a smile.

"You've grown since last we met," Innes said as he came around the desk. "I see you remain as beautiful as ever."

A fire burning in the fireplace kept the office cozily warm, but it had nothing on the warmth of Innes' hand when he took Eimarille's and brought it to his mouth to kiss her knuckles. The heat that always seemed to burn in the star god's veins tugged at the starfire that had never been extinguished in her own soul.

"You flatter me, my lord," Eimarille said, smiling at her mentor.

Innes guided her over to the nearest chair, pulling it out for her. Eimarille adjusted the skirt of her gown as she sat, the edges of the corset pressing against her hips. She settled her hands into her lap, gloved fingers folded over each other as she lifted her chin and met the Twilight Star's heavy gaze.

"How goes the farming?" she asked.

Innes waved his hand at her as he returned to the window, lazily pacing back and forth like a hunting cat. "We've acquired the necessary land in the north of Daijal. That was never going to be the issue. It's the south that is at risk of putting us behind schedule."

Eimarille resisted the urge to press a hand to her stomach. "Will the plains not work?"

"Within Daijal? No, it's too difficult to cordon off from travelers leaving the roads and wardens mapping the borders. I'm talking about the land within Solaria. It's less an issue with acreage than it is with my conniving sister who guides that country."

Eimarille would never insult a star god in such a way, but Innes wasn't bound by mortal restraint and manners. They'd always known their plans were at risk from being uncovered by Innes' brethren. Daijal was his to do with as he pleased since the civil war, but borders had never been binding on one such as himself.

"We had an experimental field near Bellingham last year," Kote said as he finished pouring tea for everyone and brought the serving tray to the desk. "My understanding is we lost the test revenants to a warden after they escaped."

"We lost them to greed." Innes glanced over his shoulder, catching Eimarille's eye, and smiled thinly. "The rulers of the House of Kimathi are not as patient as you are, my dear."

Eimarille reached for the teacup Kote set in front of her on the desk, bringing it to her lips. The smell of mint reached her nose, and she breathed it in carefully. The nausea really only affected her in the early mornings, but she still chose to drink the tea slowly.

She licked her lips after a sip and set it aside. "We need more debt slaves. The banking laws I requested be passed for my wedding present don't go far enough, but we can build on them. They'll provide us more debt slaves, with no one the wiser, once they are implemented. The banks will run an audit on all loans and collect on the collaterals."

"That will take time and political capital you can ill afford to throw away if the Ashion parliament pushes back as they have been. Bernard's decree that Amari is to be yours has rattled them. You'll ultimately need the king's backing to get what we need here. The Ashion parliament will be a harder nut to crack," Kote warned.

"I need no backing if I am queen."

Innes' mouth quirked upward at one corner, eyes half-lidded. "You'll wear that crown soon enough."

Eimarille set the teacup on the desk and stood, meeting the star god on level ground. He was taller than her, even in the heeled shoes she wore, but he'd taught her how not to give any ground but that which she was willing to lose for the greater good of her desires.

"I'm pregnant. I'll have an heir soon, and the king won't have need of me anymore. Your 'soon enough' should be now."

She'd been Bernard's ward not out of kindness, but simple political greed. Eimarille had always known she'd marry Wesley for the sole fact she could provide a child with Rourke blood to the Iverson bloodline, a child who could be raised from birth under their control, rather than gifted to them at ten years old.

Eimarille would rather cut her own throat than allow them access to the child growing in her womb.

Terilyn stood in a soft rustle of fabric, resting a hand gently between Eimarille's shoulder blades. Her touch was a reminder of support, a Blade sharp enough to protect, and Eimarille leaned into it.

Innes came to stand before Eimarille. He framed her face with both hands, looking down at her, before he brushed a gentle kiss against her brow.

"My dear child, the world will always have need of you. Why else would I have taken you out of Ashion, if not for the future you could build? The king will know his place when the time comes, and you will put him there. You have my word," Innes said.

Eimarille nodded, resisting the urge to swallow, because that was a show of nerves she'd trained herself out of performing. "Then let us discuss how to get these banking laws passed by the Ashion parliament. My preference would be a distraction big enough to turn their attention away from whatever committee is tasked with reviewing the law." Eimarille tilted her head to the side, dislodging Innes' hands. "Perhaps an attempt at expanding a portion of the eastern border by way of settlements? I know we decided against that before, but perhaps it's time we reassess."

Before Innes could give her his thoughts on that tactic, a rapid knock came from the office door. Kote frowned and strode over to answer it.

"Yes?" he demanded as he opened it partway.

Innes had stepped back, out of sight, but Eimarille was in the perfect position to see the aide in uniform salute the high general.

"Sir. A high-priority telegram came through to the Defense Council today. I was instructed to bring it to you," the aide said.

If the aide had driven all the way across the city to bring it to Kote's attention, it meant whatever news the telegram bore, it was too hot to risk sending it again over the wire. Kote took the offered slip of paper with a nod and closed the door. He turned around and unfolded it, staring down at whatever was written there.

"What is the news?" Eimarille asked.

Kote offered the telegram in silence. "The Imperial crown princess of Solaria has died in childbirth."

Eimarille took the telegram and studied the blocky text. The message was short and to the point, and no doubt the news had already reached the Daijal court if the Defense Council had the information as well. When Solaria mourned, it mourned loudly, sometimes viciously.

She looked up from the message to meet Innes' gaze. "Princess Consort Nicca was not of the House of Sa'Liandel. She belonged to the House of Kimathi before marrying the Imperial crown prince."

The Twilight Star had the fingers of one hand tucked beneath the neckline of his waistcoat, a faint smile twitching at his mouth. "She did."

Eimarille folded the telegram in half and handed it back to Kote, who promptly tossed it into the fireplace. "Is this your punishment, then? For their interference in the poison fields?"

Innes' smile got wider, a pleased look filling his eyes at what she gathered was her correct guess. "They won't see my hand in this, only what they wish to."

It was not a true admission, but Eimarille knew the truth in his words. She wondered if he would ever cast her aside so thoroughly, the way he had done with the other princess. It was always a risk, to be blessed so by a star god, but Eimarille was ever pragmatic when it came to prayer. Like with banks, you had to give up something to gain what you desired.

"You'll set the Houses against each other over this. That will complicate things."

"The Houses have always bought alliances with blood and lost them just as easily. This is no different. Callisto will have her hands full with the games the Houses play. She won't bother chasing rumors into the poison fields."

Eimarille nodded slowly, mind spinning fast, like gears in the secret war machines being built that she'd quietly backed at Kote's urging. "We'll need to tighten up the southern border with Solaria if we're to collect more debt slaves. We must ensure the Clockwork Brigade has no easy passage south for those they seek to save. We'll push them east and keep a heavy presence of debt collectors along the border there. Ashion will be no safe haven for them. Neither will Solaria."

Innes took her hand in his again, thumb brushing over the back of it. She could feel the burn of starfire in his touch, the heat of magic seeping past the thin leather of her glove.

"Do not worry, my dear. Your place is upon the throne I seek to give you."

Eimarille's thoughts went unbidden to the throne in Ashion that burned with starfire not of the Twilight Star's making. She'd walked over the bones and ash of the past in that public park there a handful of times before in the rare visits she'd taken to her birth city.

So many had tried to claim the right of rule by sitting in that seat of power, hoping their bloodline had enough connection to the Rourkes to put the starfire out. But the assassins during the Inferno had been thorough, as all Blades were. Eimarille knew no Rourke lived but herself, and she had not yet sat upon that vacant throne because Daijal was not yet hers.

One country at a time, she told herself as Innes left the office, the aether a swirl around him to distract others from his presence.

She would claim Maricol one country at a time.

Taking a breath, Eimarille smiled at Kote and retook her seat. "Let us discuss what needs to be done about the borders and when we can expect to expand them in the future."

Three

EIMARILLE

Haven was built, like all of Maricol's major cities, behind walls. When Daijal had split from Ashion after the civil war, New Haven had been designated the country's capital in the aftermath of the armistice. Istal would forever be a frontier military city, but New Haven became the Daijal court's home.

The innermost wall encircled Daijal's government heart, with the palace an ornate centerpiece amongst all the civic buildings. It had been built larger and grander than the one that burned during the Inferno in Amari.

The palace in New Haven had been built after blocks of row houses were razed to the ground, making way for the newly royal bloodline. The royal genealogies in Daijal were slim compared to ones in other countries; new blood, without the history written through the Ages. Eimarille's name had been added to them when she married Wesley, though she had kept the Rourke name instead of taking Iverson, as ordered by Innes.

It was atypical in Daijal, in a country with a heavy weight given to the male half of any bloodline. Ashion had been ruled by a queen through three Ages. Daijal's first crowned royal was a king, and that had continued for generations. Few royal women had sat in the

Cobalt Room, where representatives from parliament met with the king. Eimarille had been present within the deep blue walls since she was sixteen.

It had taken a decree from Innes to give her a seat at the table, and an immolated politician or two, but the seat to Bernard's left had been hers since then. Wesley sat across from her, ever the king's right hand despite his many absences, speaking his mind on subjects he knew little about. His favorite pastime wasn't politics, but women, alcohol, and leisure activities with his fellow contemporaries, and it showed at times, when he opened his mouth.

Eimarille remembered her lessons in Ashion by Ophelia's side. She'd learned new ones in Daijal at this table, picking out the spiderweb of power and blackmail that fluctuated beneath the glitter of the court. She knew when to speak, when to remain silent, and who to press in private to get what she wanted.

Her position was not always welcomed, but the support and favor she carried from a star god were more than enough to make the men around her think twice about what they said to her face these days. Behind her back was a different story, but Eimarille had spies in all sorts of households across Daijal. Secrets were expensive to buy, but she had a treasury at her fingertips she had no problem using under the guise of frivolous purchases.

"We have a problem in the clarion crystal mine in the north. It seems the Clockwork Brigade has stolen some of the more skilled debt slaves and incited a rebellion in the ones they left behind," Lord Angus Blackstrom said, mustache twitching with the force of his words.

He was an older gentleman, rotund in a way that made his breathing loud in the room. Seated near the end of the long table, he had to raise his voice to be heard. Eimarille was grateful for the distance. Lord Blackstrom was known for his particular love of seafood at nearly every meal. As the head of a bloodline that owned one of the biggest banks in Daijal, he had the means to indulge.

"Then inform the bloodline that owns the Star Mining Company to clean up their mess," Bernard said coolly, not taking his eyes off the memo in his hand. "This isn't the first rebellion they've had to deal with. They should know by now how to handle their property."

"The company executives have informed parliament they are short enough of the skilled workers needed for the mines that a crackdown would force the pushback of production with their business partners. Even with the new banking laws your majesty so thoughtfully signed off on after the prince's wedding, it will take time to claim collateral on loans."

Eimarille didn't frown, though she wanted to. Clarion crystals were difficult to mine, and Daijal only had claim to one mine of the source. Urova and E'ridia each had control of far larger mines inside their borders, requiring delicate trade negotiations as Daijal's slowly ran dry.

Mining was an expensive endeavor, and mining clarion crystals required a delicate touch. The great digging machines had to be used sparingly, as the veins of raw crystal would shatter if the wrong pressure was applied. Clarion crystals had to be extracted by hand, or one risked the raw, uncut crystals losing the song that helped to channel the aether.

Most magicians required clarion crystals for their wands, though she was not one of them. Eimarille had no need of a clarion crystal–tipped wand when starfire burned inside her. Other magicians could not function without that focus for their magic. Clarion crystals used to be a niche business, but their varied uses were becoming more apparent over time.

Some enterprising inventors were creating fantastical, if still experimental, devices powered by clarion crystals rather than steam. Eimarille was keenly interested in those, and had blanketed the New Haven University she was a patron of with grants to encourage the scientific advancement of such inventions.

Wesley thought it a waste of her time, but Eimarille knew otherwise, and she always kept an eye on the patents submitted to the Bureau of Patents. One invention in particular championed by the Fletcher bloodline, whose patents would never see the light of day, required a severe amount of clarion crystals to power the machinery.

Clarion crystal was the heir to steam power, though not yet widely accessible or accepted. Eimarille had always been a proponent of progress. She'd seen how stagnation could ravage a people and had no desire to find herself boxed into a corner as her mother had been. If she was to burn, it would be on her own terms.

"Were any of the damned cogs captured?" Lord Thomas Vaughn asked.

Blackstrom shot him a withering look, the ruddiness in his cheeks deepening at whatever affront he took from the question. "If they had been, you would've heard about the example we made of them."

The Clockwork Brigade had its claws sunk deep in Daijal. Its influence in Daijalan culture was something the Iverson bloodline had been incapable of excising, no matter the laws passed. People would offer up their lives for a dream, and they'd risk the same for freedom.

Having Ashion nominally under the Daijal court's control hadn't stopped the Clockwork Brigade. If anything, the Inferno had emboldened them. For all that Eimarille prided herself on knowing things, Ashion's spymaster—whoever they were—knew more secrets than she did.

The argument picked up steam amongst the parliament representatives. Bernard set down his memo, listening to the words fly back and forth with a faintly displeased expression on his face. Whether it was for the argument itself or its underlying subject, it was difficult to tell. He'd let them argue themselves into a fractious disarray that would accomplish nothing, and that wouldn't be a problem if the underlying rebellion was anywhere else but the clarion crystal mines.

Eimarille stood, drawing all eyes to her, effectively silencing the argument being tossed from one side of the table to the other. She ignored the way Bernard's mouth tightened and how Wesley frowned at her.

"Gentlemen, I understand your concerns, but there is a solution if you are willing to see it through," Eimarille said calmly.

"And what would you suggest?" one of the lords asked.

She ignored the lack of title addressed to her in favor of driving her point home. "The new banking laws allow for a broader interpretation of nonpayment. We must follow the bloodlines attributed to the debt slaves in the mines. Go through the genealogies however far back will be useful and take all of their families as collateral. Apply the debt bondage clause and make their indentured servitude the supposed rebels' punishment for this ill-advised tantrum."

Several of the men at the table dropped into murmured side conversations at her words. Eimarille remained standing, meeting the gaze of every man who chose to look at her without bowing her head. When her attention made its way back to the king, he'd masked whatever irritation he may have felt about her speaking up.

"Depending on the reach of the genealogies and who the law picks up, some bloodlines may wake up to an unpleasant surprise," Bernard finally said.

"That's the risk everyone takes when doing business with banks, Your Majesty."

"I would not see loyal bloodlines targeted."

Eimarille knew they had vastly different ideas of what constituted *loyal*. "Then we can allow them to pay the blood fine."

There were ways for the rich to sidestep the laws and pitfalls of doing business with banks. Most people paid collateral with their lives. The new law gave the option to those who were an accessory to debt to pay their way out if they had the means. In the grand scheme of things, few would be able to pay.

And that was the point of these new laws.

To provide bodies that would, eventually, die for her and become useful in a war no one knew was coming.

Bernard waved a hand at her in a commanding way, and Eimarille inclined her head at him before sitting. She'd planted the seed, and if she had her way, greed would make it grow.

It would be three more days of meetings, all of which she attended, interjecting her thoughts with the precision of a marksman, to gain the support of an action that would tear families apart. But it would pad the bottom line of several of the men seated at the table and many more in Daijal parliament, to say nothing of the king's coffers.

It was a small victory when Bernard signed off on the order that issued an accusation of treason against the debt slaves rebelling in the clarion crystal mines. The laws were clear that people paid what they owed on a loan, or they worked it off. Now, society would learn that a debt belonging to one person could ensnare generations, and its reach crossed borders.

Eimarille wanted the rebellion in the mines to be crushed. She wanted the new law to make those who gave their loyalty to an empty throne that burned with starfire in Ashion to think twice about acting against the crown she would one day wear.

"The Collector's Guild will make a pretty auron on this job," Wesley said over dinner after everything was set into motion.

Eimarille cut into her roasted chicken and dragged the piece through the buttery sauce on her porcelain plate. "As long as the Collector's Guild does its job, then yes, they will be well paid."

Bernard twisted the stem of his wineglass between his fingers and thumb. "Is this what you hoped to use these laws for when you requested them as your wedding present?"

They sat at the table in the royal family's private dining room: the king, the crown prince, the crown princess, and her Blade. The queen had taken ill after the wedding, and no amount of healing magic or medicine had cured her lungs of the rot slowly taking hold. The doctors and healers whispered behind closed doors that they didn't expect her to live another year.

These days, Queen Aleesia ate alone more often than not, in her bedroom that Bernard rarely visited. Theirs had not been a love match, but Eimarille knew the queen loved her son dearly and influenced him in ways even the king could not stop. To gain Wesley's agreement in anything, one needed the support of his mother.

Which was why Eimarille always took tea with the queen, as she had every afternoon on the first day of the week since she was a child when present at court, and let Terilyn pour for them. Habit meant no one ever suspected the root of such illness was found in the dregs of a teacup handed over with a smile.

"I only wish to expand our right to rule," Eimarille said, affecting a demur manner. She set her fork and knife down, allowing herself to smile at Wesley as if he meant the world to her when he never would. "Is that not what any parent wants for their children?"

Wesley choked on his wine, eyes going wide as he coughed to clear his throat. His gaze snapped from Eimarille to his father, then back again, disbelief clear in his eyes. "Children?"

Eimarille shifted on her chair, leaning back far enough to settle her hand over her still-flat stomach. "I'm pregnant, my dear."

Wesley's jaw went slack as he stared at her, while the fiercely pleased expression on Bernard's face wasn't comforting at all. To anyone else, the king would appear as excited, but Eimarille knew he was now counting down the days when she would outlive her usefulness to him.

"You're pregnant," Wesley repeated weakly before snapping out of his daze.

His joy seemed real when he got up from his seat and came around the table to pull Eimarille into his arms and spin her around. His laughter made her smile, because new life was always something to be celebrated in a place where poison always sought to encroach on cleansed land.

"A toast to the future," Bernard called out from his seat at the head of the table, wineglass in hand and eyes on Eimarille.

"Yes, a toast," Wesley said, still holding Eimarille close.

Terilyn said nothing, but her eyes shone with a fierceness for Eimarille alone.

The formal announcement of her pregnancy would come later, but that night they raised their glasses to a future each saw differently. In the end, only one road would hold true, and Eimarille had plans in place to ensure it would be hers.

Four

SOREN

The Celestine Lake was freezing during Second Month, though it carried no ice in its waters. Soren had done his fair share of winter training in its cold, sometimes poisonous depths over the years, and wasn't looking forward to more. Returning to the Warden's Island wasn't ever truly a respite.

Access to the island was restricted by a single port of call allowed along the lake's outer shoreline. The boathouse there was manned by a warden year-round, tending to the dock that anchored the steamboat that ferried wardens across four times a day depending on the weather.

Soren wasn't the only one returning that day, but none of the wardens around him were up for conversation, and neither was he. With their velocycles secured in the lower deck, a handful of wardens had claimed the benches in the cabin to nap their way across the choppy waters.

Soren woke when the ferry bumped up against its destination. He could hear the ferry captain and whoever was assigned to the pier calling out to each other. Soren ignored their conversation and rolled to his feet, cracking his neck, before filing belowdecks with the other wardens.

One of the crew members stabilized the ramp a dockworker had directed into place. Once everything was secured, Soren rolled his velocycle off the ferry along with the other wardens. Waiting for them on the dock was a familiar face.

Viktor was a grizzled warden who'd walked away from a lifetime in the poison fields with too many scars and a mechanical leg. The clockwork gears were well maintained, shining in the weak winter sunlight. The amputation didn't impede Viktor from chasing tithes around the training yard. His job was to teach tithes how to survive in the poison fields, not greet returning wardens, so it was strange to see him on the dock.

Viktor's flinty-eyed gaze settled on Soren. "The governor wants to see you."

Soren bit back a wince. "Can I at least stow my gear?"

"I'll handle that. Head up to the fort. You don't want to keep her waiting."

Soren wasn't going to argue an order like that, so he handed off his velocycle with all its attached gear, but he kept his pistols and poison sword. Unencumbered by the vehicle, it was an easy hike up the winding dirt road that led to the fort. The land around the imposing defensive wall was winter-bare, and he could see several automatons trundling about, their Zip guns trained on the water.

The gates were open for the day, with a warden on duty to guard the entrance. Revenants weren't as active in the wintertime, but one could never be too cautious. Soren had spent the last year on the road in western Solaria, and the uptick in revenants—both human and animal—was worrisome.

The fort was a mix of buildings from different eras, sections torn down and rebuilt depending on age and upkeep. It was a functioning mini-city that had wardens passing through its walls every day of the year. The island had no viable room for farmland, not with how they worked with poisons, so food was delivered along with tithes from the countries bound by the Poison Accords.

Everything about the place was familiar to Soren. From the barracks to the alchemy labs, he could find his way through the fort blind. Getting from the gate to the governor's office took some time as he followed paths past various buildings.

The governor's office was located in a low, squat building made to cater to the administrative side of the fort. Cramped offices filled nearly every floor, occupied by wardens who'd survived to old age and had no place else to call home.

The fort had never been home, for all that Soren had grown up there. It had housed him, though, and turned him from a tithe into a warden. If he ignored what burned in his soul, if he ignored the disjointed memories that refused to fade with every year that passed, perhaps he could pretend this was all he was.

But he'd seen what was denied him in Bellingham last year, walking in Vanya's shadow. Some part of him wanted that, and he thought he always would.

Soren climbed the stairs to the third floor, making his way to the governor's office. The position wasn't a blooded title how it sometimes was in other countries. Her door was always open, and he was expected. Soren paused in the entranceway and cleared his throat. "You wanted to see me, Governor?"

Delani raised her head, only one of her eyes focusing on him. The other was made of glass, pitch-black with gold flecks like the night sky in it. The contrast was always jarring, made more so by the monocle goggle she wore over her good eye to help with her depth perception. The leather straps keeping it in place were pulled tight over her skull, flattening her short, dark hair in those areas.

In her midforties, Delani had left the poison fields after losing her eye to revenants, along with pieces of her arm. The limb in question was scarred over and weak, making it impossible for her to safely wield a weapon. She'd spent some years teaching in the training yard before being voted into the governorship and had held that post ever since.

Delani was fair where it mattered and dug in her heels when she had to. Soren remembered the bark of her voice while standing at the range years ago, calling out minute corrections in their stances. The roughness of her voice hadn't faded, remnants of a time when she'd breathed a poisonous mist one year that not even a warden could walk away from unscathed.

Delani waved a hand at him, shoving aside a mess of papers with the other. "Come in. Sit."

Wardens didn't stand on ceremony, and Soren did as ordered. He was aware of the grit and grime clinging to his uniform, but at least none of it was blood. "I didn't think I'd be summoned so soon."

"Your reports from last year indicate there's an uptick of revenants in northwest Solaria. You aren't the only one to report such discrepancies, but you are the only one who drew the attention of someone in power," Delani said.

Soren remained silent at that statement, thinking of Vanya and the promise he'd broken by not bringing the border reports to him last autumn. "I did my duty."

"I'm not saying you failed in that regard. But the Imperial crown prince is, shall we say, persistent. He was displeased when I didn't send you with the border reports last year."

Having been the sole focus of Vanya's attention before, Soren understood keenly what that was like. "I told him that wasn't my job."

"Unfortunately, the Poison Accords allow for heads of state to dictate how they receive the border reports we give them. The empress has yet to make her position known on the matter, but that might change soon, especially after what's befallen the House of Sa'Liandel."

Soren went still, a coldness he couldn't blame on the weather settling in his gut. "What do you mean?"

Delani drummed her fingers against the desk, never looking away from him. "The Imperial crown princess died in childbirth recently. The infant survived, but the House of Kimathi has leveled accusations of murder at the House of Sa'Liandel."

The news hit like a blow, and Soren was unprepared for the worry that suffused him. The medallion that hung around his neck, hidden by his uniform, felt like a noose right then.

He'd seen news of the Imperial wedding in the broadsheets while on the road, and months after, read the announcement the princess was with child. But he'd been too busy chasing down revenants in places they shouldn't be to really care about the status of people who held a rank he never would.

Except right then, all he could think about was Vanya.

"The Houses live to kill for the throne," Soren said after a pause.

Delani smiled thinly. "It's a tradition I have never understood, but the Dawn Star allows it to continue, and so we must work around the power plays. Our duty is to Maricol, and it will remain so, no matter who wears what crown."

Soren nodded jerkily. "Am I to stay out of Solaria?"

Delani flattened her hand against the desk and leaned back in her chair. "No. You'll remain on the road in that country, but I don't want you checking the borders in any land the House of Kimathi holds sway over. I don't trust their intentions while they deal with the loss of their heir. Neither do I trust what they seem to allow to grow in the poison fields that have cropped up in their *vasilyet*."

"Ma'am?"

"You know the Wastelands in the south of Solaria are rife with revenants risen from wild beasts and the lost souls of spore-tainted frontier towns. Rixham was a garrison to keep the dead in check, but that city is lost to us by a decision made in grief. We learned too late what the empress decided about Rixham. We can't afford that same mistake now."

Soren didn't know Vanya well enough to know what the prince would do if he lost his child to the murderous schemes of another House. But Soren could guess, and it would be bloody.

"Daijal has poison fields where none should be, and the northwest of Solaria as a whole is trending in that direction, to say nothing of other countries. Revenants walk where they shouldn't, and the numbers aren't natural. Wardens have done their job and done it well over the centuries. The walking dead shouldn't be as numerous as they are," Delani continued.

Soren grimaced. In the admittedly few years he'd been a full-fledged warden, even he could see the discrepancies on the road from what he knew should be there. "Will I take the Wastelands border come summer?"

Every warden guarded that southernmost border at one point in their lives, pressing deep into the poison fields to find the hordes and eradicate them when possible. The desert sun dried the walking dead into husks that roamed the Wastelands. Keeping them confined to that area was a nonstop operation tended to by wardens with the backing of the Solarian Legion when necessary.

Guarding that border was dangerous, a task given to wardens with at least five years on the road under their belt. Soren hadn't reached that milestone yet, but if the governor sent him south, then he would go.

Delani shook her head. "You'll take the spring border reports to the Imperial court and tend to the eastern borders in Solaria."

Soren blinked. "You said last year I hadn't earned that job."

"That was before I became aware of what's growing in the poison fields. While I can't get anyone deep into the Daijal court to observe, you've given me an avenue into the Imperial one. I'll take it if it means we can keep the borders safe and cleanse the land."

"That sounds like you want me and others to spy. That isn't our place as wardens."

Delani grimaced, her mechanical eye rotating in its metal socket. "The numbers of revenants we're seeing is concerning. People are generally good at obeying the laws of their countries and burning the dead, but not everyone is. This problem is growing, and we wardens need to eradicate the roots of it. Deliver the border reports to the Imperial throne this spring and see if you can't find out something more than rumors when you do so."

It wasn't what Soren had expected to hear, but he'd do his duty as requested. And if doing so got him back within Vanya's orbit after everything that had occurred while he was on the road, well, then so much the better.

Five

CARIS

The professor lecturing about clarion crystals and their use in airships mostly knew what he was talking about, though he was wrong about how many ways the crystals could be cut.

Miss Caris Dhemlan, heir to a landless baron title and her family's plethora of patents, would've protested the inaccuracies if she was a student of Amari's Aether School of Engineering, but she wasn't. And since she—technically—wasn't supposed to be there at all, she bit her tongue and furiously scribbled into her notebook so as not to miss a single point Professor Tristan Arquette was expounding on.

The amphitheater-style classroom was packed with students, but she'd managed to claim a spot in the back row for auditing purposes. Caris had given the school's assigned guide the slip over an hour ago, and she hoped to finish listening to the lecture before anyone reported back to her mother that she'd wandered off.

Her mother was always so overprotective and had become more so since their arrival in Amari a week ago for the high-society season amongst the bloodlines. Why Caris couldn't have debuted into high society back in Cosian was beyond her. No one back home in the Eastern Basin looked askance at her fitted day jacket and trousers as they did in Amari. Fashion was different for girls her age in the nation's capital, it seemed, and it was glaringly apparent Caris was woefully unprepared to meet the social standards of the nobility out west.

She dug the nub of her fountain pen against the sturdy sheet of paper in her notebook, scowling at the airship engine diagram she'd copied down, with a few of her fixes thrown in. What did she care for the insipid gossips who only wanted a husband or a wife? Caris wanted to *learn*, she wanted to *invent*, not to marry someone more interested in her family's growing wealth than in her.

She wasn't even *interested* in anyone, for stars' sake. How could her mother expect her to like someone she knew nothing about after one measly dance?

"That's a rather interesting fix you've drawn there," the young man seated to her left said in a low voice.

Caris' gaze slid sideways, taking in the speaker. She couldn't speak about his trousers and jacket and whether or not they were of the current fashionable trend, but he was well-dressed. His dark blond hair was pulled back in a queue, and his brown eyes were on her notebook rather than the chalkboard the professor was referencing as he lectured. The curve of his mouth was kind.

"He cut the crystals wrong for that type of engine. A half cut is fine, but a quarter cut would get him quicker lift on a launch. He'd need to add another piston, though," Caris said.

Those brown eyes flicked up to meet her gaze, curiosity in them rather than the condescending humor Caris sometimes faced when people didn't know how many patents she owned at the age of sixteen. Clarion crystals sang, and Caris had been breaking down those songs since the first time her father had brought her to check on one of the filtration machines out in the Eastern Basin.

Caris knew how clarion crystals wanted to be cut. She always had. Their song lived in her like her magic did, for all that was a secret from everyone but her parents.

"How do you know?" the young man asked. He sounded curious, appearing eager to hear her answer.

Usually, older inventors who weren't aware of her work history looked down their noses at her. His manners, however, were polite, and Caris found herself wanting to answer his question. Most days she preferred machines over people, but she made an exception for him.

Caris tapped the capped end of her fountain pen against her notebook. "Everyone thinks you need a clarion crystal to power an engine, which, yes, it does that, but the engine isn't the important bit, it's the crystal."

Because the underlying mechanics would be relegated to steam power without the aether. Steam power had its place and was widely in use, but progress was never attained by sticking with the status quo.

"Most people would say the engine is more important. Even magicians can't channel the aether without their wands."

Caris shrugged one shoulder. "Most people would be wrong."

It wasn't the place for her to get into another argument about how one needed to listen to the clarion crystals and pick out which ones would work best with each invention. They needed to harmonize with the machinery, the same way they needed to harmonize with a magician's wand. Caris had learned to love her music lessons as a little girl only when her teacher revealed she'd be better able to carve a crystal once she could read the notes it sang.

She'd never mastered the piano, but she *had* mastered her father's crystal-cutting tools.

"All the inventors in history who've built what we use can't have been wrong," the young man said.

"Then they're simply uninspired."

He smiled at her words, seemingly amused. "Well said."

His agreement startled her, and Caris ducked her head a little to hide the flush that came to her cheeks at his support. She spent the remaining ten minutes of the lecture sneaking glances at him that he returned. He was handsome, but more than that, she wanted to know his opinion on the lecture.

Professor Tristan Arquette captivated her attention just as much as the young man seated beside her in those last few minutes. The professor knew what he was talking about when it came to engines. Caris absently wondered if she could apply his ideas to the next generation of filtration devices she and her father were engineering.

"Next week's lesson will be on calculating the size of an airship around the engine you build," Professor Arquette announced at the top of the hour.

He continued with a brief summary of what to expect and what chapters he wanted the students to read. Caris jotted down the name of the book the class was reading, wondering if she'd be able to order it from the bookstore back home. The students around her started to pack up their things and bustle out.

"Caris Dhemlan, *what* are you doing?"

The sound of her full name said in that tone had Caris snapping her head up and around. She stared wide-eyed at where her mother stood at the end of the row with two representatives from the Aether School of Engineering.

Baroness Portia Dhemlan was a petite woman, with the same brown hair as Caris, though it was styled in a more sophisticated manner than Caris' loose waves. She'd undone her twist after escaping her minder, the carefree style allowing her to blend in as a student more easily.

Portia's gown was simple but well-made, without the embellishments prone to a woman of high society in Amari. The dress set her apart from the students, clearly marking her as an outsider.

"Mother," Caris said with a wince as she snapped her notebook closed and tucked it away into her small satchel.

She ignored the curious eyes on her as she stood, her trousers a bit wrinkled from shifting in her seat during the lecture. Her mother looked a little frantic around the eyes, while the minder who Caris had left behind only appeared relieved.

"What were you thinking, slipping away like that?" Portia demanded in a low voice as Caris drew closer.

"I wanted to see what sort of engineering classes they had available," Caris said.

"You know we didn't have time for that, not with your final fitting happening today. As it is, we're going to be *late*."

The classroom was emptying out, and with the door at the top of the stairs, everyone had to pass by their little group on the stairs. The five people seated to Caris' right shuffled past her mother, and then she found herself standing before Portia and the fiercely disapproving look on her face.

"If I'm to come here next term, I wanted to know what to expect. Surely that isn't cause for alarm," Caris said stubbornly.

Portia frowned. "It is when you tell no one where you are going. Caris, my dear, we didn't come to Amari to spend your time here."

"*I* did."

"Pardon the interruption, but if you're worried about the quality of classes the Aether School of Engineering provides, don't be. The academics here are top-notch," her seat partner said from behind her.

Caris glanced back at the young man, looking up at him. He was quite a bit taller than her now that they were both standing, but he politely didn't loom over her.

"I thank you for your opinion, Mr.—" Portia began.

He dipped his head in a respectful little nod since there wasn't any room to bow. "Nathaniel Clementine."

Her mother arched an eyebrow. "Mr. Clementine of the Clementine Trading Company?"

"That would be my father. Please, call me Nathaniel."

"You may address me as Baroness Dhemlan. This is my wayward daughter, Caris."

"I'm not wayward, Mother. I'm exactly where I want to be," Caris muttered.

Portia sighed, gesturing for Caris to leave the row. "That is our problem right now. Come along, my dear."

"Would it be remiss of me to escort you to your destination, Baroness Dhemlan? Your daughter had some interesting opinions regarding the engine Professor Arquette was discussing, and I would love to hear more of what she thinks," Nathaniel asked.

Portia paused for a moment before saying, "You may. Our motor carriage is in the guest lot."

"That will be on the eastern side of the school grounds. I'll be happy to show you the quickest way there."

"Were you a student here, Nathaniel?"

"Yes. I graduated last year with a focus on steam train engines. Professor Arquette wasn't teaching at the time, but I've heard from several contemporaries who still attend that he's an excellent professor and quite gifted in the mechanics of airship engines. I had the pleasure of running into him at a pub some months ago, and he invited me to audit his classes whenever I have the time. We've taken tea together on occasion since then to discuss peer reports on new inventions."

"Did you find the curriculum invigorating while you attended?"

"Quite so, Lady Dhemlan."

Nathaniel glanced at Caris, who tilted her head at him. "You studied steam trains for your business here?"

He smiled brilliantly at her, but if Nathaniel hoped Caris would turn into a simpering idiot simply because he looked at her, then he would be wrong. "I did."

Caris knew the Clementine Trading Company was the largest transportation company originating out of Amari, with a fleet of steam trains crisscrossing the continent to deliver trade goods across borders. Her family's own company, Six Point Mechanics, did business with them to move their patented filtration machines.

Unlike her family, the Clementines had been offered a noble title once several generations back but had declined, causing quite a scandal. They remained top-tier merchants, though, richer than even some noble bloodlines, including her own, and Caris wasn't unaware of what it meant to have Nathaniel's interest.

She just didn't care how others might.

Portia deftly bid goodbye to the pair of guides who had been tasked with showing them both around in favor of allowing Nathaniel to escort them back to their motor carriage. The Aether School of Engineering's campus was situated on the western side of the city, having expanded over the decades by buying up surrounding housing lots to convert them into lecture halls and dormitories.

While the main campus was nestled between two inner defensive walls, it retained two satellite campuses for hands-on learning at the airfield and the railyard. Caris hadn't been able to wheedle her mother to let her tour either of those locations today, but she was hopeful it could happen after the debutante ball tomorrow.

"You seemed interested in clarion crystal cutting. Is that what you'd like to study?" Nathaniel asked.

Caris shook her head. "I've been studying that for years. I'm more interested in engine modification these days. Do you race at all? I've found the racing circuit to be rather on the cutting edge when it comes to engine innovations."

"Caris," Portia warned.

She gave her mother a wide-eyed look of faux innocence. "But he asked what I'm interested in studying."

"I can't say that I've had the pleasure of sitting behind the steering wheel of a racing carriage," Nathaniel said, sounding amused. "Have you?"

Caris would've answered, except a fearful scream caught her attention, and she rocked to a halt on the paved pathway that cut through the center common. Nathaniel immediately stepped to the side, putting himself between them and the cluster of people across the open grass being accosted by peacekeepers and several men and women in regular clothes.

"What's going on?" Portia asked quietly as she wrapped her arm around Caris' shoulders.

Caris didn't miss the way Nathaniel's hands clenched into fists or the way his jaw tightened. He looked furious, but he made no move to approach what was going on. Other students scattered across the center common had turned to watch the commotion, several drifting closer for a better look.

"A debt collection," Nathaniel finally said in a flat voice. "There have been quite a few happening on campus this spring. I had hoped no more would occur."

Caris sucked in a breath, heart hammering against her ribs as she watched the travesty unfold. She knew the risks of doing business with banks. Her father was ever careful with their accounting ledgers, and he'd taught her to be wary about taking on new loans. Collateral could be deathly expensive, and one had to weigh all the risks before signing a binding contract.

Her family was lucky in that their business thrived, but many weren't, especially with the change in collection laws. Daijal's parliament had signed off on a broadening of what the banks could use to demand collection of collateral as a wedding present for Prince Wesley and his new wife, Princess Eimarille. Ashion's parliament had yet to ratify it, but that hadn't stopped the Collector's Guild from handing out jobs to its certified debt collectors.

She'd heard rumors of families taken in the dead of night in Cosian, never to be seen again. Citizens in the eastern provinces didn't take kindly to Daijal interference, and Caris was well-read into the politics of doing business under a slowly shifting rulership. The laws were changing, and not necessarily for the good. Restrictions and regulations happened in increments that no one thought twice about until it was too late.

Like a frog in a pot set to slow boil, Caris thought bitterly.

Her parents' caution was why she'd been given private tutorship of her magic over the years and had not been sent to a magician's training school or the Star Order. More and more, if a magician did not hold allegiance with Daijal, they were looked at askance by high society. That general reaction was beginning to trickle down into the lower classes of Ashion. Nowadays, rumors of someone thought to be aligned with the Clockwork Brigade had the potential to kill.

Caris was not known as a magician and carried no wand. She'd tried to use one once and had blown the clarion crystal to pieces. For some reason, that had made her parents double down on keeping her magic a secret. It was frustrating, being unable to use what burned beneath her skin, but Caris knew her parents only wanted to protect her. That hadn't stopped the way her magic just—wanted to burst out of her lately.

"Can we do anything to help them?" Caris asked.

"Not if you don't want to be arrested. An interference charge comes with a hefty fine and jail time. While I'm sure you could afford it, you don't need the attention," a voice said from behind them.

Caris turned to find Professor Arquette staring at her with an intensity that was startling. "It's *wrong*."

"You'll find few here on campus who will disagree with you. But there is nothing you can do without endangering yourself in the process."

"Professor Arquette is right," Nathaniel said brusquely as he shook his head in disgust. "Neither of you should have to see this. Let me escort you and your daughter away from here, Lady Dhemlan."

"Please do," Portia said.

"I'll see you safely on with Nathaniel," Professor Arquette said.

The professor came to stand on Caris' other side. Hemmed in by both men, she and her mother were quickly escorted from the center common, the cries of the people being remanded into the debt collectors' custody echoing in her ears.

The whispers of what was happening behind them followed them off campus to the guest lot where the motor carriages were parked. Their driver was chatting with several others between the rows, but he immediately peeled away once he spotted them. By the time they reached the motor carriage, he had the door open for them and was prepared to offer his hand in assistance.

Professor Arquette hadn't spoken since leaving the center common, but Nathaniel didn't hesitate to properly bow to Caris' mother. "May I inquire how long your stay in Amari will be? If it's not too forward, I would ask about calling on your daughter to finish our discussion about engines."

Portia studied him, the silk shawl she wore in deference to the warm spring air staying firmly put across her shoulders with the help of a brooch. "Will you be in attendance at the debutante ball tomorrow evening?"

Nathaniel hesitated but rallied well enough. "Regrettably, it was not on my schedule, though if I had known you and your daughter would be attending, I'd have made myself available."

The shrewdness that came to her mother's gaze made Caris want to squawk a protest. She knew that look all too well.

"We're staying at our home on the eastern side of the river, at Sixteen Rose Court Garden. I'm sure my husband would not mind a visit with our daughter by one such as yourself," Portia said.

"*I* would mind," Caris said tartly. It was one thing to have a chat on her own terms, quite another to have one engineered by her mother.

Portia shot her a sharp look. "Into the motor carriage with you, my dear. It's time we're off. We're late enough for the fitting as it is."

Nathaniel stepped forward and offered his hand to Portia, and she took it with a prim smile, allowing herself to be guided into the motor carriage. When he offered Caris his hand, she thought about ignoring him and climbing inside on her own. It wasn't as if she was in a gown that would get caught underfoot. The warning look from her mother made Caris huff out an irritated sigh before thrusting out her hand for Nathaniel to take.

"I look forward to your opinion on engines," Nathaniel said with a smile as he guided her into the motor carriage.

"Thank you for your assistance," Portia said.

"I'm at your disposal, Lady Dhemlan."

Nathaniel closed the door, and Caris buckled the lap belt into place as the driver started the engine. She refused to look out the window as the driver pulled out of the parking spot, though her mother gave a polite wave as they departed.

"He seemed nice," Portia said as they headed for the street.

"Mother," Caris groaned.

"One could do worse than having the heir to such an important business asking permission to come call on you."

"Does this mean I can stay home tomorrow night if he's coming over the day after so you and Papa can discuss business with him on the side?"

"Absolutely not."

Caris scowled out the window, not looking forward to the next few days at all.

Six

BLAINE

When the Inferno ravaged half of Amari, many buildings couldn't be saved despite the efforts of the fire crews. The people of Ashion were resilient, though, and rebuilding had happened almost immediately.

The new parliament was one of the first structures to go up, as the old one in the western part of the city was far too cramped for long-term use. Eventually, a new palace was built as well, situated a block from the ruins of the old one, which had been converted into a public park. The new palace lacked Ashionen touches in favor of Daijal architectural lines, as if wanting to erase the memory of what came before.

Blaine only vaguely remembered how the palace once looked, though it didn't matter what his memory could and could not dredge up. The old queen was dead, and along with her, any hope of Ashion surviving the encroachment of Daijal rule and culture. That was what the Daijal court wanted everyone to believe.

Blaine knew differently, had known since he escaped the Inferno on that desperate airship flight east. The Clockwork Brigade shared his belief, but all they had to go by were rumors and hope, none of which could sustain them for much longer if they wanted to keep recruiting. Of the many cogs that kept the rebellion running, he could count on one hand those who knew Blaine had once been a Wester-gard. Even less knew about the child the star gods had deemed worthy of saving.

But Blaine had known what he'd seen earlier that day at the Aether School of Engineering. He'd recognized those wide gray eyes in a face growing thinner from the onset of adulthood. He might not remember the old palace, but he remembered what Queen Ophelia had once looked like, even without the help of tintype photographs. The girl who'd sneaked into his classroom had the same eyes as Ophelia, the same look about her of a family only survived by Princess Eimarille in the west.

She had the same name the Dusk Star had affirmed to him before taking her off the airship in Cosian.

He'd never seen the child again—until now.

Blaine reached up and touched his bare throat, missing the weight of the marriage torc even after a year spent in Amari. He missed it the same way he missed his husband, but he rather thought Honovi would understand the weight of determination that settled on him as he stared at the burning starfire throne across the public park.

While the new palace was walled off from the rest of the city, the old throne room was not. The throne itself had not burned amidst the Inferno by the command of the North Star, but it burned now, day and night, every inch covered in starfire.

Iron pillars held up a glass cupola, the space between them empty and open to the elements. The charred remnants of the old marble floor expanded outward past the pillars for several feet, their broken edges buried in grass. Beneath the cupola, the space around the throne itself overflowed with the bones and ashes of people who had tried to sit upon it once and claim the right to rule.

No one ever removed the remains, and there was no risk of ashes rising as revenants, driven by spores. Starfire cleansed the way nothing else could.

Blaine stood on the pathway winding around the heart of the public park, staring at what true Ashionens considered a shrine, while others viewed it as a grave. The starfire was a flicker of white-gold fire between the iron pillars, a shimmering, molten beacon even in the afternoon sunlight.

He stayed only long enough to whisper a clan prayer to the Dusk Star before moving on, feeling as if the eyes of the damned followed him. His skin prickled in a way it never did anywhere else.

The public gardens were filled with people who promenaded through all seasons. Picnics happened in the spring and summer, and there were plenty out today enjoying a garden meal. How anyone could eat near such a thing was beyond him, but then, Ashionen culture still made no sense to him some days.

Meleri despaired of him ever integrating fully, and Blaine didn't have the heart to tell her he had no plans to. The Westergard bloodline was gone, stricken from the genealogies. Blaine wasn't sure he wanted it back, not when he claimed Clan Storm as family through marriage. Still, he stayed because he was needed.

He missed his husband terribly, but Blaine had a duty, even without a bloodline, and he could not turn his back on it now.

Blaine walked through the public park as if he were enjoying the day, smiling and nodding politely to the people he passed. When he left the greenery behind for the exhaust-filled street of the civic district, he took a winding path east. Blaine popped into a bookshop at one point to peruse the front table before leaving without buying anything.

Eventually, he slipped down an alleyway rife with trash and refuse, wrinkling his nose at the smell. At the end of that alleyway was a sewer grate, the rusted-over metal slick with foul water and muck that would never be cleaned. Blaine pulled from his pocket a rectangular bit of metal, the contraption elongating to a sturdy rod with a press of a button and the click of well-maintained clockwork gears.

In the shadows of the alleyway, Blaine used the rod to lever up the sewer grate, gaining entry to the ancient passages that twisted beneath Amari on either side of the Serpentine River.

Few in the Clockwork Brigade knew all the access points to the catacombs. Even less had the keys to unlock the hidden entrances below. Blaine could only unlock six routes—twelve access points—and the one he tossed himself down feet-first was one of the more unconventional ones.

Not least because of the filth he had to walk through until he reached the door.

He slid the grate back into place above him, climbed carefully down the ladder, and nearly gagged at the stench that greeted him. Blaine swung his satchel around and pulled out a heavy cylinder tube with a glass tip. The handheld gaslight provided enough light to see by once he switched it on. Blaine aimed it at the ledge he stood on and started walking.

He breathed through his mouth, lips barely open, trying not to smell the sludge drifting through the channel past the ledge. He had to duck his head to keep from knocking it on the ceiling, counting his steps until he came to a space in the wall that wasn't any different upon first glance.

In the dark, even with the gaslight, it was difficult to see the outline of the door carefully hidden by practical means. Magic degraded over time, and any spells cast below were bound to draw attention no one needed.

Blaine ran his fingers over the wall, feeling for the indentation that would give way to the hidden lock. He found it in seconds and peeled back the covering. He slipped his hand into his satchel, reaching for the very bottom, and withdrew a key from a hidden pocket sewn there. Placing the key into the lock, he turned it, listening to the quiet sound of well-maintained gears clicking tumblers out of place.

The door shuddered in its frame. Blaine pushed it back half an inch before sliding it into a hidden casing. The grooves in the floor that allowed it to move weren't stone but metal, and Blaine stepped over them to enter the catacombs.

The air smelled stale, but better than the air in the sewer proper. Blaine slid the door back into place, listening for the click of the lock catching. Gripping the gaslight tightly, he started down the tunnel, the perfectly cut metal panels surrounding him like nothing else he'd ever seen.

Blaine didn't have a map of the catacombs. He'd been taken down this route once before by Lore and then verbally quizzed on it until he could visualize every turn with his eyes closed. Memory served him well, and he passed beneath the streets of Amari to the Auclair estate, no one the wiser.

The residence was located on the eastern side of the Serpentine River, on the border of the civic heart. The large manor house overlooked the winding waterway, with a sprawling garden walled off from the prying eyes of curious folk passing by. By virtue of its bloodline's history, the estate was a grand building, four stories tall, recently renovated, and one of the few that had survived the Inferno.

Blaine never entered the estate through the front door. He only ever arrived through the basement.

The access routes could be opened from the inside, so it was no problem sliding aside the door that led into the Auclair bloodline's home. The hard part was getting past the automaton always on guard in the basement.

The heavy shift of gears and metal reached Blaine's ears, and he stayed exactly where he was in the catacomb tunnel. In the dimly lit shadows of the basement beyond, the glow from what passed for the automaton's eyes was an eerie red.

Its left arm was bulky but human-shaped, with copper coils looped around sturdy hinged pieces of metal to act as fingers. Its right arm was a heavily modified Zip gun, and the multibarrel was currently pointed right at Blaine's chest.

"Door mouse," Blaine said.

The spell laid down over the floor of the basement just past the door flashed with magic, revealing itself in the dark. Then it went dormant, and Blaine let out a breath. His voice was keyed to the entrapment spell, and even though he had no magic, the code word unlocked it for safe passage.

"That is the last time I let Mainspring set the code word. It's ridiculous," a voice said from behind the automaton, all exasperation. "All right, stand down, Fred."

Aether made the automaton's eyes flash fiery red, the code word—

more than the other man's request—keeping it from shooting a hole clean through Blaine's body. With the defensive spell sufficiently appeased, the automaton shifted on its mechanical feet, immediately lowering its Zip gun arm.

Blaine let out a heavy breath as it shuffled to the side in rigid movements, allowing him to get eyes on Meleri's youngest child and only son. Lord Dureau Auclair flashed him a tight smile.

"You weren't due for a check-in until next week," Dureau said.

Blaine stepped into the basement, making sure to close the catacomb door tightly behind him so it locked. He didn't bother bowing. "Needs must. I'm surprised you're on guard duty."

"The clarion crystal in your key called to the one in Mother's study. We knew you were coming. We always know when a cog spins their way back to us. Shall we? Fred, resume guard position."

The automaton lumbered back into position, facing the entrance, Zip gun arm pointed at the door. Blaine skirted past it and hurried through the dark after Dureau. The other man was younger than him by six years, popular amongst his peers according to the society columns in the broadsheets. Dureau put on a good show of a lackadaisical son who'd rather spend his time with friends out on the town.

In reality, Dureau was a high-ranking member of the Clockwork Brigade, loyal to his mother and in charge of code work amongst the cogs. Dureau had a way with languages few others did, and he channeled that skill into keeping everyone's secrets safe. Locke was the name most people in the Clockwork Brigade knew him as, even if they didn't know him, and it fit.

Dureau led him to a private study on the third floor. He knocked before reaching for the handle and pushing it open. "Mother, you have a guest."

Blaine followed Dureau into the cozy, windowless space persistently lit by gas lamps. To compensate for the lack of windows, the wooden floor and wainscoting were done in a pale birch, the wallpaper white with flowering vines and birds in a watercolor style. Bookcases lined one wall, a trio of small chairs were tucked away in a corner by the door, and a credenza pressed up against the opposite wall.

Hanging from the wall over the credenza was an intricate piece of art in the shape of vines and flowers created out of metal, clockwork gears, and tiny shards of clarion crystal. At first glance, it appeared as nothing more than an homage to Ashionen flowers made to match the wallpaper.

If one knew what to look for, one could see the brass vines were twisted in such a way as to match the routes of the catacombs Blaine had just come from. Tiny clarion crystal flowers were scattered through the larger metal ones, resting on brass vines in shallow grooves. As Blaine watched, one of the flowers slowly glided along a vine in what passed for south of the city—an indication of someone walking the catacombs.

The clarion crystal flower linked to the crystal shard embedded in the key in his satchel was currently unmoving in the cluster of antiqued metal rosebuds that marked the Auclair estate. Blaine looked away from the tracking device and met the gaze of a woman who the nobility bowed to as one of the few important bloodlines left, and who was called Fulcrum by those in the Clockwork Brigade.

Meleri Auclair, Duchess of Auclair, was of average height, graceful, and demanding. Her red hair shimmered with gray and was cut in a severe style that hugged her skull. She'd never quite grown it out of the widow's style she'd chopped it to after her husband died. As the matriarch of her bloodline, Meleri wasn't bound by societal tradition.

The gown she wore was practical, high-necked, and unadorned. Her lightly wrinkled face was touched with a hint of makeup, drawing attention to her hazel eyes and the sharpness in her gaze that could skewer a man at a dozen paces. One did not become a spymaster by being meek.

"You don't ever deviate from our meetings," Meleri said.

"Something happened today that warranted it, Your Grace," Blaine said.

Meleri leaned back in her chair, the creak of leather loud in the office. "Do tell."

Blaine hesitated, thinking about the promise he'd given to the Dusk Star high in the sky, with only the cold and the wind to hear their words. But the North Star had guided the Auclairs east to him, and they knew part of the truth lost during the Inferno. Perhaps it was time to give voice to a hope few people clung to.

"The star gods left a child in Cosian. That child is here in Amari," Blaine said.

Meleri jerked forward in surprise, bracing herself against the edge of her desk with both hands as all the color drained from her face. "Are you certain?"

He closed his eyes for a moment, dredging up the shape of Caris' face and those vivid gray eyes full of life. "Yes."

Meleri drew in a breath that sounded like it hurt. "Dureau, please fetch your sisters."

"Yes, Mother," Dureau replied and slipped out of the office.

Blaine opened his eyes, watching as Meleri stood from her chair to come around the desk. He knew she could appear unassuming, but right then, the sheer forceful presence of her personality was a reminder the duchess was anything but ordinary.

"It took you a year to tell us where the child was left. Why, when we fight for the same future?" Meleri asked, studying him.

Blaine shook his head. "Your North Star gave you a decree, and my Dusk Star did the same for me. I kept my word to keep the child safe."

"And now?"

"I'm still keeping my word."

"Ever a Westergard."

He said nothing to that and kept his peace until Meleri's oldest and middle children arrived with Dureau. Blaine saw plenty of Lore these days, but he rarely saw Meleri's firstborn. Brielle Auclair was the heir to her mother's title and had claimed their bloodline's seat in the House of Lords once she was old enough.

Married, with children of her own, Brielle was neck-deep in the Clockwork Brigade, though her focus lay elsewhere. While her brother handled the sneaky aspect of codework, and Lore took charge of the cogs with their mother, Brielle's attention was on high society. It was her duty to parse the politics, to dig up the secrets hoarded by the nobility, to keep her finger on the pulse of society's mores.

It was Brielle's work in the world of false smiles and knifelike words that brought them news of the Daijal court's ever-encroaching power. Her position was such that she could corral allies still loyal to Ashion's past, but the future was looking bleak, and supporters kept peeling off. Blaine wondered how the news he brought today would change that.

Dureau closed the door behind his sisters, but he activated no spell for quiet over the room. Other than the spells in the basement and the automaton that guarded the entrance to the catacombs, the Auclairs rarely allowed magic to be used in their estate.

Their bloodline had survived the assassins on the night of the Inferno because they had no magic and starfire did not burn in their souls. Meleri had made sure to keep that distinction in the years after. While the Clockwork Brigade had magicians in their ranks, there were none allowed to work within the estate's grounds.

Secrets were kept through loyalty and the use of mind magic that allowed their servants to look the other way when visitors arrived from below. Blaine wasn't comfortable with some of the decisions Meleri made as Fulcrum, but it wasn't his place to argue.

"What is it, Mother?" Brielle asked as she moved farther into the study.

She was taller than Lore, wearing what was currently the height of fashion for Amari, with strawberry blonde hair and blue eyes that saw as much as her mother. She must have come from the House of Lords recently, for her ranking brooch was pinned to a white sash hanging off one shoulder. While in public, she was referred to by the title of Lady. Here within the walls of her mother's study, she was known as Whisper to the Clockwork Brigade.

"Blaine comes bearing news of the child the North Star helped save during the Inferno," Meleri said.

Four pairs of eyes pinned Blaine like a bug, but he refused to look away. They were all of them cunning enough not to give away their annoyance, but he heard their opinions of his decision in the exasperation found in Lore's voice.

"You couldn't have informed us before now? We've only been asking since we brought you here," Lore said.

"The Dusk Star left her in Cosian. I did not know where in that city, as I remained on the airship. I did not know if the child got to keep her name, but I believe she did." Blaine swallowed, only dimly recalling the weight of an infant in his arms. "Caris Dhemlan is the daughter of Baroness Portia Dhemlan. They're in Amari for the debutante ball tomorrow evening. Caris audited my engineering class this afternoon."

"She kept her name," Meleri said after a moment, voice tight with an old grief, though she shed no tears.

Blaine nodded jerkily. "I heard her name spoken as my class was leaving. I followed her and her mother to the center common, because I had to be sure. Nathaniel Clementine was escorting them back to their motor carriage when they witnessed debt collectors bringing someone into custody. None of them seemed pleased about that."

Brielle pursed her lips. "Nathaniel wouldn't. Neither would the girl's mother."

"What's that supposed to mean?"

"He's a cog," Meleri said. "As are his parents. Very integral cogs, I might add, as they allow the Clockwork Brigade to use their trains to transport freed debt slaves out of Daijal whenever possible. His parents work with cogs connected to the Marshall."

Blaine stared at her. "Should you be telling me this? He's not linked to me."

Cogs were linked to select other people through limited chains of communication. Only some linked to those who could be considered levers in the machine of the rebellion. Connections were vital to make it run, but the Clockwork Brigade was set up so that if one cog was discovered and broken, they wouldn't be able to implicate more than those in their immediate group and risk a cascade effect.

By virtue of who he was and the knowledge he carried, Blaine's group consisted of everyone in this study.

"He's been having tea with you when available and audits your classes. We anticipated making him known to you officially this summer," Lore said tartly.

"The Dhemlans were given a title and had their names included in the nobility genealogies slightly less than two decades ago. They're landless, with no heredity seat in the House of Lords, but they're quite wealthy through ownership of critical water purification and filtration patents. They have a daughter, their only heir, who would be sixteen. They also joined the Clockwork Brigade a decade ago. Their daughter has not," Brielle said.

Blaine always found it fascinating how Brielle seemed to have the genealogy of every noble and most of the more wealthy merchants memorized. It was useful in moments like this.

"Caris," Meleri said, testing out the name. "Caris Dhemlan. You are certain she is the same child? The name Caris isn't unheard of."

"Her eyes haven't changed," Blaine said, thinking of the fierce intelligence in Caris' gray-eyed gaze now and the color they'd been when she was an infant crying in his arms as he fled the palace before the potion kicked in to make her sleep.

"Did she carry a wand?"

"No."

Some kind of disappointment filled Meleri's gaze before fading. "Eimarille carries no wand, but she can cast starfire. Perhaps it is the same for Caris."

That was the crux, Blaine knew. One could be of Rourke blood, but one needed magic to command the starfire burning on the throne, to put it out and claim a crown. Without such power, they'd have a queen, but not one who could stand for long against what Eimarille represented.

"You say she audited your class?" Dureau asked.

Blaine nodded. "Her mother found her after it ended, which is how I learned her name. Apparently, she sneaked away from her minders, and the baroness wasn't pleased. Nathaniel said she was interested in engineering."

"Perhaps she means to attend the Aether School of Engineering."

Meleri hummed to herself, eyes narrowing. "If she is to be presented at the debutante ball, then we must attend as well."

"I'll inform the organizers we will be attending," Brielle said.

She swept out of the study, presumably to go do just that. It reminded him of the way Honovi simply expected to be included by virtue of his rank as *jarl*. It was an arrogance Blaine knew better than to question, not when it got them what they wanted.

"I don't need to attend, do I?" Blaine asked.

Lore gave him a slightly pitying look. "The name you carry here is not of the nobility."

"You gave it to me."

"Yes, because you refused the one that rightfully belongs to you. If you ever claim it again, then high society will be open to you."

Blaine had every intention of returning to E'ridia, but now that Caris was known to him—was real, after so many years of just existing in memory—he knew he would have to reassess his resolve. He'd made a promise, after all, to both his father and the Dusk Star, to protect her.

He'd made a promise to his husband, too, and at some point, Blaine would have to reconcile the two roads.

"This does complicate things, Mother," Lore said, moving to take a seat on one of the chairs in front of the desk. "Finding Caris has always been our top priority, but the rumors of that terrible death-defying machine are only growing louder. We need to ascertain the truth there, and our most trusted cogs we'd send to uncover the origins of the rumors would be the ones we'd have guard Caris."

Blaine frowned. "What machine?"

Lore made a face, smoothing the skirt of her gown over her knees. "Haven't you wondered about the excess of revenants in Ashion? The borders have never shrunk so badly as they have in the last year. Even the wardens can't explain the uptick of the walking dead. Their spring report on the borders is concerning."

"Wild beasts are one thing. Humans quite another. The dead are burned for a reason," Dureau agreed.

"What would a machine have to do with revenants?" Blaine asked.

Meleri sighed and went to take her seat behind the desk again. "There are rumors of a machine that can turn the dead into revenants."

"That's impossible."

Meleri smiled thinly, folding her hands together over the desktop. "And we never thought the coup and Inferno would happen, but here we are, stumbling through the ashes."

Blaine vehemently shook his head. "A machine like that can't exist."

"I've learned it's best not to think in absolutes when the Daijal court is involved. These are rumors, yes, but all rumors have a grain of truth in them somewhere."

"We'll find it," Lore promised.

The surety in her voice would have been laughable, but their persistence had kept the Clockwork Brigade running and had located Blaine in E'ridia. It was best, he'd come to learn over the last year, to never underestimate the Auclairs.

Seven

CARIS

"Stop fidgeting," Portia said quietly as she tucked a stray lock of hair behind Caris' ear.

"I'm not fidgeting," Caris muttered, shifting from foot to foot.

"Caris."

"Mother."

Portia arched an eyebrow in silent admonishment, and Caris ducked her head, scowling at the floor. She couldn't see her feet because of the white gown she wore, the outfit uncomfortable, especially the corset. She'd wanted to wear a stylish suit with a floor-length cape, but her mother had nixed the idea weeks ago when they'd put in the order with the tailor.

Proper debutantes wore a gown, not trousers, her mother insisted.

"If I wore something like this to the laboratory or garage back home, I'd be laughed right out for safety reasons," Caris said.

"Then it's a good thing we aren't going to either of those places. Now, chin up, shoulders back, and remember to watch your balance when you curtsy." Portia leaned in close and brushed a kiss over Caris' cheek. "I love you, my dear. Your father and I are both very proud of you."

Caris tugged at the above-the-elbow white silk evening gloves edged in lace she wore, preferring the heavy-duty leather gloves she used when working on machinery. "I know, but I'm so *bored*."

Portia sighed thickly. Caris recognized the impatience in the tone and tried not to scowl. Being presented to high society hadn't been her idea, nor her father's. But her mother had insisted, and so they were in Amari for the season, when Caris would much rather be back in Cosian.

"I'm missing the spring races for this," Caris muttered under her breath, thinking longingly of her racing carriage gathering dust in their company's garage.

"There's always next year," Portia replied.

"Not if I'm at school."

As much as she missed racing, Caris wanted acceptance into the Aether School of Engineering more. She'd much rather put her energies toward furthering her education so she could one day take over the family business than search for a husband or wife like the rest of the girls being presented tonight.

Caris leaned forward out of the line to get a quick look at the other sixteen-year-old girls waiting impatiently for their turn to be presented. Down the hall, on the other side of the rosewood double doors, was the line of escorts, young men and at least three young women that Caris could see, all of whom were dressed in comfortable-looking suits, nary a corset in sight.

"Caris," Portia warned.

She got back in line, trying not to fidget. While all the other girls and their mothers in the line seemed to know each other, Caris and Portia were the odd ones out that evening. Greetings had been polite if distant, their attendance judged by some weight they weren't privy to. Caris was shrewd enough to know it probably had to do with the fact they didn't call Amari home, and anyone of note didn't live in the Eastern Basin.

Their wealth couldn't be traced back through generations; it'd been built up in her parents' lifetime through grit and determination. Caris was proud of where she came from and what it took to live on the border. It wasn't easy some days, especially during the fiercer storms that swept poison and spores down from the Eastern Spine, but it was home.

She raised her chin high when it was finally time for her turn to walk through the double doors and make her entrance into Ashion high society. The young man chosen to escort her bowed to the appropriate degree for an heir to a barony title, and Caris placed her hand in his.

"The Honorable Mateo Garcea," the matron in charge of send-offs said.

"A pleasure," Mateo said with a polite smile.

"Likewise," Caris replied.

Mateo was a few years older than her, heir to a barony title like herself. His accent placed him as hailing from one of the western provinces of Ashion. His hand was warm through her glove, but not uncomfortably so. Caris faced forward and curled her other hand over the crook of her mother's elbow.

Portia remained by her side, standing tall and proud as the frazzled-looking matron in charge of the send-offs gestured at the doormen. The servants, dressed in matching uniforms with spotlessly shined shoes, pushed the doors open at the same time.

A rich, booming voice echoed through an amplifier, announcing, "The Honorable Caris Dhemlan, heiress to the Dhemlan barony and the Six Point Mechanics Company."

Caris counted her steps as she swept forward across the gold-veined white marble ballroom floor. The gas lamps had all been turned up to their brightest settings, and the air in the ballroom was overly warm from so many people sequestered in the space. But she remembered her cues, remembered the spot where she was supposed to let go of her mother's arm, take three steps forward, and curtsy to high society at large.

She kept her balance, remembered to dip her chin at the last second, and slowly rose to her full height. The sound of a string quartet was drowned out by the polite clapping of those in attendance.

Portia came to stand by Caris' side after the formal introduction was finished. Caris was escorted by her mother and Mateo to the other side of the ballroom, where the debutantes had formed a receiving line with their escorts.

"I'm proud of you," Portia murmured beneath the noise of the crowd before slipping away.

Caris blew out a breath, tacked on a smile, and endeavored to get through the rest of the evening without stepping on anyone's toes, metaphorically or otherwise. Mateo was polite, and he answered Caris' questions when she attempted conversation, but the moment it was time for the escorts to step back and allow the debutantes to accept new dance partners, he disappeared like fog in summer sunlight.

Caris drifted on the outskirts of the festivities, guided by her mother and father from one knot of people to the next. The polite conversations they found themselves in never resulted in any of the young men or women asking for her hand to dance. She was equal parts relieved and embarrassed as the dancing portion of the evening wore on, eyeing the golden clock above the double doors and wondering when dinner would be called.

"Lord Dhemlan, I understand your daughter is keen on engineering," a rich, cultured voice said off to the left as Caris and her parents discreetly pulled away from a group of people who very clearly knew each other and didn't care to know them.

Caris craned her neck around and stared at an older woman whose gown was by far the most expensive one she'd seen tonight. The rich green fabric was offset by a diamond-and-emerald choker necklace, emerald earrings, a diamond cuff on each wrist, and a single signet ring on her right hand.

Upon her pale, graying red hair sat an intricate diamond-and-emerald tiara that sparkled in the light from the chandeliers above. The tiara really should have been a hint of the woman's station, but Caris couldn't for the life of her figure out who she was, nor the two young ladies and younger man clustered around her. The only person she recognized in their small group was Nathaniel, which prompted Caris to smile.

"Your Grace," her father said in greeting before bowing deeply.

Caris belatedly remembered to curtsy when her mother shot her a warning look, trying to remember the proper depth for greeting a duchess. To be on the safe side, she went as low as she could go before rising back to her height in the heeled shoes she wore.

"May I introduce our daughter?" Portia said, gently guiding Caris forward with a press of her fingers to Caris' back.

"Caris Dhemlan, Your Grace," Caris said.

Meleri Auclair, Duchess of Auclair, wasn't a tall lady, but she carried herself with the air of a person well used to being recognized and acknowledged for her station. If she was aware of the glances thrown her way and the whispered conversations around their little group where she was the subject, the duchess gave no sign of caring.

The smile she offered Caris appeared genuine, though, but the veneer high society kept up in public was never the truth. Even as far away from the capital as her family lived, Caris knew that.

"A pleasure. Allow me to introduce my daughters, Lady Brielle and Lady Lore, and my son, Lord Dureau. I understand you have already made the acquaintance of Mr. Nathaniel Clementine," Meleri said.

"Yes. He told me he wasn't attending the ball tonight."

"Caris," her mother hissed, sounding vaguely horrified.

Nathaniel bowed deeper than was required, the morning tails and trousers he wore a far more comfortable attire than her corseted gown. "Her Grace was kind enough to invite me along. I was hoping we could continue our conversation about racing carriages. Perhaps while we dance?"

He was the only person, outside of her escort, to invite her to dance all evening, and Caris knew she couldn't decline. That it was Nathaniel made it at least bearable. She nodded and extended her hand for him to take. The first notes of a waltz started up, and Caris found herself guided onto the ballroom floor and into the circle of Nathaniel's arms for the dance.

"I'm terrible at dancing. I may step on you," Caris warned.

Nathaniel smiled down at her and chuckled. "I've had plenty of practice having my toes stepped on by my younger sisters."

He led her into the steps and turns of the waltz. Caris would've kept her attention on her feet if Nathaniel hadn't drawn her into conversation.

"Do you own a racing carriage?" Nathaniel asked as they spun about the ballroom amidst other dancers.

"We own several. I race my own."

"Is that what you do for fun in Cosian?"

"It's far more enjoyable than this."

Nathaniel laughed, the amusement in his eyes kind as he spun her in a circle by one hand on the beat of the music. "I find I would probably agree with you if I'd ever had the pleasure of racing one."

"Amari has races."

"I've been to the spring races here as a spectator, not a driver. I'm afraid my skills in that area would be nonexistent."

Because he didn't assume racing was easy and something anyone could do made Caris reluctantly approve of his attitude. Racing at the speeds the altered motor carriages ran at wasn't for the faint of heart. She'd been racing since she was fourteen after spending a year begging her parents for permission and enjoyed it immensely.

"How do you know the duchess?" Caris asked.

"Our families do business together. I've only heard good things about yours."

"My family or our business?"

"Both."

Caris raised an eyebrow, staring up at him. "If you come calling, my father will want to talk business with you."

"Only if you're there as well."

That he didn't immediately assume she wouldn't take over from her father rather than sell the company, as so many other people did, made Caris carefully consider her opinion of him. "Did you enjoy your time at the Aether School of Engineering?"

"Immensely."

Nathaniel talked at length about the classes he'd taken and the wealth of knowledge that awaited her so long as her parents let her attend. Caris hungered for what he spoke about—the limitless desire to learn, to invent, that gave rise to the new inventions seeping into everyday life.

By the time Nathaniel led her off the dance floor, Caris was pestering him about the expected course load for a first-year student. Her father seemed fondly amused at their choice of conversation upon their return to the little group that had somehow become the epicenter of the ball. Her mother appeared resignedly exasperated.

"I had hoped you would at least remember your conversation classes and what topics were fit for tonight," Portia said on a quiet aside.

Caris lifted one shoulder in a shrug, smoothing down the skirt of her gown. "Did you know the graduating engineers have a tradition of tossing an automaton off the clock tower at the end of their last term? I want to do that."

"That sounds strangely exhilarating. Your father was just telling us about your patent exploits," Meleri said. "I must say I'm impressed."

Caris shifted her attention to the older woman. "Gears make sense."

She was keen enough not to mention that sometimes people didn't. Caris was terrible at making small talk if it wasn't about business. She spent hours in the laboratories outside her schooling and preferred an engineer's coveralls to a dress or suit. She preferred racing carriages on the dirt track to dancing, liked the freedom she could find there from the restrictive manners high society exacted on creativity.

Caris liked inventing things that helped people, as her father did. She wanted to make a difference in people's lives. Figuring out what made the world tick began with the machines that ran it.

"I've invited you and your mother over for tea tomorrow. I hope to chat more with you about the future of your education."

Caris glanced quickly at her mother, unable to read the expression on her face. She didn't appear angry or worried, but even Caris knew being invited to tea by the duchess was an honor rarely bestowed on anyone newly presented. When all was said and done, in the absence of the Rourke bloodline, the Auclairs were the oldest, unbroken bloodline left in Ashion. Gaining their favor would've been like gaining the favor the old queen.

She knew *that*, at least, from her lessons.

"I look forward to tomorrow," Caris said, dipping into a quick little curtsy after a raised eyebrow from her mother. "Thank you, Your Grace."

The duchess studied her for a long moment before smiling. "Have you met the Palmers yet, my dear?"

"No."

"Let me introduce you to them before we're seated for dinner."

Caris and her family could only follow in the duchess' wake, pulled into the delicate dance of introductions to some of the more well-known and respected bloodlines in Ashion. It was a stark contrast from the beginning of the evening, when they'd been relegated to the outskirts of what passed for high society within these walls.

But the duchess paved a way they couldn't, and Caris found herself incapable of escaping from being judged by people she didn't know. It was unsettling, in a way, but she stood tall beneath the many assessing gazes turned her way and hoped to do her parents proud.

Eight

MELERI

Meleri finished signing her name on a letter with a slight flourish when Lore poked her head into the study. "The steward informed me the Dhemlans are here."

Meleri set down her fountain pen and put the letter aside to mail later. It wasn't a missive needed by the Clockwork Brigade, merely a general correspondence to one of many received that morning. Their time spent at the debutante ball last night had served well as a reminder to the other families that the Auclairs could and would take an interest in high society's children.

It's something Ophelia had done, in her capacity as queen, and it left Meleri with a brief ache in her chest. She did her best to uphold the tradition best carried by those who sat upon the throne, but she was no queen. She had no desire to be. The North Star guided her down a different road, and it had finally led her somewhere with purpose.

"Excellent. Let's greet them, shall we?" Meleri said as she stood.

For today's visit, she'd chosen a simple, high-necked gown with minimal embellishments, but the color was a vibrant blue. Everything about it—from the bodice over the corset to the petticoats beneath the gown—was made of high-quality silk, tailored precisely to her frame.

Sometimes it was the lack of adornments that could showcase a person's wealth.

Meleri knew the Dhemlans were wealthy, courtesy of their business, but they extensively lacked social wealth. She'd begun the task of amending that deficiency last night and hoped it would continue if her plans worked out.

Meleri left her study for the hallway, where Lore waited for her. Meleri locked the study door behind her with the master key she carried in her pocket. No spells adorned the door or her study, because magic like that would only indicate she had something to hide. While Meleri made a business about keeping secrets, one couldn't advertise that fact. Precautions were needed and executed within reason. The servants in the estate knew better than to enter where she worked.

"Nathaniel escorted them. He called upon Caris this morning, and apparently he wasn't the only one," Lore said as they started down the hallway.

"We did give her our favor. That was never going to go unnoticed," Meleri said.

Lore glanced at her mother, the features of her face her own this afternoon. Half the time Meleri never saw her daughter's face, hidden as it was behind a veil when she worked.

"Are you certain she's the one?"

Meleri paused at the top of the stairs leading to the next level, one hand resting on the thin metal railing. She closed her eyes, mind drifting to the past and the life she'd once led in a glittering court only seen in photographs, paintings, and history books these days.

"She has her mother's eyes."

The same shade, the same shape, the same fiery stubbornness and curiosity that had existed in Ophelia's burned in the girl's. Meleri wanted to believe Caris was the long-lost princess, the one who could sit upon the starfire throne without being burned to ash.

The one who could save them from Eimarille and the Daijal court's insidious encroachment of their sovereign right as a free country.

The one the North Star had promised her.

"Let us hope the stars haven't guided us wrong," Lore murmured.

Meleri opened her eyes and nodded in quiet agreement before starting down the stairs until they reached the ground floor. The pair of them swept into the parlor where the servants had gotten Caris, Portia, and Nathaniel settled. All three rose to their feet at Meleri's arrival, and Nathaniel bowed while the other two curtsied.

Caris was not, Meleri noted, wearing a dress this afternoon but instead wore a stylish day jacket and trousers in a pale dove gray that offset her eyes. Rather than morning tails, a cape fell from her shoulders to just past her hips. The blouse she wore was cream-colored, the buttons pearlescent. Her brown hair was loose, falling a little past her shoulders in a tumble of thick waves. She held Meleri's gaze well enough, no hint of artifice in her eyes. Perhaps there was something to be said of growing up in the outer provinces. Caris seemed far more practical than others her age.

"Welcome to my bloodline's home. I'm pleased you could join us," Meleri said.

"It's an honor, Your Grace," Portia demurred.

Portia had opted for a gown that was both fashionable and practical. She didn't seem one to flaunt her wealth how some of the families did, perhaps because it wasn't the custom back east or because she saw no need to.

Lore was still assessing Emmitt and Portia's placement as cogs in the Clockwork Brigade, while Brielle was completing her due diligence on the Dhemlan bloodline. All that aside, Meleri had liked what she'd seen last night in how the family handled themselves amidst high society's veiled teeth.

A formal tea spread sat on the rectangular table by the glass windows overlooking the garden. Lore politely prompted everyone to find their seat at the table, as indicated by the placeholder card.

The pair of servants standing at attention nearby stepped forward once everyone was seated. They poured tea for Meleri and Lore first, then their guests, offering dishes for them to choose from without needing to pass the food among themselves. Once everyone had their pick of the delicate pastries, savory mini quiches, and seasonal fruit, Meleri took up the reins of conversation.

"I understand you're interested in attending the Aether School of Engineering. Will your family move here for your studies?" Meleri asked.

"We haven't quite discussed that yet," Portia said before Caris could answer.

"I want to go. I like learning, and I like inventing," Caris argued.

Meleri hummed thoughtfully. "It *is* the premier school for that in Ashion."

She guided the conversation with a deft hand, letting Caris speak about her desires and judging Portia's response to such wants accordingly. It was a lively discussion they had, and Meleri was intrigued at the range of knowledge Caris already retained.

A good foundation to build on, she thought.

Eventually, when everyone had their fill of the afternoon tea, Lore invited Caris and Nathaniel for a walk about the estate's garden, leaving Meleri with Portia to discuss a future neither could predict.

"I can tell you love your daughter and only want the best for her," Meleri said once the table was cleared of dishes and the servants had disappeared.

"As any mother does," Portia said.

"As a mother, I know well the worry we have for our children. Cosian is a long train ride from Amari, and passage on airships can get expensive. If you choose not to uproot your home and business, I can perhaps offer you peace of mind and a place in my household for your daughter."

Meleri's opinion of Portia went up a notch when the other woman didn't immediately gush over the honor of such an offer. Indeed, the other woman met her gaze from across the table with a steadiness that Meleri approved of. "You hardly know us, Your Grace. Why would you open your home when we have nothing to offer you in the way of prestige? Our bloodline was only elevated into the nobility genealogies barely two decades back."

Meleri tipped her head to the side, pleased by the question asked of her. "Despite what gossip you might read in the broadsheets, I've always had an interest in the next generation and what they can contribute to our country."

"And what do you think my daughter can contribute?"

She didn't say *everything*, but the word rested on her tongue regardless. "I think it would be a crime to see one such as your daughter lose her innovative curiosity. This is the Age of Progress, after all. I've always been a great believer in change."

The sort of change Meleri yearned to see needed to be carried by someone capable of shouldering it. If she had to teach Caris how to stand beneath that weight, then so be it.

Meleri paused a moment before committing herself to a truth she wouldn't be able to take back without the aid of a magician well versed in mind magic. "My role as Fulcrum is built on that belief, after all."

Portia froze in her seat, eyes going wide even as she went so pale in the face she looked sickly. Meleri watched her mouth part, but no words were forthcoming.

"You trusted my Clockwork Brigade and what it fights for enough to become a cog. Will you not trust me to keep your daughter safe?" Meleri asked gently.

"Caris isn't a cog," Portia rasped out.

"Not yet, she isn't."

Portia pressed her lips into a thin line but said nothing in the face of Meleri's assumption that Caris one day *would* become one.

"Think on it, and let me know," Meleri said into the quiet at the table.

Portia inclined her head slightly. "I shall."

In the end, after Portia had taken her leave with Caris, and Nathaniel had gone to confer with Lore about the latest debt slaves needing transport out of Daijal, Meleri returned to her locked study.

She was unsurprised to find the North Star waiting for her within.

Aaralyn sat behind Meleri's desk, flipping through the coded messages that had been locked away in the hidden drawers of her desk. The ink magic on every sheet came to life beneath the star god's touch.

"How fares your rebellion?" Aaralyn asked, not looking up from the paper in her hand.

Meleri shut the door behind her, the lock clicking quietly into place. "You could have given Ophelia's daughter to me all those years ago. The Eastern Basin is a harsh place to live and grow up in. I would have raised her here, and I would have loved her like my own."

"You would have molded her into what you thought she needed to become, and it would be a lie she'd have hated you for. The girl needed to find herself first before returning to her birthplace."

"She's sixteen. She knows nothing of what we intend for her. She wants to be an engineer."

"Of course she does." Aaralyn set down the message and spread her fingers over the paper, the words on its face shining bright like stars. "What better thing to build than the world?"

Nine

BLAINE

Cap pulled low over his face, Blaine looked both ways down the street before unlocking the side gate and slipping past the iron fence that surrounded the E'ridian embassy in Amari.

He'd been given a key to the entrance by the current ambassador, who had held the post for the past few years. Blaine had heard from Brielle that the ambassador had been recently recalled, and he didn't know who was the replacement.

The embassy was the size of two city blocks, one-third of that space committed to the hangar. Blaine's destination was the third floor of the main building, where the long room dedicated to telegraph machines was located. He didn't care for the hangar. His father had been murdered there, after all, and Blaine didn't want to walk where he'd died.

Blaine dodged around the illumination from gas lamps on his way to the side door where deliveries were handled for the embassy. The guards patrolling the grounds were some of the few people Blaine ever came into contact with, and they knew to let him pass. Mind magic ensured they'd forget he'd ever been there, and that precaution still left a sour taste in his mouth. Lore had been adamant about it, and the *Comhairle nan Cinnidhean* had reluctantly allowed for the interference.

Better the clans as a whole knew nothing about what he did to their people for their own safety. Blaine knew plausible deniability was important when it came to subterfuge.

Pulling the key out of his pocket, Blaine unlocked the side door he'd come upon and entered the embassy. He pulled a gaslight from his satchel and turned it on, letting it guide his way to the telegraph room.

The embassy staff slept elsewhere, in a cluster of buildings located several streets over in a more residential section of the city. The Promenade on both sides of the river had become commercial and civic areas over time, save for the land held by some of the oldest bloodlines. That meant no one should have been around other than the guards, so it was a shock to find the telegraph room occupied at this hour.

Even more shocking was who greeted him.

"Hello, Blaine," Honovi said from his spot at a work desk close to the door.

The gaslight nearly fell from Blaine's hand before he remembered to tighten his grip. He stared in shock at where his husband sat, not comprehending the sight for a few long moments. Then he shook his head, taking an uncertain step into the room.

"Honovi? What—how are you here?" Blaine asked, speaking E'ridian for the first time in months and months.

"I told you I'd find a way to come west and be with you."

Blaine drank in the sight of his husband, taking in the kilt and the fitted jacket with its plaid hanging off his shoulders, the torc around his throat that hadn't ever been removed. Blaine keenly felt the absence of his own mark of their marriage, had missed it since the moment Honovi had taken it off to keep it safe in their home.

Honovi stood, the small gas lamp on the desk throwing shadows across his face. "I knew I couldn't visit you at that school or send a message. The previous ambassador said you came once every two weeks or so to send your reports, but she said the day always changed. I've stayed late every night this week waiting for you."

He looked—exactly how Blaine had left him standing on that dock in Glencoe's airfield a year ago. He looked like home, and Blaine didn't waste any time standing in the doorway. He closed the distance between them in a handful of strides, practically throwing himself at his husband. Honovi met him halfway, kissing him with a ferocity that spoke of counting every night they'd been apart and hating the absence of each other in their separate beds.

"What are you doing here?" Blaine asked between breathless kisses.

"I'm the new ambassador to Ashion," Honovi replied, the words mumbled against Blaine's lips.

"You're a *jarl*."

"I can be both."

"Honovi—"

His husband growled something wordless before pushing Blaine backward and up against the nearest wall. A heavy hand pressed against his chest, keeping him in place as Honovi kissed his way down Blaine's throat for a few glorious seconds before falling to his knees. Blaine dropped the gaslight and didn't care where it landed, too busy reaching for Honovi's braid to grip it instead.

He'd dreamed about his husband's touch—about his mouth—but those half-remembered moments that fled in the light of day paled to reality. Blaine's head smacked against the wall when Honovi got his trousers undone and shoved down his hips, warm lips sucking at the tip of his cock. He slapped his hand over his mouth, biting down on the meat of his palm there as Honovi swallowed him down like a starving man.

Blaine wasn't going to last, not after a year of falling asleep in an empty bed, not with Honovi's mouth working him over with a sureness that almost hurt. Honovi drew Blaine's orgasm out of him in minutes, leaving him panting and wrung out and barely able to string two words together.

He still had enough sense of mind to pull on Honovi's braid and drag his husband to his feet. Blaine tugged him into a messy kiss, tasting himself on Honovi's tongue. Honovi pressed up against him, bracketing him in, and Blaine didn't want to be anywhere else but where he stood right then.

"I missed you," Honovi said, dragging his nose over Blaine's cheek to kiss his temple.

Blaine laughed hoarsely, finally letting go of Honovi's braid to do up his trousers. "I couldn't tell."

He could feel Honovi's hardness against his hip through the kilt, but Honovi seemed in no rush to tend to himself. If Honovi wanted to rub off on Blaine, he wouldn't move from his spot, much like he never had in their narrow bunk on the *Skyborne*.

Blaine wrapped his arms around Honovi's waist, holding him close, breathing in the familiar scent of him. "How did you get the *Comhairle nan Cinnidhean* to agree to make you ambassador?"

"Lena's term was up. I argued I should go in her place, because I could speak for the *Comhairle nan Cinnidhean* when she couldn't."

"Why would you need to?"

Honovi let out a heavy breath, tickling Blaine's skin. He pulled back just enough so he could press his forehead to Blaine's, eyes closed, hands gripping Blaine's hips hard enough to bruise. Blaine didn't mind the pressure.

"Daijal recalled their ambassador in Glencoe over winter. They sent a new one after the crown prince married. They've been demanding E'ridia acknowledge Daijal's sovereign right over Ashion."

Blaine grimaced, thinking of Eimarille and who she'd become—everything a Rourke wasn't. "Because of who he married."

"Yes."

"Ashion has its own parliament."

"Whose laws more and more require approval from Daijal to pass. We've been having better luck in Daijal getting trade done than in Ashion over the last couple of years."

"Is that why you're here, then? For Ashion?"

"For you."

Honovi finally pulled away enough for Blaine to look him in the eye. He reached up and cupped Honovi's jaw, stroking his thumb over warm skin. "Mainspring won't like that you came."

"I don't care about what that woman likes or dislikes. E'ridia needs me to be here, and so do you."

"I need to care, because of what I've discovered." Blaine paused, sighing. "*Who* I've discovered. I was coming here tonight to report on it, even though Mainspring would rather I didn't."

Honovi's grip got tighter. "You found her?"

His voice was barely louder than a whisper, and Honovi didn't say her name, but his gaze was heavy in the dim glow of the gas lamp. It was as if he knew the risks of giving voice to a truth Blaine had hoarded for years.

Blaine nodded, a tightness in his chest that wasn't easy to breathe through. "Yes, and that means I have to stay."

He had a promise to keep, and he couldn't do that if he stayed on the other side of the Eastern Spine. It was something that had become more and more apparent as the months drifted by since he'd first come to Amari—this duty he'd thought left by the wayside with his bloodline.

The encroaching cultural changes pushed by Daijal were causing friction in the populace that wouldn't be contained forever. And Blaine doubted, with everything he was learning, that the borders between countries would be enough to keep Daijal in check.

Honovi touched his fingers to Blaine's jaw. "Blaine."

"There's more. The Clockwork Brigade has uncovered rumors of a machine. Something that can turn the dead into revenants. It's just stories, we think, but there have been more revenants in supposedly cleansed lands here in Ashion lately that it merits looking into."

Honovi frowned, eyes narrowing. "Everyone burns their dead in every country. The star gods gave that decree when they first fell through the skies to Maricol. To disobey that is anathema to the Star Order."

"I said it was rumors, not that it was true."

"But you believe it could be."

Blaine opened his mouth, then closed it, biting at his lip. "Who's to say turning the dead into revenants isn't impossible when spores do it already? New inventions are being patented all the time. Would this so-called death-defying machine be any different?"

"I'd ask what reason someone would need a machine like that, but I can see what Daijal would do with it."

"Can you?" Blaine gently pushed Honovi back, giving them both room to breathe. Blaine shifted on his feet, grimacing at the way his trousers and underclothes chafed at his skin now. "I didn't believe it at first, but the rumors are terrifying."

"That isn't the only concerning issue. The *Comhairle nan Cinnidhean* has been discussing Mainspring's warning since you left. The majority think the Eastern Spine will be enough of a barrier to keep anyone out if the worst comes to pass. Some don't believe they would even try."

"Do you?"

Honovi met his gaze, jaw set. "I think Daijal has craved power since cleaving itself from Ashion in their civil war. They've never respected borders."

"Do you know the king expanded the collateral laws for banks as a wedding present to Prince Wesley and Princess Eimarille? The risk of debt bondage has broadened because of that change, and not just for Daijalan and Ashionen citizens. Those of other countries can be found liable as well and taken by debt collectors."

"E'ridia won't stand for that."

"It would be an act of war if any clan attempted a rescue of one of their own. I think Daijal is hoping for a situation such as that."

"You think they'd call for war?"

Blaine shrugged. "What would you do if you had that chance?"

Because Blaine could see it like parts of a machine, all the disparate pieces coming together in a slow-going build years in the making. Hindsight showed the blueprint now, and the Clockwork Brigade had its work cut out for it if Meleri's cogs were going to break what Daijal was building.

Honovi leaned forward to kiss Blaine slow and sweet on the mouth before pulling him into a hug. Blaine let himself be held, curling into the warmth of a body he'd achingly missed over the long months they'd been separated.

"Your hair is still short," Honovi murmured against the side of Blaine's head.

"It's considered fashionable here." Blaine reached around and tugged on Honovi's braid. "I miss what you cut. When this is over, when I can come home, I'll grow it out again."

Honovi didn't say anything, just held him tight. Blaine closed his eyes against the glow of the gas lamp, content to stay in his husband's arms for as long as he could.

Ten

SOREN

Calhames was a city built for heat, birthed from desert sands that crept up from the Wastelands on the warm winds. It sat on cracked earth scorched by the summer sun, fed by the Tahir River flowing from the eastern hill country. Settled far from the coastal swamps on the east coast and the small rainforest along the western shore of Solaria, Calhames was a capital that rarely felt cold.

Soren always regretted that state of affairs, especially with the way his field leathers stuck to his skin. One of these days, he would be assigned to a cold, northerly border, where he'd have to worry about staying warm rather than staying cool.

The steam train's horn sounded loudly, smoke billowing away from the chimney and over the carriages as it sped down the tracks. Soren had caught passage up in Karnak after crossing the Solarian border rather than taking the slower route over the road. He wasn't on border duty for this trip but traveling in his capacity to deliver the biannual border report to the Imperial throne.

That meant an extra stipend for travel expenditures, as governing bodies never appreciated late reports. What it didn't mean was comfortable seats.

Soren shifted on the hard wooden bench at the back of the train carriage. His third-class ticket meant a packed carriage with every available seat taken save the one beside him on the bench. Normally, Soren would be grateful for the extra legroom, but it had come about only because the woman who'd been assigned it had refused to sit by him.

His status as a warden was apparent in his clothes and his weapons. His velocycle was stored in the cargo carriage, the cost for that more than his ticket, but one the wardens' governor had been willing to pay.

Soren rested his head against the window, soot from the chimney having speckled the glass on the outside, turning the world speeding past into a haze. Calhames was easy enough to make out as the train approached the station on the outskirts of Solaria's capital. The vaulted roofs of the city's buildings arched beyond the top of the wall, interspaced here and there with large domes belonging to Star Order temples and government buildings.

The closer the train got to the station, the higher the wall became in the sky, until it obscured most traces of the city. Then the tiled, vaulted roof of the station replaced the sky as the steam train slowed to a stop at its platform.

The sudden bustle of people leaving their seats had Soren remaining in his until the crowd had mostly exited the train carriage. He finally stood, hauling down his small travel bag that carried his poison antidote kit, pertinent paperwork, and extra ammunition for his pistols. The poison short sword hadn't left his back, and he rolled his shoulders to readjust the weight after sitting in a cramped space for so long.

Soren exited the train carriage and made his way against the crowd for the cargo carriage. After showing his paperwork to the platform supervisor and porters offloading luggage, Soren was allowed to haul himself inside and retrieve his velocycle, wheeling it out of its locked cage and onto the platform.

The crowd cleared a path for Soren after a few shouts from himself and passing station personnel. He exited the station through the gate meant for cargo, queueing up behind a porter pushing a motorized cart overflowing with luggage to get through customs.

Soren wheeled his velocycle into the sunlight once he was cleared, squinting against the brightness, the heat of midday an almost oppressive thing. He took a moment to get his gear settled and pull on his helmet and goggles before slinging a leg over the seat. He started the engine and pointed the velocycle down the road for the city gates, driving at a slow pace in the lane designated for vehicles.

He drove through a short tunnel that spanned the width of the wall before emerging onto a street teeming with motor carriages and pedestrians. The gate to Calhames' north train station was a busy intersection, and it took a bit of maneuvering for Soren to leave it all behind.

The warm breeze smelled of exhaust and a city packed to the brim with people. Calhames was a capital, which meant its outward growth over the centuries could be counted in the many defensive walls ringing its ever-expanding borders. Soren knew the route to the warden resupply station, but that wasn't where he was headed today.

The Imperial Senate, the Imperial palace, and other bureaucratic buildings that kept the country chugging along were located at the very center of Calhames, inside its first and oldest defensive wall. Soren had to get through nearly a dozen checkpoints to reach it, because the Houses were ever wary of attacks, and none more so than the one that currently sat upon the Imperial throne.

Soren's status as a warden was enough to get him to the gates of the Imperial palace but not inside. The medallion that hung around his neck, tucked out of sight beneath his shirt and leather waistcoat, was a heavy weight that Soren didn't want to rely on.

The *praetoria* legionnaires guarding the gold-plated gate were armed and in uniform, heads protected from the sun by crimson and white *effiyehs*. The guardhouses on either side of the gate held yet more soldiers, while spiderlike automatons like the ones guarding the shores of the Warden's Island scuttled after the soldiers on mechanical legs.

Their Zip guns were a newer model, with handles for a soldier to take control of and direct the automaton's fire if necessary. Someone had painted the automaton's casing Legion crimson, with the roaring lion's head of the House of Sa'Liandel standing out in gold paint on two sides.

The legionnaires were deft at managing the flow of people onto the palace grounds, from bureaucrats to everyday workmen and women. One needed the proper paperwork to enter, and the writ given to him by the wardens' governor for delivery of the border reports was enough.

The legionnaire with a single gold chevron on his shoulder studied Soren for a long few seconds before nodding sharply. "Leave your velocycle. I'll take you inside."

Soren shook his head. "It goes with me."

He thought he would have to argue more, but the officer just made an annoyed sound and waved at him. Soren dismounted his velocycle to walk it through the golden gates and into the massive courtyard of the Imperial palace.

Palace wings stretched toward the walls surrounding the massive building. The exterior arcades stretched down one wing, across the curved front of the palace, and down the other wing, providing sheltered walkways for officials and servants. The officer kept a steady pace across the flagstone courtyard for the pillared main entrance with its vaulted roof section rising over a pair of massive double doors.

Soren knew he couldn't bring his velocycle into the building and reluctantly left it parked outside. He pulled the ledger containing the border reports from the satchel and tucked it under one arm. Several legionnaires stood at the entrance, and Soren nodded at the closest one.

"Make sure no one touches my velocycle," he said.

"No one will touch it," the officer replied.

The grand foyer they walked through was filled with a tiled mosaic that covered the walls and floor in an array of colors. Gas lamps in sconces provided clear illumination, adding to the brightness that came through the open windows near the ceiling that vented hot air.

The officer seemed to know where he was going, which was a good thing, because keeping track of the winding path down a dozen different hallways and up a level left Soren wondering where they were. He'd never been inside such a massive building before. It was like a mini-city with the number of hallways, inner courtyards, and a whole mess of people they passed.

"Sit," the officer said when they finally made it to a large, surprisingly airy antechamber.

The officer disappeared behind a guarded door. Soren eyed the full benches along the wall, the people sitting in clusters on the floor, and didn't miss the wary looks given him. For all that wardens provided an integral job for every country, the citizens were never quite welcoming of them. Wardens had the right to cross borders everywhere needed to cleanse the poison fields, but it was the poison they worked with—that ran through their veins—that made people not want to be around them.

Soren shifted out of the way and resigned himself to a long wait with everyone else. He was surprised, then, when a beautiful woman in a flowing white dress mantled at the shoulders with colorful feathers swept into the antechamber. Everyone clamored for her attention, but she ignored them all in favor of Soren.

She bowed to him. "Chief Minister Caelum will see you, warden."

Soren bit his tongue, wondering how he'd earned an audience with the Imperial empress' highest ranked advisor so quickly, but he wasn't going to question it. He nodded at the woman and followed her into a large workroom filled with clerks all clattering away at their typewriters. They didn't stop, moving deeper into a separate, grand office decorated with a wealth most people would never see in their lifetime.

Chief Minister Caelum sat behind a large, ornate desk. The paperwork covering it was neatly organized, as were the bookshelves filled with folios and ledgers lining one entire wall. Windows overlooked an inner courtyard beyond a narrow arcade, allowing for continuous shade from the sunlight. The room wasn't stifling hot; the mechanical fan hanging from the ceiling and the one standing in the corner with its face pointed at the desk helped with that.

"We were told to expect you last autumn. Instead, someone else delivered the border reports. His Imperial Highness was displeased," Caelum said in the trade tongue.

Dressed in the robes of his office, head covered in an elaborately patterned and decorated brimless, round cap, the Chief Minister was a man who looked to be at least three decades Soren's senior. His face was tanned, the wrinkles at the corner of his blue eyes deeply entrenched from years of squinting through sunlight. He had an air about him that spoke of confidence and power, but it wasn't enough to make Soren bow before the man.

"I'm a warden. I go where my governor tells me to," Soren said.

Caelum studied Soren with unblinking eyes, letting nothing of his opinion about that fact show on his face. "His Imperial Highness gave strict instructions regarding your arrival when he returned from Bellingham last year. You are to be accorded all manner of support and access to the private wings of the palace. You come bearing the border reports?"

"I do."

"I will see to them."

Soren didn't offer up the ledger. "I was instructed by Vanya to give the reports to him."

"His *Imperial Highness*," Caelum stressed the title, "is briefed on the reports, as is his mother, the empress. They do not handle the minutiae of what you bring us."

"Are you going to sit there and tell me to ignore a direct order from your Imperial crown prince?"

Caelum frowned deeply, but Soren remained rooted where he was. He had his orders, both from the governor and from Vanya. He wasn't about to ignore his duty no matter what the Chief Minister would prefer.

Perhaps the Chief Minister was well acquainted with the stubbornness of wardens, for the man stood and picked up the telephone handset on his desk. He turned the dial a couple of times, the different sounds of each number coming through the receiver as tinny noise.

Caelum pressed the handset to his ear, speaking into the bottom portion. "Send for His Imperial Highness' majordomo. A warden has arrived who has been ordered to meet with him."

Caelum hung up the handset on the brass cradle, ending the call. Then he waved at one of the armchairs situated near the windows. "Sit there."

Soren did as directed and got comfortable. He didn't know how long it would take for the majordomo to arrive. He didn't even know who the majordomo was in relation to Vanya. When the majordomo eventually arrived in the Chief Minister's office, she didn't appear pleased to see Soren.

The woman wore a flowing if well-tailored sleeveless gown that fell to her ankles. A metal ring was hooked to her thin leather belt that cinched tight around her small waist. Numerous keys of varying sizes hung from it. A plain-cased televox was clipped to her belt as well. Her arms were bare save for the matching golden cuffs she wore, bright against her pale freckled skin.

Her blonde hair was twisted off her neck into a high knot held in place by delicate bone combs inlaid with semiprecious jewels. Around her neck hung a thin chain, the golden pendant attached to it small and pressed with the Sa'Liandel crest. She looked to be about ten years older than Soren, but he couldn't be sure and knew better than to ask.

"So you are the warden His Imperial Highness gave favor to," she said in flawless trade tongue with a disapproving frown. "I'm Alida, majordomo to the Imperial crown prince's household. If I'm to add you to it, I must affirm your name."

"I can't be part of the House of Sa'Liandel," Soren protested as he stood.

"I said household, not House. You will be held within the Imperial crown prince's circle of employ at his request. It does not tie you to a House. Nothing but blood can do so. Now, your name. I will have it."

"Soren."

Alida nodded sharply. "It matches my records, and you've the look of the man we were told about."

"I have not had him tested for spells," Caelum said, not looking up from his work.

Soren couldn't squash the affronted expression that slipped across his face. "I'm a warden, not a magician."

Alida's smile was all teeth, and her eyes were still not friendly. "It would not be the first time a rival House has attempted entry to the palace by impersonating a warden, for whom all borders are open to. Follow me."

Soren scowled in annoyed disbelief at the thought of anyone pretending to be a warden when they weren't. No perks came with the job, after all.

He was led out of the Chief Minister's office and through half a dozen hallways, crossing two inner courtyards before arriving in a windowless room whose floor, walls, and ceiling were covered in black marble shot through with gold veins. Etched into the floor and the ceiling were six concentric circles, each golden line made up of repeating constellations. Standing inside it was like standing surrounded by the night sky and nothing else.

"Stand in the center," Alida said before sweeping out.

Soren warily did as requested as someone new stepped inside, the door closing behind him. The gold veins in the marble pulsed with a light that was all magic powered by the aether, a soft glow that gave off no heat.

The newcomer was a man clad in the robes of a Star Order priest, a wand made of metal and tipped with a clarion crystal in his hand. The star priest said nothing, merely made a gesture with his wand that caused every bit of gold in the room to burn with magic.

Heat stole through the bottom of Soren's boots, making him shift on his feet. His skin crawled with magic, aether lines snaking all around his limbs, pricking at his uniform. Whatever spell the star priest had cast didn't go deep enough to touch what Soren had been so careful to ignore over the years.

If you do not acknowledge it, then it can never burn.

The Dawn Star's words whispered through his thoughts. Soren ignored the part of him the star god had tried to lock away as he always did, focusing on the present instead of the past. Whatever magic the Dawn Star had left behind inside him was enough to turn aside mortal spells without anyone the wiser. The star priest lowered his wand and turned on his heels, leaving without saying a single word to Soren. Alida stepped into the open doorway a moment later and beckoned him out of the room.

"That's it?" Soren asked as he rolled his shoulders, trying to shake off the sensation of foreign magic.

"You wear no veil woven by thread magic, and you are as you say you are according to the star priest. I'll take you to the Imperial crown prince's rooms now," Alida said.

Unbidden came the memory of his last stay in one of Vanya's rooms. Even a year's distance wasn't enough time for him to forget what it had felt like to have Vanya's hands on him.

Alida led him into a richly decorated wing of the palace where servants were in abundance. Despite the late spring heat of Sixth Month, the halls they walked down were cool. Whichever long-dead architect had designed the Imperial palace, they'd managed to keep air moving and letting it rise to be let out in places.

Soren found himself deposited in a receiving room that overlooked an inner courtyard. A low wall was all that separated the room from the outside, and Soren could hear the gentle bubbling sound of running water coming from the well-tended greenery beyond.

"Make yourself comfortable. I'll inform His Imperial Highness you are here," Alida said.

She left. Soren looked around at the extravagant receiving room, with the murals painted on the walls and the intricate mosaic floor, the exquisitely carved furniture, and took a seat on a chaise rather than the large lounging pillows on the floor. He set the satchel on the floor by his feet and the ledger with its border reports on the cushion beside him and waited.

And waited.

A servant came and brought him a pitcher of cold red wine and a tray of fresh fruit, stuffed dates, and cheese wedges. Considering all he'd had was jerky and oat bars to eat on the train ride south, Soren did his level best to decimate the food.

It was an hour later, the minutes counted off by his pocket watch, before Vanya arrived. Soren hadn't seen any hints of mourning in the palace, either in the form of decoration or clothing, but Vanya wore mourning bands on his upper arms over the thin material of his robe's sleeves. Soren stood, leaving the ledger on the cushion, caught by the intensity of Vanya's gaze as the Imperial crown prince entered the receiving room.

"I didn't think you would come," Vanya said in greeting.

Soren dragged his gaze away from the other man's face, taking in the vibrant cobalt robe Vanya wore. The underlying trousers were a cream color that offset the blue, both shades standing out against his dark skin. Cream thread embroidered in intricate swirls curled away from the center of the robe where it was clasped together. The ranking medallion glittered golden against his chest, and the thin circlet he wore was more elaborate than the one Soren remembered.

"I was needed in Daijal's southern border over winter. We wardens had to run a grid search for revenants. There's been a strange surge lately."

"You could have come to Calhames in autumn."

"I go where the governor tells me to." Soren made an aborted gesture with one hand, meeting Vanya's eyes. "I heard about the loss of your wife. I'm sorry."

Vanya frowned, gaze unwavering as he stared at Soren. "I did not know Nicca well, despite our arranged marriage. But she was kind enough while she lived here, and I will always be grateful for our daughter, who survived."

"What happened?"

The question was past his teeth before Soren could bite back the words. It wasn't his place to pry into royal affairs, but everyone knew the murderous games the Houses played. He wanted to believe Vanya wasn't cruel enough to murder his own wife, but anything was possible. Despite the handful of days they'd spent together on the road and the vow hanging from Soren's neck, they didn't know each other.

He shoved down the desire of wanting to because wardens weren't allowed to *want*.

"She died in childbirth. Hemorrhaging and a clot in the lungs, or so the doctors said. The magician's magic couldn't save her in time, but they were able to save my daughter." Vanya shook his head, mouth twisting. "There was no poison involved, no murder intended by anyone of my House, despite the rumors the House of Kimathi spreads now. I married Nicca to align our Houses, not break them apart further than they were before."

Soren did not pretend to understand the intricate histories of the Houses, with all their blood feuds and vows and ever-shifting alliances that tied them all together. "Will you remarry?"

Vanya's gaze became scornful. "And lessen my daughter's right to the throne? Never. Raiah is my first and only born. That will make her a target all her life, but if I were to remarry, whatever House I tied myself to would demand their children be my heir in place of her, and that includes any branch of the House of Kimathi. I refuse to be the architect of my daughter's grave when I have already lost my wife."

Soren could say nothing in the face of that fierce promise. It wasn't his place to offer comfort, even if he wanted to. "I hope your daughter grows up safe."

Vanya stared at him for a long moment, dark eyes locked on Soren's face. "Would you like to meet her?"

It would be impolite to say no, even if Soren had no experience whatsoever with children of any age. His tithing cohort didn't count. "Do you want me to?"

"I wouldn't ask otherwise."

Soren floundered internally for a moment, wondering what sort of game Vanya was playing here, because the Houses ever played such things. "I came to deliver the border reports like you asked. If you want me to see your daughter, then I will."

"And what of the vow? Have you thought of a repayment I may offer you yet?"

Soren shook his head. "You owe me nothing, princeling."

Vanya sighed, lifting a hand in a commanding gesture for Soren to follow him. "You'll find that debt remains until you want *something*. Come, let me introduce you to Raiah, and then I'll have Alida show you to the bathhouse. I still have business with the Senate this afternoon, but you may rest here until I finish, and we'll have dinner together."

Soren couldn't say no to an order like that, and in truth, he didn't want to. Being out in the poison fields was never restful, and he'd had a taste of what luxury royal life could offer, enough to know he'd take whatever he could get. Besides, the governor had said to stay as long as needed to glean what information he thought was useful about the encroachment of revenants where they shouldn't be.

"I wouldn't mind washing off the travel dust."

Soren retrieved the ledger from the chaise and followed Vanya out of the room, putting himself into the prince's care.

Eleven

VANYA

The Senate's session regarding water allocation ran past sunset. Vanya stayed until the end, shepherding the arguments how he'd seen his mother do in the past. With Empress Zakariya Sa'Liandel in Oeiras hammering out another trade treaty with the Tovan Isles, Vanya was tasked with keeping the Senate on track because the heat of summer was yet to come, and water was a resource the Houses had gone to war over before.

The water used for Solarian bathhouses was filtered and cleaned after use. Once all the soap and oil and other grime were removed, the water was used for crops, supplementing what was drawn from aquifers and the country's rivers. Water rationing was law, especially during the dry seasons, and rights to that precious resource were always something to be argued over.

"Your daughter sleeps, Your Imperial Highness," one of the wet nurses reported when he entered the nursery guarded by two *praetoria* legionnaires.

Vanya quietly approached the low crib, staring down at his sleeping daughter. Not even a year old and she had a strong personality. Raiah's dark hair wasn't as curly as his own, and Vanya could see hints of Nicca in her nose and the lighter coloring of her skin. She had his eyes, and the stubborn way she cried until she got her way was him as well, according to his mother.

Vanya gently stroked a finger down his daughter's round cheek, not seeking to wake her but still wanting that connection. He loved her, had loved her when she was first put into his arms after the desperate hecticness of her birth and the thinned-out grief that followed. He wanted to give her the world, give her the Imperial throne, and he'd do everything in his power to do that. Not remarrying would ensure her succession, and Vanya had given that vow to the stars.

"Is the evening meal ready?" Vanya asked.

"In the courtyard," one of his daughter's servants said with a bow.

"And the warden?"

"Waiting for you, Your Imperial Highness."

Vanya left the nursery, the low-lit gas lamps in the room casting shadows behind him. The ones in the hallway beyond were set brighter, lighting his wing of the Imperial palace as bright as day.

He found Soren in the private courtyard, already seated on a cushioned bench at the low glass table. Well-tended ferns and small trees in various-sized ceramic pots were scattered around the mosaic floor, while a fountain burbled away in the center, filters and pipes keeping the water clean and moving. Flowering vines hung from balconies that overlooked the courtyard. The space above was open all the way through four levels, the night sky a starry blackness overhead.

The courtyards were the center of any home in Solaria, and the palace had been built around many of them for the Imperial family's personal use. This one belonged to Vanya and his daughter. A meal such as the one prepared tonight, held within the Imperial family's private space, was an honor afforded to very few outside the House of Sa'Liandel. Vanya wondered if Soren even knew what it meant for him to be here or if he even cared. In Vanya's experience, wardens cared for very little beyond their duty.

Vanya stepped into the courtyard and was pleased to see that Soren had indulged him by wearing the clothes he'd instructed the bathhouse attendants to provide rather than slipping back into his uniform.

The white robe was made of thin gauze, banded at the wrists by gold cuffs with thin gold chains that connected to the delicate fabric by way of neatly placed grommets. It fell open over his torso, no shirt beneath, showing off the golden medallion Vanya had gifted him last year, as well as several old scars. A delicate gold chain hooked into two grommets that rested over his collarbones, keeping the robe from sliding off his shoulders. His loose trousers were of thicker material, but only just, and as white as the robe. They were open from knee to thigh, secured by a tie on the side of each hip, with no belt to aid in keeping them up. Someone had given him house sandals, but he'd kicked them off beneath the table.

"Did you enjoy the bathhouse?" Vanya asked.

Soren watched him approach with unblinking eyes. "Better than any I've found on the road."

"I'm sorry I couldn't join you."

Vanya truly did regret being unable to join him. Having his way with Soren would've been far more enjoyable than watching the Senate argue for hours over a needed allocation law. In the well-lit courtyard, it was impossible not to see how Soren's gray eyes dilated a bit at that statement. Vanya was trained to notice and catalogue a person's reaction in any situation. Soren's was encouraging for how Vanya intended the evening to end.

"You had your duty."

"And yours brought you here." Vanya sat at the other end of the small square table, the serving platters and bowls between them over-flowing with food. A servant had already poured their glasses full of the cold red wine swimming with fruit Solarians enjoyed during the hot months. "Though, duty aside, I am glad you came."

Soren hooked a thumb beneath the gold chain of the medallion he wore and lifted it for Vanya to see. "I still have no answer for you about this."

"Remember what I said in Bellingham last year? You will come to me with the border reports twice a year, or more, if you like, and someday, you will have a need that I can provide for."

Soren let the vow he carried settle back against his chest and sighed. "You're so stubborn, princeling."

Vanya's mouth quirked a bit at the hint of what one could maybe call fondness in Soren's voice. "One must be to survive what Maricol throws at us."

He had no qualms about speaking so openly of the vow in the palace, in the wing that was his. The servants who tended to him were loyal to his House and, aside from that, were bound to silence by way of mind magic cast by a magician. His mother had become far more stringent when it came to those employed in the palace after the attack last year that should have, by all rights, killed him.

Loyalty could be bought, and it could be sold, but it could also be a collar tight enough to choke someone.

One of the servants stepped forward from her spot by a potted tree. She reached for the serving spoon in the spiced rice bowl and scooped some out onto Vanya's plate, then Soren's. The meal was served family-style, with more than enough to feed a group of people rather than just the two of them. Soren hesitated only a moment before he started to eat.

The flatbread was warm and garlicky, a perfect vehicle for the rice and stewed meat. Vegetables charred a bit from the grill surrounded a bowl of cool herbed yogurt there for dipping. Vanya was pleased to see that Soren tried a little bit of everything, though there were one or two dishes he didn't try twice.

They ate in silence for a time, servants standing attentively nearby, ensuring their wineglasses were always topped up. Soren ate with a single-minded focus that Vanya remembered from their brief time on the road last year. Here, he wouldn't need to watch his rations, though, and Vanya would rather he want for nothing while within the palace walls.

"Did you come here from the poison fields?" Vanya asked when Soren had finished most of the food on his plate.

Soren shook his head and reached for his wineglass. "Took a train from Karnak. I'm to head southeast after delivering the border reports. The wetlands there need deeper mapping."

The towns in that part of the country were few and far between, and most relegated to commercial harvesting operations. It was a hard, if lucrative, living. Many of the companies with stakes in that area had once belonged to the House of Rixham before his mother thoroughly annihilated that House. She'd parceled out the ownership of such businesses to various other Houses over the years, buying bits of loyalty in order to sway politics.

If the wardens thought the wetlands needed deeper mapping, it could be a sign of trouble. That area had a history of losing settlements to poisoned mists and fog that carried spores in its depths. Hunting revenants in murky, low-lying water and thick tree coverage was always dangerous.

"Anything of particular note I and my mother should know about?"

Soren shrugged. "The northwest is more of a problem than the southeast right now. It's in the border reports."

They ate, and they talked, looking for common ground they'd never find. Soren spoke bluntly, offering no deference to Vanya, but it was refreshing in a way to be treated as someone other than a prince.

The servants cleared the meal when they finished, whisking the dishes and plates away. Other servants arrived with a platter containing a multitude of small desserts. Soren went right for the flaky, nutty square of pastry drenched in honey, getting his fingers sticky. He shoved it in his mouth and licked his fingers clean.

Vanya leaned back on the low bench, eyes on Soren. "Come here."

Soren raised an eyebrow, but he stood from his bench and came around the glass table without argument. Vanya settled his hand against the side of Soren's knee, dragging it up hard muscle shown off by the trousers' design. He slid his fingers beneath the fabric, fingers splaying against the curve of Soren's ass, thumb resting against the tie there on his hip.

He tipped his head back and met Soren's half-lidded gaze, gray eyes gone dark with something they both wanted. The quiet between them was as heavy as the hot evening air and charged like a thunderstorm.

"You'd make a fine courtesan," Vanya said after a moment.

Soren snorted. "I noticed you had your servants hide my uniform. I'm not walking around the palace in this tomorrow."

Vanya dug his fingers a little harder into warm skin. Soren rocked forward a bit on his feet. "You did so today."

"I walked inside your walls, not where the public could see. What would your people say of their prince so openly fucking a warden instead of a whore?"

"Some of my country's best assassins were whores. And I'm sure there would be nobles who would wonder what House had superseded your duty."

Soren tilted his head a little, staring down at Vanya as the servants bustled about the table, removing the dessert tray and discreetly leaving behind a smaller one filled with tiny vials.

"If you couldn't trust your courtesans, is that why you married when you did? Because you wanted someone in your bed?"

"There is very little difference between a sacrifice and a spouse when it comes to marriage between the Houses."

"That sounds more like a gamble than love."

"I told you before why I married. She sleeps in the nursery."

Vanya had simply neglected to tell him what was lost in their marriage bed after Nicca died in childbirth. He trusted Nicca to provide him an heir, because that was what both their Houses had wanted, had contracted for. Perhaps in time he could have trusted her not to kill him at the behest of her mother, but they hadn't even had a calendar year together before she was burned to ash.

Vanya did not trust easily and never would. There were many ways for the Houses to slip an assassin into his bed. He should know, as he'd worked with his mother to send such hidden threats as gifts to recalcitrant Houses in the past. He slept alone most nights in order to see the dawn.

Soren's hand settled over Vanya's, callused fingers stroking over skin. Then he moved to undo the ties on the trousers, letting the fabric pool around his ankles. Vanya tightened his grip, letting his gaze drop from Soren's face, down his faintly flushed chest beneath the gauzy robe, to the half-hard cock between his legs.

"Is this what you want when I bring the border reports? Me in your bed because you know I won't put a bullet in your back?" Soren asked.

Vanya dragged his hand up over Soren's stomach and down to curl his fingers around Soren's cock, giving it a firm stroke. The way Soren rocked forward, a breath hissing between his teeth, made him remember all the little sounds he'd forgotten the warden had made the last time they'd been together like this.

"Does it matter? I want you, so I'll have you, and you'll let me, won't you?"

To prove his point, Vanya gripped the edge of the gauzy robe and pulled Soren onto his lap. Soren went without protest, settling across Vanya's thighs, knees pressing into the soft cushion of the bench. Vanya reached up and caught Soren's chin, pulling the other man down into a slow, deep kiss that tasted of honey and cinnamon, sweet like the dessert he hadn't gotten to try.

This was better.

When they finally broke apart, Soren's lips were clean of honey, and the depth of his desire could be felt in the hardness pressing against Vanya's stomach. Vanya leaned forward and pressed a kiss to Soren's chest, lips catching on the thin gold links of the medallion's chain.

"No one will care that you're in my bed. You're a nameless, state-less warden, who I owe a debt they know nothing about, but it is a cost I can easily pay when you finally come to me with hand outstretched," Vanya murmured.

You're safe was what he didn't say, because he knew better than to speak of things that could never be taken back.

Vanya turned his head, lips brushing against soft gauze as he placed his mouth over one dark nipple through the see-through fabric. He sucked hard on it, running his tongue over the fabric and the quickly hardening nub. Soren shifted on his lap, hands coming up to cradle Vanya's head as he bit gently at the skin beneath his teeth.

"The wardens will care," Soren murmured when Vanya finally lifted his mouth from the tender ministrations he'd provided. The robe was damp over both Soren's nipples, skin reddened beneath it, and the flush to his chest had gotten deeper.

Vanya leaned forward far enough to retrieve a vial from the small tray on the table, pressing a kiss to the side of Soren's neck. "The Poison Accords will not be broken by me having you."

And have him Vanya did, there in the courtyard as the servants went about their evening duties around them. Vanya had never minded an audience, and Soren didn't seem to care, not when he had three of Vanya's fingers pressed deep into his body, mouth fallen open around quiet moans of pleasure. Vanya sucked kisses into warm skin, teeth catching on fabric, on gold, as he stroked Soren to a slow hardness before bringing him over the edge with sure hands.

He sounded like Vanya remembered when he came, curled forward, fingers gripping Vanya's heavier robe hard enough to almost tear as he blocked out the sky above. When Soren finally caught his breath and lifted his head, his eyes were more black than gray, dark with desire. Vanya ignored his own throbbing ache for the moment in favor of raising his hand to Soren's mouth, who needed no guidance to lick Vanya's fingers clean of his spend.

He sucked on them until Vanya could no longer ignore his own need. Vanya pulled his fingers free and undid his own trousers, freeing his cock. He gripped Soren's hips and urged him higher. It was easy to push inside, to swallow Soren's quiet moan as Vanya pulled him down onto his cock with firm hands. When Soren finally settled on his lap, gasping against Vanya's mouth, he rolled his hips upward, driving his cock as deep as he could into that tight warmth.

Soren took the hint and used Vanya's shoulders to leverage himself up before sinking back down. He'd already come, but that didn't stop him from giving up what Vanya wanted. He moved with a fluid ease that only came from years of knowing how to use his body in the field. Soren tipped his head back, swallowing thickly as he rolled his hips, the gauzy robe sticking to his skin from sweat.

Vanya held Soren close as he came, driving in deep to the willing body sprawled over his, listening to the way Soren's breath stuttered in his chest, half-hard again from his efforts of bringing Vanya over the edge.

When Soren moved as if he was going to get up, Vanya dug his fingers into warm skin, nipping at his jaw. "Stay."

Soren sighed, his breath ghosting over Vanya's neck, but he didn't protest the request or when Vanya finally moved them from the courtyard to his bed.

In the morning, when Vanya woke from a night of indulgence, Soren was still by his side.

Twelve

NATHANIEL

Paradis was a burlesque club and brothel that catered to the merchant class, located on the eastern side of the Serpentine River, snugged up against an inner defensive city wall. The neighborhood wasn't the best, but neither was it the worst, and the pubs that lined the street ensured Paradis always had customers stumbling through its red door.

Nathaniel and Blaine didn't stumble so much as drunkenly stagger into the establishment after drinking at two pubs. The smell of perfume in the low-lit foyer made Nathaniel's nose twitch, but it wasn't enough to send him back out into the street. Especially not with the greeting they were given.

"Hello, darling," Scarlette purred as she sauntered down the hallway toward them.

"My dearest Scarlette," Nathaniel said, doffing his hat in a tipsy sort of bow to the madame of the house. "You look as beautiful as ever."

"Flattery will get you everywhere, Mr. Clementine."

Scarlette had the body of a dancer, all firm curves and precise control over her long limbs. Her hair was dyed an unnatural red that matched her lip rouge, the shade bright and gleaming beneath the chandeliers. She wore her hair pinned up, not loose like some of the girls and boys she supervised. The black stockings and red corset she wore with its feathered skirt surrounding her hips matched the color of her hair.

Her choice of colors also matched the blooming bouquet of roses tattooed on either side of her neck, the leaves of the flowers arching toward the center of her throat. Hidden beneath the ink was a set of bank numbers Nathaniel had asked about only once when he didn't know any better.

Scarlette's exquisitely painted face dominated by green eyes was ageless, and she looked the same now as she did back when Nathaniel was fifteen and staying out late with his friends, daringly unsupervised. Scarlette had made a living on the stage here as well as between the sheets of her bedroom upstairs. Nathaniel had visited her in both places over the last few years, and while he enjoyed his time with her, he was smart enough not to fall in love with her like nearly all the rest of her returning customers.

Besides, there was a whip-smart young baroness Nathaniel wanted to call on, either here in Amari or in Cosian if need be. Scarlette, he knew, would never begrudge him his change in desires. She was a businessperson as much as he was and understood when desires needed to be renegotiated.

What's more, she was a cog he was connected to within the Clockwork Brigade, and he was here tonight to introduce her to Blaine.

Scarlette cocked a hand on one hip, the heels she wore putting her at eye level with Nathaniel. "Who's your friend?"

Nathaniel put his hand on Blaine's shoulder, smiling widely, still tasting the alcohol from the last round of beers they'd had on his tongue. "May I introduce you to Tristan Arquette, a professor at the Aether School of Engineering and a newly made friend of mine."

"A pleasure," Blaine said, bobbing his head a little before listing to the side.

Nathaniel tightened his grip to keep the older man upright. The sloshy feel of too much drink was getting to them both.

"You've a bit of an accent. Do you travel much, Professor?" Scarlette asked.

Blaine paused a moment before saying, "I spent some time in E'ridia for my engineering education."

"That's the lilt I'm hearing. Do you know any aeronaut captains? My girls and boys do so love when they stop by."

"Tristan is more interested in airships than their captains," Nathaniel interrupted. "But we aren't here to chat about work. Rumor is you have a new show this season."

Scarlette smiled and easily slipped between them, hooking her arms around theirs. "Rumor would be correct, darling. Let me show you to your table."

She led them down the hallway toward the source of the music and laughter that echoed through the walls. The beaded curtain that blocked their way was easily parted, and they stepped into a warmly lit room filled with booths, tables, and chaises. Almost every spot in the small theater was filled, men and women alike being tended to by servers for drink, dancers for future tips, and those there to coax willing partners to a room upstairs.

Scarlette dealt in pleasures, both the reality and illusion of them.

"Only the best seat in the house for you, Mr. Clementine," Scarlette said with a wink and a smile as she deposited them at the only empty table in the center of the audience.

It faced the stage head-on, allowing them to see the dancers without needing to crane their heads around. The stage was currently empty and low-lit, the velvet curtains pulled around the curved shape of it while the band sat idle off to the side.

Nathaniel and Blaine took their seats beneath Scarlette's watchful eye before she said her goodbyes with a flirty smile. She wandered off between the tables, stopping here and there to chat with the customers there to be entertained.

"On the house," a server said as she twirled up to their table, setting a pair of small glasses down before them with a flourish.

"I can't possibly drink any more," Blaine groaned, but he reached for the glass anyway.

The glass was red in color, and the drink it carried was tinted blue. It smelled like alcohol even if it didn't taste like anything. Magic helped with that, and Nathaniel drank the potion in one quick swallow.

Its effects were immediate. His head pounded like a drum, his stomach roiled like he was standing on an airship flying through a storm, and the nausea that assailed him was almost overwhelming for the few seconds it lasted. Then the sensations faded to a clarity not hazed by drunkenness, forced sobriety an aether-provided gift.

"Wow," Blaine said, staring at the glass. "Someone needs to patent this stuff."

"Scarlette already has," Nathaniel said.

Nathaniel pushed the glass aside and leaned back in the wooden chair, making sure to keep his expression easygoing and attentive. No one came to Paradis and stayed in a bad mood. The women and men who worked for Scarlette were very good at their jobs, and the entertainment they provided always put a smile on everyone's face.

They stayed through two new performances, erotic dances that left Nathaniel feeling a little hot under the collar. The cold water doctored to look like alcohol gave him something to do with his hands even if he could do nothing about the ache in his trousers. The gossip had been right. Scarlette's new show *was* exquisite.

When one of Scarlette's girls settled onto his lap, dressed in a satin corset not meant for dancing, to undo his cravat and whisper a request into his ear, Nathaniel wasn't one to say no. Quirking an eyebrow at Blaine, he nodded in the direction of an entrance whose velvet curtains were tied aside.

"Care to join us? She has a friend upstairs for you, if you like," Nathaniel said with a casualness he had perfected after his first few visits.

He'd had long practice cultivating enjoyment of carnal pleasure in Paradis to hide the real reason he visited. Blaine had no trouble agreeing to Nathaniel's request, and the brothel worker led them out of the theater through the velvet curtains for the stairs that led above.

Two very burly-looking men armed with pistols stood guard at the foot of the stairs. Scarlette wasn't one who allowed abuse of her workers, and she employed several strong men and women to help keep the peace without involving peacekeepers.

They went upstairs and were taken to a bedroom decorated in deep green and brilliant gold, the bed elegantly made. It always was between customers. The heavy velvet curtains had been drawn over the only window, hiding what happened within. Instruments and draughts for pleasure were neatly laid out on the credenza, though Nathaniel didn't go over to peruse them.

"Let me go find my friend. Feel free to get comfortable," the woman said with a laugh before closing the door behind her.

Blaine craned his head about, taking in the room, before pinning Nathaniel with an irritated look. "I've never been one for brothels."

Nathaniel didn't know Blaine's history beyond what Lore had told him—an Ashionen who'd spent years in E'ridia before making his way home at the behest of the Clockwork Brigade under an assumed identity. He knew nothing about the life Blaine had lived in another country, only borne witness to his deft hand at making engines sing for the sake of his students.

But Meleri, in her capacity as Fulcrum, had elevated Blaine to a level of trust within the Clockwork Brigade that Nathaniel had no choice but to accept. Nathaniel's position was such that he was allowed to learn Blaine's real first name but was not given his last. There was no way for anyone to track Blaine through genealogies without it, and perhaps that was the point.

"Don't worry. We won't be staying long," Nathaniel promised.

Less than a minute later, the door opened again and Scarlette slipped inside. The smile on her face dropped away the second the door shut behind her.

"Do you have it?" she asked in a low voice.

Nathaniel slipped his hand beneath his tailored jacket and pulled the folded-up copy of a manifest from the inside pocket. "Of course."

He passed the manifest to her, the information there proprietary and belonging to the Clementine Trading Company. Within its neatly typed columns was the monthly schedule for the dozens of company steam trains that rode the rails across every country on Maricol save the Tovan Isles and E'ridia. His family's company couldn't cross an ocean, and the threat of poison and revenants in the Eastern Spine had always curtailed railway expansion in the east.

Cities and way stations were listed out beside train numbers and timetables on the manifest, but the only ones that mattered were those Nathaniel's father had marked with a red star. Those columns and rows were the ones Scarlette memorized, because those trains would be the ones ferrying escaped debt slaves out of Daijal with the aid of cogs overseen in that country by the Marshal.

Paradis was first and foremost a place of entertainment, but beneath the veneer of pleasure it provided was a place for those escaping debt bondage to rest. Scarlette would have built her business to be a haven whether or not she'd joined the Clockwork Brigade. She'd been a debt slave once, after all, and become the muse of a man in Daijal who loved her so much he'd paid her debts and freed her.

Scarlette had returned his misplaced idea of kindness by clawing a notarized copy of her loan discharge paperwork from the bank and fleeing east. The first thing she'd ever done with her second chance at life was to bury her past in colored ink to hide black numbers. It was tradition these days for freed debt slaves to carry intricate cover-up tattoos on their necks and have copies of their loan discharge paper-work deposited in multiple places.

The Collector's Guild was notorious for not caring about a person's status when they'd once been a debt slave. Their reach had grown deeper into Ashion as a whole and was entrenched in Amari this long after the Inferno. The laws coming out of Daijal that were eventually mirrored and passed in Ashion meant getting rid of the Collector's Guild was nearly impossible.

Scarlette was too well-known, with far too many cultivated busi-ness relationships, for any debt collector to openly harass. Her noto-riety meant she couldn't evade scrutiny, but the Clockwork Brigade had long ago decided what shelter and aid she could provide was worth the risk.

Many people walked through her doors and enjoyed themselves in private rooms in Paradis. No one on the premises kept track of who entered and who left. No one watching would ever see smuggled debt slaves with their bank tattoos painted over with makeup slip inside and down into the storage basement. They would not see one of Scarlette's artists tattoo necks with flowers beneath the glow of a gas lamp with gentle hands.

They would not see the debt slaves escape to freedom with falsified loan discharge paperwork and newly bought train tickets in hand to ride the rails into as desperate an obscurity as they could find.

That was why Nathaniel did this. That was why he'd become a cog, like his father and mother: because debt bondage was a nightmare they hoped to help eradicate. And while their family's business could not carve out the wealth attained on the backs of debt slaves, they could use that same business to help free as many people as possible until the nightmare was over.

"Helpful, as always," Scarlette said with a sharp nod.

She folded up the manifest, but rather than return the copy to Nathaniel, she retrieved a match from a box on the credenza. Once it was lit, she stuck the corner of the manifest into the flame. It caught fire immediately, and she dropped the paper into the small fireplace, a luxury only her room had in Paradis.

The manifest burned until nothing was left but ash.

Scarlette turned to face them, professional smile back in place on her painted lips. "Now, where were we? I believe you boys are here for a good time."

Nathaniel dipped his head at that but didn't move toward the bed. Blaine, he saw, had a pained look in his eyes the other man couldn't quite hide. "I think perhaps a game of cards will suffice."

Scarlette blinked at him before throwing back her head and laughing. "Cards, is it? And who might have stolen your heart these days that my bed no longer entices?"

Nathaniel wasn't sure about his heart but definitely his attention. Given enough time, he was certain he could lose both to Miss Caris Dhemlan. "A young lady who enjoys racing carriages."

"She sounds anything but boring, darling. You know what I think about boring."

He did, and Nathaniel didn't stop the smile that came to his face at her words.

Blaine looked far more relieved now that he knew they weren't going anywhere near the bed. He'd come along tonight because Meleri had wanted someone else to know this particular duty that had been Nathaniel's for the last several years. If Nathaniel was unable to perform the handoff, they needed a backup.

"I'll go find us a set of cards and something to drink. Make yourselves comfortable," Scarlette said before sweeping out of her bedroom.

"You heard the lady," Nathaniel said as he settled on the floor. "I hope you're okay with losing money."

"Fancy yourself a card shark?" Blaine asked as he sat with his back up against the footboard of the bed.

"Not in the least, but Scarlette could steal your life savings even with a bad hand."

Blaine smiled at the warning, and Nathaniel settled in for the hour of time brothel-goers were expected to spend in one of Paradis' bedrooms.

Thirteen

PORTIA

Portia had lived all thirty-nine years of her life in the Eastern Basin. Dry and arid, the plant and animal life that flourished there did so in spite of the environment, not because of it.

The motor carriage Caris drove hit a pothole in what passed for a dirt road, causing Portia to nearly slide off the back seat. She braced a hand against the roof of the motor carriage, the other keeping her wide-brimmed hat from falling off.

"Sorry!" Caris yelled over her shoulder without turning her head.

The windows were cranked down halfway, and the hot air felt like a weighted blanket all around them in Seventh Month. The dust blown up by the tires didn't help any, even if the gas mask and goggles Portia wore did. The sucking sound of her breath through filters was as familiar as anything else out here.

"This isn't a racing carriage," Emmitt called out from beside her.

"I know!"

Portia shared a glance with her husband through the tempered glass of their goggles. Caris had a lead foot and steady hands, but that didn't mean either of them cared for the speed she liked to travel at. Their motor carriage's engine had been modified by Caris, which meant the vehicle carrying their employees and hired gunslinger had a difficult time keeping up.

"You were the one that let her behind the wheel," Portia said.

"I like how she's my daughter when she's acting like a madwoman and not yours," Emmitt said cheerfully.

The motor carriage bounced through another pothole, and Portia steadied herself. In the front, Caris kept her right hand on the gearshift, changing gears as needed as she drove them deeper into the wilderness of the Eastern Basin.

They were a three-hour drive from Cosian, less than that between two desert towns, following a route Emmitt and Caris had argued over for the past two days. Hydromapping was something their company did several times a year. It enabled them to find the best places to put their filtration machines in the rivers and streams that ran down from the mountains and pooled in the arid province.

Living in the rain shadow of the Eastern Spine meant water was a precious resource everyone had learned to ration through their lifetime. Living out here in the borderlands of Ashion gave a person grit Portia hadn't found in almost anyone back in Amari.

The Eastern Spine wasn't cleansed land, and Portia doubted it would ever become so. The wardens kept the borders up to the base of the mountains and did not venture into the peaks and valleys that separated Ashion from E'ridia. That meant the poison inherent in the land there filtered and flowed into the Eastern Basin—as did the revenants.

Water was routinely contaminated and required filtration for use. Poisonous mists saturated with spores had been known to wipe out desert towns and turn their inhabitants into revenants. It was why every person was issued a gas mask and carried it on their person wherever they went.

It was also very useful when her daughter was behind the steering wheel and persisted in kicking up dust with the speed she drove at.

Emmitt was in charge of navigating them to this stretch of land populated with twisted trees and low-growing shrubs. The sun overhead was bright and hot, and Portia was looking forward to washing off the grime once they made it back home.

"There's the field marker up ahead," Emmitt shouted, pointing over the front seat.

Portia squinted through her goggles at the metal post with its curious-looking top rising from the ground some distance away. The field marker had been placed years back by the wardens to help monitor the poison level in the area.

Six Point Mechanics Company had gotten permission from the wardens to piggyback some of their own devices off the field marker for data collection. It helped them extrapolate on what to expect in the rivers and aquifers so they could recut clarion crystal as needed and adjust their filtration machines accordingly.

They'd had better results once Caris started cutting clarion crystal. She'd always said the crystals sang to her, and that was a secret Portia had struggled to get her daughter to keep when she was a child. Caris was better at keeping her magic under control now, even if Portia knew she hated to bottle it up. She'd gone unnoticed in Amari, though Portia hadn't felt relief until they'd made it back to Cosian some weeks ago.

Caris braked to a stop near the field marker and turned off the engine. She opened her door and slid out, the coveralls she wore a match for Portia's. "Can I take off my gas mask now?"

Emmitt shoved open his door and stepped out of the motor carriage, staring down at the handheld device he used to check the air for poison levels and spores. Portia slid out after her husband only to stand on the foot ledge to get at the travel trunks they'd strapped down to the hard roof. The other motor carriages finally reached them and parked nearby, the workers spilling out.

Emmitt finally nodded. "Levels are within normal range."

Portia didn't remove her gas mask until she had the ropes undone, allowing access to the travel trunks. A hand settled on her waist before she could climb up farther, and she glanced down into her husband's face.

"Let the boys get those," Emmitt said, eyes narrowed against the midday sunlight.

Portia gladly switched spots with one of their workers so she could remove her gas mask. The first breath of fresh air was nice, despite the heat. She pulled a kerchief from her pocket and wiped away the sweat beading on her forehead, taking in the area.

The mountains rose high in the distance, with snow on some of the highest peaks even during summer. Everywhere closest to them were shades of brown and tan, with hints of dark green amongst the plants that thrived in the arid environment.

Caris was already at the data-collecting device, satchel left on the ground, notepad and fountain pen in hand to jot down measurements recorded over the last month. One of the engineers hauled a folding table over to set up a makeshift work area. Caris looked happier here than she had back in Amari save for her time spent at the Aether School of Engineering.

"What do you think of the duchess' offer?" Portia asked when it was just herself and her husband standing by the vehicles.

Emmitt raised a hand to shield his eyes from the sun. "I think to deny Caris an education would be cruel. You know how she was as a child. We couldn't keep her out of the laboratories."

"But we could keep her here."

Portia ached with the thought of their only child living far from the safety of their home. That she would be the ward of the highest-ranked noble bloodline in the country couldn't outweigh a mother's concern.

Caris was theirs and had been ever since the night a star god had placed her in their care.

The memory of that moment was thin and fuzzy, like a dream half remembered, but Portia knew the truth, old and aching as it was. Portia had long since buried her grief for the child she'd borne and lost to a star god's decree, choosing to love Caris as her own—and Caris *was* hers. No one else had fed her, had rocked her to sleep, had watched her grow from a child to a fiercely intelligent young woman primed to shepherd their bloodline's company into the future.

Primed for more, if the magic she stifled was anything to go by.

Even in Cosian, even this far east from the border that divided Ashion from Daijal, it was impossible to escape the reach of the Daijal court. Everyone knew King Bernard had orchestrated the horror that was the Inferno even if the courts couldn't prove it. Everyone knew the Ashion parliament was now a puppet system of government slowly having its strings restrung.

The Clockwork Brigade that Portia and Emmitt aided as cogs had yet to draw Caris in. If she went to Amari, if she found herself under the duchess' tutelage and care, Portia wasn't sure they could keep Caris safe. But to keep her here would be to watch her wither to a shadow of what she could be. That, in itself, was a painful sort of prison.

Emmitt tipped his head in Portia's direction. "I would like to think the duchess would keep Caris safe. The duchess' loyalty lies with Ashion, not Daijal."

It had been a shock to realize Meleri was Fulcrum, head of the Clockwork Brigade and the keeper of all manner of secrets. Portia and Emmitt had secretly provided tools and resettlement guidance for escaped debt slaves under the supervision of other cogs for many years. They'd kept Caris ignorant of that area of their work because they hadn't wanted to burden her as a child.

Portia sighed. "I worry."

Emmitt touched a hand to her arm, smiling softly when she looked over at him. "We don't have to decide just yet."

No, but Portia rather thought he already had. Emmitt was just waiting for her to catch up.

Portia pasted on a smile and headed to where Caris had taken charge. They had a lot of work to get through in only an hour before needing to turn around and drive home. One never wanted to be caught past the city walls after night had fallen.

Everyone they'd brought along with them knew their job. Work went quickly enough, with information being taken from the data-collecting device and compared to current numbers. Production of filters couldn't begin until they figured out the adjustments.

They were all so focused on the task at hand that Portia didn't realize the gunslinger hired for security purposes had stepped away from their group, staring out into the distance. She didn't realize there was a problem until the man barked out a warning.

"Get back to the motor carriages!" the gunslinger yelled.

Portia squinted against the sunlight, trying to see what had put that sort of panic into the gunslinger's voice. Then she saw them, hunched over and rotten, but moving with a quickness that meant they'd been dead for quite a while, long enough for the spores that saturated bloated flesh to gain complete control.

Long enough for that dangerous, insidious contamination to find a pathway to spread.

"Revenants!" one of the engineers screamed.

Portia's feet remained rooted to the ground even as her head snapped around, gaze searching for her husband and daughter. Emmitt was by the folding table, snatching up what ledgers and devices he could grab, leaving everything else behind.

Caris was some distance away, hands tangled in the hard wire of the transmitter device they'd come out here to set up, the generator only half put together beside her. Beyond her, pushing themselves off the dirt where they'd been crawling for who knew how long, were more revenants.

"Portia!" Emmitt bellowed, staring at her with horror on his face.

Her feet finally moved, and she lurched around in time to see the revenants *behind* them, running or staggering forward, putrid hands reaching outward. Somehow a horde had surrounded them, and they'd have to fight their way to the motor carriages, because there was no outrunning a horde like this.

A gun going off reminded Portia of the one she carried, and she yanked her pistol out of its holster. She couldn't hear anything over the sound of her frantic breathing. Her hands weren't the steadiest, but revenants never were ones to dodge when faced with taking a bullet to the chest.

She cursed the fact none of their bullets were poison-tipped, merely iron, and she knew—she *knew*—what weapons they had wouldn't be enough to keep the horde at bay. Reports had come back from travelers the past few weeks that passage had been easy, unexciting, but everyone knew Maricol was a land of poison and risk.

And they'd risked it to come out here because the press of business demanded it. No one had reported back of a village or town engulfed in a poison fog and left to the mercy of drifting spores. Some distant part of Portia's mind whispered that a census count would show otherwise. Somewhere beyond here a town had turned into a graveyard, its inhabitants dead and risen to walk again.

She was a decent shot when it mattered, and this mattered, but she wasn't a crack shot. Fear and adrenaline made Portia's hands shake, pulling her aim off-center, sending her next bullet into the dirt rather than a revenant.

She could smell them now, close as they were, having been downwind and out of range most of the time as the crew worked. Portia gagged at the rancid smell that assailed her but kept shooting.

One of the engineers screamed in that high-pitched, wild animal way one did when they were dying. Portia couldn't look, but the wet tearing sound that reached her ears and the ragged, wordless scream eventually cutting off was evidence enough of the revenants getting their hands on the living. He wasn't the only one to die, and Portia's ears rang with the sound of screams.

She couldn't tell if any of the dying voices belonged to Emmitt or Caris.

Portia yelled wordlessly, stumbling back when her pistol clicked empty. Terror swept through her like a flash flood when she realized she didn't have any extra ammunition on her. Her fingers trembled against the trigger of the pistol, but no matter how hard she pulled on it, her predicament didn't change, because there were still two revenants left coming her way.

Bone bleached to a dirty white peeked through ragged hanging flesh. Desiccated eyes sat far back in dried-out eye sockets, muscle peeling apart between the jaws as their mouths worked, but no sound came out. The skin was stained a deep burgundy in areas—evidence of the spores that propagated in dead flesh and forced it to move.

If the revenants killed her, or if she got bitten and the wound festered—

Portia stumbled when she stepped back, heel catching on a rock. Her ankle rolled, the pain cutting up through her calf as she went down. Her teeth clacked together, and dirt puffed up around her, all the pain forgotten in the face of the dead lunging toward her.

She thought she screamed. If asked later, she would swear she had.

But whatever sound her voice made was drowned out in the roar of a conflagration that heated the air to something untenable. Brilliant starfire scorched the area around Portia, burning through the revenants with a ferocity that was too focused, too powerful, to be anything but magical.

Portia held her breath and fumbled for the gas mask hanging off her belt. She yanked it free and pulled it on over her face, sucking in air through the questionable protection the filters provided against such heated air. Her skin felt as if it would crack from the temperature, and her eyes stung.

For a long moment, all Portia could hear was the ragged sound of her own breathing. Then the starfire disappeared as if it had never been, leaving behind scorched dirt, the ashy outlines of bodies, and brittle pieces of bones—all that remained of the revenant horde that had attacked them.

Portia's eyes watered as she tried to take in her surroundings. The motor carriages had survived the fire, and that was the only blessing to be found amidst the remnants of torn apart people.

"Caris!" Portia gasped out through numb lips. "Emmitt!"

"Here," her husband croaked out from somewhere behind her.

Portia shoved herself to her feet, hissing when she put weight on her twisted ankle. The boots she wore would have to be enough support for the moment until they could get back to Cosian. Emmitt caught her when her ankle wouldn't support her weight all the way, and Portia huddled against him, too numb from terror to even think about crying.

"Where is she?" Portia rasped, voice coming out tinny through the gas mask she wore.

Emmitt wasn't wearing his, and the ledgers he'd tried to save and had abandoned were indistinguishable from the ash of bodies drifting on the breeze. No one else from the group who'd traveled out with them was alive, but their daughter had to be.

"Caris!" Emmitt shouted as he tugged Portia along with him.

They made their way to where Caris had last been sighted, finding her sprawled on the dry, cracked earth, the shrubs nearest her blackened to char. When Portia brushed against one, the entire thing crumbled to the ground, a dusty outline of a once living plant.

She yanked herself free of Emmitt's arms, falling to her knees beside their daughter. She pulled Caris' unconscious form into her arms, rocking her the way Portia had done when she was younger and the magic growing inside her pained her more than growth spurts. Emmitt kneeled on Caris' other side, holding Caris' lax hand in one of his.

Portia undid her gas mask, and Emmitt took it from her before she could drop it to the ground. She patted Caris' cheek with a firm hand, calling her name with increasing desperation. Caris was so pale, and the blood trickling from her nose stood out so brightly. When Portia tried to wipe it away with the sleeve of her blouse, it smeared over Caris' cheek like badly applied rouge.

"Caris," she said desperately, shaking her daughter to try to wake her up.

"She sleeps."

The woman's voice that came from behind them had Portia crying out in surprise even as Emmitt raised his pistol to aim over Portia's shoulder. His hand was steady, years working with intricate machinery and delicate gears giving him better control than Portia had in the moment. Her pistol was—somewhere. Empty and useless. She hadn't cared about much of anything except her daughter after the starfire burned.

Emmitt's eyes went wide, lips parting in shock. He didn't pull the trigger, though he did lower the gun. Portia finally found the wherewithal to take her eyes off her daughter in favor of their impossible visitor.

The North Star stood amongst the charred earth, wearing the robes of a star priest and a headdress that framed her skull like a halo as much as her thick auburn hair did. The golden circles and spikes dripped starfire around her body, the same white-hot burn that Caris had summoned in defense of them. She was like a vision, all hazy heat on the horizon, a figment of Portia's imagination or mind magic pushed through the aether—she couldn't decide.

Aaralyn held Portia's gaze as the star god walked ever closer, the weight of her presence heavier than the hot summer air that shimmered all around them. Memory dragged itself from the depths of Portia's mind, a blurred face shadowed in a nursery finally coming into sharp relief after so many years.

"Your brethren gave us our daughter," Portia said.

"And I gave Nilsine my country's future," Aaralyn replied. "But Caris can't be known just yet."

Aaralyn stood over Portia, and the hand the North Star seemingly placed on Portia's head sent ice trickling down her spine. Portia's eyes watered as she stared up at the apex star god who guided the whole of Maricol but had chosen Ashion as her children so long ago.

"My lady."

Aaralyn smiled, and maybe someone else could find comfort in it, but Portia only felt a creeping sense of unease settling in her bones. "Keep her secret for a little while longer."

Portia stared at the blackened ground that stretched around them. "She called starfire. How do we explain that?"

Her voice came out no louder than a whisper. Even this far east, in the middle of nowhere, she knew the risk of what giving voice to that fact meant. Magic was found in every country, wielded by magicians and star priests, but those that commanded starfire were few and far between. Ashion's royal genealogies had dwindled to one name after the Inferno, even if the count was wrong.

Portia tucked that thought away, buried it deep, and tried to forget. What mind magic that lingered inside her helped with that, or perhaps it was Aaralyn's doing. All Portia knew was she came back to herself, thoughts murky and gaze blurred, in the motor carriage with Emmitt in the back seat and Caris slumped between them.

"Mama?" Caris groaned.

Portia raised a hand to cradle her daughter's head against her shoulder, everything that had happened sleeting through her mind, too quick to make sense of.

Everything but Aaralyn's promise as the star god drove them back to Cosian, real and solid and dressed as a warden now, her words from before an echo in Portia's mind.

"Trust me, child. No one will see the truth unless I will it."

Fourteen

JOELLE

Joelle Kimathi of the House of Kimathi had borne much grief in her years, but nothing was so bitter as the loss of her grandchild who had married into the House of Sa'Liandel. She mourned Nicca, but she mourned the loss of an avenue to power more.

"Why have you not called for a blood feud?" Karima demanded, hazel eyes bloodshot from the tears she'd cried every day for months since Nicca's death.

Joelle had cried, too, but only as long as the mourning period required. There was little to be gained from the dead, and it was the living she needed to focus on.

She looked at her eldest daughter, garbed in a high-necked black gown, hair piled high on her head, and wondered when Karima would deem it time to wear color again. "Because Raiah is half our blood, and if we call for a blood feud against the House of Sa'Liandel, we call it against her. Would you see your granddaughter and my great-granddaughter dead?"

"I haven't seen my granddaughter at all."

Karima's bitterness was shared by Joelle, but she hadn't allowed grief to keep her from moving forward. "And that is why I will not call for a blood feud. We still have a claim to the Imperial throne through Raiah. A blood feud would deny her our House and forever associate her with the House of Sa'Liandel."

"They do so already. Zakariya refuses us our right to bring Raiah to Bellingham. You refuse to let us go to Calhames. Raiah will not know us, her true family, if we cannot be in her life."

"To go to Calhames and beg for the chance to see my great-grand-daughter diminishes our position. The House of Sa'Liandel murdered Nicca once they got an heir off her. To be conciliatory toward them is to forgive, and I will not allow such lies to perpetuate," Joelle said tartly.

Karima's hands curled into fists, the intricate design stained onto her hands from pigmented paste showing up bright over her knuck-les. "You leave an heir in the viper's nest."

"That heir will ensure we have a claim to the Imperial throne until we can seize it ourselves." Joelle softened her tone, reaching out to settle her hand over Karima's. "I grieve as much as you do, but do not let your grief override our search for justice."

Karima nodded jerkily before uncurling her hands to clasp Joelle's between them. "We should have never agreed to the marriage contract."

Joelle said nothing to that, because there was no marriage contract she would not have approved and signed on behalf of their House if it would tie them to the Imperial throne. Karima was to be *vezir* one day. She should know the sacrifices that had to be made for prestige and power. Grief should not have dissuaded her from that road. It made Joelle wonder if it would be prudent to choose her son over her daughter to succeed her.

Artyom and his wife had only borne sons. Joelle knew from her spies that the Imperial crown prince enjoyed both men and women in his bed, but an heir could only be begotten from a wife. She'd chosen Karima because of Nicca, but with Raiah born and Nicca ash, Artyom might be the better choice for the future of their House.

"I have a meeting," Joelle said, pulling her hand free. She cupped her daughter's face, ignoring the ache in her swollen knuckles to draw Karima close to press a kiss upon her brow. "Don't spend all day in prayer."

Joelle pushed herself to her feet, taking a moment to adjust the fall of her robes and the angle of her headdress. The weight of the gold and onyx felt heavier these days, but she would never leave it by the wayside, even within the vast estate of their House.

Bellingham was the heart of the *vasilyet* that the House of Kimathi ruled over, the one which all other minor Houses within their rule of Solaria looked to for guidance first if they knew what was good for them. The House of Kimathi kept the northwestern borders of Solaria and guarded the trade routes with Daijal for the good of Solaria.

Joelle guarded her political relationship with the crown princess of Daijal's military advisor for the good of her House and herself.

The handmaidens that followed in her wake wherever she went waited for Joelle out in the hall and bowed at her arrival. The women varied in age, but their loyalty was never in doubt. A touch of mind magic from a magician helped with that. The four handmaidens escorted her out of the family wing of the estate to the civic wing where her office was located.

Artyom was already there, having been responsible for seeing High General Kote Akina to the estate with no one the wiser. Secrecy had to be kept in getting the man south across the border to Bellingham. His visits always coincided with his time spent traveling to field-train Daijal soldiers. His presence was more easily missed when he was not in New Haven.

The Daijalan military officer wasn't dressed as such, though Kote held himself with the bearing of a man who preferred a uniform over the Solarian-style robes he wore. But the disguise was necessary, as communication through telegrams was too easily intercepted, and Joelle had never trusted telephone calls.

Joelle's actions today and all the days before where she parleyed with Daijal's shadow ruler were considered treason by her country's standards. It didn't matter that she did this *for* her country. There were many Houses that would never understand her reasoning.

Kote bowed in greeting. "*Vezir* Joelle of the House of Kimathi. My queen sends her regards and heartfelt prayers for your granddaughter lost earlier this year."

"Eimarille is not queen yet," Joelle said as she settled into her plush leather seat behind the wide desk. "And prayers cannot return Nicca to my House."

Kote said nothing in the face of her statement, disinclined to rise to the veiled insult Joelle had given regarding Eimarille's rank. A princess did not make a queen, no matter the guidance of a star god.

Joelle sighed, curling her hands together over the desktop. The ache in her bones was a side effect of having survived an assassination attempt by her brother fifteen years ago. Poison had damaged her nerves before a magician was able to counteract what they could. Damage from poison was difficult to heal from, and there was no miracle cure for what ailed her these days.

In retaliation for the harm sustained, Joelle had ordered her brother's death and refused to have his name written on a memory wall. She hadn't stricken his name from the nobility genealogies, but she still could, and the threat of it mostly kept his surviving children in line.

Her House could be so troublesome at times.

"What is it that Eimarille desires now?" Joelle asked.

"I have been authorized to speak on my queen's behalf. The banking laws in Daijal have expanded the breadth of collateral. While that means we're coming into more debtors, we need more room for experiments."

"If I carve any further land in my *vasilyet*, I risk the attention of wardens. They will, in turn, bring such reports to Calhames. If Eimarille wishes to use my land for your country's experiments, then I want assurances in writing I will have her backing to take the Imperial throne."

Kote gave a slow blink at that demand. He was a difficult man to read; very much Daijalan to his bones despite the Tovanian look to him. "My queen anticipated such a request."

Joelle smiled thinly. "And does she agree?"

"After her child is born, she will go on a royal tour through Daijal to introduce her heir to the country. She'll be in Helia for some of that time during winter. Send your proxy to sign an accord with her in that city, *vezir*. In exchange for more land, you will have our support for your endeavors here in Solaria."

"How much land must we give away to foreigners, Mother?" Artyom demanded. "We risk our own people with these hideous experiments you insist on conducting."

"Enough that it gets us what we want. The wardens can cleanse what land is poisoned after we hold the Imperial throne and our House rules Solaria," Joelle said.

That was a prize all Houses wanted. The House of Sa'Liandel had held the Imperial throne for too long. If the Dawn Star would not favor the House of Kimathi, Joelle would look to the Twilight Star instead.

Kote nodded at whatever he saw in Joelle's eyes and stood. "I must leave to catch my train back across the border. My queen will see your proxy in Helia over winter."

He gave her a bow worthy of her station, no more and no less, before leaving her office. Artyom frowned at the high general's exit, arms crossed tightly over his chest.

"You will go to Helia when it is time," Joelle said.

Artyom's head snapped around, eyes widening before narrowing when he caught her gaze. "Shouldn't that task fall to Karima?"

"She grieves, and grief has no place in the fight ahead."

It wasn't a formal repudiation of Karima as her heir, but it was near enough that Artyom would do whatever Joelle demanded if it gained him favor. He turned to face her fully and bowed as one would to an empress.

"Whatever you ask of me, I shall provide," Artyom said before leaving her office with a spring in his step, no doubt prepared to tell his wife of the news.

He left the door open upon his exit, and one of Joelle's handmaidens stepped inside the office. "Chai, *vezir*?"

Joelle uncurled her hands, fingers throbbing. "Yes, and send for Dalma."

Her family's personal magician would hopefully be able to get rid of the ache in her bones so she could get through the day's tasks. Ruling a House and governing a *vasilyet* was never-ending some days.

Fifteen

TERILYN

After an eighteen-hour labor, the sound of Eimarille's child finally being born and crying was all Terilyn wanted to hear.

"Congratulations, Your Royal Highness. It's a boy," the doctor said.

The doctor handed the squalling newborn off to a nurse to be seen to. Terilyn tracked where the woman went in the bedroom Eimarille shared with Wesley. The room was overfull with the doctor, his nurses, a midwife, a magician, and servants who fetched whatever was required of them.

Eimarille hadn't once let go of Terilyn's hand during the labor, but she let go now as she slumped back. Terilyn pressed a hand to Eimarille's damp dark blonde hair, holding the younger woman close. The nightgown Eimarille wore was soaked with sweat, the braid her hair was in loosened from all the times she'd writhed in the bed as she pushed.

And while Eimarille's son was born now, it was up to Terilyn to see her lover safe.

"My son?" Eimarille murmured, voice a rasp from exhaustion.

Terilyn kissed the top of Eimarille's head, watching as the nurse who held the infant boy left the bedroom with him. "Do not worry. I'll return shortly."

Terilyn extracted herself from the spot on the bed she hadn't left since the labor started. Her gown was wrinkled from not being removed for over a day, but her weapons were still in place underneath. Terilyn left the bedroom, bare feet making no sound as she tracked the nurse with sharp eyes.

The antechamber was crowded with the Daijal royal family, the head recorder from the star temple who was responsible for updating the royal genealogies, and various others that King Bernard thought prudent to be present for the birth. They'd arrived within the hour when it became apparent Eimarille's labor was finally progressing, and the room smelled of cigars, making Terilyn's lips curl in distaste.

"Your son, Your Royal Highness," the nurse said with a curtsy before offering the crying newborn to Wesley.

He seemed thrilled, though not as thrilled as the king. Terilyn took in everyone's expression in a swift scan of the room like she'd been taught as a child. There was no one present she trusted with her lover's child.

"I have a son," Wesley said with wonder as he cradled the infant close.

Bernard gestured commandingly at Wesley, handing his cigar off to a courtier so he could hold his grandson. "Let me have a look at him."

"I will take Prince Lisandro," Terilyn said, cutting through the chatter. "His mother wishes to have him returned to her."

Wesley's smile faded as the two men turned to look at her. Terilyn met their gazes calmly, not reaching for the blades strapped to her thighs and easily retrieved through the carefully tailored slits in her gown's skirt, though she dearly wanted to. She'd dreamed, sometimes, of the way it would feel to carve a thin red line across their throats.

"Prince Lisandro, is it?" Bernard said as he cradled the still-crying baby close.

Terilyn stepped closer. "As blessed so by the Twilight Star."

No king liked to be reminded of his failures in public, whether anyone knew of them or not. Terilyn knew her presence in the palace and by Eimarille's side all these years was one Bernard hated. He had tried to banish her once before. He must have remembered that failure and what it cost him—a finger as a reminder of his insolence, but he kept his head and his life—because he offered the baby to Terilyn with a false smile on his face.

"It is, as you say, much too soon for mother and son to be parted. We shall celebrate his birth while my daughter-in-law rests," Bernard said.

Terilyn accepted the baby into her arms. She dipped into a curtsy but didn't bow her head. "I wish you much merriment, Your Majesty."

She retreated back to the bedroom, feeling the weight of the king's attention like a bullet to the back. But he did not demand she stay, and Wesley did not protest her leaving. Terilyn kicked the door shut, muffling the chatter that rose up behind her of men celebrating an effort they had no part in.

Eimarille still lay on the bed, face turned toward the door, her gray-blue eyes overly bright in her face. The magician had replaced the doctor at her bedside. Terilyn could only hope that meant whatever bleeding had been ongoing had finally stopped.

"Darling?" Eimarille murmured.

"I have him," Terilyn said quietly.

Eimarille's mouth curved in an exhausted smile. "I know."

Terilyn settled on the bed beside Eimarille, ignoring the people moving around them. The only people who mattered to her were now safe within her care, and she placed Lisandro back into his mother's arms with a gentle smile.

"Here," she said. "He missed you."

Eimarille hummed softly, staring down at her son with wonder on her face. Terilyn smoothed her hand over Eimarille's hair, tucking the sweaty strands out of the way. Eimarille touched a finger to Lisandro's round cheek, smiling sweetly at him.

"I'm going to give you the world," she promised.

Terilyn leaned closer, wide-awake and unwilling to move from her own world's side.

Secrets

934 A.O.P.

One

SOREN

Rixham was a dead city. There was nothing living in Rixham.

The old Solarian mantra settled in the back of Soren's thoughts as he rode his velocycle around the still-standing walls of the city of the dead. The Wastelands were finally to the south of him, but the red sand from the desert dunes felt as if it had settled in his skin, in his clothes, in the gears of every weapon he carried on him.

The Wastelands hugged the southern part of the continent, the coastal dunes touching the Gulf of Helia, the Southern Ocean, and the Constellation Sea. The farther north one went found the dunes dwindling into gravel plains that aided in the spread of desertification. The Wastelands were poisoned land that sustained no towns or cities.

What they did sustain were revenants.

Wild animals that died and were brought back to life by spores drifting on the wind called the valleys between the dunes home. Humans who succumbed to poisonous fog in frontier towns walked again after dying, their bodies urged onward by deadly spores looking to propagate amongst the living.

Wardens kept watch on the border, annihilated and burned what hordes they could find, and tried to keep revenants from finding their way north. Rixham used to be a city they could work out of and deploy from. These days, Rixham was nothing but a walled-off grave, just another border for wardens to guard.

Soren eventually made it to the damaged road ruined by the Legion's war machines during the siege on the city. It was more holes and cracks than anything else now, leading to a city gate that had been welded shut by flame-throwing automatons. Wardens had barricaded it after the fact and built another iron gate over it as a precaution in case the hinges on the original didn't hold against the elements.

The dead still walked those city streets, after all, and even wardens weren't brave enough to enter a city with a horde over several hundred thousand strong.

The warden's watchtower consisted of a solidly built one-story building, with a rising tower accessible only from within protruding from the roof. A two-story-tall, human-shaped automaton was positioned near the building's entrance, the machine's clockwork gears quiet and its Zip gun arms pointed at the ground rather than a target. Whoever was on watch duty had the control device and could easily activate the sentinel-class automaton.

It wasn't the only automaton guarding Rixham. Some of the best inventors of war machines for Solaria's Legion had created the sentinel class, whose sole purpose was to patrol Rixham. They carried enough firepower to hopefully contain a breach, but as a breach had yet to occur, they hadn't been tested. Soren had driven past a few on his way to the watchtower.

The two wardens assigned to the watchtower met him at the front door, the younger woman waving at him in greeting. Neither had their poison swords strapped to their backs, but each carried a pistol and had a few blades holstered on their bodies.

"You're a little early to be Jalissa's replacement," the older woman said. Her eyes were a piercing blue in a nut-brown, weathered face, hair an even mix of gray and brown.

Soren rolled his shoulders to adjust the weight of his poison sword as he cut the engine on his velocycle. "I'm here to pick up your border reports."

He wouldn't have driven around the swampy wetlands to get to

Rixham otherwise. The railroads that used to run to the city of the dead were rusted from disuse these days. There was no hope of catching a train this far southeast in Solaria.

"Ah, we have those for you. I'm Petra."

"Soren."

She blinked at him. "The same warden who saved the Imperial crown prince a few years back?"

Soren shrugged. "It was either that or leave him to revenants."

"Might have been the better option, with the way the Houses are. You heard the news yet?" Petra asked as she retreated into the watchtower.

"I've been in the Wastelands. I haven't heard anything."

Jalissa grimaced. "The Empress and Emperor Consort are dead. Poison is the running bet with the bookies, according to the broadsheets. The prince is taking over the Imperial throne."

It might have been Second Month, but it was still warm enough in the middle of the day this far south. Warm enough that the sudden chill that shot through Soren made his teeth clack together. Unease settled heavily in his gut. He reached up and scratched at his cheek before shoving his brass goggles on top of his riding helmet.

"Got a broadsheet I can catch up with?" he asked.

"Inside. We'll get you chai as well."

The watchtower wasn't homely, reminding him more of the barracks back on the Warden's Island. Weapons were laid out on a table in the main work area on the first level. Petra shuffled through folios on a wooden desk against one wall while what looked like a clockwork cat sat perched on the stool beside her. It wasn't a wind-up version or looked to be steam-powered. When it turned its head to stare at him with bottle-green crystal eyes that glowed, Soren had the intense desire to go for his pistol.

"What is that?" he asked, going still.

Petra looked over her shoulder at him and then dropped her gaze to the clockwork cat beside her. She half-smiled, reaching out to pat the dull brass metal piece welded between the clockwork cat's ears.

"A present from an old friend who never made it off the poison fields. Tock here is one of a kind," Petra said.

The clockwork cat moved with a fluidity most clockwork devices and automatons didn't have. Deep within the bulk of its gears and metal plates, flickering over every screw and gear teeth, was the glow of magic drawn from the aether.

Whatever spell animated the clockwork cat hadn't faded with its caster's death. The magic resonated with Soren in a way that made his skin itch beneath the leather of his uniform, the same way it always itched when a magician with particular strength was flinging spells about. The aether clawed at him, and he tried to ignore the metaphysical ache it left behind.

"How does it work?"

"My friend was a magician as well as a warden, and I'm only one of those. I never asked him, so I couldn't tell you."

Soren didn't press the issue, but he steered clear of the clockwork cat and instead sat at the sturdy dining table tucked against the wall between two bookcases. The shelves were neatly organized, and there was a stack of broadsheets sitting haphazardly on top of one.

Jalissa came back with a small tray holding a couple of mugs and a teapot. Soren could smell the spice in the chai from halfway across the room. "Those broadsheets are old. You'll want this one."

She set the tray on the table and then handed him the broadsheet she'd had tucked beneath one arm. Soren took it with a nod and unfolded the paper. The date on it was from last week, which probably meant some other warden had stopped by with it. The articles were all in Solarian, but his grasp of the language as a whole had gotten better over the last few years.

Soren had made it a point to stop by Calhames whenever possible. He was obligated to show up twice a year to deliver the border reports, but he'd found it impossible to give up Vanya's touch in between that. Wardens weren't supposed to get involved with matters of state, but Delani had yet to rescind her order to use his connection to spy on the Imperial court.

So he stayed with Vanya for days, sometimes weeks at a time, watching Raiah grow up and reluctantly learning the ways of the Houses. More and more, Calhames—or whichever city Vanya stayed in—was becoming Soren's home. He doubted that's what Delani had meant when she asked him to spy, but Soren was reluctant to leave Vanya's bed for anything but his duty.

That duty had become more difficult to complete in parts of Solaria. Too many revenants were crawling out of the poison fields in the northwest, and the House of Kimathi was territorial of its *vasilyet*. The Poison Accords granted wardens passage along every border, but Soren wasn't the only one who had been hounded away from towns and villages in that area of the country as of late.

The Imperial throne could have ordered the House of Kimathi to grant unhindered passage, but it was even odds if they'd have listened. Ever since Nicca had died, there'd been no peace between the House of Kimathi and the House of Sa'Liandel.

Soren's chai grew cold as he read the articles in the broadsheet. In the end, it wasn't the words that kept his attention, but the printed photograph of Vanya seated on the Imperial throne.

Petra came over and set a thick folio on the table. "I have the records for our Rixham patrols. Will you stay for lunch?"

There were no more trains that came to Rixham, and the ride north would take several days between stops at way stations. According to the broadsheet, the coronation was for this week, and he'd miss it if he stayed.

Soren picked up the chai and drained the mug in a couple of long swallows. "No, I need to get on the road."

Petra nodded. "We'll pack you a couple of sausage rolls and replenish your bullets. We had a supply run delivered last week, so we won't be hurting. It'll be better than the hard bread and jerky you've probably been eating while in the Wastelands."

"My thanks."

He folded up the broadsheet and would have put it back on the stack, but Petra shook her head. "Keep it."

Soren tucked it away between the pages of the border report for Rixham. It only took a couple of minutes for Jalissa to scrounge up the promised food and just as long for Petra to procure a couple of boxes of ammunition.

The two wardens followed Soren outside to his velocycle. The strange clockwork cat crouched in the watchtower's doorway, staring at him with those eerie glass-bottle eyes, still glowing with magic. Soren didn't turn his back on it.

"Safe travels down your road," Petra said.

Soren kicked the stand up and revved the engine of his velocycle, everything secured in the travel compartments. "May you ever keep the watch."

They didn't stay to see him leave, heading back inside, because they were all wardens, and they knew their duty. Soren turned his velocycle north down that cracked black road and headed toward his.

Two

SOREN

Calhames was draped in black-and-gold fabric, the sign of a city in mourning. The walls surrounding Solaria's capital were covered in tapestries, and the line for travelers to get through the main city gate from the trade road looked to be hours long.

Soren bypassed it completely, weaving his velocycle through the traffic of motor carriages, larger trucks, and other velocycles. Calhames had two major train terminals, the northern one and the western one, with the main trade gate situated between the two. The airfield was to the east of the city, and Soren could see airships dotting the clear sky above as they came in to land.

"Halt and state your business," a legionnaire ordered when Soren reached the gate.

Soren pulled off his brass goggles and undid the straps of his metal-plated leather helmet, shaking free some of the dust from the road. He rather thought the hilt of the poison sword sticking out over his shoulder should have been identification enough but opted not to argue.

"I'm a warden. I'm here for a resupply," he said.

Which was true, even if he wouldn't be going to a resupply station. Vanya always got vaguely insulted when he tried. Soren did have to admit that Solaria's Legion had vastly superior grades of weapons, and he was always appreciative of what he could walk away with from the royal munitions stores.

It took longer to get through the checkpoint, and Soren attributed that to the crush of people hoping to be present for the coronation of their next emperor. A darker reason was to perhaps limit the number of threats aimed directly at the person who now occupied the Imperial throne.

Soren got through the main gate, and it took almost two hours for him to get from the outermost wall to the center of Calhames, where the grounds of the Imperial palace resided. When he finally drove up to the security perimeter held by *praetoria* legionnaires, he thought he'd have to argue his way past them.

But several of the legionnaires recognized him from all the times past that Soren had visited Vanya. He was waved through the golden gates and into the grand courtyard of the palace without argument.

He knew his way around the palace these days, and the servants knew how to attend to his velocycle whenever he arrived. By the time he braked to a halt near the building's entrance, a servant in white robes was there to oversee its care. Soren took with him his satchel of poison samples and antidote vials, the border reports from Rixham, and his own field reports.

"Everything else will be brought inside for you," the servant promised with a bow.

Soren trekked through the cool hallways of the palace to the private wing that had been Vanya's for so many years. But when Soren got there, the usual bustle he expected was missing, and the rooms he passed through had been stripped of every hint of décor Vanya had favored.

"I'd heard you had arrived," Alida called out from behind him.

Soren turned and watched Vanya's majordomo walk toward him down the wide hallway, dressed in a more elaborate robe than he'd ever seen her wear before. The blue fabric was detailed with golden embroidery that had desert flowers blooming across her shoulders and down the sheer sleeves of her robe.

Soren frowned at her. "I've been in the Wastelands the last few months. I only just heard about what happened. Where are Vanya's things?"

Alida sighed as she came to a stop some feet from him, clasping her hands together in front of her. Her makeup was pristine as usual, and while it helped to hide the circles beneath her eyes, Soren could see the exhaustion in her gaze. "His household has moved to the main family wing, where his parents kept theirs."

Soren swallowed. "Right. Because he's the emperor now."

Alida arched an eyebrow. "He's spent much of his time of late with Raiah. They'll both be pleased to see you. Come. I'll take you to them."

Soren nodded, trying not to feel awkward and out of place as Alida led him through the palace to an area he had never set foot in before. Usually, when Soren stayed at the palace, he rarely left Vanya's bed, much less the private wing.

The grandly decorated halls and rooms they passed through were filled with numerous servants and other officials in more formal roles. Furniture, artwork, and all manner of decorations were being removed and replaced. Soren wondered if this was tradition, to erase the ghosts of one's familial past in favor of the living. He didn't ask.

The organized chaos was a sound in Soren's ears that didn't fade until Alida led him into a set of private living quarters decorated in a style Soren was familiar with, even if the layout of everything was new. Vanya had a preference for creams, golds, and crimson, and those colors were resplendent here.

There were fewer servants and far more *praetoria* legionnaires present than Soren remembered from all his previous visits. The men and women in uniform eyed him with various expressions of recognition or disapproval on their faces.

"The warden should not be armed," the woman with ranking chevrons on her sleeve said.

"The warden is of His Imperial Majesty's household," Alida replied, her stride never slowing.

She gestured imperiously at Soren, and he could only obey the silent order. Maybe her position as Vanya's majordomo outranked even those assigned to protect him. He nodded at the legionnaires in passing anyway but didn't bother with any sort of conversation. Alida was already slipping through the doorway up ahead, and Soren hastened to follow her.

"Raiah, that's to play with, not to eat."

Vanya sounded tired, and he looked it, too, when Soren finally got eyes on the other man. The slump of his shoulders wasn't normal as he watched his daughter play with a clockwork train. The two-year-old Imperial crown princess sat in the center of the circular tracks, chewing on one of the blocks that had held up a now knocked-over tunnel. Her dark, curly hair had been neatly tied into small twisted knots over her skull, held in place by ties rather than pins. She'd grown in Soren's absence, but her smile and laughter were still the same.

"Your Imperial Majesty," Alida said with a deep bow.

Vanya didn't look away from Raiah. "I asked not to be disturbed for at least the luncheon hour while I spent time with my daughter. Surely you can handle the household transition without me? I know the Senate is preparing the coronation law in my absence without needing my oversight."

"Your warden is here."

Vanya turned his head with a sudden jerk, piercing dark eyes landing unerringly on Soren. He was too much of a royal, too much of a politician in some ways, to visibly show how he felt, but his dismissal of everyone in the room was enough of a hint. It made Soren's gut tighten, being the focus of Vanya's formidable attention.

"Leave us," Vanya ordered brusquely.

The handful of servants in the room silently left, with Raiah's governess being waved off by Vanya. Alida shut the door behind everyone, leaving Soren alone with Solaria's new ruler. Vanya stood from the chaise, moving to pick up Raiah. She shrieked in glee but became shy when she caught sight of Soren, tucking her head against her father's shoulder.

"I'm sorry." Soren swallowed tightly, not knowing what else to say. "I was in the Wastelands for months."

Vanya held Raiah close as he approached, expression shuttered, the gold circlet on his head far more elaborate than the usual one he wore. The ranking medallion was missing as well, though Soren supposed if it was for the heir, Raiah was too small to wear it. She might also try to eat it.

"I thought you wouldn't come," Vanya said.

Soren carefully deposited his satchel on the nearest table, knowing better than to leave it on the ground where Raiah could get at it. She'd been crawling the last time he was here, and she looked to be of age for walking now.

"I read the news in a broadsheet at the watchtower when I was picking up border reports. I came here instead of heading for the Warden's Island."

He was expected back there to deliver the reports for record-keeping, but for once, Soren was being selfish. He'd give his report late, but the governor would get it eventually. Delani might not appreciate the delay, but there'd been nothing that constituted an emergency in his area of the Wastelands or in Rixham.

Vanya needed him more right now.

Once Soren had divested himself of his baggage and the folios, if not his weapons, he went to Vanya's side. Lifting a gloved hand, he touched the taller man's cheek, fingertips skimming over the shadows beneath those dark eyes.

"I'm sorry," he said again.

Wardens understood death better than anyone. He'd grown up in a tithe group that was whittled down by alchemy. He went into the poison fields where threats from revenants, wild beasts, and spores were an undying and never-ending threat. He walked in the footsteps of the dead, and grief was a distant emotion Soren sometimes didn't know how to carry.

Vanya carried his in his eyes, in the rigidness of his muscles, in the way his jaw stayed tight when Soren brushed his fingers over it. Vanya kept his grief locked up like a tomb of old, hidden from everyone. Soren only hoped Solaria wouldn't lose another city how it'd lost Rixham in the past.

Vanya's gaze never left Soren's face. "You have your duty."

"Yes." But he'd still come anyway, and that said something Soren didn't want to dwell on for long. It didn't change where they stood with each other. It couldn't.

Vanya lifted Raiah higher in one arm before snagging Soren's wrist so he could turn his head and kiss Soren's palm. His lips were cool and dry, a little chapped from the winter air outside. Familiar, when Soren knew they shouldn't be.

"Stay."

Soren pressed his fingers over the shape of Vanya's face, careful to angle his body away from Raiah's curious, grasping hands so she couldn't get at his poison sword. "As long as I can."

A warden wasn't supposed to want, but Soren did. He blamed Vanya for that on the days he didn't blame the star gods for his lot in life and the road he walked.

But the vow that hung around his neck wasn't any easier to keep, not when it'd been given by a prince and would be paid by an emperor.

If Vanya survived.

Soren eventually pulled his hand free, crossing his arms over his chest. "The broadsheets said it was poison. Quiet killer?"

Perhaps it was too blunt of a question, judging by the way Vanya swallowed, but Soren couldn't take the words back. "Quiet killer and a knife through the heart while they were in Oeiras for treaty talks with the Tovan Isles. The assassins weren't willing to take any chances the poison would be enough."

"A Blade?"

"There were no eyewitnesses, so we can't be sure." Vanya pried one of Raiah's hands off Soren's vest. "No House has claimed victory."

"But you have your suspicions."

"My parents were targeted. I and Raiah were not."

"You think it's the House of Kimathi?"

"Nicca's family hasn't set foot in Calhames since her death and have sent no representatives to be present for the Conclaves of

Houses. At most, they allow their senator to be present when the Senate is in session, but their hatred for my House is not hidden."

Soren glanced at Raiah, who was trying her best to get her chubby little fingers around the leather strap slung across his shoulder that held his pauldron and poison sword in place. He prudently took a step back.

"I need to use one of your telegraph machines," Soren said.

"A telephone might be quicker if you have need to speak with the wardens' governor."

Soren made a face. "She'd order me back if I spoke with her."

Vanya shifted Raiah on his hip, adjusting to her wriggling from lots of practice. "Telegraph it is."

Vanya lifted his free hand and curled it around Soren's neck. Soren let himself be reeled in close for a bruising kiss that reminded him of everything he'd missed while in the Wastelands.

Three

SOREN

On the morning of the funeral for Vanya's parents, Soren kept a promise Vanya had asked into his skin the night before.

"Raiah will need to be present for the funeral rites after the prayers are done at the star temple, but I don't want her walking the procession route," Vanya had said.

There were so many risks involved with a crowd of that size that Soren could only say, "Do you want me to stay behind with her?"

"No. I want you to walk with me. You can carry her afterward."

The request had stilled his hands on warm skin, but Soren hadn't said no.

Perhaps he should have. In the light of day, senses not clouded by lust, Soren could see how badly he'd miscalculated in agreeing to Vanya's request. As a warden, he shouldn't be anywhere near such political upheaval. Except a vow hung from his neck that Soren had yet to ask payment for, and the second he did, he knew Vanya would not keep him close.

The funeral rites at the star temple had taken hours. The procession back to the Imperial palace looked to take just as long. Legionnaires lined the route as protection against the crush of people come to say goodbye or good riddance, depending on quietly held allegiances.

The air was thick with incense from the star priests' funerary devices. The smoke blew over those walking behind the twin caissons that trundled down the cobblestone streets, each pulled by a pair of golden *Akhal-Teke* horses.

The bodies of the empress and emperor had been transported from Oeiras by airship days ago, and the length of time the royal mourning period and funeral took left Soren uneasy. Whenever he came upon the dead in the poison fields, he burned the bodies immediately. No sense risking the dead rising into revenants, but apparently the past rulers of Solaria didn't feel the same way. Mourning royalty in Solaria was a grand pageantry that happened more often than in other countries.

Despite it being winter and the plains having withered from the cooler temperatures, people had still found flowers to throw at the caissons. Soren's boots crushed petals and leaves with every step he took, the floral scent mingling with the incense.

He felt out of place, walking at the front of the column which held the *vezirs* or equivalent representative from nearly every major and minor House in Solaria. The senators marched behind them, followed by Legion officers and various civil leaders. The organization of the procession came down to rank and authority. Soren knew he had disrupted every sense of social propriety when Vanya had ordered him to walk with the Houses.

His skin prickled with the weight of unwanted attention, acutely aware of how easy it would be to take a bullet in the back.

"Calm yourself," the *vezir* to Soren's left said quietly in the trade tongue after the dozenth time Soren sneaked a look over his shoulder. "Those of the Houses will not harm you."

"Is that so?" Soren asked just as quietly, his lips barely moving.

The man ducked his head in a pretense of watching where he set his elaborately carved cane on the cobblestone. The action hid the faint smile that twitched his lips beneath the thick mustache framing his mouth. "You are a warden. I have always heard it said your kind is difficult to kill."

Vanya had dressed Soren in Solarian robes that morning in the colors of his House but hadn't been able to convince him to leave all of his weapons behind. The robe was loose enough that Soren could still reach the only pistol he had on him. The *vezir* seemed to understand what the aborted jerk of his hand meant.

"Peace. I and the House of Vikandir mean you nor His Imperial Highness no harm."

Soren blinked at the name, recognizing the House as one whose loyalty to Vanya's was over a century old. "*Vezir* Amir."

"I see you've heard of me."

Soren looked straight ahead, gaze riveted on Vanya's back, watching the way the golden fur lining his crimson mourning cape fluttered in the breeze. "Every warden knows the names of the major Houses and who leads them."

Because it was their duty to report any discrepancies to the people in charge of granting wardens passage to do their jobs. The House of Vikandir held the *vasilyet* in the northeast of Solaria, their seat of power embedded in Karnak. The wardens rarely had issues with that House.

"Your name is becoming known as well."

Soren grimaced. "It doesn't need to be."

"If you hadn't wanted notoriety, then perhaps you shouldn't have saved Vanya's life four years ago. But if that was the case, you would not be here, and someone else would sit upon the Imperial throne."

"You?" Soren couldn't help but ask in a low, biting tone.

Amir smiled wistfully. "It is power of the likes which my House has held several times in the distant past, but it is a costly crown to keep. I would rather my House live than be eradicated."

"So you are loyal, but you do not want to rule."

"The same could be said of you."

"I'm a warden."

"Yet here you walk."

Soren clenched his teeth together and let out a slow breath through his nose.

Here he walked indeed.

The sun was past its zenith when the procession finally wound past the Senate building, aiming for the Imperial palace down the wide boulevard. The trees lining either side were nothing but bare branches from the winter. People had climbed them to sit above the crowd, watching as the caissons with the bodies wrapped in elaborate shrouds rolled past.

The whole ordeal was a precisely choreographed affair that saw the procession be whittled down to only the major Houses by the time they reached the private star temple located on the palace grounds. Legionnaires coordinated everyone else's removal from the procession with military precision, allowing palace servants to guide them away for much-needed refreshments. A feast for the dead was planned for the afternoon, which was probably where everyone else was headed.

Soren remained to stand witness with those chosen few for the last, intimate affair of laying to rest the dead. He wondered what more prayer needed to be said over the bodies before cremation happened. He wondered if they'd burn on an outdoor pyre, witnessed by the guests. In Soren's exploration of the palace over the last few years, he'd never once seen any hint of a crematorium on the palace grounds.

The bearers of the dead removed the coffins from the caissons. The flag of Solaria was wrapped around each one, unmoving in the stiff breeze, much how Vanya looked. Soren studied Vanya's profile while everyone else paid their respects with deep bows as the bearers of the dead walked past.

"I don't agree to the warden's presence," someone behind him said.

"His Imperial Highness has willed it," Amir replied calmly.

"The warden is not welcome and should not be here."

"*I* say who is welcome here. The warden stays," Vanya said without looking back.

In the fraught silence that followed his words, the high priestess of the Star Order in Calhames stepped forward. Her face was hidden by an elaborate headdress and mask that extended away from her skull in gold spikes and starbursts. The bottom edges curled like flames, obscuring her features.

"Now, we lay the dead to rest in the arms of Callisto," she said.

Vanya, Soren, and the *vezirs* of what major Houses that had presented themselves for the funeral followed the high priestess into the private star temple utilized by the Imperial family.

It was like most other temples in Solaria: intricately carved walls on the outside depicting iconography of the star gods, the constellations, and the country's guiding star. Inside, the mosaic floor was a riot of color, the windows made of stained glass, and the frescoes on the inside of the dome brilliantly painted.

The bearers of the dead carried the coffins to the center of the temple, and everyone else could only follow. Soren looked back at the sound of the temple doors being closed and locked by acolytes, barring anyone else from entering.

Raiah's laughter rang through the air, catching Soren's attention. "Papa!"

Waiting for them in front of the altar, held in a star priest's arms, was the Imperial crown princess. She made grasping hands at Vanya, who went to her like a moth to a flame. He murmured to her, words too soft to hear, before carrying her to where Soren stood.

"There are rites I must attend to below. I cannot hold her while I do so," Vanya said.

There were Houses present who should have had the right to guard her more than him. Soren wasn't Solarian, wanted nothing to do with the games the Houses played, but here he was, playing them.

Raiah was a difficult child to say no to, after all.

Soren took her into his arms, propping her onto his left hip so he could more easily reach his pistol. She was a delightful distraction from the collective attention of the *vezirs* standing around, watching the interplay.

"*Vezir* Amir of the House of Vikandir. Will you do me the honor of bearing witness on my daughter's behalf?" Vanya asked, not looking away from Soren.

Amir bowed over his cane, robes rustling softly about his large frame. "It would be the honor of my House to do so, Your Imperial Highness."

Vanya leaned in to kiss Raiah on the cheek, using the gesture to shield the words he spoke to Soren. "When we go below, do not say a word."

Maricol was a harsh mother to love in the poison fields and along the borders wardens guarded. The traditions wardens abided by, and the alchemy that built them, were all geared toward survival. The tradition of a country in mourning was a nuanced dance of prayer Soren didn't know the steps to.

If he had—if any warden had known over the centuries—he would have done anything to stop it all.

For the Houses coveted power above all else, but they kept secrets better than anyone on Maricol.

Soren stared at Vanya, wondering what was meant by that warning but knowing better than to voice his concern where the Houses could hear. He pressed his lips together as the bearers of the dead hitched the coffins they carried from waist height onto their shoulders. The high priestess tapped her golden ceremonial staff against the mosaiced floor.

"Let us pray them unto the stars," she said.

The acolytes surrounding them became a choir, their pitch-perfect voices ringing through the air. The high priestess placed the butt of her ceremonial staff in a spot on the floor in front of the altar that depressed downward from the weight of it. She used both hands to twist the staff. The grind of clockwork gears vibrated beneath Soren's feet, and he reflexively held Raiah tighter to him.

In the center of the temple, the intricate mosaic consisting of the six constellations surrounding a roaring lion's head broke apart. The floor opened up in sections, revealing stairs that led below into darkness. The high priestess twisted her staff a second time, and light flickered into existence in the shadows, gas lamps coming on one after the other.

The bearers of the dead marched toward the stairs. Vanya followed after the high priestess, and Soren had no choice but to join the pared-down procession, Raiah squirming in his arms. The *vezirs* of the major Houses took up the rear as everyone descended into a cold, carved-out space of earth that resolved itself into underground corridors and spaces filled with statues and coffins.

So many coffins.

The interlocking light gray stone was smooth beneath his feet and along the walls, unpainted save for within each open tomb where an external iron coffin lay. Those stone walls were painted with the emblem of whichever House had held the throne for the historical time neatly carved above. The curved ceilings were painted like the night sky, with thousands of tiny golden flecks resembling stars dotting the frescoes and catching the light from gas lamps.

While the paintings might have been beautiful, there was nothing beautiful about what they watched over.

Soren heard the scratching first as the procession passed down the halls, faint scrapes he could have passed off as scurrying rats. But he'd seen no sign of rodents, and when the faint, rasping sound started up the farther they got away from the entrance, he could no longer pretend to not know what was buried in the tombs.

Bodies of the royal dead turned into revenants, their bones and embalmed flesh trapped for eternity.

And there were hundreds of them buried in the royal crypt beneath the palace.

Soren clenched his teeth so hard his jaw ached, heart beating a furious drumbeat against his ribs. This place was anathema to the rigid tradition that every country adhered to regarding the dead. Everyone who died was cremated, their deaths added to genealogies and their names to the memory walls that encircled every columbarium.

Solaria was a country born out of the Dying Times during the Great Separation beginning in 301 A.O.S., along with all the other countries. That was several thousand years of the Imperial throne being in existence. Several thousand years to collect the country's ruling dead.

And Vanya, with his House having held the Imperial throne for the last few hundred years, must have known how the royal dead were handled. Every major House that had ever held it must have known, and the wardens had been kept in the dark about an unguarded border between the living and the dead for countless generations.

This was worse than the grave of Rixham, because at least Rixham was walled off and watched over by wardens, and would be until the spores finally faded from the last revenant. Here, the crypt was unguarded, and the key held by the high priestess was too easy to steal and duplicate. The temple above was a cover, not a lock.

What have the Houses done?

The thought tumbled through Soren's mind as the procession continued through the winding hallways of the crypt. Solaria had broken the Poison Accords, perhaps since their very inception, and the cost of that would be a punishment no governing body liked to contemplate.

Solaria would be required to cover the tithes for every country for the equivalent number of years they'd broken the Poison Accords. That was hundreds and hundreds of people Solaria would have to tithe for decades to come. An oversight committee of wardens would need to be set up to preside over permanent laws that could not be overturned by any future governing body or monarch on how the dead were handled.

No ruler liked to be overruled, but then again, Soren could not recall at any point in history where a country had broken the Poison Accords so acutely, so dangerously.

Revenants had been a threat since the stars fell to Maricol and guided their ancestors home. For all the progress wardens had made in the poison fields, the spores had never been eradicated. The Poison Accords had been created for a reason, and that reason was to keep the living alive and make sure the dead had no chance to rise.

No wonder Vanya had told Soren not to speak while they walked through a nightmare created by Solaria's past and present rulers.

The procession finally stopped in front of an empty tomb that held two iron coffins on a low dais. Soren stayed silent through the burial ceremony performed by the high priestess that saw the bearers of the dead lower the wooden coffins inside the larger metal ones. The heavy metal covering was lowered in place again, but Soren didn't see any locking mechanism that would secure it.

Vanya stepped forward, the golden circlet he wore glittering against his dark hair and skin, a flash of brightness in the low-lit crypt. "*Vezir* Amir, if you would stand as witness."

The *vezir* of the House of Vikandir stepped forward to stand beside Soren and Raiah. "Bound as my House is to the House of Sa'Liandel through blood, I can attest that all surviving members of the ruling House are present."

The high priestess rapped her staff lightly against the stone floor. "It shall be recorded."

Vanya raised his hands, palms up, and called forth starfire.

Soren felt the flow from the aether, the way it made the hair on his skin stand up with the buzzing power of the magic Vanya commanded. It tugged at something buried deep inside him, trying to draw it to the surface, and Soren wrenched his focus away from that terrible temptation, that biting need he wasn't allowed to want or have.

Starfire leapt from Vanya's hands, cascading over the edge of the iron coffin where the covering and base met. The heat of the starfire made sweat trickle down Soren's skin despite the cool temperature of the crypt. It grew in intensity, forcing him to step back and around the opening of the tomb to shield Raiah.

He peered around the corner, watching as Vanya sealed the iron coffins that contained his parents' bodies, welding both shut with starfire. The metal along the edges glowed orange after the starfire faded away. Four acolytes moved to stand at the head and foot of the iron coffins to keep watch. For how long, Soren didn't know.

Raiah squirmed in Soren's arms, but he refused to put her down.

Only when Vanya turned and left the tomb, coming toward them, did Soren finally give her up. She tumbled into her father's waiting arms, wrapping her own small ones around his neck.

Soren met Vanya's gaze and said nothing as he'd been asked. Then he turned and left the way the Houses had come, fury and fear making his fingers tremble where they were curled tight against his palms.

Four

VANYA

The traditional gifts of mourning from the Houses crowded the table in Vanya's private living area within the royal wing of the palace. The redecoration was nearly complete under Alida's watchful eye. All hints of his parents' life had been boxed up and stored away, because the only way to show the strength of the House of Sa'Liandel was to move forward. Grief had no place in politics.

Anger, though, that was a familiar passion.

A hint of it stirred in Vanya when he finally left his bedroom, body servants still fussing at the fit of his elaborate robes, and found Soren not wearing the robes he'd been given for the feast.

"Why aren't you ready?" Vanya demanded.

Soren sat on a chaise in his warden uniform, flipping a fountain pen between his fingers. The notepad resting on the cushion beside him was opened on a blank page. Those sharp gray eyes slid away from Vanya to the servants still orbiting around his royal person.

"I need to speak with you alone," Soren said.

It wasn't phrased as a request but an order. More than one *praetoria* legionnaire standing guard in the room scowled at the show of disrespect.

Vanya gestured in the direction of the door. "Everyone, leave us."

The servants left without a backward glance, while the legion-naires were slower to make their exit. The arched door to the private living area finally closed with a sharp sound that reminded Vanya too much of the metal coffins he'd buried his parents in.

Soren didn't move from the chaise. He carefully set aside the fountain pen, keeping his attention on Vanya. "You bury your dead."

Vanya grimaced. He supposed it was too much to hope that Soren would hold his tongue until after the feast. "Every House who has ever sat on the Imperial throne does so. It is part of how we worship our goddess of death. The records go back to our country's founding."

"There are revenants in those tombs, Vanya."

He knew that. He'd known that since he'd followed his mother and father into the crypt when he was eight years old to bury Iosiv. He'd stood in his brother's tomb several times over the years, offering up prayers and trying not to think about the terrible scratching sound that came from the iron coffin his brother's body resided in.

Sometimes the wind carried spores. Sometimes it didn't. One never knew which ancestor would dance among the stars and which would endlessly claw at a prison in the dark.

"Starfire seals the dead in their final resting place. None have ever risen."

Soren stood in a fluid motion, anger in every line of his body. It radiated off him with an intensity Vanya could almost feel, a crackle to the air that reminded him of the aether.

"You're telling me Solaria has been breaking the Poison Accords for centuries and none of you care about the threat buried beneath your feet?" Soren stepped into Vanya's personal space in a way no one else would ever dare, face flushed with anger rather than pleasure, the difference notable. "You have an unguarded border in that crypt that puts your entire capital at risk!"

Vanya grabbed Soren by the elbow, drawing him in. "The star temple on the palace grounds is watched around the clock by star priests and *praetoria* legionnaires. It has *never* gone unguarded."

Soren pressed his hand against Vanya's chest, shoving him backward with a strength that forced distance between them. "A warden has never walked that border."

"You said it yourself. Our tradition goes against the Poison Accords, but that is how we've always prayed to our goddess of death. We bury our royal dead in honor of Callisto. The wardens were never supposed to know."

Soren laughed harshly, yanking his arm free from Vanya's grip. "Then why show me?"

Vanya's gaze strayed from Soren to the table that overflowed with mourning gifts from the Houses. "Do you know it is tradition for the Houses to provide a star cake for the royal altar of the dead when a ruler passes away? Every House has one delivered by a servant who wears no indication of the House they serve in their clothing. The offerings are meant to be eaten. No one ever partakes. Some are poisoned. Some are not. But the House that sits upon the Imperial throne will never know which House sent which cake. We never know where their true loyalty lies."

"Gifts that kill are no gifts."

"We would not be Solarians if we weren't trying to kill each other." Vanya looked back at Soren, meeting that steely gray-eyed gaze without blinking. "I asked you to come below because of what is happening in the north."

"Of Solaria?"

"No. *North*, in Ashion and Daijal." Soren went still in a way that made Vanya frown. "My spies have brought back rumors of a death-defying machine. I do not know if it is real or what it does. What I do know is that our border with Daijal is overseen by the House of Kimathi, and I don't trust them to do right by Solaria."

"Wardens have mapped more poison fields in the northwest of Solaria in the last decade than we have in a hundred years prior. You aren't wrong to worry, but if you know they're a problem, then you should do something about them."

Vanya hissed out a breath between his clenched teeth. "I'm aware of the reports you bring, but you must understand my position. My parents are *dead*. I'm to be crowned emperor tomorrow. My daughter is my only heir, but her mother was of the House of Kimathi. The assassins that targeted my parents did not target Raiah or I. It has been two years since Nicca's death, and Joelle has not called for a blood feud. If I die and Raiah lives, the House of Kimathi takes the Imperial throne regardless of which House claims my murder."

"Then don't die."

"My mother took what debts are owed to our House to her grave. They do not fall to me. The Houses who stood with mine before now may no longer do so. I do not have time to focus on what is happening in the *vasilyet* the House of Kimathi governs when I must negotiate loyalty from all the rest in order to secure my power."

"None of this explains why you showed me the crypts. I'm a warden, Vanya. You must know I have to report to my governor about this. Even the other *vezirs* knew I shouldn't have been down there."

Vanya closed the scant distance between them, cupping Soren's face in both hands. The flush of anger to his cheeks had warmed his skin, and Vanya rubbed his thumbs over the lingering heat.

"The House of Kimathi has ruled before and knows about the crypts. They weren't present today because they have not set foot in Calhames since Nicca died. They send their senator, and that is all. I don't trust them with my country's borders, and I don't trust them with my country's dead. Someone outside the Houses needs to know the threat Joelle and her House represent. Whatever machine my spies are searching for, if it deals with the dead in any way, Solaria has two cities' worth I would not see fall under the House of Kimathi's control to bargain with."

Soren licked his lips, letting out a slow breath that ghosted between Vanya's wrists. "The major Houses know you brought a warden to the crypts. You put a target on my back."

"That wasn't my intention."

"Then what *was* your intention?"

"To get you to stay."

It wasn't a truth Vanya would have given voice to before he'd received his parents' bodies in the airfields days ago. He'd told himself since the train wreck where they'd met he had no need of the comfort

Soren provided him. Only now, with the Houses circling and Daijal never a country to be trusted, Vanya found himself wanting to rely on someone he shouldn't.

Soren's expression twisted, some mix of emotion Vanya couldn't read crossing the younger man's face. "I'm a warden. My job is to guard the borders."

"You said it yourself that the crypts are a border. So guard it here, with me."

Soren jerked out of his grip, gray eyes dark like a storm. He said nothing as he turned on his heel and stalked to the door.

"Soren, wait."

Vanya might have been a prince, about to be crowned an emperor, bowed to by every Solarian alive, but he had no power over a warden. Soren reminded him of that fact by walking away, leaving Vanya to face the Houses at the feast of the dead alone.

Five

TERILYN

"Your escort is here for your protection. You will have access to the quarry, the laboratory, and your rooms in the barracks. Interaction with the workers outside required communication is forbidden," the Solarian quarry master said in the trade tongue upon their arrival at the makeshift airfield in what seemed like the middle of nowhere in Solaria.

"I was promised access when and where I liked, just like last time," Samuel Fletcher said while looking down his nose at the other man. Which was a feat in and of itself, considering the highly sought-after inventor was inches shorter than the Solarian who had greeted them.

"We've had increased forays from wardens in the area lately. The restrictions are necessary to keep them from discovering our work." The quarry master turned and inclined his head at Terilyn, giving her a degree of respect he hadn't shown her travel companions. "I hope you understand the precautions, my lady."

Terilyn nodded, keeping her expression serene. "They are acceptable."

Samuel scowled, drawing himself up to his full height and puffing out his chest. Terilyn let her attention rest on him and wasn't surprised when he wilted beneath her icy stare. Unlike Wyatt Lehan, the silent, haunted-eyed inventor Samuel had brought along with him, Terilyn had no fear of his social standing. She was Eimarille's lady-in-waiting in public, lover in private, and personal Blade. Her status was tied to Eimarille's, and Samuel could not match it.

"We will abide to maintain secrecy," Terilyn said.

Terilyn was here in Solaria on behalf of Eimarille, working to ensure Eimarille's orders were enacted. They'd contracted with Samuel because they'd needed to, but eventually, the man would outlive his usefulness.

Samuel was an experienced inventor, part of a family whose bloodline had been elevated into the nobility genealogies some years ago. He was of the opinion that gave him unfettered power, and Terilyn took pleasure in making him learn otherwise.

If they didn't need him still, Terilyn would gladly slide a knife between Samuel's ribs, into his heart, and leave him in the poison fields. At nineteen, Wyatt was a promising inventor who didn't have the household name Samuel did, but whom Eimarille hoped to train up to act as their liaison at the laboratory here. It was far easier to control someone young and in fear of their position and debt over someone with an inflated sense of ego.

"Very well," Samuel finally huffed out. "Show us to our quarters so my assistant may unload our things."

He made a sharp gesture at Wyatt, who reached behind him to grab the handle of the motorized cart that held numerous travel trunks. Activating the miniaturized steam engine with a push of a button, Wyatt gave the cart a firm tug to get it moving. Terilyn watched him steer it after Samuel and followed them at a sedate pace toward the row of barracks farther down the dusty street.

The quarry master fell into step beside her, eyes on Samuel. "The *vezir* despises that one."

Terilyn hummed softly. "Samuel has his uses."

So did the *vezir*, though Joelle always liked to think she was the one using them. Eimarille had reached out to Joelle some years ago because the House of Kimathi was one of the easier noble bloodlines subverted for their cause.

Whatever sort of alliance Joelle thought she'd made with Eimarille, it wasn't truthful. Terilyn knew Eimarille offered conditional support because destabilizing the Houses would keep Solaria busy while they took back Ashion. The *vasilyet* Joelle governed would eventually, with time, come under Daijal rule—as would the rest of Solaria and the entirety of the continent.

The Twilight Star had decreed it, after all.

Eimarille was to be queen in this Age of Progress as it turned into a new Age, and Terilyn would stand by her side always.

Until then, Terilyn would do her queen's bidding. If that meant ensuring each of the death-defying machines remained functioning, then she would cross borders to do so.

It wasn't often Terilyn left Eimarille's side. When she had to, they gave excuses that the Star Order required Terilyn's presence for further training. The lie about a brief sabbatical allowed for Terilyn to travel where Eimarille couldn't, acting as her queen's voice. She'd visited every country on the continent, stood in the poison fields, killed those who needed removing, and enslaved others that were useful.

Her last excursion had taken her to Matriskav, her birth country's capital. Unlike that icy city, Thornton was a tiny frontier town in the Southern Plains of Solaria, southwest of Bellingham, and walled off from the grasslands by metal fencing. It was as far removed from the cold of the north as one could possibly be.

Outside the town's wall was the Thornton Quarry, a venture started fifty years ago before going idle two decades after its inception. The recent resurgence of work in the area had little to do with mining and everything to do with why they'd all flown south on false papers.

Terilyn waited outside the barracks while Wyatt unloaded some of the travel trunks. Samuel threw a fit about the quality of his accommodation—namely, the lack of it—but the quarry master was unmoved. Terilyn ignored the byplay, more interested in the townspeople curiously watching the display of bad manners. She was ever on guard against potential threats, and while she was dressed as a Solarian, one could never be too careful.

Once Wyatt finished, the quarry master flagged down several workers to load the remaining trunks onto a truck. In the process, one clearly marked fragile was nearly dropped, and Samuel almost had an apoplexy.

"Watch it!" Wyatt called out frantically.

Terilyn stayed out of the way while the workers grappled with the trunk and got it lashed down. The quarry master barked out orders to his people while Samuel merely got in the way. When he was uncere-moniously shoved back for the third time, nearly falling on his ass in a most unbecoming way, Terilyn closed the distance between them.

She stood in front of him, staring into his reddened and sweaty face, having slipped one hand into her robe's pocket to access the knife strapped to her thigh. "You are not in charge. Remember that, Mr. Fletcher."

He went, if possible, even more purple, but the anger writ clear across his face was never given voice to. His gaze flicked down to her hand, hidden in the folds of the robe, and the red faded to a sickly white. Memory served him well enough in that moment, and he held his tongue.

Samuel swallowed hard before rallying himself in the face of Teri-lyn's pointed dismissal. He stepped past her, shoulders curved in a vaguely defensive way. "Let them handle the trunks, Wyatt. We'll be taking the motor carriage to the quarry."

The motor carriage in question had been outfitted with rugged tires that raised the frame of the vehicle higher than those driven in a city. The quarry master got behind the wheel of the truck, revving the engine. Terilyn chose to join him in that vehicle rather than the one Samuel picked.

The small convoy left the safety of the walled-off town and drove down a bumpy gravel road to the edge of the quarry several miles away. There were two ways down into the quarry: a lift for personnel purposes, and the winding road used to move machines and stone. The pit wasn't their destination, but rather, the fenced-off processing factory and the warehouses built beside it, hiding a specialized laboratory.

Terilyn climbed out of the truck, shielding her eyes against the sun with one hand as she took in the area. Workers swarmed the truck to empty it of cargo. Everything was set on several motorized carts, of which Wyatt took charge of without needing to be told.

"Hurry up," Samuel called out as he headed toward the open bay door of the factory. Workers armed with pistols and shotguns stood guard at the entrance, nodding at the quarry master in greeting as their group approached.

The quarry master gestured at Terilyn. "The contract holder's representative is here with a personnel and equipment delivery. You remember the inventor. He and his assistant are to be granted full access to the quarry and laboratory while here."

The guards merely nodded but said nothing, allowing everyone to enter with the motorized carts. Terilyn blinked rapidly to adjust her eyesight to the shaded interior.

Gas lamps burned from the ceiling, the illumination kinder on her eyes than the winter sunlight. The entirety of the factory floor had once been used to process stone. Now, those machines were all gone. In their place was an enormous machine that reminded Terilyn of a spider sitting in a web with all the piping and coils that twisted everywhere. Clarion crystals glowing in shades that ranged from carnelian to a yellow gold powered pistons that pumped within the depths of the machine.

The center bulk of the machine was a chamber made out of brass hexagonal plates, shaped into a large dome with a set of doors on opposite sides. Clear tubes connected to that center portion, pumping green-tinged gas into the chamber.

One set of chamber doors was easily accessible by laboratory workers. The other set of doors opened up into a walled-off pen that Terilyn couldn't see into. Workers paced around the pen in the catwalks above, the shotguns in their hands pointed at whatever was kept imprisoned below.

Around them, packed into cages, were dozens and dozens of debt slaves.

"I see the banking laws have helped to keep you well-stocked," Terilyn mused.

A woman turned away from the machine's controls. "Well enough, though I'll never say no to a shipment of product."

The woman in dusty coveralls, with a pair of elaborate goggles pushed on top of her head, crossed the laboratory floor to meet them as the bay door was winched shut. She was older than Wyatt but younger than Samuel, with blonde curls trimmed short around a thin face. Terilyn didn't notice the mechanical prosthetic until she was closer, thinking at first it was a glove.

Her right hand was made out of metal rods and clockwork gears. The contraption was strapped to her forearm, powered by chips of clarion crystal, the metal engraved with a spell. The fingers moved easily enough when she planted that hand on one hip, tendrils of magic coiling in the gears.

"I wasn't expecting you for another day," she said to Samuel.

"So quick to berate, Poppy. It shouldn't matter if I'm a day early or a day late. I'm here, and I expect an update," Samuel said with all the haughtiness of a man used to being obeyed.

"We both do," Terilyn added, prompting Samuel to snap his mouth shut.

Poppy made a clicking sound with her tongue, not cowed by Samuel's presence at all. She turned her attention to Terilyn, rightly inferring who was in charge. "I take it you're our rich benefactor?"

"I represent them."

"I'm in the middle of a transmutation process right now. I can't power down the machine for your upgrade until it's finished."

"I was told the upgrade will take several days. I'd like to see the results of this batch before we get started."

Poppy pursed her lips. "You and your guests will all need to put on some safety gear when it's time to open the chamber doors."

"We are no guests. Mr. Fletcher works for my benefactor, and his apprentice will be our liaison here. He will be in charge of applying any further upgrades to this particular death-defying machine."

Poppy stiffened at her words. "I need no oversight, especially not from someone half my age."

Terilyn bared her teeth in a smile. "What you want doesn't matter. You're being paid handsomely to do a job that my benefactor oversees. I am here to ensure you do it correctly."

Her tone was mild enough, but whatever threat Poppy saw in Terilyn's eyes was enough to make the other woman swallow nervously. "Of course."

"Mr. Fletcher's presence is required in Daijal and he cannot keep making trips down here while we are in transition. Wyatt will report back to him personally regarding the progress of fine-tuning the death-defying machine's applications while you continue doing the job you are being paid so handsomely for."

Poppy pursed her lips before nodding grudgingly. "As you say."

She wasn't savvy enough when it came to politics to hide her annoyance. Terilyn could see it in her face, the way she clenched her jaw. Unlike Samuel, she didn't press the issue, though she still seemed displeased when she stalked back to her work area.

Terilyn trailed after her, allowing Samuel to overtake her to the control panel. Wyatt, she noticed, remained hovering on the outskirts of their little group, ever watchful but not intruding. He'd need to learn to make his presence known if he was going to be working at the quarry.

She turned her attention back to the analytical engine the control panel was erected around. Terilyn wasn't gifted with knowing the intricacies of engineering. She was an assassin, not an inventor. But even without that knowledge, it was interesting to see what the design she and Eimarille had gone over some years ago had ultimately become.

"How has production been?" Terilyn asked.

"Well within initial output." Poppy stared at the control panel before pressing a few buttons. "We've found it best if the product is newly dead before initiating the transmutation process. The spores' activation period works better that way."

"How long does the transmutation process currently take?"

"We've cut it down from three days to one and a half days. I started this latest batch yesterday."

Samuel curled his fingers over the lapels of his day jacket, glancing at Terilyn. "The upgrade should shorten that timeframe. We've discovered a new pattern cut for clarion crystals that speeds up the spores' propagation period when a magician applies the aether to the device. We've been implementing it up north with spectacular results. I'm eager to duplicate it here."

"We're a little short on magicians. The last one you sent got bitten when he failed to adhere to the safety protocols in place and a revenant escaped the pen."

Terilyn frowned. "What happened to him?"

"He ended up becoming part of the experiment rather than assisting with it," Poppy said dryly before glancing over her shoulder at Wyatt, gaze cool. "I do hope you listen better than your predecessor."

"Of course," Wyatt replied evenly.

"What of wardens? Have you had to deal with many?" Terilyn asked.

Poppy shrugged, flipping a couple of toggles and twisting a dial. "Here and there. The ones that demand the right to come inside our walls end up in the chamber."

"You need to be careful about that. We don't need scrutiny from the wardens."

"*Vezir* Joelle has promised to distract them. It's what some of the revenants will be used for."

"The wardens are one issue. Lack of a magician is something else entirely."

Terilyn let a hint of dissatisfaction filter into her voice, and she watched how Poppy's shoulders tightened before she forcibly relaxed. "It happened earlier this week. I sent a coded telegram to New Haven, but you must have already departed."

"I'll procure you another one when I return to Daijal. Unfortunately, the bargain we have with the House of Kimathi states we cannot use Solarian citizens for any part of this experiment other than as cover with the quarry work."

"We'll make do until the replacement arrives."

Samuel frowned, reaching out to tap his fingers against the edge of the control panel. "How much longer will the transmutation process take?"

Poppy pulled a pocket watch from her coveralls and thumbed it open. "At least another hour for this one."

"Plenty of time for us to go over the new blueprints."

Terilyn had no part in that conversation, though she sat with the trio while Samuel spread the blueprints of the death-defying machine out on a worktable. The mechanics of it all were different than the alchemy she witnessed used by the *Klovod*. That still, to an extent, dealt with the living.

This machine only dealt with the dead.

An hour later, Terilyn stood upon the catwalk with Samuel, Poppy, and Wyatt, watching as the second set of doors to the death-defying machine's chamber were opened.

"Wonderful, wonderful. We'll corral these ones and ship them back to Daijal and let them loose on the eastern border. For now, no more revenants will be created until the upgrade is complete," Samuel said as they watched the walking dead stumble about the holding pen below.

Terilyn never thought this would be her road—making a mockery of the Star Order's teachings—but Innes had promised Eimarille a new path forward. She had faith in her queen and the Midnight Star that both would guide her true.

Six

VANYA

The ceremonial bathhouse on the star temple grounds was a place of unparalleled beauty that had washed away the sins of every emperor and empress who claimed the Imperial throne. Intricately carved white stone walls and pillars supported a golden dome painted around the base with Callisto's constellation. Inside, the inner dome was covered in frescoes depicting daily Solarian life while the walls and floor were covered in exquisite mosaics.

The mosaics on the floor glittered from gold and pearl pieces, the color swirling up the walls into richer shades. Only one pool filled the space below the dome, its warm waters hitting waist-deep. The edges of the pool were painted gold, giving it a sun-like look.

Vanya stood in the center of the pool, scented oil and fragrant flower petals covering the water until one couldn't see the bottom. Several acolytes from the star temple were in the water with him, heads bowed in supplication as they sang in quiet voices. Their thin white shifts had become saturated from the water they waded through as they ritualistically washed Vanya's body clean for his coronation.

An altar made out of white marble flecked with gold and dedicated to Callisto overlooked the pool. All the oils and perfumes and other accoutrements required for the ritual cleansing were set up on the table below the shrine. A star priest stood in front of it, his strong tenor leading the prayer songs the acolytes gave voice to.

Vanya allowed himself to be turned and guided by the hands drifting over his skin, his body not his own in that moment as the ceremonial ablutions were tended to. The oil being rubbed into his skin held a scent that reminded him of his mother—floral and spice that would fade slowly. Vanya had to bite the inside of his cheek to stop himself from asking it be washed off.

His coronation was a precisely scheduled set of ceremonies that had begun with dawn prayers at the royal family's star temple. Vanya had then been escorted from the palace to Calhames' main star temple for the cleansing ritual. When it was finished, he would be dressed in an elaborate set of coronation robes before being escorted into the adjacent star temple for the confirmation prayers. From there he would be driven to the Senate in the city center, where the coronation would happen.

Vanya wished the day wasn't happening at all, so he welcomed the disruption Soren provided when the warden entered the bathhouse uninvited. The prayer song broke off at Soren's appearance. He was followed by a frantic acolyte who bowed apologetically to the room at large.

"Forgive me, Your Imperial Highness, but I could not stop him," the acolyte said.

Vanya hadn't seen Soren since he walked away after the burial yesterday. He'd slept alone last night, when he'd slept at all, and had thought Soren had left without saying goodbye. A first in the years Soren had been visiting him, and one Vanya despised. He despised just as much the traitorous lurch in his chest that came with knowing Soren hadn't left him after all.

"We need to talk," Soren said.

"We're in the middle of a ceremony. You shouldn't be here," the star priest snapped.

"Vanya gave me right of passage anywhere he is. The legionnaires had to let me in."

Vanya tugged his arms free from the acolytes who had paused in their ministrations. "I'll speak with the warden alone."

The star priest opened his mouth as if to argue, but one slashing look from Vanya made him hold his tongue. The acolytes in the pool with Vanya glided toward the stairs off to the side and exited the pool. Their soaked gowns clung to their skin as they walked away, petals falling away to the tiled floor.

Vanya kept his eyes on Soren, neither of them speaking until they were alone. The only sound between them was that of the faint hum from the heaters and pumps beneath the bathhouse. Vanya spread his fingers over the top of the water, petals clinging to his oiled skin.

"I thought you'd left," Vanya said.

Soren crossed his arms over his chest. "I was going to."

"Why didn't you?"

Soren's mouth twisted and he didn't speak for half a minute. "You have an unguarded border. It doesn't matter if the tombs are welded shut with starfire. A warden needs to guard it."

"So guard it. I will not argue with you on that."

"The wardens' governor is responsible for assigning border patrols."

"And did you inform her of what I showed you?"

"I called her about the crypts and the state of the Houses early this morning."

Vanya glided toward the steps to exit the pool, feeling Soren's gaze on him as he walked naked over to the altar where the ceremonial bathing robe was laid out. Tradition dictated a star priest should dress him, but Vanya didn't call back any who had left. He pulled on the crimson robe edged in gold to ward off the faint chill from leaving the warm waters of the pool. He didn't belt it, which caused the front edges to fall open, hiding nothing.

When he turned to face Soren, he found the warden walking toward him around the pool. Vanya watched him approach, seeing the glint of a gold chain beneath the open collar of his shirt. Even now, Soren hadn't removed the vow.

Soren came to a stop beside Vanya, head tipped back some to look him in the eye. "I asked the governor to hold off on announcing sanctions against Solaria."

Vanya arched an eyebrow. "Did you?"

"Wardens aren't meant for politics. We aren't supposed to interfere with matters of state, but when governments put the borders at risk, we are obligated to respond. We've charted the rise in revenants in the northwest of Solaria, as well as in Daijal and Ashion. I told the governor the House of Kimathi can't be trusted and that any move toward sanctions against Solaria as a whole will make it more difficult to find out what's going on in that *vasilyet*."

"Did your governor agree with your reasoning?"

Soren nodded slowly. "She told me to stay and guard the border between the living and the dead beneath your palace. She won't initiate the sanctions clause in the Poison Accords just yet. But Vanya, you have to know your country will be punished with them in the future."

"I'm well aware of what Solaria will owe. We'll pay the tithes if I sit on the Imperial throne. If another House rules in my stead one day, then it will be up to them to pay. If they refuse to do so, I know you wardens will hold them accountable. That's why I brought you down into the crypts yesterday."

"I don't appreciate being manipulated. You could have just told me."

"Would you have believed me? Would you have understood such a threat if you hadn't seen it with your own eyes?"

Soren took a half step closer, eyes flashing with the same sort of anger Vanya remembered from yesterday. "Don't play your House games with me."

"Such games are all I know."

"Vanya."

Vanya reached out and hooked his fingers beneath the chain Soren wore, pulling out the roaring lion head medallion. He slid it open, revealing the dried blood still smeared over the metal there from the vow he'd given several years ago.

"You ask things of me for your duty but never for me to pay you what is owed. Will you have me pay it now when I am still a prince or in several hours' time when I am crowned emperor?"

Soren pulled the medallion free from Vanya's grip. He snapped it closed before tucking it beneath his shirt and vest. "I've told you for years you don't owe me anything."

"Yet you still wear my vow." Vanya settled his hand against the side of Soren's throat, thumb pressing into the hinge of his jaw. "You still come to me. Why?"

Soren's gaze tracked up and down Vanya's body, lips parting slightly as his tongue flicked out to wet them. "You know why."

"Would you still come to me without the vow or a border to guard or reports to deliver?"

"Wardens exist to guard. We're not supposed to want, not the way I want you, even when you do something so idiotically stupid as break the Poison Accords because of *tradition*."

The aggravation in his voice made Vanya's lips twitch. "So I'm an exception."

Whatever bit of mirth that had been creeping into Soren's gaze fled at that statement. "Exceptions are a dangerous weakness for a warden."

Vanya slid his hand up to cradle Soren's jaw. "I won't be a weakness."

"You already are, princeling."

Soren gripped the edges of Vanya's ceremonial bathing robe and tugged him closer, rising up on his toes to slant his mouth over Vanya's to silence any protest. Vanya tightened his grip on Soren's throat, forcing his head to a better angle that allowed him to deepen the kiss. He licked his way into Soren's mouth and tried to breathe for both of them. When they finally broke apart, Vanya realized his fingers were pressing bruises into Soren's fair skin.

"Guard your border for however long you must, but you'll stay with me while you do so," Vanya said.

Soren splayed his fingers over Vanya's chest, swallowing tightly against his grip. "You focus on the future with the Houses. I'll focus on your past mistakes."

Vanya thought of Iosiv and his parents and Nicca and the buried dead scratching at their iron tombs. He thought of the quiet killer poison he'd swallowed on that train to Bellingham and the chance he'd chased it with at Soren's urging.

What might have been, what could have been, wouldn't have seen Vanya walk into the star temple later that morning. But that winding road led him to kneel before the high priestess and accept the crown his mother had once worn to thunderous applause that was meaningless. The senators and House representatives weren't applauding his ascension so much as they were applauding his hopeful demise.

As he turned to face the congregation of *vezirs*, senators, military officers, ambassadors, foreign dignitaries, the press, and others given invitations to the coronation, Vanya forced himself to smile. The gold crown was heavy on his head as he raised his hands in front of him, calling forth starfire.

It formed between his curved hands like molten gold, magic of a strength few could wield. Starfire curled around his fingers and palms, drifting around his wrists as he proved he had the right to rule how the star gods had decreed at the birth of their country.

The high priestess rapped her ceremonial staff on the floor, using a voice amplifier to call out, "By authority of the Dawn Star, in her graciousness, the Star Order acknowledges His Imperial Majesty Vanya of the House of Sa'Liandel, holder of the Imperial throne, ruler of Solaria. Long live the emperor."

The answer to that announcement was an acknowledging roar as the crowd stood from their seats. The Solarians in the audience bowed, as did the foreigners. The only one who didn't bow in that sea of people was Soren, seated in the first row reserved for the family and close allies of the new ruler. The House of Vikandir took up the majority of that row, but Vanya only had eyes for Soren.

Which was why he didn't see the assassin until it was nearly too late.

As Vanya stepped down from the altar, the crowd surged, and someone screamed, *"Gun!"*

The *praetoria* legionnaires around the dais rushed forward, seeking to protect him as the *crack* of a pistol discharging echoed in the star temple. Screams replaced the cheers as the crowd panicked and rushed for the exit at the rear of the temple. The legionnaires surrounded him in a flurry. One raised his wand to cast a shield spell that erected a wall of magic between them and the panicked audience, hexagonal shapes glowing in the air.

"Come with us, Your Imperial Majesty," one of the legionnaires barked at him.

The legionnaires whose sole duty was to protect the Imperial throne and whoever sat upon it would do their duty and get him to safety. Only Vanya refused to start his reign cowering in what passed for safety.

And he wasn't leaving without his daughter.

"Where is Raiah?" Vanya snapped as he was forcibly dragged aside, surrounded by legionnaires. "Raiah!"

She'd been left in Alida's care under Amir's watchful eye since the House of Kimathi had refused to send any representative, not even their senator, to his coronation. Vanya looked at the bench she should have been in, but he didn't see his daughter or her minders.

"*Raiah!*" he shouted again, a sickening sort of fear making his chest hurt.

The *praetoria* legionnaires assigned guard duty during the coronation had overtaken the crowd. A cluster of legionnaires was detaining the shooter in the aisle, but they missed the woman who stepped onto a bench, her robes indicating no House affiliation, but the pistol in her hand was all the proof of where her loyalty didn't lie.

Her arm moved in an arc, pistol aimed unerringly in Vanya's direction, but she never got the shot off.

Soren got his off first.

The warden's bullet found its home in the center of her face, exiting out the back of her head with an explosion of blood and brain matter. More bullets tore through her flesh barely half a second later. The would-be assassin fell over, body jerking from the bullets still tearing through her.

Vanya's attention was riveted on Soren as the warden turned to face him, Raiah held close in one arm, his daughter's face tucked tightly against Soren's throat. Relief coursed through Vanya so quickly he staggered, causing several legionnaires to look at him in a panic.

"Your Imperial Majesty!" one of them cried out.

Vanya violently shrugged off their hands, trying to push his way toward Soren and Raiah. "I'm fine."

The *praetoria* legionnaires refused to move. A tall woman with auburn hair shot him a fierce look from beneath her *effiyeh*. "Stay *here*. We can't protect you if you run off, Your Imperial Majesty."

The chaos of the attack was dying down, with legionnaires and quite a few acolytes forcibly bringing everyone to order. Vanya had eyes for none of it, all his attention riveted on Soren and Raiah as the warden approached with his daughter.

"Lower the shield," Vanya snapped.

The hexagonal shapes parted with sharp little snaps down the center, allowing Soren to step through with Raiah. Vanya could hear his daughter crying, her sobs muffled against Soren's body.

The *praetoria* legionnaires moved to bring Soren and Raiah into their circle of protection as the shield expanded around them. Vanya reached for Raiah, pulling his daughter into his arms with a shaky sigh of relief. He kissed the top of her head, holding her close.

"Thank you," Vanya rasped.

"I told Alida to take cover under the bench. Raiah didn't want to go," Soren said.

Vanya freed one hand to grab Soren above the elbow, pulling him closer. "You're all right?"

Soren rolled his eyes. "I wasn't their target. I thought you said everyone would be screened for weapons before being allowed inside?"

"They should have been." The only people allowed to carry weapons of any sort during the coronation—pistols or wands or knives—were the high priestess, legionnaires, and Soren.

Soren nodded, gray eyes dark. "I'll check the bodies."

Vanya tightened his hold on the other man. "You should stay here."

"I guard the borders, remember? And the dead will always belong there."

It was a pointed reminder of the argument they'd recently had, and Vanya could only let him go. The legionnaire magician parted the shield again, and Soren slipped away.

Vanya steadied himself, focusing on Raiah to try to get her to stop crying. A minute or so later, the shield parted again and Alida stepped through, hair a mess and wild-eyed from fear. She bowed shakily once past the legionnaires.

"I'm sorry I couldn't protect her," Alida said, gaze downcast, nearly crying.

Vanya shook his head, knowing that in a fight, Soren was the only one who could have got Raiah to safety. "You did enough until Soren reached you. I need you to take Raiah back to the palace. The *praetoria* legionnaires will keep you both safe."

He had to believe that. Raiah was the Imperial crown princess now, his only heir, and a target as much as he was. He needed to think about her safety and the future of the empire, and keeping her out of harm's way was the next logical step.

The *praetoria* legionnaires separated into two groups without being asked. The magician went with his daughter, the small group hurrying toward the side entrance that led to the back hallways of the temple. Vanya stayed, because it was his duty. He was emperor now, despite the attempted assassination, and he needed to prove he was strong enough to rule. Hiding wouldn't help with that.

He headed to where Soren stood in between the pews, where the woman he'd killed now lay. Vanya and the legionnaires stayed in the outside aisle, keeping their distance from the dead. Her face no longer existed, so there would be no hope in identifying her.

Soren pulled something from around the woman's throat, lifting up the ragged ends of gossamer-thin fabric and a metal clasp. "She wore a veil."

Vanya's lip curled upward. "Her face will be false in photographs, then."

"That's not all." Soren's gaze flickered over Vanya's shoulder at the men and women surrounding him. "Come here. I need to show you something."

Vanya waved for the legionnaires to stay where they were before making his way between the pews. Soren had the body laid out on the bench, the front of the woman's robes a tattered mess from bullet holes and blood. Once Vanya was close, Soren ripped the fabric wider, exposing deep vivisection scars crisscrossing her chest.

The scars were ropy and pink, long healed, but she was no revenant.

Soren raised his head, a grim look in his eyes. "She's dead now, but she was alive when she was trying to kill you."

"What is she?" Vanya asked in a low voice, staring down at the body.

"I don't know, but this is one body you *will* burn after an examination."

Vanya wouldn't argue against that. "Until we know what she is, I don't want any other House to know of what you've found. Can you keep control of the bodies?"

"Are you asking me to keep state secrets?"

"You already do."

Soren scowled at him. "I have leeway from the governor. That's the only reason I'm saying yes to this."

"Good. I'll tell the peacekeepers you're in charge."

"Fine." Soren glanced past him. "Where's Raiah?"

"I sent her and Alida back to the palace under armed guard."

"You should head back there as well."

"I will as soon as the motor carriage arrives out front."

"Please don't tell me you're going to still persist with a damn parade, princeling."

"I'm an emperor now, in case you missed that."

"I missed you being *rational*. You can't know if there are others like her out there waiting to take a shot. We don't know what she is or who sent her."

"Even if there are, I can't start my reign letting the Houses think

I'm weak. The only way to prove otherwise is to continue as if this didn't happen."

Soren straightened up and blew out a harsh breath. "That's a good way to end up dead."

Vanya smiled slightly. "I seem to have a knack for not dying when you are around. That's twice you've saved my life."

Soren shot him a look. "I don't need another vow from you."

"Enough people shot at her that it would be impossible to say whose bullet reached her first. If you like, I can give credit to the legionnaires on duty."

Soren seemed relieved about that. "You do that. I'll deal with the dead in here. Get out there and show your people that you're still alive."

Vanya badly wanted to kiss him, but there were too many witnesses. He had to settle with gripping Soren's hand in thanks instead, before retreating back to the legionnaires. They formed a protective circle around him before guiding him toward the entrance of the star temple, pistols out and held at the ready.

The coronation guests hadn't gone far once it became apparent the threat was neutralized. The crowd beyond the temple gates hadn't dispersed either. Vanya pushed his way past the legionnaires to stand before his people at the top of the steps. He spread his arms wide, starfire flickering at his fingertips.

"As you can see, your emperor lives," he called out, pitching his voice to be heard across the courtyard.

The cry that erupted at his words was one of relief that segued into raucous cheers. The pop and flash of cameras going off from the press who hadn't gone far would provide everyone with proof in that evening's broadsheet that the House of Sa'Liandel still held the Imperial throne.

Seven

SOREN

Soren missed the coronation feast, not that he was in any mood to eat the food Vanya said waited for him at the palace when he came around hours later. With both hands buried in the chest cavity of the would-be assassin, Soren's interest in meat was nowhere to be found.

"You shouldn't be here," Soren said as he pushed the dead woman's rib cage open wider.

Vanya arched an eyebrow, staring at the mess Soren had made in the crypt's embalming room. It turned out there *was* something like a crematorium beneath the palace, or at least the rooms used for body preparation. Currently, Soren was using the embalming room for his examination of the dead.

"The festivities are over, and I put Raiah to bed. She asked for you," Vanya said.

"I've been busy."

"I can see that. Have you found anything?"

Soren grunted when bone cracked, the dead woman's ribs splayed open like butterfly wings. He stared through his goggles at the mess of organs below. "Come here."

Vanya approached the worktable to stand by Soren. The light in the embalming room was bright, throwing everything in high relief and glinting off the metal in the dead woman's chest.

"What is that?" Vanya asked sharply.

Soren used his gloved hands to move aside the lungs. He hooked his fingers around the clockwork metal heart buried in the chest cavity and gave it a yank. The tiny screws and washers connected to the veins and arteries to keep them in place ripped through the delicate flesh as it came free. He cradled the intricate machine in both hands, tilting it for Vanya to see.

He wiped at some of the blood on the framework, revealing the intricate spellwork carved on the metal. Chips of clarion crystal were embedded throughout the device, none of them active.

"The other two assassins don't have this sort of machine in their chests. I've never seen it before," Soren said.

He knew the machine had pumped blood at one point, because the woman he'd killed had been alive. Her flesh wasn't rotten. She'd been a living person, not a revenant, walking around with a metal clockwork heart in her chest, no one the wiser.

Vanya extended his hand toward the device, but Soren jerked it out of reach. "Don't touch it."

"I won't, but let me try something. Put it down. I don't want you holding it while I check the spell components."

Soren set the clockwork heart back in the chest cavity. It sank a little against the organs there. Vanya held his hand over it, fingers splayed, and aether pooled against the palm of his hand. Not starfire, but still magic that drifted like rain down on the clockwork heart.

Which promptly broke.

The clarion crystals shattered while the framework cracked along every weld, the spellwork hissing with foreign magic that abruptly dissipated, leaving behind melted slag where the inscription had sat. Soren swore, glaring down at the mechanical mess now nothing more than bits in a dead woman's chest.

"Very helpful," Soren said irritably.

Vanya grimaced and drew his hand back. "The spell had a self-destruct component to it. That's all I got off it before it was destroyed."

"I'll draw what I can remember seeing of the spellwork."

Soren stepped away from the worktable and stripped off his gloves and the heavy work apron he'd appropriated from the room's storage cabinet. He dug into his rucksack and came up with a notebook and fountain pen. He quickly sketched out a rough shape of the device before flipping the page to write out what pieces of the spellwork he'd seen.

He'd meant to take photographs of it, as he'd done with the body before he carved into it, but that was a useless endeavor now.

"The bodies need to be burned."

"The high priestess is prepared to remove the bodies tonight and send them to a crematorium owned by the Star Order. They'll be taken care of."

Burning the bodies still left them with more questions than answers. Coming on the heels of his discovery of the crypt, Soren couldn't know what the governor would make of this.

"I need to return to the Warden's Island," Soren said as he put away the notebook.

Vanya went still. "Tonight?"

He looked over at Vanya, taking in the more neutral robes the older man wore and the crown that still sat upon his head. The intricate gold filigree of the crown's spikes was inlaid with rubies along the wide circlet. No House emblem could be found in its design, for it predated the Houses. But every emperor or empress that sat on the Imperial throne had worn it, a symbol of Solaria's power.

He reached out and brushed his knuckles over Vanya's cheek. "Tomorrow. I'll want to say goodbye to Raiah."

Vanya blew out a breath before nodding. "If you are finished with the dead, the living have use for you."

"Let me gather my things."

He took with him his rucksack and the camera with its few tintypes packed up in a separate case. The delicate remains of the clockwork metal heart were placed in a storage case Soren appropriated by emptying it of embalming tubes. Vanya took charge of that, despite Soren's protest.

"Of the two of us, who can use the aether?" Vanya asked.

Soren bit the inside of his cheek so hard it bled. "Just don't let it break any further."

Vanya smiled a little at that jibe and waited while Soren washed his hands with an old bar of soap and hot water. Then he followed Vanya into the corridor, where two star priests still waited by order of the high priestess, the only people outside the Houses allowed below.

"Cremate the bodies," Vanya ordered.

The two star priests bowed deeply. "By your will, Your Imperial Majesty."

Soren had retrieved all he could from the dead, and they took what mattered back aboveground. The star temple was nearly empty, but beyond its doors, the legionnaires ever guarded it.

The escort wasn't something Soren was used to, though he supposed this was how things would be from here on out. He wondered what else would change, now that Vanya wore the crown that gave him the right to sit upon the Imperial throne. The disquiet stayed with him through the walk back to and through the palace to the royal wing and the bedroom there. The rooms were different than what he'd grown used to. Soren wasn't sure he'd get the chance to learn the walls of this bedroom as he had the other one.

He set his rucksack and the camera bag in the trunk that had, at some point, found its way into Vanya's furnishings for Soren's use. Then he undid the pauldron and sheath that secured his poison short sword to his back and laid it on top. Vanya still carried the storage case, which he passed on to a *praetoria* legionnaire and gave strict instructions to have it guarded by magicians in another room.

"I'll have the servants provide you a better traveling case for it tomorrow," Vanya said as he closed the bedroom door behind the legionnaire.

"You're not going to demand to keep it?" Soren asked.

"As you said before, the dead are your duty, though I would want you to inform me of what the wardens find."

"There's the princeling in you."

A hand caught him by the elbow, pulling him back against a familiar body. Warm lips kissed the side of his neck over the collar of his shirt. "You forget I was crowned emperor today."

Soren lifted a hand so he could run his fingers through Vanya's short dark hair around the crown, gripping what he could. "You'll always be a princeling to me."

Vanya chuckled, the sound low and deep and making Soren shiver, because he knew that tone, knew the mood Vanya was in. "Is that so?"

He tilted his head to the side, biting his lip when Vanya slid a hand between his legs with firm intent. "Stubborn and full of yourself. Of course you'll always be that. It's in your blood. It's in your House. No one ever tells you no."

Vanya kissed the shell of his ear, the hinge of his jaw, and Soren could only rock into the touch between his legs. "You do."

He turned his head, twisting his torso enough so he could find Vanya's mouth. "Someone needs to."

Vanya made a sound that was all want, pure and simple, as he kissed Soren until they were drunk on the taste. He kissed with a fierceness that Soren didn't back down from. They stumbled toward the bed before parting long enough to shed their clothing, and in Soren's case, the rest of his weapons.

He hadn't worn his whole set to the coronation, but he'd been thankful for the pistols. He left the belt with the holsters and pistols on the nightstand, within reach in case any other threat made it past the *praetoria* legionnaires on duty around the palace.

The only thing he didn't remove was the vow hanging around his throat, the gold medallion warm against his skin. When Vanya pulled him onto the bed, the glint from the golden crown was a match for the vow.

He leaned up to steal a kiss, fingers pressed to where gold rested against dark skin, thinking about the day when he wouldn't have this anymore. "What do you want?"

"You," Vanya said as he bore Soren down to the bed, settling between his legs, exactly where he belonged. "Whenever I can have you."

Soren groaned, hooking a leg over Vanya's hip and arching against him. "I'm here tonight, so have me."

And Vanya did, with such exquisite thoroughness that Soren was reduced to begging by the time Vanya slid into him. Soren tilted his head back, mouth open on a wordless moan when Vanya snapped his hips forward and began fucking him in earnest.

Here, in this bed, it was just the two of them in ever-changing roles, but the want they shared, that was a truth Soren clung to. He urged Vanya on with hands and mouth, rocking into every thrust that had heat pooling in his gut.

Fingers scrabbled at his chest, tangling in the gold chain there, gripping it tight. When Vanya pulled on it, Soren could only follow, propping himself up on his elbows so he wouldn't choke. Vanya's hand slid up his back, pressing between his shoulder blades, and he found himself hauled upward, rocking forward onto Vanya's lap.

He sank with a groan onto Vanya's cock, the new position driving the other man deeper, feeling split open as he panted against Vanya's mouth. The crown sat askew on Vanya's head but hadn't fallen off, and Soren would've fixed it, but Vanya thrust up into him with enough force to punch the air out of his lungs.

The metal links of the medallion's chain bit into his skin as Vanya twisted it around his fingers again, keeping Soren in place. His eyes were nearly black beneath the crown he wore as he fucked Soren, fingers digging bruises into scarred skin.

"Tell me what you want," Vanya said, voice a rasp as he chased his pleasure in Soren's body.

Soren knew if he ever did, he could never have this again. That Soren wouldn't have the right to Vanya's time, his touch, his life, now that he was emperor. In that moment, as Soren tipped over the edge and came with a gasp against Vanya's mouth, fingers curled over the crown, keeping it in place, he knew he'd do anything to stay.

It was a dangerous thing, he realized, to make a person your home.

"No," Soren said against the seam of Vanya's lips, giving himself up to the other man's pleasure because he could at least offer that.

When Vanya finally came, fingers tangled around a vow he'd given and clutching Soren close, there was nothing between them but everything that mattered.

Flash Point

⁓

936 A.O.P.

One

MELVIN

Helia was a city of decadence and filled with all manner of pleasurable escape for the wealthy. Overlooking the Gulf of Helia, the seaside city was the escapist heart of Daijal, second only to the Daijal court as a place to see and be seen.

The buildings behind the city walls that kept out revenants were painted a riot of color, easily seen through the thick fog that rolled off the waves throughout the year. Unlike Istal, with its lasting frontier grit and military feel at times, Helia was vibrant and welcoming to those who could pay. It was less so to those who could not.

The crown jewels of the city were, of course, the casinos. Owned by rival bloodlines, the grand casinos competed for patrons everywhere in the city. Scattered between the inner defensive walls, with one or two of the oldest situated on the cliffside, their gaudy exteriors —brightly lit with colorful gas lamps—were merely a precursor for what one would find within.

The Shipwreck was one of the more well-known casinos, its namesake taken from the scaled-down clockwork-model sailing ship perched above its entrance. The mechanical ship rocked back and forth on lit-up waves, the Daijal flag on its mast fluttering in the breeze. The Shipwreck needed no barker to entice gamblers into its den, and its doors were always open to revelers around the clock.

Inside, the Shipwreck was done up in an ocean motif, with dark wood and rich blue velvet for the card and dice tables. The sconces and chandeliers were designed to look like the grasping legs of creatures from the deep. Low betting card and dice tables took up half the ground floor, with the glittering slot machines set up in the rear.

The chime of the occasional winner at a slot machine and the clanking sound of gears turning with the pull of a lever was a nonstop companion to the music pouring out of phonographs scattered throughout the space.

Waitstaff scurried between gamblers and the bar, ferrying drinks and small plates of shareable finger food to casino patrons. Smoke made the air hazy, but no one ever minded, even if getting the stench out of clothing was always a chore.

The smoke that clung to Melvin Khaur's clothes and hair was always something he needed to wash off after leaving his family's casinos. In his late thirties, married for over ten years, Melvin belonged to a branch of the Khaur bloodline. The connection meant his name was written down in the nobility genealogies, but he did not carry the title of lord.

He did, however, carry the title of Marshal for the Clockwork Brigade in Daijal.

Normally, Melvin and his husband, Ezra, worked out of Istal. That city was their domicile, close to the eastern border and their contacts in Haighmoor. Melvin's position meant he knew more cogs than most in the chain of smugglers working to free debt slaves and escort them out of the country.

Melvin had held the title of Marshal for nearly two decades, guided by his uncle—the current Lord Khaur—who had held the title before him. The trips to Helia were generally used as a break to visit family, catch up on the minutiae of official business, and reassess everything else. Details concerning the Clockwork Brigade were only ever done in person, with no record of the meetings.

Which was how Melvin and Ezra ended up at the Shipwreck,

making themselves available to the public at a poker table in the high-rollers parlor on the second floor of his family's casino. A bowl of tuber chips sat half-demolished between them, and while Melvin was savoring his scotch and the decent hand of cards, Ezra had finished half his beer. Melvin's husband still had a fondness for the stout he'd drunk growing up.

Ezra's name hadn't been written in the nobility genealogies until he'd married Melvin, and his introduction to high society had taken some getting used to. He was years past the point where appearing in public in expensive clothes made him uncomfortable.

Melvin eyed his husband and the cut of his suit with an appreciative look. Ezra's blond hair was tied back in a queue, the neatly trimmed beard he'd started growing some years back a faint ginger hue. His blue eyes appeared lighter than they were in the glow of a gas lamp.

Melvin pulled out his pocket watch to check the time. "It's nearing the top of the hour."

Ezra took a sip of his beer and laid a card down on the table when it was his turn. "Just a little longer, and then we can head out. It's been ages since we got to visit a casino."

The response was said lightly, his husband giving no hint of the reason they were staying out late. The pair of them excelled at double-speak, as any cog would if they wanted to survive and not bring down the chain.

"One more hand after this, and then we must be off, darling," Melvin conceded.

Ezra flashed him a warm smile, no hint of worry in his eyes or voice. After all these years, they were both very good at lying. "As you say."

Melvin won the current round by virtue of being a card shark when it came to poker and knowing how to count cards since he was a young lad. Since his family owned the Shipwreck and several other casinos—both large and small—he was in no danger of being escorted off the premises by the hired peacekeepers.

The older gentleman who had lost bid them a good night before leaving the table. A young woman took his place, dressed in a fine gown, the lacy shawl wrapped around her shoulders a burnt-orange shade. Melvin made a note of it, settling his free hand on Ezra's thigh to give it a warning squeeze.

Their cog had arrived.

"Darlings! You didn't tell me you were back in Helia," Lady Sabine Garnier scolded with a friendly smile.

"We arrived earlier this week. Mother requested our presence. Apparently a cousin is getting married," Melvin replied.

The Khaur bloodline was vast, with many different cadet branches shooting off the main tree, and it held distant ties to the Auclair bloodline in Ashion. The casinos were a lucrative business that sustained them all, as well as their efforts with the Clockwork Brigade. They had family in every major city and medium-sized town in Daijal, which meant visits were easily explained away.

The Garnier bloodline was only two generations old and barely established in Helia's high society. Melvin and Ezra had been introduced to Sabine at a social party some years back. The more official introduction as cogs had come after by Fulcrum.

Sabine handled emergency extractions for the Clockwork Brigade in Helia. She had the societal clout to know the best avenues in and out of the coastal city, could provide funds for bribes, and was married to a Navy captain. She smuggled out people and information and was a critical lynchpin to their efforts against debt bondage and the Daijal court's insidious spread of power.

That she'd requested their help days ago through a dead-drop message exchange was the entire reason they were meeting now.

Sabine smiled, the dimples in her lightly rouged cheeks deepening as she slid some poker chips into the center of the card table. "Let's play a hand, and then you two fine gentlemen can escort me home."

"How is Payton doing?" Ezra asked.

The dealer doled out cards after a thorough shuffle, building a hand for each player with a flick of their wrist. Melvin kept half his attention on his cards, the rest on Sabine.

"He's still on a two-month patrol of the coast. He's scheduled to return in a couple of weeks. How long are you staying in Helia?"

"Not long enough to welcome your husband back," Melvin said, affecting a disappointed tone.

They chatted amicably through the game, which Melvin allowed Ezra to win. Sabine laughingly gave up her winnings before sliding out of her seat. "Shall we?"

Melvin offered his arm to escort her out of the high-rollers room and to the exit. Sabine's touch remained casual, her chatter light as she caught them up on gossip people would expect her to pass along. The only gossip Melvin cared for was the reason they'd come out tonight.

Ezra got behind the steering wheel of the motor carriage borrowed from the family's motor pool while Melvin sat in the back seat with Sabine. Once on the road, with the windows rolled up, Sabine finally spoke.

"We have a high-priority target who needs extraction out of Daijal immediately. Tonight if you can manage it," she said quietly.

Melvin frowned. "That's very short notice. I haven't heard anything from Fulcrum about moving quickly for anyone lately."

"Because Fulcrum doesn't know yet. I have a cog who will travel with the target who will masquerade as his wife to keep attention off him. She'll bring the news to Fulcrum's cogs, but I need you to get them into contact with that chain." Sabine hesitated before continuing with, "It's about the death-defying machine."

Melvin went still, and her words were enough to cause Ezra to look over his shoulder at them. "Are you certain?"

Sabine nodded sharply. "A Daijal inventor came into contact with one of the cogs in Bellingham. You know that city hasn't been safe lately for the flowers we pluck."

"Other cities in Solaria still are."

"Not Bellingham. The cog there worked to smuggle the inventor back over the border and bring him here. The frontier towns weren't safe, what with the numbers of revenants the wardens have been dealing with in that area of the country. We've passed him through the chains on a priority push because of what he knows and what he carries with him."

"Which is?"

Sabine shook her head, her face gray-looking in the glow of passing gas lamps. "You need to see it for yourself."

Melvin grimace. "Where is this inventor now?"

"At my home."

"Sabine!" Ezra hissed from the front seat. "You know how dangerous that is."

She reached up to pull her shawl tighter around her shoulders. "I *know*, but I had no other choice. There's a bounty on his head. Rumor is it's driven by a high-ranking noble for stealing proprietary patents. Debt collectors are looking for him, and nowhere in the lower tiers of Helia is safe."

"Nowhere in the *upper* tiers is safe if a noble is pushing the bounty. If anyone saw you bring him in—"

"They wouldn't have."

She slipped her hand into a slit in the skirt of her gown, retrieving the brass-made wand with its clarion crystal tip. Sabine laid the wand flat over her lap, the sight of it a reminder of her secretive station not even her husband knew about. For Sabine had been born with magic and trained as a magician in secret because her mother had been and still was a cog in the Clockwork Brigade.

Sabine's very particular skill with mind magic meant she was very, *very* good at separating a truth from a lie or creating a lie from a truth.

Melvin's wand was secured in its case at the small of his back. He was a known magician who had cultivated a reach of mere parlor tricks, when in fact his magic was far more useful than that. Secrets were the livelihood of the Clockwork Brigade and always would be.

"I kept him from being noticed," Sabine said.

"We've never doubted your dedication or precautions toward the cause. But you're a cog we can't lose," Melvin gently reminded her.

Sabine slipped her wand back into her pocket and whichever form of carrying case she wore beneath her skirts. "The cause is more important than one cog."

The Clockwork Brigade was a machine that ran on the backs of people working to provide freedom to others who no longer had it, but also against the encroaching reach of power the Daijal court sought. Melvin and Ezra were rarely required to be present in New Haven. Others in the Khaur bloodline had that responsibility.

King Bernard was a man who didn't rule on a whim, unlike some of the past kings. Reunification with Ashion was closer than it ever had been before, despite what the puppet prime minister and parliament in Ashion espoused. Melvin knew the eventual erasure of the countries' shared border wouldn't fix the rot in Daijal. It would only make everything worse across a broad swath of the continent.

The rest of the drive to Sabine's mansion was made in silence. No one would think anything amiss of her being escorted home by a pair of married friends or that she'd invite them inside for a late-night drink. Sabine was known to be devoted to her husband and had never been followed by social-ruining rumors. That veneer of properness helped hide her actions as a cog.

Melvin and Ezra, for their part, were known to both be upstanding citizens of a prominent Daijalan noble family. It would have been rude of them to decline Sabine's offer.

"This way," Sabine said as she led them to the front door of her cliffside home.

City walls didn't extend along the white stone cliffs, where homes owned by the rich sat on tiers carved into the land. Sabine's had been built behind an iron fence, overlooking the Gulf of Helia. Space was a premium on the tiers, which meant the mansion was on the small side. What it lacked in space, it made up for in décor.

Sabine's taste was expensive, and it showed in the thoughtful design of each hallway and room they passed through after sending the only servant up off to sleep. She led them to her private parlor, curtains drawn over the windows that overlooked the small rear garden.

Melvin locked the door behind them and waited with Ezra as Sabine went to one of the bookcases built into a wall. She pulled a statue off a shelf and pressed a hidden button underneath it.

351

The bookcase swung inward with a soft click of gears. The hidden space behind it couldn't be called a room as it was barely large enough to be called a closet. A man was curled up on the floor in a nest of blankets. He squinted at them, clutching at a leather-wrapped cylindrical case of the sort used to transport architectural blueprints or paintings.

"Wyatt Lehan, these are some of my associates. They're here to help," Sabine said.

Ezra made a startled noise in the back of his throat, causing Melvin to glance at his husband. Ezra caught his eye and grimaced. "I'd heard he was a promising inventor before he basically fell off the map some years ago."

Ezra was still a toymaker who excelled at creating new devices to entertain the masses. The Toy Trunk in Istal provided a nice cover for the Clockwork Brigade, and Ezra still oversaw it plus the rest of the stores in the company he'd built up. Ezra kept a finger on the pulse of the talent coming out of the Inventor's Guild, both for their business and the Clockwork Brigade.

The inventor in question slowly got to his feet and stepped into the parlor proper. He was younger than them by quite a few years, with a haunted look to his eyes that Melvin had seen on far too many people throughout his lifetime. Wyatt clutched the travel case close to his chest, gaze flicking from Melvin to Ezra.

"You put yourselves in danger helping me," Wyatt said.

Ezra shrugged. "We're used to it. Sabine said what you carry is important. May I see the blueprints?"

Wyatt hesitated and only offered up the case after an encouraging nod from Sabine. He unslung the case from his shoulder and passed it over. Ezra took it, and Melvin followed him over to the writing desk tucked against the other wall, where he spread out the blueprints and began to peruse them.

"They're copies which I made here. I couldn't risk taking the originals."

"Copies are still useful so long as they are accurate."

"I have an eidetic memory."

Ezra's attention never strayed from the intricately drawn blueprints. "I can see that."

"There's a bounty on your head, Mr. Lehan. Quite an expensive one. Do you have any idea who might have authorized it?" Melvin asked.

Wyatt grimaced, pressing a fist against his stomach. "Samuel Fletcher."

Melvin managed to hide his wince, but it was a near thing. "He's noble through a distaff branch of that family, but not a lord."

"It wouldn't matter. That whole family is trouble," Ezra muttered.

Melvin had been briefly acquainted with Claudius Fletcher during the time he'd first met Ezra. He'd long since rectified that societal mistake and hadn't had anything to do with the Fletcher bloodline outside attending the same parties during the high-society season.

"Have you checked Wyatt's memories?" Melvin asked Sabine.

She nodded, mouth twisting. "There's been no tampering. His mind is his own."

Ezra's sharply inhaled breath had Melvin stepping closer to his husband. "What is it?"

The wide-eyed look Ezra shot him was filled with so much horror that Melvin had an instinctual desire to grab his husband and *run*. Ezra's gaze flicked past Melvin to Wyatt, hands pressed flat to the blueprints. "Does it work? Does this death-defying machine of yours *work?*"

Wyatt nodded, lips pressed into a hard white line as he stared into the middle distance. "It was Samuel's design initially, and he forced me to upgrade it. But yes, it works."

The hoarse confession made Ezra briefly close his eyes. Melvin reached out and settled a hand on his husband's lower back. "What does it do?"

The bleakness in Ezra's voice was a tone Melvin had never heard before. "It transmutes the dead into revenants in far less time than spores ever could on their own."

Melvin's stomach sank low and fast, nausea settling in his gut. "What?"

Ezra never took his attention off the blueprint and the schematics copied on the paper, notes and numbers meaningless to Melvin but not to his husband. When it came to the intricacies of clockwork gears and engines, to say nothing of clarion crystals, Ezra was the expert in their relationship.

Ezra straightened up and turned to face Wyatt. "You saw it work?"

Before Wyatt could respond, Sabine spoke up. "He *used* it. Conducted experiments on debt slaves."

Wyatt flinched with his entire body, but he didn't deny it.

"If he's been part of this—this *atrocity*, how can we trust him?" Melvin asked.

Sabine sighed tiredly and rubbed at her forehead. "Because I saw in his mind that he didn't want to have any part of what is happening in Bellingham. He wasn't lying when he stated Samuel forced his hand. Wyatt's desire to escape and pass on the information doesn't absolve him, I know that, but we need him."

"The information we need, yes. I'm not so sure about the messenger," Ezra said.

Sabine shrugged tightly. "He's built and upgraded portions of the death-defying machine. He knows how it works. Fulcrum will want that."

She was right, damn her, and Melvin knew it. That didn't make it any easier to stomach. "There's a Clementine Trading Company train scheduled to depart for Foxborough in the morning at dawn. We'll get Wyatt and the cog who will act as escort smuggled into the rail yard tonight. It's a freight train, and not ticketed. Its final destination is Amari."

"The cog who will be going with him has familiarity with such escorts. She'll keep him safe as much as possible, but a veil would be helpful."

"We'll pass one along," Melvin said, mind already spinning through the massive task ahead of smuggling a highly wanted man carrying critical information out of Daijal and into Ashion.

There was no room for error, not with this. Error meant too many people would die, and enough already had if Sabine's and Ezra's reactions were anything to go by.

Melvin glanced down at the carefully copied blueprints depicting the inner workings of a machine that was anathema to every country's law when it came to the dead. "May the stars guide us through the night."

Two

CARIS

Caris held her head high as she made her way through the crowd of graduates to where she knew her parents, Nathaniel, and Meleri would be waiting. She clutched the smooth leather folio that held her newly given engineering degree to her chest, giddy with the knowledge she was now a graduate of Amari's Aether School of Engineering.

Four years of hard work had paid off, so much so that she'd added to her family's patents during her schooling. She'd received several job offers in the last few weeks from businesses who either weren't aware she was tapped to take over Six Point Mechanics Company or didn't care.

She discreetly wiped sweat off her brow as she walked. The graduation gown she wore over her tailored trousers and day jacket was stifling in the heat of Seventh Month. Caris eventually reached the staircase that would lead to the temporarily erected mezzanine for VIP guests. The usher guarding the staircase let her pass after a quick conversation. Caris clambered up the spiral metal steps and cleared the top moments later, searching for her family in the groups of people before her.

"Caris!" her mother cried out, leaving good manners by the

wayside in the heat of the moment as she bustled forward. "Oh, I'm so proud of you."

Caris caught her mother up in a hug, still a little surprised at the fact she was a full head taller than Portia now. As an educated young woman of twenty, Caris had grown so much in the last four years, and seen her parents so little, that she'd been stunned at the difference when they arrived last week.

Portia stepped back to hold Caris at arm's length, tears in her eyes but a smile on her face. "Look at you. My darling little girl. You're an engineer now."

"Just like you and Papa," Caris said, beaming.

"Ready to take over the family business, then?" Emmitt teased with a smile.

Caris went to him for a hug, breathing in the familiar scent of his cologne and the hint of tabac he smoked in his pipes. "Certainly someday."

She caught Meleri's eye over her father's shoulder, sharing a look with the woman who had been her teacher, confidant, and a motherly figure ever since Caris had become her ward. Caris had learned a lot about being an engineer at the Aether School of Engineering. She'd learned secrecy, politics, and quiet rebellion from the duchess and the Clockwork Brigade the spymaster oversaw.

Truly, it had been a shock one year into her stay when Meleri had sat her down and opened her eyes to aspects of the world Caris hadn't known about. For all that the Auclairs had shared with her their life's work in upholding Ashion values in the face of Daijal encroachment, Caris hadn't been as forthcoming.

She still kept her secret of starfire, though it was becoming more difficult by the week to ignore. Ever since letting it rage loose four years ago, the urge to let her magic burn through her kept rising. The clawing need to use the aether for magic or science was something Caris routinely warred with lately. With a quiet sigh, she pulled away from her father and adjusted her grip on the folio containing her degree.

"Shall we head to the restaurant?" Meleri asked.

The duchess had kindly reserved a private room at one of the most well-known and expensive restaurants along the Promenade for the celebratory meal. Caris had eaten there several times before with the Auclairs. She was greatly looking forward to the flambéed fruit desserts.

"I think that's a fantastic idea," Nathaniel said, smiling at Caris.

She returned the smile and didn't hesitate to take his arm when he offered it to her. They'd become friends after that initial, awkward meeting in Professor Arquette's lecture several years back. Nathaniel was kind and funny and smart, always polite, and never falsely interested in her mechanical designs.

Caris' stomach swooped a little every time she saw Nathaniel these days, something she hadn't experienced growing up in Cosian. Her school-aged friends always seemed to have crushes, gossiping about the latest boy or girl who'd caught their eye, and yearning to be courted. Caris hadn't understood that desire, not until it had oh so slowly unfurled in her own heart through the last few years of getting to know Nathaniel.

She cared for him deeply, perhaps even loved him, but she couldn't quite bring herself to tell him. Caris worried about putting him in danger because of her association with the Clockwork Brigade, and at some point, she needed to return to Cosian. He hadn't officially asked permission to court her yet, but that hadn't stopped him from calling on her. Caris never declined his request because he hadn't ever demanded anything from her that she wasn't willing to give.

"When you're ready, I will be here," he'd always said within earshot of her chaperones.

And here he was, present at one of her milestones, something Caris appreciated more than she could say.

Getting through the crowd of families and graduates was easier with the escort that arrived at the bottom of the spiral staircase to see them off campus. The two men who worked for the Auclair bloodline carved them a way out through the press of people.

"Would you like me to carry that for you?" Nathaniel asked.

Caris tightened her grip on the folio and shook her head. "Thank you, but I have it."

The motor carriages that had chauffeured them all to the school for the ceremony were parked in the lot beneath the shade of a tree. The drivers opened the doors of the vehicles as they approached, the party splitting up. Caris followed Nathaniel to his motor carriage, with her mother acting as a chaperone.

The drive to the Serpentine River and the winding Promenade took a little longer than usual because of the crowd. Caris spent that time chatting with her mother and Nathaniel. She didn't mind the delay—right up until the warning sirens went off in their section of the city. The sound was a piercing, haunting noise that reverberated through the air.

The warning was only issued for tornadoes or revenants, and the sky above was clear and blue. Then a static-edged voice came through the speakers attached to the siren posts, cutting through the siren.

"Revenants in the Serpentine River, north of Hollows Bridge. All citizens to clear the area and shelter in place. All wardens within the city limits to lend aid."

Caris froze, staring wide-eyed at her mother, who sat between her and Nathaniel in the back seat. "Mother?"

The Promenade, with its winding pathway through grassy parklets dotted with trees, was to their right. People who had been out for a leisurely stroll along the Serpentine River panicked, spilling into the street around their vehicles. The reason for their terror came climbing over the side of the river, waterlogged flesh bloated around bone, the dead come in search of the living.

Nathaniel leaned forward, barking out an order. *"Drive."*

"I can't!" the driver exclaimed. "I'll hit someone if I do!"

People streamed past their motor carriage as they ran from the walking dead. Several women had fainted and were being carried away from the danger by men, but the lack of speed was costly. The revenants on the Promenade weren't newly risen. The spores must have had time to sink into the dead and get control of the bodies.

These revenants moved with a speed that, while not as quick as a living person, was still quick enough to be a threat. Caris watched in horror as one of the revenants swiped at the gown of an unconscious woman being carried away from the Promenade in front of their vehicle. The skeletal fingers snagged on the bright blue fabric, and the man who'd tried to save his companion gave her up to the dead. He ran, and the revenant wasted no time in tearing through the woman's clothes for her skin below and the organs beneath that. The sound the woman made when she was eviscerated was something Caris would hear in her nightmares.

Nathaniel hit their driver on the shoulder with his fist. "Bloody hell, just *drive*! We can't stay here."

The driver slammed his foot on the gas pedal, face pale in the rearview mirror. Caris jerked forward against the lap belt, losing her grip on her folio. It tumbled to the floor, but she didn't try to retrieve it.

The warning sirens hadn't stopped, the noise ringing in Caris' ears as the motor carriage swerved around the revenant and its victim, only to slam into another revenant. The force of the blow split the revenant in half, with the motor carriage's wheels rolling over the lower half of the revenant's body while its upper slammed onto the hood locked over the engine.

Portia screamed, hands going to her hip for a pistol she wasn't carrying. Nathaniel shouted at the driver, who sat frozen behind the steering wheel. The man didn't react in time, and it cost him his life.

The half of the revenant lying on the motor carriage's hood dragged itself forward and slammed its rotting arm through the thin glass of the front windshield. Glass shattered as the grasping hand missing a finger gripped the driver's face. The horrible, rotten stench of the dead filtered into the motor carriage, and Caris gagged.

"Get out!" Nathaniel shouted.

"It's not safe outside," Portia protested.

"It's not safe in *here*."

Caris fumbled at her lap belt buckle, jabbing at the button to release it. She did the same to her mother's before curling her fingers around the door handle and shoving it open. She slammed it into a revenant trying to stand on one leg, pitching it over to the ground. Caris threw herself out of the motor carriage, fingers wrapped tight around her mother's arm as she hauled Portia out with her.

Breathing rapidly, hands shaking, Caris was reminded of that moment in the wildlands of the Eastern Basin some years back and the horde that had attacked them. That same fiery heat burned in her chest now as it did back then, making it difficult to breathe. Her fingertips stung like when she touched a charged clarion crystal by accident.

Portia's hand dug into her shoulder, and the hissed, frantic warning from her mother was nearly drowned out by the warning sirens.

"*Don't*," Porta begged. "Don't let it out."

Caris swallowed against the pressure in her chest, not knowing where to focus. The pressure made her teeth tingle, made it difficult to breathe. Then Nathaniel was there, yanking both Caris and Portia out of reach of the revenant she'd slammed the door into and which had twisted around to lunge at them.

"Head off the Promenade," Nathaniel shouted.

The crowd had thinned out, but the revenants weren't slowing down. Running wasn't necessarily a way to safety, but it was all they had at the moment. Caris fumbled at the clasp on her graduation robe, slipping free of it as she ran toward the motor carriage with the duchess and her father. They were hemmed in by vehicles behind them, to say nothing of the revenants clawing at the motor carriage.

Someone had dropped a cane in their haste to leave the area. Caris leaned down midstride to retrieve it, gripping it how one would a bat.

"Caris!" Portia shouted behind her.

The revenant blocking the rear door of the motor carriage had cracked the window using its head. The rotten skin had split over the skull, smearing the fractured glass with blood and strips of putrid flesh. Caris raised the cane over her shoulder and swung at the revenant's head. The force of the blow pushed the revenant back, and she swung again, the cane slamming against its chest to topple it over.

"You should have run!" her father yelled as he shoved the motor carriage door open.

"I wasn't leaving you behind," Caris said.

"Infection of spores through a bite isn't a way I would ever want you to die."

Emmitt reached behind him without looking, offering the duchess his hand. She took it, moving with a speed someone of her age and rank only achieved through desperation. Caris tightened her grip on the cane, scanning their immediate area with wide eyes.

They no longer had a clear path to the intersection ahead where others had escaped. Half the horde of waterlogged revenants was headed their way, and the street behind them was packed with abandoned vehicles and more revenants.

Caris swallowed thickly, flexing her fingers. "Mother?"

Portia shook her head, her carefully set curls having come undone from their pins. "No, Caris."

"I can't—"

"Take cover!" a deep voice shouted.

Caris' head snapped around, eyes going wide at the sight of a warden riding his velocycle down the street behind them, dodging cars with practiced ease. He flung his arm forward, and something shiny arced through the air.

The sphere hit the ground between their group and the revenants, rolling toward the threat. Mechanical legs sprouted from the grenade, and it scuttled forward to do maximum damage amongst the horde.

Caris grabbed her mother's arm and dived for cover behind an open motor carriage door. Her father, Nathaniel, and Meleri managed to hunker down next to a vehicle right as the grenade went off with an ear-piercing *boom*.

The blast tore the revenants apart, shattered bone and ripped-to-pieces limbs careening through the air. Caris threw herself over her mother's hunched form, doing her best to shield Portia from what rained down around them. The wet sounds of ruined flesh hitting the motor carriages and ground around them made her stomach churn.

Something wet hit her back before siding off and landing on the ground with a sickening splat.

She was never wearing this day jacket again.

Caris gagged at the stench wafting around them as she lifted her head to see what was happening. The warden had driven past them and flung himself into the midst of the remaining revenants, firing poison-coated bullets at the walking dead. The toxins on the bullets caused the revenants to collapse, momentarily incapacitated. In that brief lull, the warden drew free a machete strapped to his back, dispensed poison from the hilt so it coated the blade, and started cutting off heads.

Caris looked away from the scene, stomach trying to crawl up her throat. She swallowed back bile as she moved away from her mother, letting go of the cane long enough to hastily shrug out of her stained day jacket.

"We need to find somewhere safe to hunker down in. The inner gates will have closed and won't reopen until the wardens give the all clear," her father said as he scrambled over to them.

The warden had the situation well in hand, unbothered by the few revenants left who lunged at him. Emmitt helped Caris and Portia to their feet. Caris retrieved her cane, holding it tight in one hand. Nathaniel carried Meleri in his arms, the duchess pale and grim-faced in the wake of the revenant attack.

They left the warden behind with the revenants, escaping the Promenade and their ruined motor carriages for the questionable safety of Amari's twisting streets.

As far as graduations went, Caris' certainly was memorable.

Three

HONOVI

The Gilded Songbird wasn't gilded, and certainly anyone singing there would be singing off-key. The pub was located in an outer neighborhood of Amari, popular with airfield workers, and just the place Honovi wouldn't be looked askance at as he rendezvoused with his husband. It helped that the pub wasn't anywhere close to where the revenant incursion had occurred, even if it was all anyone could talk about.

"Not E'ridian whiskey, but it'll do," Siv said as she came back from the bar with four pints in hand.

She set the glasses on the rickety round table they'd been able to lay claim to after a group had left. The tabletop was sticky from spilled beer, and crumbs from the fried food the kitchen offered were mushed into some cracks. Someone had set the phonograph to play, but either the record was poorly made or the machine was, because the music coming out of it was choppy at best and utter noise at worst.

Honovi lifted his glass and hid his grimace behind a swallow of slightly too-sour beer. "Next time, find a better pub."

Siv tipped her head in Honovi's direction but didn't promise anything. The younger woman was a member of Clan Mountain and

an aide who Honovi had relied on since taking over the ambassador-
ship. Trading with Ashionens on a business level was a far cry from
negotiating on a national level with politicians and a prime minister
who couldn't exactly commit to deals without the approval of King
Bernard. The puppet government E'ridia was dealing with meant any
new deals were slow to form, and nothing had been agreed to yet.

Perhaps his predecessor would have settled for something more
than the nothing they currently had, as Siv had so tactfully explained
after one brutally long negotiating session with Honovi's counterpart.
But Honovi was a *jarl*, and he knew intimately what the *Comhairle nan
Cinnidhean* would and would not accept in a trade treaty.

Two years of a careful political dance, hoping for better terms, had
gotten them nowhere. Honovi had a sinking feeling, growing worse
over the last season or so, that it wasn't so much his and his country's
demands holding everything up. The Ashionen government was
focused on whatever Daijal wanted these days, and Crown Princess
Eimarille was known to favor laws that went against ones already on
the books in Ashion.

Honovi had done a deep dive into Ashion's political history of the
last decade when he first arrived in Amari. What he'd gleaned from it
all had guided his hand in negotiations for the last two years. Expansion of debt bondage requirements, granting legal authority to the
Collector's Guild to do business in Ashion, interference in Ashion's
army recruitment process, and other laws that sought to transfer
power west had crept through Ashion's parliament.

All at the behest of Crown Princess Eimarille.

Oh, it was King Bernard's signature approving those laws, but the
authorial sections of the bills all had Eimarille's name on them.

It painted a picture that left a hum of disquiet in the back of
Honovi's mind. He'd noted his concerns to the *Comhairle nan Cinnidhean* when he'd send his quarterly reports back by way of a diplomatic
messenger on an E'ridian airship. Some information could not be
safely discussed over a wire, and a diplomatic telegram written in
code was the only option.

Honovi leaned back in the wooden chair, staring out at the

crowded pub filled with off-the-clock workers, half of whom were E'ridian. Honovi had left his ranking hair adornments at the embassy, keeping to a simple braid. He wore the flight uniform of an aeronaut captain rather than clan-affiliated plaid, the marriage torc around his neck something he never removed.

They'd chosen this pub because of its mix of people, making it less likely anyone would think it odd that an Ashionen professor and an E'ridian aeronaut would run into each other. The pub had a few side rooms used for card games and illicit meetings everyone pretended weren't happening. The Gilded Songbird wasn't a brothel, but that didn't stop people from finding a little pleasure in the shadows.

Normally, Honovi would have met Blaine at the embassy after hours, where they were assured a modicum of safety they couldn't find anywhere else in the capital city. With the revenant incursion two days ago, that area of the city, which included the E'ridian embassy, had been restricted for investigation purposes and cleanup.

Blaine had sent a message through Lady Brielle Auclair during Honovi's official office hours within parliament. Their pleasantries had happened under the guise of politics. The folded letter she'd left behind on his desk from Blaine had been burned after the message was read.

Which was how Honovi had ended up here, waiting for his husband to arrive, flanked by E'ridians he'd grown to trust while in Ashion. The diplomatic corps was insular in the way an airship crew could be, but they'd welcomed him with open arms regardless.

Honovi kept drinking, kept chatting, exchanging his beer for a whiskey on the next round. The dregs had settled at the bottom by the time he caught sight of Blaine.

It was always a shock to see his husband with short, unbraided hair. It fell to Blaine's shoulders these days, barely long enough to tie back in a queue—certainly not long enough to showcase clan braids. His casual trousers and button-down shirt were a far cry from the suits he normally wore when visiting the embassy. The outfit replaced the flight leathers with its plaid panels and shirt that kept them warm in the high altitude or the kilts when on the ground at Glencoe.

Everything about him screamed Ashionen, and Honovi supposed that was the point.

It didn't stop him from wanting to bring his husband home.

Blaine took his time getting a drink at the bar, chatting with some of the men and women crowding the counter. Honovi kept half his attention on Blaine, the rest on everyone else, occasionally interjecting a comment in the conversation happening at his own table.

Eventually, Blaine headed toward the back of the pub, slipping down the narrow hall that led to the private rooms. Honovi shoved his chair back, nodding at those with him. "I'll return shortly."

He made his way through the crowd. The music wasn't as loud in the back, but the smoke was thicker, the smell of cigars heavy in the air. Honovi squinted against the haze, seeing Blaine at the far end of the hallway, waiting at the door which led into the alleyway between two buildings. He slipped through it, and Honovi lengthened his stride to join him.

Outside, the muggy evening air smelled worse than the cigar smoke–choked pub he'd left. Garbage and other refuse was piled against the walls, waiting for the trash pickup later in the week. Honovi breathed through his mouth and tried not to let it bother him as he turned to where Blaine stood in the shadows.

"Honovi," Blaine said quietly, already reaching for him.

He let himself be drawn into a tight embrace, holding Blaine close. Honovi tucked his nose into Blaine's hair, drawing in a deep breath. The cologne his husband wore wasn't a scent he recognized.

"I'm here," Honovi said.

Blaine nodded, hands digging into Honovi's back. Meeting like this —in secret, in the shadows—for the past two years was wearying. Honovi's bed felt empty every morning he woke up alone. He missed flying with Blaine by his side, missed their language, their food, their *home*.

"We don't have much time," Blaine said after a moment, pulling back enough that Honovi could just make out his face. It was difficult to read his expression in the darkness between buildings. Light from the streetlamps didn't penetrate this far.

Honovi lifted a hand to trace the edge of Blaine's jaw. "You said you had something to tell me. Is it about the incursion?"

He'd read about the attack in the broadsheets, mourning the victims but quietly afraid for the ones who had escaped. The Duchess of Auclair had been named in the stories as a survivor, along with others, but hers was by far the most striking identity. She had known sympathies for the monarchy of the past, was stridently opposed to continued Daijal interference, and had a stranglehold on the nobility that mattered. There was a reason Honovi had cultivated a political relationship with Lady Brielle, aside from that bloodline's connection to his husband through the Clockwork Brigade.

Blaine reached into his pocket and pulled out something that could have been a pocket watch. When he opened it, the internal face of beveled clarion crystal glowed softly, the light hidden from the mouth of the alleyway by Honovi's body.

"A moment," Blaine muttered.

He toggled a tiny switch on the side of the casing, and the crystal flickered like candlelight. The rose-colored glow faded into a dark purple hue, the aether that powered it clearly running some sort of spell.

Blaine closed the covering, cutting off the glow. "We're in the clear. No one is listening. It would have turned green if anyone was close by and eavesdropping."

"Nifty device," Honovi said.

"It does come in handy." Blaine tucked it back into his pocket. "As to your question, no, I didn't want to meet with you about the incursion, but that's still of concern amongst those of my acquaintance. The revenants could have attacked anywhere, but it happened too near the duchess for anyone's peace of mind."

"And your charge?" Honovi was careful not to use Caris' name, but Blaine understood who he spoke about regardless.

"Safe. We can't rule out they were both targets. Everyone is a bit paranoid right now and sticking close to home. I can't. There's a package heading to Amari on a train out of Foxborough tomorrow night. It needs to be extracted off the train before reaching the station here."

Honovi frowned, letting his hand drop to Blaine's waist. "Do you mean to hijack the train?"

Blaine shook his head. "No. That doesn't allow for a quick escape. We're to extract via airship. There's a crew, and I'm to be part of it."

Honovi tightened his grip on Blaine, displeasure deepening his voice. "How *exactly* is this extraction supposed to happen?"

"That's what I wanted to talk to you about. It's a risky night flight, and I don't trust anyone behind the controls for something like this except you."

"Blaine."

His husband leaned closer, ghosting his lips over Honovi's, voice so low he could barely hear the words. "I know I shouldn't ask you. That it goes against what the *Comhairle nan Cinnidhean* allows. That it's outright interference in a sovereign nation's affairs if you give aid. But Honovi, the package is *important*. We can't risk losing it."

Honovi swallowed, breathing against the faint pressure of Blaine's lips on his. The thought of Blaine participating in what amounted to a nighttime raid in an airship that would certainly not be up to E'ridian standards sent a chill down his spine. Because it could go terribly wrong, and he'd lose the only person he'd ever loved if that happened.

"Let someone else take your place," he said.

"I *can't*. Fulcrum asked me to go personally."

Honovi pressed forward, kissing the breath from his husband's lungs with a fierceness that hurt. "I'm asking you not to."

Blaine broke the kiss but didn't let go. He pulled on Honovi's braid until he could press their foreheads together. "You know why I need to do this. I just don't want to do it without you for once. Please, Honovi. Captain the airship for me."

The right answer for E'ridia would be *no*.

But that wasn't the right answer for Honovi. It never would be.

He dragged Blaine close, into another kiss, one that left him aching inside. "No one can know I'm doing this. I'm no cog."

"I'll get you a veil," Blaine panted against his mouth, slumping against him in relief. "We're meeting at Hangar Thirty-Eight tomorrow after the sun goes down."

Honovi wrapped his arms around Blaine, holding on with everything he had. "I'll be there."

Agreeing to the job was the only way he'd ensure Blaine would live to see the dawn.

Four

BLAINE

Hangar Thirty-Eight was attached to one of the smaller piers in the airfield, used more for short-haul airships that ran domestic flights in the western provinces of Ashion. Night flights weren't uncommon for airships launching out of that hangar. The flight manifest filed with the control tower listed the airship heading northwest to Haighmoor. In reality, it would be heading south.

"A cog on the ground confirmed the train in question has passed the last way station stop on the schedule," Anya said in greeting when Blaine approached the gangplank. She frowned at the person trailing in his wake. "Crew is complete. Who is this?"

"Our captain," Blaine said calmly as he glanced over his shoulder at Honovi.

It wasn't his husband's face staring back at him. The veil Blaine had logged out of Lore's personal stores ensured Honovi looked Ashionen. The flight uniform was familiar, even if it lacked the fur-lined leathers E'ridians preferred. Blaine wore something similar, and the wool wasn't quite as soft as he was used to.

Anya crossed her arms over her chest. "Really, Tristan? I wasn't informed of a personnel change."

Blaine was well used to responding to the false name he'd been living under for several years now. He plucked a folded piece of paper from his front pocket, passing over the message Lore had written in code. An order given by Mainspring herself wasn't one to be ignored. Anya's displeasure was written clear on her face, but she, like the other cogs on this mission, weren't ones to disobey an order.

"You're informed now," Blaine said.

"Caleb won't appreciate being demoted."

"He can take it up with Mainspring, then."

They and their crew were the only ones in the hangar, which was why Blaine could speak so openly of things usually not given voice to in public.

Anya jerked her head in Honovi's direction. "What are the bloke's credentials?"

"More than your current captain's," Honovi replied evenly.

Veils couldn't change a person's voice, but Honovi had spent two years learning to lose his accent when necessary. He sounded Ashionen enough to pass, but it still made Blaine twitch.

"I'll believe it when we're in the air." She turned on her heels, gesturing for them to follow her up the gangplank. "Let's get this done."

Blaine's background as an engineering professor dovetailed neatly with the applicable skill he'd acquired in E'ridia. His inclusion in the mission hadn't been questioned, but everyone seemed to question Honovi's.

"This is ridiculous. I'm perfectly capable of flying the airship," Caleb snapped after Anya passed along Mainspring's order.

"Mainspring changed the lineup. We will all abide by it," Blaine said.

The entire crew of the airship consisted of those needed to get it flying and those tapped to handle the extraction of the package from the train. The cogs assigned for that hailed mostly from the Ashion army, soldiers who'd been heavily vetted by Mainspring and Fulcrum for their loyalty.

One of the cogs carried a wand hanging from a slender case on their belt. She was a magician, one who gave Blaine an intensely odd look when he arrived on board, but said nothing when Anya introduced him as the one in charge.

Everyone on the ship had been slotted into Blaine's chain of cogs for this mission, and that included the package they aimed to retrieve. He outranked everyone and was backed by the people who were in charge of the Clockwork Brigade. None of the crew members were of a rank to argue their orders, and they all knew what was at stake. Caleb gave up his spot at the controls with a scowl and a muttered curse but no further arguing.

Honovi stepped up to the control panel in the flight deck, eyeing the buttons, levers, and steering mechanism. It wasn't quite the same setup that E'ridians used, but similar enough it wouldn't pose a problem. Blaine had gone over the airship's specs with Honovi on their way to the airfield. The airship was small on the keel and balloon, but what it lacked in size, it more than made up for in a modified engine.

The make of it was all Blaine's creation, designed for low altitude, steep dives, and quick takeoffs. The outside decking had been cleared of unnecessary gear, providing space for the soldiers who Mainspring had promised were skilled in jumps. Blaine could only take her word for it, and he hoped they wouldn't lose anyone tonight.

But Honovi was one of the most skilled night fliers Blaine knew. If anyone was going to fly an airship in a nighttime raid on a moving train and make it back into the air in one piece, it was his husband.

"Let's get in the air," Honovi said as he took his seat at the controls.

Blaine went and took his place by the engine controls. Caleb took up a post near the navigator, the flight deck crowded with four people. When they were cleared to launch, Blaine set the engines for an ascent, and Honovi guided them out of the hangar and into the night sky.

Navigating by stars was second nature to him and Honovi. Following a ground route through the dark was far more difficult. The railroad tracks weren't marked and illuminated, but the towns and way stations were. All they needed to do was follow the tracks heading south and hope the navigator assigned was up to the job of figuring out where their target was.

Honovi took charge in a way only a captain could, in his element barking out orders to the crew. Blaine adjusted the engines as needed, keeping an eye on the gauges that indicated air pressure in the air balloon. The thrum of the engines was something he'd missed during his time on the ground.

Honovi flew them northwest first until Amari was a dim glow on the ground, barely visible by the crew on the outer deck. When he judged the distance far enough, he steered the airship back around, banking east and then south back toward Amari.

Before the city came into view again, Honovi reached for a set of switches on the control panel. "We're running dark until we put Amari behind us."

The lights in the flight deck went out, plunging them into darkness. Thankfully, the engine gauges weren't affected, backlit so they could still be read. Honovi called for an adjustment in power, and Blaine manipulated the engine to help them ascend a little higher.

Amari was a sprawling sea of lights through the windowpanes of the flight deck as they flew around it. Honovi didn't switch the running lights back on until they'd lined up with the train tracks, heading south, the city behind them once more. The triangulation of their route on the navigator's map against the stars and a sextant was all they had to rely on to guide them.

Night flying was dangerous at the best of times, but to pull off what needed to happen required a captain with great skill. Blaine felt steadier knowing Honovi was in command, and it was almost like they were back in E'ridia, flying their own airship. He could have gone on pretending for a little while longer, except a crew member shattered the daydream an hour into the flight, judging by the clock bolted to the wall.

"We got us a light below," she said, voice muffled through the scarf wrapped around the lower portion of her face.

"The train?" Caleb asked.

"We're en route." Her gaze cut to Honovi. "Nearly right on top of them."

"We should—"

"We'll descend and come up from the rear. Warn the crew to hold tight," Honovi interrupted, causing Caleb to scowl at him. "Make sure the soldiers are ready to jump."

"The package is supposed to be on the second-to-last cargo carriage with their escort," Blaine said, eyes on the engine gauges as he worked a couple of different levers. "Ballonets are prepared to be filled. Ready to descend."

"Going dark. On my mark."

Honovi switched off the running lights and counted down with a steady voice. When he finished the count, Blaine engaged the engines to fill the ballonets with air at a speed that normally wouldn't be safe if the engine was Ashionen make. E'ridians were masters of the sky, though, and Blaine's foundation was in their science, not the one he taught.

The airship shuddered, engine thrumming hot for a couple of seconds before the noise died down. His stomach swooped in the way it always did on a fast descent, the wind howling past the windows and over the decking outside.

Honovi steered the airship after the train, descending in a tight circle as he positioned them behind and to the side of the train. As the airship dipped toward the black earth, Blaine could see the glow of a headlight cutting through the dark up ahead on the ground below,

Blaine worked the engines to keep a steady level of air in the ballonets to maintain buoyancy as Honovi guided them lower and lower. At least on the Northern Plains, they wouldn't have to worry about mountains, but trees were a concern. Running dark meant they couldn't use the spotlight to keep clear of any risks as they aimed for the tracks and what air clearance they'd provide.

All of the risks involved with such a night flight were why Blaine had wanted Honovi captaining the airship. His husband brought them down low over the train with a skill that had their navigator giving a low whistle. The sound of the train's wheels churning over the rails was a counterpoint to the thrum of their own engine.

Blaine checked the gauges one final time before calling Caleb over to take his place. "Keep an eye on the ballonet levels. Don't let that gauge drop below the red line."

Most crew members had enough passing knowledge of other stations in the flight deck to take over if necessary for a short period of time. Since Blaine was the only one the duchess had given the code word to for verifying the identity of the package, he had to get on the train.

Honovi looked away from the front-view windows, giving him a grim little nod. "Good luck."

Blaine wanted to kiss him goodbye just in case, but they weren't supposed to be anything more than acquaintances. Blaine left the flight deck without a backward glance, stepping onto the decking where the soldiers were prepping their grappling ropes on the railing. Anya relayed their position back to the navigator for Honovi to adjust their position over the correct train carriage.

As a professor, Blaine shouldn't have the skill he possessed in rappelling himself off an airship. As an E'ridian, he'd done this hundreds of times in emergency training scenarios, and it was muscle memory at this point. When one of the soldiers passed over a coil of rope and started to explain what they had to do, Blaine listened with half an ear, intent on checking the gear with a thoroughness that eventually had the soldier going quiet.

"We're ready," Anya shouted over the wind.

With no time to lose, Blaine followed the soldiers over the aft side of the airship, pitching himself into open air above a moving train. The wind buffeted them, and the noise of the train in the darkness was a reminder of the danger below. Then the magician with them cast an illumination spell, the glow dripping from her wand like viscous fluid to the train carriage below.

It crawled across the roof, spreading like a puddle, providing enough light to see by that hopefully they wouldn't tumble off to the tracks once they landed. The special gloves they all wore with magnetized fingertips would hopefully help with that.

Blaine relied on his upper-body strength to rappel himself down the swaying rope to the train carriage roof. His feet found the carriage seconds later, and he let go of the rope, dropping to a crouch and getting his gloved hands onto the roof. The magnets engaged automatically, providing much-needed support as the rest of the soldiers landed around him.

The train was going at a speed that would be deadly if any of them fell off. The sway of the train on the tracks reminded Blaine of an airship. Moving while balancing wasn't as tricky as it could have been.

A soldier made her way toward the front gap between train carriages, satchel bulging with explosives. Blowing the coupling to separate the train was a last resort if things went badly. Blaine hoped it wouldn't come to that because it would draw far too much attention to why the train was targeted.

One of the soldiers tapped Blaine on the shoulder and pointed at the side of the train roof. "Ladder is on this side."

Blaine nodded and deactivated the magnets on his gloves with a press of the small button accessible on the inside. He stayed low, head ducked against the wind, and carefully followed the soldier over to the ladder that protruded from the side of the train carriage. Being a freight train meant the door was on the broadside, with no accessible, additional entry over the couplings.

Since Blaine was the only one out of all the cogs with the code phrase, he was the one who had to confirm the package. Gritting his teeth against the juddering of the train, Blaine carefully twisted around and over the edge to get his feet on the ladder rungs and maneuver himself down. The magician with them remained flat on the cargo carriage roof, wand in hand, eyes wide in her face.

"Be careful!" she called out.

Blaine didn't know everyone's names, as the cogs were tied to Lore and the duchess, not his chain. Identities were best kept secret, even amongst themselves sometimes. But the magician's vaguely accented voice was familiar in a way he couldn't place.

Taking a steadying breath, Blaine looped an arm around a ladder rung before pulling a key—a copy made from the master of the Clementine Trading Company—out of his pocket.

He reached for the lock that kept the cargo door secured in place.

It took a couple of tries for him to slide the key into the lock and turn it. From there it was a matter of twisting the handle and sliding the bar upward. Blaine pocketed the key before shifting position to stretch his leg out and get his foot against the edge of the door. With a grunt, he shoved it open a little, the metal screeching against the grooves.

A pair of hands appeared from within the cargo carriage, hauling the door open partway. A young man peered cautiously out, face lit from the glow of a lantern inside. "I suppose you're our pickup?"

"You'd suppose right," Blaine yelled to be heard over the sound of the train and the wind. "I'll need your code phrase."

The young man rattled off a rhyming phrase that matched what the duchess had given Blaine. The quote from a children's book was an odd choice.

Dureau is right. Lore picks out terrible code words.

Blaine rattled off his own response to the code phrase, and the young man's expression became one of relief. Blaine let go of the ladder with one hand to point at the airship still easily keeping pace with the train. "We'll get you on board."

Even as he spoke, the soldiers on the roof were already signaling the airship crew. Blaine clung to the ladder, watching as a soldier grabbed a line, attached it to a clip on his belt, then rappelled over the side of the cargo carriage. He swung into the cargo space with practiced ease, landing in a crouch.

It was a matter of moments for the soldier to secure the young man to the line with an extra belt harness. Then the soldier threw them out of the train, swinging in the open air, before someone on the airship started winching them up at a rapid pace.

The woman left behind in the cargo space crept to the side of the open door nearest Blaine. She set down the lantern before sliding a leather travel tube off her shoulder. Then she braced herself against the side of the train and extended her arm to offer him the traveling case.

"He made these copies, but the Marshal didn't want them left in Helia," she shouted over the clacking of the train wheels.

Blaine reached for the leather tube. His fingers had barely curled over the shoulder strap when a burst of gunfire cut through the air. The woman jerked, eyes going wide as flecks of something dark and wet splattered against the underside of her jaw and over her throat. She swayed for a moment, hand dropping from the tube, before she crumpled in a slow fall that sent her pitching sideways off the train.

In the weak glow of the lantern, Blaine saw her body get caught by the train wheels and dragged beneath them, tearing to pieces as they moved down the tracks.

He jerked his gaze away from the cog's bloody remnants and found himself staring down the barrel of a Zip gun attached to a spider automaton clinging to the side of the cargo carriage.

"Tristan!" the magician yelled.

He didn't hear the Zip gun go off, but he heard the impact of the bullets crashing against an aether shield that solidified between him and the unexpected threat in the shape of connecting trapezoids. The magician jerked her wand toward the automaton, dragging the shield with her, and smashed it into the machine.

The force of the blow dislodged the automaton. It fell to the ground, one of its mechanical legs getting caught in the train's wheels and dragged beneath them. Loud popping sounds came from the tracks as some of the bullets in its internal magazine careened through the air and impacted the train.

Blaine slung the leather tube over one shoulder before scrambling up the ladder, nearly losing his footing near the top as he flung himself back onto the roof. He activated the magnets on his gloves to keep himself from sliding off, watching as the magician hurled a fiery ball of aether from the tip of her wand at a second Zip gun wielded by a spider automaton crawling up from the end of the cargo carriage. Her attack knocked it off, but more were appearing.

"Where did they come from?" a soldier asked.

"Who cares? We need to get off the train!" someone else shouted back.

"I'm betting debt collectors have control of them," the magician said grimly.

The thought made Blaine's stomach twist. "If they knew the package was on the train, then that means the chain might be compromised."

It was a terrifying thought, because if they lost the Marshal, they would lose too much of the ground the Clockwork Brigade had fought to keep in Daijal.

The magician flung another spell at yet more automatons, her magic the only thing standing between them and getting turned into pincushions. Some of the automatons took aim at their transport instead. Blaine looked up in fear as bullets pinged off the underside of the thin metal plating that curved beneath the balloon. The modification was one Blaine had overseen, an addition found on E'ridian airships more than Ashionen ones.

The soldiers left on the train roof sought to make themselves as small a target as possible behind the magician's trapezoid shield. Wind slammed against them as the airship readjusted position in the air, Honovi keeping it stable and flying apace. Blaine watched as a couple more automatons took aim at the airship—so the magician took aim at them.

She cast a spell that sent bullets of magic cutting through the air and through her shield, finding a home in the automatons. Magic crackled around the machines as they shuddered and wound down, the motion of the train forcing the ones that had been hit to go sliding off the roof. She snapped her wrist, sending another wave of aether-shaped magic bullets toward the remaining automatons.

"I'll hold them off! Get everyone back on the airship!" the magician shouted.

Someone signaled the airship with a handheld gaslight, and more ropes were thrown overboard. The soldiers wasted no time hooking themselves to the ropes and getting winched back up. But even with the magician's shield, the soldiers in the air were targets. One cried out, going limp on his line but not falling due to being clipped in. He was hauled up as literal dead weight along with the rest of the soldiers, before two more lines were tossed overboard.

Blaine caught one, staying balanced on his knees with one gloved hand magnetized to the train roof. The travel tube slung across his back bumped against his head as he turned to look at the magician.

"Come on!" Blaine yelled. "It's our turn!"

The magician slid her way toward him in an ungainly sprawl, wand still in hand. As she drew closer, Blaine realized that the clarion crystal embedded in the tip of her wand wasn't glowing. She wasn't channeling her magic through the wand but through herself.

Oh, no, he thought, something like horror blooming in his chest. He only hoped it didn't show on his face.

The magician snagged the line where it swayed in the air and connected it to her belt. She gave it a firm tug before grinning at Blaine, a manic gleam to her brown eyes. "Ready when you are. I'll shatter the shield spell once we're on board."

Blaine had nothing to say to that. Everything he wanted to say and do—shake her until the damned woman saw reason and lock her away to keep her safe—he couldn't. Instead, Blaine called up to the decking, and the rope jerked with a heavy tug, hauling him into the air. The magician joined him, and she kept her wand pointed at the train below them that suddenly grew smaller as Honovi abruptly gained altitude, flying away from the tracks.

Blaine looked back, seeing more automatons clamoring onto the cargo carriage in the glow of the magician's shield. Then the spell shattered with a flick of her wand, the aether brightness snuffed out at her command.

The wind that blew around them was cold as the airship picked up speed. As they were hauled to hull height, Blaine kicked his legs out to brace against the metal-lined wood, walking up it. Hands reached for them both when they made it to the railing, hauling them to safety.

The moment his feet hit the decking, the airship engines changed pitch as they ascended rapidly, putting the train behind them. Blaine sucked air through his teeth at the sound of the magician's breathless, disbelieving laughter.

"A word, if you will, miss," he snapped, getting a stranglehold on his temper.

She stared guilelessly at him as she tucked her wand into its holster. "Of course."

Blaine spared a moment to pop his head into the flight cabin and give Honovi a nod to show he was all right before leading her belowdecks. She took the steps slower than he did, not having the years he had under his belt at finding his balance in an airship running at speed.

He led her a little ways from the stairs before turning to face her and raising his hands. "If I may?"

She blinked at him but gave him a nod anyway. Before she could step back, Blaine reached for the pendant sitting at the hollow of her throat and undid the clasp there. She took in a sharp breath and made to jerk away, but it was too late. The veil came undone, magic sliding away, the face she'd worn throughout the night becoming her own.

Blaine stared at Caris, heart hammering against his ribs, as she looked back at him in alarm.

"I can explain," Caris said as she hastily reached for the clasp of the veil to do it all up again. The magic glimmered like a haze on a hot day, her visage once again becoming someone else entirely.

"You're not supposed to be here—" He pointed at the holstered wand. "—with *that*."

"I wanted to help."

"You're not known as a magician. You *can't* be known as that right now."

Those brown eyes—not gray like he'd grown used to seeing over the years—narrowed at him. "And what do you mean by that?"

Blaine realized too late he'd backed himself into a corner he hadn't even known was there. Before he could respond, the sound of footsteps on the stairs reached them. Honovi came into view seconds later.

"We're heading to the rendezvous point." He frowned at them. "Is everything all right?"

"Perfectly fine," Caris said with all the haughtiness of the title she'd been born to in her voice.

She spun on her heels and hurried back abovedeck, leaving the two of them alone in the narrow hallway lit by a dull orange gas lamp. Honovi watched her leave before returning his gaze to Blaine.

"What was that about?" he asked in E'ridian.

"*That* was Caris, doing what she pleased when she shouldn't," Blaine replied in the same language, keeping his voice low lest they be overheard.

"Then why do you look as if you saw a revenant?"

Blaine swallowed thickly, remembering the way she'd flung magic about on the train roof, knowing now she'd channel aether without the need of the wand required by nearly everyone else. He knew what that meant—for her and for the country.

"She has the ability to cast starfire."

He said it with a certainty he'd felt only once before, when he'd said his vows to Honovi and accepted the marriage torc around his throat. And Honovi, stars guide him, understood the weight of that statement. Even through the veil he wore, Blaine could see the worry in his eyes.

"She'll be a target."

Blaine's mind dredged up the distant, smoky memory of the night he escaped Amari with Caris in his arms, the both of them leaving everything behind. "She was always a target."

And it was his job, wrapped up in a dead bloodline's duty, to somehow protect her and bear witness to her being seated on the Ashion throne.

Five

MELERI

Meleri wasn't prone to losing her temper, but when faced with the dangerous exploits of her soon-to-be former ward, she found she misplaced her manners quite entirely.

"What were you *thinking*?" Meleri demanded, unable to keep her voice from rising. "Stealing a veil from the stores, attaching yourself to a mission you had no part of, and putting yourself in danger?"

In the gas lamplight of her personal study, Caris looked less repentant than she first had when she and Blaine had returned to the Auclair estate an hour or so ago by way of the catacombs. The package was currently hidden away in a safe house and scheduled to be smuggled out of the city in two days after the required interrogation. Blaine had returned with a travel tube of blueprints that Lore had immediately taken control of. Which left Blaine the sole audience of Meleri's temper, because her children were either abed asleep or handling the fallout of a disastrous mission.

Admittedly, Caris didn't seem cowed in the least. If anything, the young woman was just as angry as Meleri but for a vastly different reason.

"I wanted to *help*," Caris snapped back, her own voice rising.

"This wasn't the way to do it."

"Then, pray tell, what way should I have gone about it? You took one of my cogs when I had offered to go in the first place."

"I have told you before that you aren't meant for missions like this. They're too dangerous. It puts you too much at risk. Just look what happened! Automatons attacked, and you were caught in the crossfire. You very nearly died."

Which was in itself a massive problem. Peacekeepers had met the train at the railway yard to investigate the theft of cargo that wasn't on any manifest. But the more insidious problem was no one should have known the package was on that train in the first place.

Yet someone had.

The implications were enough for Meleri to want to drink an entire potion bottle from the nearest apothecary to get rid of the headache pounding right behind her left eye. The Clementine Trading Company now had the glaring attention of Daijal-backed government officials trained on it. Which meant every route out of Daijal the Clockwork Brigade relied on with that company was most likely compromised.

"You are too much like your mother," Meleri said, thinking not of Portia but of a woman long since burned and her ashes dancing amongst the stars.

Caris glared at her, wavy brown hair still a mess from the flight. In the trousers and work shirt she wore, Caris didn't resemble the noble-woman Meleri had tried so hard to shape her into being. Her own daughters knew the worth of their bloodline, but Caris didn't know hers, and if she kept putting herself in danger, she never would.

"What's that supposed to mean?" Caris demanded.

Belatedly, Meleri realized she'd misjudged her words. Portia was never one to make waves; that had always been Ophelia. "Nothing meant as an insult, so do not take it as such."

"You should hope so, because you are *not* my mother."

"Your mother would be appalled at the way you put yourself and everyone else in danger if she knew."

Portia never would be told, though. For all the Dhemlans were cogs within the Clockwork Brigade, their chains did not overlap.

Caris was mostly outside everyone, placed nearer to where Meleri and her children were in the workings of the rebellion. They'd tasked her with cogs who attended her university, all of whom were screened by Meleri herself.

It was for Caris' own safety, the same way Portia and Emmitt had been kept separate from their daughter in terms of clandestine work. All the secrecy was done to insulate Caris from any fallout.

She'd been chafing more and more the last year at the restrictions placed upon her. For all that Meleri had tried to instill in her the pride of a noblewoman, Caris more often resembled the world her parents had come from: merchants and inventors, people who built things rather than governed or ruled. Ones who called the far-flung borders home and not the beating heart of Ashion.

Oh, Aaralyn. You should have left her with me.

Meleri snuffed out that regretful prayer, hoping the North Star didn't hear it. She pulled the edges of her fur-lined dressing gown closer together. Despite the summer weather, Meleri was old enough to take a chill in the morning. Being woken from her sleep and needing to immediately deal with the fallout from last night's raid hadn't given her time to call her lady's maid and dress for the day.

Meleri huffed out an angry sigh before carefully sitting down behind her desk. What she wouldn't do for some tea at the moment, but until this whole mess was addressed to her satisfaction, breakfast would have to wait.

"Your antics put everyone sent out last night at risk—yourself included. When I made you a cog, I impressed upon you the need to keep the chains intact. Haring off on your own risks breaking every chain present on the airship last night," Meleri said.

"I never meant—"

Meleri held up her hand, cutting Caris off. "You are not to oversee any Clockwork Brigade mission until I say otherwise. Until I know you'll put the country first over your need for adventure, I cannot rely on you right now."

Caris jerked back a step, something like shame flashing across her face before her shoulders stiffened and she raised her chin. "If you'll excuse me, I think I'll visit my parents for the remainder of the day."

Without waiting for permission, Caris left, shutting the door loudly behind her. From the corner where he'd watched the argument play out, Blaine said, "You do realize that will only drive her to action you will not like."

"She should have never gone with you to begin with," Meleri snapped.

"I didn't know it was her until the automatons attacked. She wore a veil and didn't speak to me until we were on the train. Even then, she used an accent."

Meleri closed her eyes, trying not to think of all the horrible ways Caris could have been injured or killed last night. "The moment you knew it was Caris beneath the veil, you should have sent her back to the airship. How am I to trust you'll keep her safe when you let her fight?"

Blaine moved away from the corner, a simmering sort of anger in his eyes. "I have done nothing but try to keep her safe since you brought me to Ashion. You forget who I was."

"Your bloodline died in the Inferno."

Blaine sketched a mockery of a bow to her, the crispness of his Ashionen accent fading a little into the rolling burr of his E'ridian one. "Yet here I am."

"You would've stayed in E'ridia if given a chance."

"I came back because I knew my duty. I *always* knew it, even while living in Glencoe. I have done my duty by staying by Caris' side. You're teaching Caris to know hers, but keeping her blind to the truth helps no one, least of all her."

"She is too important to risk."

Blaine stepped closer to the desk, planting his hands on it and leaning forward so he could look Meleri in the eye. She stiffened but refused to draw back. "Caris cast magic holding a wand, but she didn't channel the aether through it. The clarion crystal at the tip never glowed. You must know what that means."

Meleri drew in a sharp breath, lips parting in surprise as her heart lurched. She'd wondered—for years—if Caris had any magic to her. But the girl had come to Amari with no wand, despite her exquisite skill with cutting clarion crystals. There'd been no indication of magic from her, not a hint.

Until now.

Meleri's hopes soared at that revelation before they were promptly choked off by the realization of who was to arrive tomorrow at the height of the social summer season. As Meleri's ward for so many years and a noble in her own right, Caris would be obligated to appear at any party she was given an invitation to on behalf of the crown princess.

Blaine straightened up, never blinking. "I'll guard her, but you would do well to let her know the truth of her bloodline. She needs to know."

Meleri swallowed dryly. "Not yet. It isn't safe."

"It never will be. Would you rather a living queen that Ashion can rally around or a name on a memory wall bearing a bloodline that was never meant to be hers?" Blaine smiled tightly before turning to leave. "I know my preference, Your Grace."

Blaine left, closing the door quietly behind him. Meleri let out a shuddering breath, cognizant of the dangerous road that lay ahead and all the pitfalls beneath her feet.

Six

EIMARILLE

The royal airship juddered upon anchoring, but Eimarille barely noticed it in the suite she, Terilyn, and her son were in. Eimarille had never been fond of courtiers, and none had journeyed with them to Ashion. She'd taken a contingent of her staff, royal guards, and that was it. Servants bustled about, readying them for departure once the crew allowed it, but Eimarille's focus was on Lisandro.

"Come here, darling. Let me fix your collar," Eimarille said.

Her four-year-old son tore himself away from the port window to return to her side. His shorts and tiny button-down short-sleeved shirt were a deep navy and a crisp white. Eimarille knelt to be on his level, expertly straightening his shirt collar before smoothing down his blond hair.

Lisandro took after her more than Wesley, and his temperament was certainly more hers than his father's. He was a sweet child, with the spark of starfire in his soul that Eimarille had felt since the moment he was placed in her arms.

Eimarille smiled before brushing a quick kiss over his forehead. "There we go. Now, remember not to let go of my hand."

"Yes, Mother," Lisandro said in that high, sweet voice of his.

Eimarille straightened up, carefully smoothing out the skirt of her gown. The deep blue silk was picked through at the hem with golden embroidery depicting the six star god constellations. The delicate white lace shawl Terilyn draped over her shoulder was dedicated to Innes alone in its making.

"We'll be ready to depart shortly," Terilyn said.

Her lady-in-waiting had opted not to wear a gown for this trip and instead wore a tailored pale blue suit with a day jacket fitted with morning tails. Eimarille could easily pick out the places where tailoring hid her lover's weapons only because she knew the spots Terilyn preferred to carry her knives and derringer. Terilyn preferred ease of movement whenever they came to Ashion, and Eimarille would never fault her for that.

Eimarille took Lisandro's hand in hers and drew him close to her side. Terilyn coordinated with the royal guards before ushering her charges out of the suite. The moment they came abovedeck and reached the gangplank, the crowd waiting for them in the private hangar came to life with a roar. The flash of camera bulbs went off for the tintype photographs that would run in the evening broadsheets.

Sawyer Clark, Prime Minister of Ashion, was decked out in a smartly tailored suit, top hat, gloves, and cane. He bowed deeply to Eimarille as she and her son stepped off the gangplank to the arrival platform.

"Your Royal Highness," Sawyer said.

Eimarille smiled, holding the pose long enough for the press to get the picture, before stepping closer. "Prime Minister. It's lovely to see you again."

Sawyer straightened up, giving her a respectful nod at her words. The man was the second prime minister appointed by King Bernard to oversee the Ashion parliament. He was head of the Ashion government in the absence of a monarch, a position that would eventually become obsolete once Eimarille took Bernard's crown, throne, and court. Ashion would have no need for its own form of government when she was queen.

"We here in Ashion are always pleased when you grace us with a visit."

He lied well, but Eimarille knew half the bloodlines in Ashion would rather see her dead, treating her as a traitor to a throne none of them had the right to. The Clockwork Brigade certainly had its sympathizers, especially here in Amari. While many in the western border provinces had bent well to Daijalan propaganda over the years, the eastern provinces and the whittled down military had not.

It was why Eimarille had traveled east so many times over the years on a progress that saw her visit large cities and small towns across Ashion. Putting a human face to a name most people only ever read about in broadsheets could sway public opinion more than quoted statements from an article.

Eimarille went through the formalities of greeting with polite enthusiasm. She bent to accept a bouquet of flowers from a prettily dressed young girl who curtsied to her. She smiled through the accolades and respect given to her by select members of the Ashion parliament who had joined the prime minister for the occasion. Their faces and names were familiar to her through reports provided by Daijalan spies and official messengers.

Terilyn remained to her right and a step behind, ever a faithful shadow as the royal guards escorted them off the arrival platform and down to where the motor carriages awaited. Theirs carried miniature flags of Daijal and Ashion at the front over the headlamps, while the Daijalan royal crest was painted on each door.

The motor carriage windows were nearly wrapped all the way around, providing a mostly unobstructed view of the streets they drove down after leaving the airfield behind. The route was lined with well-wishers, the sidewalk impossible to see beneath the feet of the crowd in places.

Landing in the western airfield meant it took some time to make it across the Serpentine River via Hollows Bridge and to the eastern half of Amari. The palace they were driven to had stood for two decades, and it was nothing like the one she remembered from her childhood. She supposed that was for the best. Eimarille had no desire to rule in the memory of her mother's shadow.

The motor carriage drove through the open gates into the royal grounds. The fountain in the center of the courtyard bubbled away, with some birds preening in the higher pools. Servants and guards lined the main entrance to the palace, all bowing or curtsying when Eimarille was helped out of the motor carriage. The last time she'd been here was two years ago with Wesley. He hadn't been fond of the palace or the city, preferring New Haven and the adoration of its citizens.

Here, though, in this eastern city, was a place where Eimarille was adored more and more. The older generations remembered when the Rourke bloodline once ruled. Eimarille had been told more than once —usually as an insult behind a smile—that she was the spitting image of her mother, save for her eyes.

Alasandair had their mother's eyes.

The thought flitted through her mind, a distant recollection. With it came an old curiosity. Eimarille had always wondered if the child Ophelia had been pregnant with and died with would have had eyes like their mother's or their father's.

Eimarille pressed her lips together, offering up a smile to the steward in charge of the palace employees instead of the frown that pricked at the corners of her mouth.

"Welcome home, Your Royal Highness," the steward said.

And it was home, this city—this country, even. She'd been born here, after all. Raised within these city walls for her childhood before Innes stole her away from beneath the North Star's guidance. Ashion was a country without a queen, but not for too much longer, if Eimarille had anything to say about it.

They were escorted through the palace to the royal family wing. Along the way, they passed a veritable army of workers preparing the palace for the ball tomorrow night that would officially welcome Eimarille's presence in the city.

Eimarille and Lisandro took introductions of their assigned personal servants in a blue-and-gold parlor, while Terilyn stalked the private rooms on silent feet with guards at her side. Her Blade was ever resourceful when it came to securing their safety, and Eimarille let the Urovan take as long as she liked to be satisfied.

When Terilyn slipped back into the parlor, long black hair falling loose down to her waist, expression serene, and no weapon in hand, Eimarille let herself relax. Moments later, the servants were dismissed to handle their travel trunks and bring tea and a light meal while Eimarille saw to Lisandro's comfort.

"I want to see my room," Lisandro demanded.

Eimarille raised an eyebrow at Terilyn, who smiled down at her son and offered up her callused hand to him. "I know just the one you'll like, *malynshka*."

The Urovan endearment was one Terilyn offered no one else, and Lisandro always delighted in it. He let go of Eimarille to take Terilyn's hand, chattering at her all the while about what he'd seen on the drive through the city. Terilyn glanced at Eimarille, sharing a sweet smile over her son's head that was just for her.

Eimarille was glad she had taken the trip alone with just Lisandro and Terilyn for company. Wesley could bed whichever mistress he pleased in her absence, and Eimarille would get to sleep beside the only person she'd ever loved before her son came into her life.

The bedroom Terilyn led them to was decorated in soft greens and pale browns, the wallpaper an intricate design above the wainscoting. It had clearly been decorated with her son in mind, with one set of doors opening up onto a nursery filled with toys, including a large clockwork horse that would rock back and forth on its own if wound up. Lisandro gasped in delight before scampering into the nursery to play.

Eimarille and Terilyn stood just past the doorway, both of them watching as he explored. After a moment, Terilyn reached into the inner pocket of her day jacket and pulled out a folded slip of paper, handing it to Eimarille.

"I will need to meet with the Blades here in the city tonight. They may have information regarding our missing inventor," Terilyn said.

Eimarille unfolded the piece of paper and reviewed the address typed on it, along with a time. Beneath it were a few handwritten sentences in Urovan that Eimarille could read only because Terilyn had taught her the language growing up.

She was unsurprised the missive had been delivered to them. Blades were deft at getting in and out of places without being seen. They'd done so during the Inferno, after all.

Eimarille held no ill will toward the people who had murdered the governing body of Ashion. She used to as a child, but that was before Innes had explained it had all been for the greater good, that he'd done it for her, his favorite child. Blades dedicated their lives to the Twilight Star. The ones who had followed his orders on that long-ago night did so because they believed in his cause, not simply for a king's money.

Terilyn had dedicated her life to Eimarille at the behest of two star gods. Such guidance was unheard of within the secretive sect of worshippers. To that end, Blades were far more willing to give aid to her when needed, even if it went against a current contract.

Eimarille was to be queen of Maricol one day. It was written in the stars, and Blades were ever mindful of what the stars told them.

"Kote promised to keep us apprised of any new information he receives in New Haven. Tomorrow we have the ball, and as much as I would love for you to bring back the traitor's head, I'd rather you remain by my side," Eimarille said.

They'd been informed of Wyatt Lehan's disappearance in Solaria the other week, and Eimarille had melted an entire tea set with starfire in her quiet rage. Terilyn had taken it upon herself to head up the search for the missing inventor while here in Amari. Blades were useful for cutting through so many things.

"And the *Klovod?*"

Eimarille pursed her lips, thinking about the one person who was responsible for all the puppets she'd gathered in her travels over the years. "You'll meet with him as planned."

"As my queen commands."

Eimarille reached out and tucked a long lock of hair behind Terilyn's ear, searching her lover's face. So many courtiers saw the other lady as an impassive shadow, never seeing the mirth that danced in her brown eyes, never knowing truly what she was, only knowing that she was Eimarille's.

Terilyn grasped her fingers and turned to press a kiss to Eimarille's palm, lips lingering against her skin. "I've missed getting to taste you."

It'd been weeks since they'd last had time together. Eimarille was determined to rectify that. "Tonight, darling."

Terilyn smiled, heat burning in her gaze for a brief moment, before she released Eimarille's hand to go and entertain Lisandro. Eimarille watched them play for a few minutes, finding joy in her son's laughter and the smile on her lover's face, before she joined them.

Seven

CARIS

The Dhemlan bloodline's two motor carriages drove behind the ones that carried the Auclair bloodline into the palace grounds. Normally, being a newer bloodline and low on the social hierarchy, Caris' family would not be accorded an arrival honor with the duchess. But since she'd been Meleri's ward for the past several years while attending university, the Dhemlan bloodline was treated to the same sort of respect by virtue of association.

"Promise me you will be on your best behavior," Portia said as she stared out the window at the attendees making their way into the palace.

"Of course, Mother," Caris said.

The entirety of Ashion's noble bloodlines was expected to attend the ball tonight. Caris hadn't even protested wearing the gown Meleri's servant had delivered to her family's small estate for the evening's festivities. It wasn't often Crown Princess Eimarille Rourke returned home to Ashion, and her scheduled time here in the capital had been the talk of the city for weeks in the lead-up.

It was inescapable, the palpable excitement in the air as their motor carriage rolled to a gentle stop. Tonight's ball was *the* event of the season, and if one were to miss it, they surely would be considered socially worthless.

A servant opened their motor carriage door, offering his hand to Caris and then Portia as they exited the vehicle amidst the flashing bulbs of the press cordoned off to the side. Caris discreetly smoothed down the skirt of her ball gown. The rich dark blue tulle of the skirt was pinpricked with gold thread that resembled stars falling down from her waist. The golden detail followed the bones of the corset she wore, and the off-the-shoulder look allowed for the gold-and-sapphire choker she wore, loaned out by the duchess, to show off the line of her throat and clavicles.

Caris' thick, wavy, shoulder-length hair had been tamed into more defined curls. She wore no headdress or tiara, unlike the duchess, who looked like a queen in the deep green gown and diamond tiara with emeralds she wore. The silver metal cane she carried was topped with a clarion crystal, though she had no magic. Caris wondered if there were any spells attached to the cane, as it wasn't one she'd ever seen the duchess use before.

"Come along, my dear," Portia said, touching Caris' elbow.

She fell into step beside her mother, her father playing escort for Portia. Meleri's children had joined the duchess in front of the wide steps that led to the palace's main entrance. Lore and Dureau lacked an escort, while Brielle stood with her husband, their children left at home for the evening.

"Shall we?" Meleri asked, smiling as Caris and her parents approached.

Caris bit the inside of her lip, still angry about how the duchess had treated her the other night. She hadn't been able to confide in her parents about what she was feeling when she'd stormed inside their small Amari home. Caris had ended up taking out her temper on what devices her father had brought with him from Cosian to work on, setting about repairing them to distract herself until she cooled off.

That tangle of fury and—yes—embarrassment came rushing back as she and her parents joined the Auclairs. Caris averted her gaze as she curtsied to the duchess, hoping the rouge on her cheeks was enough to hide her flush.

In hindsight, perhaps she owed Meleri an apology of sorts, but now wasn't the place to give one. Besides, Caris still had to figure out a way to talk with her old professor and beg him not to say anything about her magic. That, more than Meleri's anger, was what made Caris want to bite her nails.

All her life, her parents had told her to hide her magic, and she *had*. But lately it felt as if her skin wanted to split over her bones and let the aether flow out of her as if she were a waterfall. It's why she sneaked veils from the duchess' secret stores and sometimes took missions she should have passed on to others.

Caris wanted to *help*, and her magic let her, even if she wasn't supposed to use it.

Her heavy thoughts kept her company up the stairs until Lore glided over and nudged her discreetly with an elbow. "You look far too glum for such a grand party we're about to join. Cheer up, Caris. I'm sure Nathaniel will be happy to see you."

"I suppose," Caris said, some of her anxiety fading away at the thought of getting to dance with Nathaniel.

Despite his family not being ennobled, they'd been invited because their company was one of the largest and most successful in Ashion. Only a handful of merchant families had been extended the invitation, and they'd accepted before the Clockwork Brigade had targeted one of their trains.

Caris had gone to the shops with her mother yesterday for last-minute purchases before the ball. She'd heard the whispers trailing in their wake about the Clementines and the scrutiny that family now faced. All manner of rumors were percolating through high society, and Caris wasn't immune to it, having accepted Nathaniel's attention, if not formal courtship, for years. Before she could be reunited with him, her family and the duchess' had to get through the formalities of arrival.

The palace was brightly lit by gas lamps in sconces and in crystal chandeliers. The artwork on the walls consisted of pastoral scenes from Daijal, because Ashion was landlocked and had no coast or dense forest its citizens could cavort through. The painted scenery transitioned into cityscapes with airships flying above, but Caris didn't recognize the places.

She did recognize the portraits of the Daijalan royal family that preceded them into the ballroom. Her gaze lingered on the one of Crown Princess Eimarille, the artist having made every effort to include imagery of Daijal and the Iverson bloodline within the painting. As if he could erase Ashion's past staring out of the princess' eyes here in this place.

Caris ducked her head slightly as they passed by the portrait and entered the ballroom proper. The who's who of high society filled it from wall to wall. Music from a dozen orchestra players huddled in the corner and overseen by a conductor was a counterpoint for the chatter filling the air. The noise picked up with their arrival as the guests nearest them recognized the duchess.

No formal announcement heralded their arrival, but one wasn't needed. The duchess stood out amongst the crowd and always would. Caris and her parents followed in the Auclairs' wake, and the duchess never forgot they were there.

Caris took a champagne glass from the tray of a passing server and took a small sip. Dancers waltzed on the black wood of the ballroom floor while those not asked or not inspired to huddled around it in little groups.

Lore stayed by Caris' side when her parents were drawn into a conversation with another family as new to a title as they were. Whenever she went to one of these events, Caris was never left alone for an instant. Over the years, the duchess had introduced her to nearly every Ashion bloodline in existence.

All save one.

The loud crack of a staff against the floor at the end of the waltz cut through the air. Every head turned toward the double doors that had been closed at some point. The dance floor cleared in moments, with everyone jockeying for a spot up front as politely as possible.

"Announcing Her Royal Highness, the Crown Princess Eimarille

Rourke," the majordomo of the palace called out in a deep voice that carried.

Uniformed servants smartly opened the double doors with a flourish, allowing the crown princess to enter in a swirl of silver fabric, escorted by the prime minister. The ball gown Eimarille wore sparkled from thousands of crystals embroidered on the skirt, like tiny stars that flickered beneath the light.

Her blonde hair was twisted back in a neat, formal bun unadorned with any combs, the sleek and simple style a backdrop for the diamond tiara she wore. More diamonds were wrapped around her throat in a choker, layered loops falling over her bare shoulders. The white, above-elbow-length gloves she wore offset the silver of her gown.

Behind her came the royal entourage, and Caris wouldn't have cared about any of them, except Lore leaned close, pitching her voice low beneath the furious sound of everyone clapping.

"They say the princess never goes anywhere without the Urovan. I've heard it's said she acts as the princess' voice at times," Lore said.

The words were barely louder than a whisper, and Caris had to strain to hear them. She stared at the woman in question, one whose ice-white gown was a complement to Eimarille's. Her long black hair had been swept back by combs and curled. Her escort was the prime minister's son, who looked absolutely besotted with the woman, but Caris noticed how the lady never took her eyes off Eimarille.

"They say her words cut like a blade."

Caris stiffened slightly at the phrasing, careful not to let anything show on her face. She didn't look at Lore, because everyone was looking at Eimarille, and to do otherwise was to draw attention. The clapping hadn't stopped, and Eimarille basked in the reception she was given, beautiful in an icy way that Caris didn't trust.

The music started up again, and the crowd surged forward to fill in the space. Lore looped her arm through Caris' and pitched them in the opposite direction, well away from the crown princess and her entourage.

"Let's see about finding something to nibble on. Remember the last time you drank on an empty stomach?" Lore said.

Caris grimaced at the reminder and eyed what remained in her glass. "Yes, let's find something to eat."

Dinner was to be eaten under the stars in the palace gardens in the hour after sunset. To tide people over, servants were tasked with ferrying trays filled with finger food around the ballroom. Lore waylaid one such servant and picked up a thin wedge of toasted bread with a spread of some sort on it. She passed it to Caris before taking another.

"I haven't seen Nathaniel yet. Have you spotted him?" Caris asked as she nibbled on the toast. The spread was minced fish heavily mixed with a dense cheese and flavored with dill. It was tasty.

"He should be about."

Lore kept them moving, pausing every now and then to chat with someone when drawn into a conversation. Caris held up well enough, but mostly everyone was talking about finding a wife or a husband for their children who'd yet to be married.

"I'm sure we're boring you, Lady Lore," Lady Sylvie Bloyer said with an impolite smile. "All this talk about husbands and you've yet to marry."

Lore returned the viscountess' smile. "I'd rather marry just the once, and I'm willing to wait to do so."

Caris covered her smile with her champagne glass as the viscountess could say nothing to that jibe, having been married five times in her lifetime. The woman was a notorious social climber. She'd hoped to nab a duke and a title when she was younger, but the most she'd ended up with was a viscount who, if rumor was correct, spent far more time with his mistress than in their marriage bed.

The pair chatted a few minutes longer before taking their leave, continuing their circuit of the ballroom. When they made it to the set of double doors that led into the large hall of crystal and mirrors, a replica from the old palace, Caris was grateful to leave the music behind.

"Shouldn't we pay our respects to the crown princess?" Caris asked. The last time Eimarille had been in Amari, Caris had been taking exams and couldn't get away. She was overdue for an introduction.

Lore hummed wordlessly, attention on the crowd around them. "Eventually."

The hall of crystal and mirrors was an exquisite room, and when the original one had burned in the old palace, those who had seen it mourned its loss. The replica they stood in was brightly lit by gaslight crystal chandeliers. The illumination reflected on the wall of mirrors to Caris' left. Each mirror was carved to match the size of the window it sat opposite. During the day, she was certain the hall dazzled from the sunlight that poured in.

The carved columns and arched ceiling were painted gold, with bits of clarion crystal embedded in the deeper reliefs. The frescoes painted on the ceiling in sections outlined in gold relief depicted the star gods, with the Twilight Star taking pride of place where the North Star should be. More clarion crystals acted as stars above, twinkling in the gaslight.

There was a nearly soundless hum to the air, beneath the music, that came from the cut clarion crystals. It pricked the edge of her hearing, catching Caris' attention in a way she'd always been attuned to. Whoever had cut the clarion crystal had been skilled, but not skilled enough that some sour notes weren't present.

Caris' fingers twitched with the need to recut and fix what had been created back when she was a young child. She shook her hands to try to get rid of the itch beneath her skin, smiling in the face of Lore's curious look.

"It's nothing," Caris said. It wasn't as if she could explain to Lore that the hall they stood in made her ache for the aether she so rarely got to touch.

The crowd shifted around them, gazes cutting askance, and a familiar figure eventually appeared, whispers trailing in his wake.

"Miss Caris. Lady Lore," Nathaniel said with a smile, shoulders tight amidst the stares. "I don't believe you've had the pleasure of meeting Ambassador Honovi tonight."

The tall E'ridian was decked out in a formal kilt and plaid, the colors of which Caris knew meant he was from Clan Storm. His head was shaved on the side while his long braid was intricately wrapped with beaded leather ribbons and metal hair ornaments that indicated he was of significant rank.

Caris dipped into a curtsy that honored his position. "Ambassador."

"Miss Caris," Honovi said, brown eyes studying her with an intensity she couldn't find a reason for.

She turned her attention to Nathaniel, closing the distance between them to stand by his side. She peered up at him with a straightforwardness she'd never been able to give up, despite all of Meleri's teachings. "What's wrong?"

The edge to Nathaniel's smile softened into something far more like himself. "It's nothing. How are you this evening?"

Caris glanced back at Lore. "Well enough."

"Perhaps we should—"

The chatter of the crowd became far more excited, and Caris turned to face the entrance they'd come from. She was tall enough in the heeled shoes she wore to catch a glimpse of the tiara worn by Princess Eimarille over everyone's head.

"Lady Lore," Nathaniel said sharply.

The look Lore shot him was one Caris couldn't read. "I hear the gardens are open for the evening? Perhaps we should all adjourn there?"

"I fear I may tarnish your reputations if I joined you."

"What is that supposed to mean?" Caris asked sharply. "And shouldn't we wait to be introduced?"

Before Nathaniel could respond, the crowd shifted around them, giving space for the guests of honor who had made their way farther into the hall. Nathaniel offered Caris his arm, and she didn't hesitate to curl her hand around his elbow and let him guide her back some into the crowd. Lore stood partially in front of Caris, making it so she had to peer around the other woman to see anything.

The prime minister was introducing Eimarille to those standing in the front of the crowd, which meant they could not escape an introduction. Leaving would be considered an insult, so they could only stay and wait for the moment the guest of honor was given their names, though Eimarille seemed to know some of them already.

"Lady Lore," Eimarille said with a polite smile.

Lore curtsied deeply, the skirt of her gown fluttering around her as she dipped down. Caris followed her lead, even though she hadn't yet been introduced. Nathaniel clicked his heels together before bowing to the degree reserved for royalty, if not a monarch. Honovi bowed as well.

Eimarille nodded at Honovi. "Ambassador Honovi, it's a pleasure to have you this evening."

"The clans are honored by the invitation," Honovi said in accented Ashionen.

Eimarille's gaze shifted from the ambassador to Nathaniel. "Mr. Clementine. I heard what happened to one of your company's trains recently. It's such a pity the Clockwork Brigade has targeted your family's business."

"It's an unfortunate side effect to success, Your Royal Highness," Nathaniel demurred.

"Yes, isn't it?" Eimarille's attention drifted to Caris, those icy blue eyes narrowing ever so slightly. "And you are?"

"Caris Dhemlan, Your Royal Highness. It's an honor to meet you," Caris said, remembering her manners. Eimarille's attention was a heavy thing, and Caris felt pinned in a way she never had before.

Eimarille smiled slightly. "The Duchess of Auclair mentioned you when we chatted earlier. You were her ward for several years, were you not?"

"Yes, Your Royal Highness."

"How have you found living in Amari?"

"Quite to my liking, thank you. The duchess and her family have been nothing but kind."

"I'm sure."

Eimarille studied her for a few seconds more without saying a word before moving to the next guest. Caris let out a breath she hadn't been aware she was holding, tightening her grip on Nathaniel's arm. The princess' attention was a weight she was glad to be rid of, along with the Urovan lady-in-waiting's regard.

Caris could have done with some air, but leaving would've been rude. Lore and Nathaniel maneuvered their small group deeper into the crowd, allowing others to take their place for introductions. Honovi chose to stay with them.

They mingled, because that was expected of them. Caris found herself keeping up sides of conversations she had no interest in. Everyone gushed about the princess, and Caris was hard-pressed to find a lie in anyone's words.

She knew some of the bloodlines present weren't in favor of Eimarille, even if they paid lip service to the Daijal court. Everyone did that night—through dinner, through more dancing, and through the end for the fireworks that exploded over the capital above the new palace.

The spectacle was made more extravagant by the addition of starfire cast by Eimarille. The white-hot burn of magic streaked away from the princess' raised hands to erupt against the starry night sky. A pressure dug roots through Caris' chest, coiling deep, as Eimarille called forth starfire. Caris' hands twitched as she stood there in the garden, surrounded by the elite of Ashion, a secret burning in her soul.

Cool fingers wrapped around her left wrist, squeezing tightly. Caris glanced sideways, meeting her mother's clear-eyed gaze.

"Don't," Portia warned, the word barely a sound falling from her lips, but the fear in her eyes was easy enough to read.

Caris swallowed thickly and faced forward again. As she did so, her gaze caught on the face of a woman dressed in a long-sleeved gown who wasn't staring at the night sky but right back at her. Caris blinked, and when she opened her eyes again, the woman had disappeared, as if she'd never been.

Frowning, Caris cast her gaze upward, watching starfire explode amidst fireworks, yearning for something she could not explain.

Eight

MELERI

Meleri had chosen a spot deep in the palace gardens to watch the fireworks show. She was accompanied not by any of her children, but by the North Star herself.

"The aether calls to the girl," Aaralyn said from her spot on a marble bench.

Meleri gripped her cane tighter, keeping her eyes on the star god and not the sky. "Should we be discussing this here, in this place, with the princess in residence?"

Aaralyn looked over her shoulder at Meleri, the star god's eyes shining in her face. "My husband holds no sway here, no matter what he likes to believe."

"Eimarille does, for she is still a Rourke."

"If that were the case, she would have taken her chance with the starfire throne well before now. She hasn't, and there is a reason for that."

Meleri walked farther into the small area of the garden, with its bubbling fountain and high hedges that kept them hidden from the crowd. If it were anyone else out there with her, Meleri wouldn't trust their conversation could be kept secret.

"Did you know that Caris had magic? That she needs no wand to channel the aether?" Meleri asked.

"I am the North Star."

Meleri pressed her lips together, hands shaking with a sudden fury that left her light-headed. "She's headstrong and stubborn. We could have lost her on that raid."

"You didn't, but you will lose her anyway if you block her from the road she is meant to walk."

"She is meant to rule, not to fight."

"What is ruling but a type of war?" Aaralyn stood, the Wolf constellation tattoo on her right arm shining through the sleeve of her ball gown. "She will not learn to survive if you do not let her fight. Allow her the freedom of her choices, or the queen you hope for will be a bitter ruler lost to you."

Aaralyn walked away into the darkness, leaving Meleri alone beneath a cascade of fireworks. The explosions echoed in her ears, the sound not loud enough to block out the North Star's admonishment.

Meleri straightened her shoulders, chilled despite the warm evening air, and made her way back to the main crowd scattered throughout the garden. She was mindful of where she placed her cane as she made her way back to where her children stood. Spellwork was carved on the inside, protection against mind magic and other threats in company such as this.

Which was all for the best, considering who glided out of the crowd like a ghost, all sharp-eyed and knifelike smile.

"Were the gardens to your liking, Your Grace?" Terilyn asked.

Meleri had spent years learning to mask her true feelings and emotions. Not even a purported Blade could carve the truth out of her on a night like this. She held faith in the North Star and the prayers Aaralyn answered.

"They're different from the ones I walked as a child," Meleri said.

"My lady remembers the ones you speak of. She quite prefers the flowers that bloom today."

"It's a blessing to have the princess with us."

She meant what she said, even if it wasn't about the woman Terilyn served. Words were a game Meleri had played since she was a child learning to speak them. They were a weapon in their own way, and Meleri wielded them with the skill of a professional.

Terilyn studied her without giving anything away before finally stepping aside, allowing Meleri to pass her. Meleri continued on her way down the garden path, cognizant of the threat she left behind.

Her children must have been keeping an eye out for her, because Dureau suddenly appeared by her side, offering his elbow. "Mother."

Meleri took the offer of support with an easy smile. "Thank you, my dear."

"That's some company you were keeping."

She thought of Aaralyn in the garden and the Blade in the path and could only agree.

Nine

BLAINE

Blaine was in Meleri's study in the private wing of the Auclair estate when Lore swept into the room. He straightened up from where he'd been bent over copies of the inventor's blueprints, hearing his spine crack a bit from the motion. His shoulders felt tight, and he rolled them a few times to loosen the muscles.

Lore cleared her throat. "I need an escort."

Blaine rubbed at the bridge of his nose, sighing irritably. "You have a brother."

"He's busy. You'll do in his stead." Lore came around to stand by the writing desk, reaching out to touch the corner of one of the blueprints. "Information has come in from a cog about strange goings-on at an apothecary in the southwest of Amari."

Blaine shifted on the chair so he could better see her. "Your mother wants my report on this death-defying machine sooner rather than later. Rumors won't help with that."

"The apothecary may be important. Word is people go in, but they do not come out."

"Perhaps it is over a catacomb entrance."

"We've checked the map. It's not."

Blaine leaned back in his seat and crossed his arms over his chest. "If it's as dangerous as you make it sound, you shouldn't be going. Send a different group of cogs. Make sure one of them is a magician."

"With the princess present, and her Blade, my cogs are leery about moving. I told Mother I'd handle it. We'll have veils to limit identification."

"We?"

Lore grimaced. "The information came from a cog linked to Caris' chain, some university student still attending the School of Engineering a year behind her."

Blaine's mouth tightened into a hard line, not liking where this was going at all. "I don't care where the information came from. Caris shouldn't be helping you surveil any place in the city you think might be connected to the death-defying machine."

"She's insisting she joins me, or she goes on her own. What would you have me do?"

"Lock her in her bedroom, if need be. Veils won't save either of you from a bullet. Give her a mission if she wants, just not this one."

Lore gave him a scornful look. "Since when has that worked in the past? She followed you onto that train, remember? Mother didn't want her to go with me, but Caris said it was her cog who brought the information, so it was her responsibility to see this through."

"Your mother is Ashion's spymaster. She handles cogs, and Caris is one such piece. Make her stay put."

Lore made a cutting gesture with her gloved hand. "The North Star wishes Caris to handle this mission."

Blaine rolled up the blueprints and tucked them back into the leather tube. "Does she, now? And your mother is fine with such a plan?"

"The North Star was present at the ball. She met with Mother in the gardens. I was not privy to their conversation, only what my mother would share after the fact."

"Which is?"

"The North Star wishes Caris to fight."

Blaine's mouth curled at the corners, but it didn't feel like a smile. "The star gods didn't fight for her during the Inferno, yet they wish her to take up their idealist mantle now?"

"They *saved* her. She is why we fight."

"You fight for a memory. Caris was raised in Cosian. She is of the Eastern Basin and all that entails. She is a child of the borders. The four years you've spent trying to teach her the ways of high society and a culture she doesn't feel in her bones won't make her what you wish her to be. Even I can see that."

"She is meant to be queen."

"Yes. For everyone in Ashion, not just those whose bloodlines are written in the nobility genealogies."

"If you have such little faith in what we hope for her, why do you stay?"

"Because she is my duty, even if she is not what my heart desires."

"Ah, yes. You Westergards did your duty well during the Inferno when the lot of you died."

Stung, Blaine stood so they were on even footing. "My father died to see her safe. Don't belittle his sacrifices."

"Then don't mock our hope. Caris is who we've been waiting for."

Ashion needed a queen, one who could claim the throne and put out the starfire that burned on it. Blaine knew that. Not even Eimarille dared sit on the relic the Rourke bloodline had once ruled from. That veneer of hesitancy was what kept half the country's noble families from caving to Daijal's promises, but it was a constant battle. The duchess had promised them the impossible, and at some point, she had to deliver.

At some point, she would have to introduce Caris as someone other than her ward.

Blaine knew the day that happened was the day a war would start.

He ground his teeth, hating that he couldn't argue against a star god's decree. He wanted Caris to have a choice, but at the same time, he needed to keep her safe to make it. "If the North Star wants Caris to join you on this endeavor, then I suppose I'll act as escort."

411

Lore smiled thinly. "You're too kind. Were all Westergards so attentive?"

"That bloodline is dead."

Lore flicked her gaze from his head to his toes and back up again. "It looks perfectly alive to me. We leave in an hour. It's a long walk through the catacombs to get where we need to be."

With that said, she exited the study to go handle whatever needs the Auclair household currently had. Blaine knew Meleri was in parliament with Brielle, overseeing whatever damage Eimarille sought to do to their country and try to mitigate it. They'd left after Blaine had arrived from the catacombs, heading off to deal with a problem that had no easy answer. Ashion's government was a slowly eroding puppet that had given up power too easily over the years.

The Auclairs were determined to stop that slow death, and if stubbornness could fix anything, they'd fix this. Blaine had come to understand over the last few years why that family fought, why the Clockwork Brigade existed. It wasn't just to free debt slaves but to push back against laws that would harm Ashion.

Blaine sighed, rubbing at the back of his neck. He knew the Auclairs saw Caris as their savior and didn't want her to fight. Keeping the young baroness from the line of fire was becoming more difficult by the day. Caris was stubborn, and that trait was on display hours later when he and Lore met her in the basement.

"What is *he* doing here?" Caris asked with a scowl as she glared at Blaine, the gas lamps in their sconces turning her skin sallow.

Lore shrugged. "He's our escort."

Caris' eyes narrowed. "Do we really need one if we're going as someone else?"

Her fingers were clenched around the shimmery fabric of a veil, her face yet her own for the moment. Like Lore, the younger woman was dressed in sturdy boots, trousers, and a well-worn linen blouse—the typical outfit a working-class girl in the outskirts of the city might wear.

The places they were going weren't exactly popular with high society, and so they had to play the part. Blaine's own veil was tucked away in his trouser pocket, a pistol holstered at his lower back. He knew Lore was similarly armed, having pocketed two aether-powered smoke bombs from the weapons store that could help hide their retreat if necessary. She'd holstered her derringer around her right ankle, the small pistol hidden by the wide cuff of her trouser leg.

Caris, he noted, wasn't carrying a wand of any sort. Despite the revelation of her magic, no one wanted her to use it. The North Star may have ordered Meleri to allow Caris fieldwork, but there were limits to the duchess' obedience. Caris was not to tap the aether, and that was for everyone's safety. Blaine only hoped she listened.

"Yes," Lore said.

"You could have picked anyone else but Tristan."

Blaine hadn't yet found the time—or been given permission—to tell Caris that Tristan wasn't his real name. He still lived under a false identity where she was concerned, and he knew the longer he went without telling her the truth, the more trouble it would cause.

Lore gestured at the entrance to the catacombs that Fred guarded, the automaton having not moved from its post. "Shall we?"

Getting into the catacombs was the easy part. Navigating the underground tunnels was something else entirely. Blaine knew some of the routes, but Lore had memorized the safe passages as a child and so led the way.

The Clockwork Brigade wasn't the only organization to access the catacombs. The Collector's Guild had sought to lay claim to the underground world from time to time, but the Clockwork Brigade never let their access remain for long. Inevitably, people died, buildings were burned, and records were forcibly lost to help keep a city's secrets.

Lore's handheld gaslight was a bright point in the dark. It was cold below, making Blaine's skin prickle. None of them had worn anything warmer than summer clothes, because it would draw too much attention once they made it across the city to their destination.

Where they were going was the Pemberry neighborhood, named

for the type of flowers the prostitutes who worked the corners and alleyways outside of pubs wore in their hair in the summer months. The petals were as red as their lip rouge and the blood that sometimes stained the streets during territory fights of the local gangs.

None of that mattered in the chill of the catacombs, the strange metal walls lacking the rust other metals in use gained after time passed. Lore had always wondered about what ancestors had built the tunnels belowground, and why. The Northern Plains weren't dangerous if one were behind walls, and the catacombs stretched farther than even where the city walls currently stood.

The only sound below was their breathing and footsteps in the dark as they traversed the seemingly never-ending tunnels. By the time they reached the ladder that would take them up to a grate covering, Blaine's feet ached.

They huddled by the ladder, looking up as Lore clicked the handheld gaslight off, plunging them into near darkness. Water dripped from a distant pipe, and the smell was atrocious, but the ladder leading to the grate appeared sturdy enough. Blaine squinted through the iron bars, barely able to see the darkening sky above.

"The grate is located in an alleyway rather than the street. I'll go up first and check our surroundings," Lore said.

She took a moment to put on her veil, and Blaine followed suit, as did Caris. The world shimmered like when one broke the surface of the water while swimming, flecks of light scattering across his vision. Then it settled, the fabric a ghostly touch against his skin, some other face, he knew, stretched across his own visage now.

Lore tucked the handheld gaslight into her trouser pocket and climbed up the ladder. After a moment, he heard a muffled pounding from above as Lore worked the mechanism to get the grate to move. Clearly, this was a route rarely taken.

Moments later she got the grate open and Blaine winced at the creaking sound the hinges made. Lore climbed out, disappearing from view. Then her head popped back into view and her voice called down to them in a hiss. "The way is clear."

Blaine glanced at Caris as he gestured at the ladder. "After you."

Caris said nothing, merely climbed up the ladder with an easy swiftness. Blaine followed after her to the alleyway. It was empty at the moment, even if the street past the mouth of the alley was not. Blaine knelt and carefully replaced the grate. It locked automatically, no one the wiser of its secrets.

"Where to now?" Caris asked, clearly not oriented.

"We find ourselves a good time," Lore said.

Which could have meant a drink, a game, or an illicit affair conducted in public. The opportunities, while not endless, were at least typical of the neighborhood, and they were here to play a part while spying. Lore hooked her arm around Blaine's and Caris belatedly did the same. One man with two women went unremarked on beyond drunken leers of passers-by.

Blaine got eyes on a street sign screwed to a building half a block later. He tilted his head in that direction, silently asking Lore for directions. She smirked and tugged on his arm, leading the way. The catacombs had apparently spat them up a quarter mile away from the apothecary, and the way to their target was accessible by winding, cobblestone streets.

The Pemberry Apothecary was located down a narrow street filled with dingy storefronts selling wares no one in the center of Amari would buy. Not fashionable by high society's standards, less-than-stellar craftsmanship for the goods, and in general, meant for the poorer segment of the working class.

"This way," Lore said right before pulling them into the apothecary, ignoring Blaine's hissed warning.

"Wait," he managed to get out before clamping his teeth shut on the rest of his protest.

A bell jingled overhead as the door opened. Lore stepped inside with a loud giggle and Blaine could only follow, pasting a smile on his face. The space wasn't large, with a glass display counter taking up a prominent spot. Vials and jars, along with pillboxes, were neatly lined up inside. Rows of shelves on the wall behind it were filled with yet more medicinal-type offerings.

The place smelled faintly of chemicals, making his nose twitch.

Caris stepped away from them to go peruse the locked glass case on the other side of the shop. The apothecary was empty for another minute before the chemist came out from the back, the door to the back swinging open on squeaking hinges. The woman wasn't tall, though she was a little on the heavier side. Blaine was still able to look past her, getting a brief glimpse of two people in what looked like a messy workroom.

The woman in a rich, plum-colored tailored suit had her back to them, long black hair contained in a thick braid down her back. The man stood next to a worktable, face in profile, a jagged, circular scar pock-marking his cheek, like something had tried to bite off his face. He wore a pair of lab glasses, the brass of it dulled.

In the second before the door shut, the man turned his head slightly, meeting Blaine's gaze through yellow-green lenses. Blaine had met the eyes of many people over the years, but never before had he seen such coldness. The man's gaze cut straight through Blaine in a way that made the hair on the back of his neck stand on end. Then the door shut, hiding the two from sight. The prickly feeling in his skin didn't fade.

The chemist didn't seem pleased at having customers, judging by her glare. Blaine watched as Lore gazed blithely at her. "Evening. We're wanting your draught for sustained pleasure."

Caris made a faint choking sound that she forced into a giggle to hide whatever her true feelings were on Lore's request. Blaine merely smirked when the chemist addressed him.

"Having a bit of trouble below the belt?" the chemist asked.

"More like these ladies would tire any man out," Blaine replied with a chuckle. Lore made sure to eye him flirtatiously and simpered when he winked at her. "Do you have what we're looking for?"

The chemist sniffed disdainfully before moving down the display case. She pulled out a small pillbox and set it on the glass countertop.

"One pill taken with dinner will aid your predicament. I sell them in packs of five." She used her fingernail to undo the clasp of the pillbox, revealing five deep red pills nestled inside. "Fifty aurons for the lot."

Blaine winced. "For five pills?"

Lore dug into her pocket for some bills, handing over the money. "We'll take the lot."

The chemist eyed the bills for a moment before taking payment with one hand while sliding the pillbox toward them with the other. "I'll write you a receipt."

Lore pocketed the pillbox. Blaine kept an arm wrapped around her waist, playing the part of an eager lover. When the chemist came back with the receipt, Lore took it with a murmured thanks.

"Enjoy yourselves," the chemist said.

The woman didn't retreat to the workroom, which meant they weren't given the privilege of getting a peek at what was going on. Blaine gestured for Caris to follow them to the door. The bell jingled again as they stepped back outside.

The gas lamps on the street were flickering on, gaslights burning behind dingy glass. The mugginess of the evening lent the air a thick feel to it, but it still wasn't enough to chase the lingering chill Blaine felt.

Caris sighed. "That seemed fruitless."

Blaine shook his head as they walked. "Not quite. Did either of you get a glimpse at who was in the workroom?"

"A man and a woman, but I only saw the man's face," Lore said. "The woman was expensively dressed. She could be nobility."

"Or she could be masquerading as such. We can't know, not without seeing her face."

"And that's if she wasn't wearing a veil. What about the man?"

Lore frowned thoughtfully. "He could have been a customer."

Blaine shot her a narrow-eyed look before lowering his voice as they walked past a man slumped against the side of the building, empty beer bottle in hand. "The information we received said the apothecary may have connections to the Collector's Guild. That man could pass as a bounty hunter."

"Who do you think he's hunting?" Caris asked when they reached the intersection.

As they turned the corner, Blaine caught movement out of the corner of his eye, and he glanced back down the way they'd come. The crowd wasn't nearly thick enough to hide the hooded and cloaked figure striding down the street, the plum-colored suit appearing almost like the color of blood in the approaching twilight.

"She's hunting us," Blaine said around a mouth gone suddenly dry with the horrible knowledge that they'd somehow been found out.

Ten

BLAINE

Caris' question echoed in Blaine's ears, but he didn't look over his shoulder. His focus was on Caris and making sure she got out of this mess alive. He let Lore go to free his arm. His pistol was holstered to the small of his back, hidden beneath the linen shirt he wore. The weapon wasn't atypical for a man in this part of the city, and he was glad he'd come prepared.

But preparation would only be useful if the person following them wasn't a magician. Blaine lengthened his stride, forcing the ladies to keep up as he led them to a street they'd passed by before, one filled with pubs and restaurants and a crowd large enough to hopefully get lost in.

Blaine gripped Caris' wrist, pitching his voice low. "Whatever you do, don't use your magic."

Caris shot him a wary look, gaze cutting to Lore, who didn't appear surprised at all. Meleri must have told her. The veil Caris wore had her looking like a dark-blonde young woman with muddy brown eyes, though it couldn't hide the sharp intelligence of her gaze. "I didn't bring a wand."

He thought about lying to her, but the Auclairs had done enough of that in his opinion. If the North Star wished to allow Caris to dance in the thick of things, then so be it. He would do his absolute best to ensure she survived.

"We both know a wand wouldn't stop you. But your magic is attention you can ill afford." Caris sucked in a sharp breath, something akin to fear replacing the wariness in her face. Blaine forced a smile he knew probably looked more like a grimace. "Don't draw from the aether. *Don't* use your magic."

"I won't promise that."

"Now is not the time to discuss this," Lore hissed.

Blaine finally spared a glance over his shoulder, seeing the woman who'd been following them had disappeared. He cast his gaze upward to the roofs of the densely packed buildings. Being crew on an airship meant they looked down as often as they looked up for threats. It was habit those who lived their lives on the ground never quite mastered.

In the darkening twilight, Blaine could make out a figure nimbly traversing the roofs, and hoped the bounty hunter in question didn't have a ranged weapon.

"She's above us. We need to go," he said.

"We can make it to the catacombs entrance from here."

"There's no guarantee we can lose her, and that's a secret you don't want to give up."

"Then what do you have in mind?"

Blaine shouldered his way past a couple of drunkards, aiming for a rowdy pub with music pouring out of the open windows across the street from the buildings their hunter was racing across. "We try to lose her."

What he wouldn't give for an escape by way of an airship pickup. But that wasn't an option, and right now, he needed to make sure Caris was safe.

The pub they entered was hazy with pipe smoke. The scent of sour beer and unwashed bodies in close proximity made Blaine breathe through his mouth. The singer on the rickety stage was missing some teeth, but the bawdiness of her song had the crowd roaring approval. The floor was sticky underfoot as they pushed their way through the crowd for the rear of the pub, ignoring the annoyed looks tossed their way.

"There should be a back entrance to the alleyway where rubbish is collected. I didn't see the entrance on the street we just left, which means it hopefully exits onto a different one," Lore said.

Blaine was familiar with the way Amari's blocks were laid out between the numerous city walls. Buildings were clustered together in little islands, with streets winding around them and through designated gates carved into the inner city walls. The layout was a little different from Glencoe, which prided itself on accessibility.

The one good thing about Amari was that it was easy to get lost if one wanted to. And they desperately wanted to. It was a pity they couldn't.

They'd made their way down a narrow hall that smelled of piss from the nearby toilets, the back door lit by a flickering gas lamp. Lore had very nearly reached it when the door was shoved open, their way out blocked by the woman hunting them.

She reached up with one gloved hand to pull the hood back, letting the dark fabric pool around her shoulders. Blaine sucked in a breath as Eimarille's beloved lady-in-waiting stared back at them with unblinking eyes. Hers was a face he'd seen many times in the broadsheets as of late, always a step behind the woman she served.

He realized then that she'd let them see her face because they weren't expected to make it out of the neighborhood alive.

"I'm curious what your faces look like under those veils you wear," Terilyn said.

Blaine had no idea how the people in the apothecary had seen past them, and he had no time to dwell on that miscalculation. Terilyn snapped her wrist, a knife dropping down into her hand from a hidden forearm sheath. Her fingers had barely curled around the hilt when Lore tossed a smoke bomb between them. It exploded instantly, filling the narrow hallway with dark smoke.

Blaine spun on his feet, dragging Caris with him back to the main area of the pub, Lore right on their heels. He pulled his pistol free as they ran from the Blade, careening into the raucous crowd. Blaine shoved a burly man with a reddened face out of the way, earning a startled yell for his efforts.

"Watch yourselves!" someone shouted.

"Get to the exit!" Lore yelled.

The singer's voice trailed off, even if the upbeat tempo of the music did not. Blaine shoved Caris ahead of him before spinning to get eyes on Lore. She was between him and the Blade, frantically tipping over a card table and earning the ire of the players.

The crowd went from drunken friendly to drunken vicious in seconds. Someone grabbed Blaine's arm before he could take aim at Terilyn, and he jerked his finger off the trigger so he didn't inadvertently shoot someone else by mistake.

A bottle smashed over the head of the man holding him, beer and blood dripping down his face. He let Blaine go, howling in pain as he clutched at his head and stumbled away. Blaine looked back at Caris, who had already tossed the broken bottle aside and was looking for another one to use as a weapon.

"I told you to run," Blaine snapped.

"I'm not leaving both of you behind," Caris retorted.

Someone grabbed her arm and twisted it behind her. Caris shrieked in pain before slamming her foot down on the man's instep and snapping her head back with a brutalness no high-society lady should know.

But the borders were a place only the strong survived, and the Eastern Basin wasn't kind to those who didn't know how to fight. Blaine heard the crunch of the man's nose breaking even over the yelling of the crowd. Caris wrenched herself free, then turned and kneed the man in the balls. He fell to his knees, nose a bloody, crooked mess, no longer a threat.

Beyond Caris, in the dirty mirror over the bar, Blaine caught movement coming up behind him. He barely had time to jump aside and refrain from getting skewered like a beetle by the Blade's knife.

Terilyn moved like a dancer, all fluid, unwasted motions that were deadly in their intensity. Blades were fanatics, dedicating their lives to the Twilight Star. Their existence was furiously denied by the Star

Order out of Daijal, but denials meant nothing when one danced with a Blade.

Blaine jumped back to keep his stomach from being opened up, keeping his eyes on Terilyn and hoping to lead her away from Caris.

"My lady is always pleased when I bring her gifts. Your head will do this evening," Terilyn said.

She'd ditched the cloak, fighting in the plum-colored suit that no one else in the pub could afford. Blaine raised his pistol and took aim, firing off a shot that didn't find its target. But it hit someone, judging by the scream that cut through the smoky air. Blaine would feel bad about that—later—when the night was over.

If he lived that long.

Someone hooked their arm around his throat, squeezing tight. Blaine choked as his right arm with the pistol was yanked upward. Fingers dug into the tendons of his wrist, sending shooting pain down his arm and through his hand. His fingers uncurled on their own, and the pistol fell to the ground.

Terilyn dodged forward, arm extended, the blade of her knife glinting in the lamplight. Blaine frantically kicked his feet against her midsection, shoving her backward, but not fast enough to stop the tip of her knife from tearing through the veil.

The world melted, color bleeding all around him, and he couldn't even blame it on the arm choking him out. Another smoke bomb went off, the distraction sending people clamoring for the exit and the clean air out on the street. Blaine would've given anything right about then to simply be able to breathe.

The man holding him grunted harshly as wooden pieces of a chair rained down around Blaine's face. The arm around his throat slid away, as did the man. Blaine ripped himself free, gasping for air. Twisting around, he grabbed the man's arm and shoved the taller, heavier man into a nearby table. Both the man and the table pitched over, getting in the way of Terilyn.

Lore tossed the remnants of the chair aside and yanked at Blaine's arm. "Your face is showing."

Blaine locked eyes with Terilyn, and he knew there was nowhere in the city they could go right then where she wouldn't follow. Blades were known for murder above all else. Giving up the chase wasn't an option.

She'd keep coming, and they couldn't lead her to the places where the Clockwork Brigade existed in secret.

They couldn't lead her to Caris.

Blaine didn't see a way out of the predicament before them. He shouldn't have been surprised that Caris did.

Starfire exploded between them, catching the tipped-over table alight with white-gold flames. The heat was enough to make Blaine throw an arm over his face to shield his watering eyes. People all around him yelled in shock, many of them rushing for the exit. He squinted through the heat shimmer in the air, searching frantically for Caris.

"Over there," Lore said.

She left his side, hurrying around tables and scattered chairs as the starfire grew with a rapidness that was dangerous. He couldn't see Terilyn through the starfire, and he wondered if she'd been immolated.

He could only hope.

Lore's shout reached his ears. "I need your help!"

The pub was rapidly emptying as starfire ate away at the wooden structure. He vaulted a table and ran to where Lore struggled to haul a swaying Caris off her knees. She was white-faced even through the veil, and her outstretched hands trembled violently for a moment longer before she clenched them into fists. The starfire flickered, becoming smaller, until all that remained was scorched wood. In its wake, Terilyn was nowhere to be seen, and there was no ash on the floor that meant a body had burned.

Caris' eyes rolled up, and she passed out in Lore's arms, causing the older woman to stagger. She shot Blaine a frantic look. When he reached them, he picked up Caris and started for the door.

"We'll head to the catacombs. Can you lead us to a neighborhood where we can hot-wire a motor carriage?" Blaine asked as they hurried out of the pub and into scattered chaos on the street.

"Yes, but wouldn't it be better to stay below?"

"I can't carry Caris across the city, and we need to move fast."

Lore took the lead while Blaine hefted Caris higher in his arms as they ran away from the smoking pub. He scanned the rooftops and the crowd around them, but he saw no sign of the Blade.

He doubted, though, that was the last they'd ever see of her.

Eleven

HONOVI

The residential building that housed the E'ridian ambassador's rooms was located several streets over from the embassy itself. The cluster of buildings surrounded an inner courtyard that past attendants had tended to with cuttings from E'ridia. The garden that bloomed there reminded Honovi of home, especially during summer.

He could see it from his bedroom. What he couldn't see was the street and the trouble that drove up that evening close to midnight. Honovi was abed reading a book for pleasure rather than work when the steward knocked on his bedroom door.

"There's someone here who is demanding to speak with you," Milas said through the door.

Honovi lifted his gaze from the book with a frown, glancing at the clock ticking away on the nightstand. "Who?"

"A Clan Storm member asking for aid."

Honovi immediately set the book aside and climbed out of bed. The sleeping pants he wore hung low on his hips, and he didn't bother with a shirt. When he opened the door, Milas frowned at him, more for his state of undress than anything else, Honovi assumed. The steward was a member of Clan Sun, the smallest clan in E'ridia, and they were always a stickler for propriety.

"Where are they?" Honovi demanded as he strode down the hallway barefoot.

"The receiving room."

Honovi made his way to the room on the first floor located near the building's front door. The receiving room was exactly what it sounded like, decorated with historical objects and E'ridian artwork. Honovi saw none of it when he arrived, all his attention focused on Blaine.

"Oh, good, you're here," Blaine said tiredly in E'ridian.

Something hot unfurled in Honovi's chest as he caught sight of the bruises around Blaine's throat and the rips in his clothes that didn't come from snagging on a nail or screw. Honovi had so many questions, chief of which was who had harmed his husband and where were they so Honovi could mete out his own form of punishment.

Swallowing back his concern, Honovi glanced at the entrance to the receiving room, where the steward waited in the doorway. "Leave us, please."

Milas nodded. "I'll stay awake if you need anything, *jarl*."

He stepped back into the hallway and closed the door. The sound of his footsteps faded after a moment. When Honovi knew they were alone, he strode across the room to pull his husband close, cradling Blaine's face in both hands.

"What happened?" Honovi demanded.

Blaine settled his hands on Honovi's waist. "I have two cogs in a motor carriage a street over. I need you to take them home while I dispose of the motor carriage. It's stolen."

"Blaine."

"One of them is my duty, and she's hurt. I need to get her to safety, but I need to hide our trail, and the only person I trust to take my place right now is you."

Blaine's voice cracked on the words, and Honovi leaned down to rest his forehead against his husband's, staring into those tired hazel eyes he'd missed so. "What were you doing that put her at risk?"

"One of her cogs brought information about an apothecary being used as a front by Daijal. We were told debt slaves were being brought in but never coming out. We went to investigate."

"What did you find?"

Blaine shifted on his feet, and Honovi pulled his hands away, settling them on his husband's upper arms instead. "We scouted the apothecary and were going to stake it out overnight. But there was a man and a woman in the back room. They somehow knew we were wearing veils, and the woman turned out to be a Blade."

Honovi's grip tightened, realizing how close he'd come to losing Blaine that night. "How did you escape?"

Blaine licked his lips, gaze shuttered. "Starfire. But that's not the worst of it. The Blade was Eimarille's lady-in-waiting. I'm assuming she didn't hide her face because she had every intention of killing us."

An icy knot settled in Honovi's gut. "You are certain it was her?"

"I'd know her face anywhere."

"What interest does the crown princess of Daijal have for an apothecary that she would send her closest attendant to it?"

"Your guess is as good as mine, and none of them are good."

Honovi blew out a breath. "Let me get dressed, and I'll drive your duty home."

Blaine blinked a couple of times before surging forward. Honovi let himself be drawn into a kiss, feeling his husband's fingers curl around the gold marriage torc wrapped around his throat.

"Thank you," Blaine said in a low, tired voice.

Honovi wished he could wipe away Blaine's concern, wished he could take his husband home. But he knew Blaine would not leave Caris, especially not with the threat of the death-defying machine and what it could possibly do hanging over everything.

He wrapped one hand around Blaine's wrist and tugged his husband toward the door. Honovi led Blaine back to his private rooms, where he ransacked his closet for a set of Ashion clothes. No sense in announcing his affiliation if he could avoid it.

Blaine watched him with hooded eyes as Honovi got dressed. The trousers and button-down shirt were well made, if plain, and the knee-high boots were sturdy. As Honovi shrugged into the casual jacket, Blaine pushed away from the wall and came closer. His fingers ghosted through Honovi's long hair, catching on tangles that he gently unknotted.

"Let me tie back your hair," Blaine murmured.

The shaved sides of Honovi's head and the length of his black hair falling from the strip on top was a clear denotation of his nationality. Ashionens didn't grow their hair out to the length E'ridians or Urovans did.

He stood still as Blaine found a brush and quickly ran it through the length. Honovi couldn't remember the last time someone had braided his hair for him. He closed his eyes, relishing the way Blaine tugged at his hair, setting it to rights in a neat, three-strand braid. He finished it off with a beaded leather tie. Honovi opened his eyes and turned, hating the wistful look in Blaine's eyes.

Blaine smiled wanly. "I miss getting to do this."

"I miss letting you," Honovi confessed.

Blaine leaned forward just enough to rest his forehead against Honovi's shoulder. Honovi held him close, and they stood like that for a breath or two, before Blaine shook himself into motion. "Let's get this over with."

They left the bedroom and then the building by way of the garage. Honovi opted for one of the plain black motor carriages that didn't have any E'ridian symbols painted on the doors or adhered to the registration plate. He'd made sure there was at least one vehicle present in the motor pool that couldn't be easily traced back to the embassy.

Blaine directed him where to go, and Honovi drove three blocks over, parking behind a motor carriage that was blocking the mouth of an alley. They both got out, shutting the motor carriage doors as quietly as possible. As they approached the other one, the barrel of a pistol greeted them through the window.

"It's me," Blaine said, not breaking stride.

The pistol disappeared, replaced by a face Honovi didn't recognize. "It's about time."

Honovi did recognize the voice from that meeting in E'ridia so long ago and the ball the other night. "Mainspring."

Even in the shadows, he could see the grimace on her face through the open window. "Don't call me that here."

"Lady Lore, then."

"Oh, that's worse. Do be quiet."

Blaine went around the other side of the motor carriage and opened the door. "The two of you are going with my contact. He'll drive you back while I dispose of the motor carriage we stole. Has she woken up yet?"

"No. She hasn't even twitched."

Blaine let out a soft grunt, and when he came back in sight, he was carrying a slim young woman in his arms. She was limp in the way of true unconsciousness, head lolling against his shoulder. A far cry from the vibrant young lady Honovi had met at the ball.

Blaine carried her to the motor carriage they'd arrived in, depositing her in the back seat. Lore climbed out of the motor carriage on her own, limping a little. As with Blaine, she'd clearly been hurt in the bar fight but was gamely pressing on.

"Drive it into the Serpentine River if you must, but make sure no one can find it," Lore said.

Blaine shrugged. "If I must."

Lore got into the back seat of the motor carriage and closed the door behind her as quietly as she could. Honovi met Blaine halfway between the two vehicles, allowing himself to lean down and steal one more kiss.

"Send me a message later that you're all right," Honovi said.

"I don't think we were followed. We traveled through the catacombs for half the way before coming above and stealing a motor carriage."

"Send it anyway."

Blaine smiled slightly before leaving with a regretful look in his eyes. Honovi let him go, because they both had made promises when they'd come to Ashion.

Honovi got behind the steering wheel of the motor carriage and started the engine. He drove away before Blaine, the other vehicle disappearing in his rearview mirror once he turned the corner.

"Where am I taking you?" Honovi asked.

Lore slouched deeper in her seat. "Your accent has gotten better. I noticed that at the ball."

"My accent has no bearing on my driving. Where are we going?"

Lore sighed quietly, the sound barely distinguishable over the thrum of the engine. "The Auclair estate."

Honovi kept to the speed limit, kept off the main roads until they made it to Hollows Bridge. They were the only vehicle to cross the Serpentine River past midnight, and Honovi took a winding route to where he knew the Auclair estate was located on the eastern side of the city.

He'd been a guest there twice before since coming to Amari as his people's ambassador. The formal dinners had been a way to introduce Honovi, his fellow ambassadors, and other important members of society to each other. Since Ashion had no queen and no court, despite the palace, Meleri Auclair, the Duchess of Auclair, had been a decent stand-in. She'd been kind and charming, Honovi recalled. She was less so tonight when she greeted them from the top of the stairs in the foyer.

"What happened?" the duchess demanded.

Lore reached for her throat, deft fingers undoing the clasp there. "We ran into a Blade, Mother."

Honovi hefted Caris higher in his arms as he watched Lore remove her veil. The face she'd worn shimmered, peeling away into true flesh and bone. The features there were the same as the ones that had stared back at him during the meeting with the *Comhairle nan Cinnidhean* several years ago. He hadn't seen her at the dinners he'd shared with the duchess, nor in parliament, or anywhere else where politics grew here, until the ball. Honovi wondered if that had been deliberate.

"Caris needs to lie down. Where shall I put her?" Honovi asked, attention on the duchess.

The older woman leaned heavily against the railing for support.

431

Her dressing gown was definitely not proper attire for greeting anyone outside of family, but she didn't seem to care.

"A Blade?" the duchess asked, voice trembling slightly.

Lore stepped forward, her feet making no sound on the plush rug covering the hardwood floor. "Princess Eimarille's lady-in-waiting, to be precise."

Even in the low lighting, Honovi saw the way the duchess flinched. Her face paled, but she rallied well enough after a moment. With how open Lore was with her mother, Honovi had his suspicions about the duchess' place within the Clockwork Brigade.

He carried Caris up the stairs, following Lore to a bedroom that had some engineering tools scattered around and picked-apart clockwork pieces covering a desk. Lore switched the gas lamp on, and Honovi went to lay Caris on the bed. Then he stepped back and let Lore get the young woman's boots off, as well as the veil she wore.

The face, once revealed, was pale from overuse of magic. The skin beneath her eyes was bruised a faint purple, and her shoulder-length brown hair spread over the pillow in loose waves.

"You should call for a magician," Honovi said.

"We can't. No one can know she uses magic," Lore said.

"Lore," the duchess said in a sharp voice.

Lore retrieved the throw blanket from the foot of the bed and draped it over Caris' sleeping form. "He's Blaine's husband, Mother. He already knows."

"I am aware, but he doesn't need to know everything."

Lore smoothed her hand over Caris' forehead, pushing back some hair, before turning around to face her mother. "I don't know why you think Blaine hasn't broken confidence with him about everything that matters. They meet every couple of weeks at the embassy and have since the ambassador arrived in Amari."

The duchess studied her daughter before that piercing gaze turned Honovi's way. "We should speak frankly, Ambassador."

Honovi nodded in agreement. "I think it's time we had such a conversation."

Lore settled in the desk chair. "I'll keep watch."

The duchess left the bedroom. Honovi followed her out and found himself led upstairs through the private family floor he'd never been privy to during the dinners he'd attended. They arrived in a study with no window that didn't appear as if it held a country's secrets, even if it did.

The duchess settled behind her desk, drawing her dressing gown tighter over her shoulders. "Apologies for my lack of proper dress, Ambassador."

Honovi waved off the apology as he took a seat. "I've captained an airship in nothing but my underclothes before. Emergencies never announce themselves, Your Grace."

"An apt observation. I'm curious about what else you might have observed tonight."

Honovi met her gaze across the desk, studying her in the soft glow coming from the nearby gas lamp. He'd learned a lot about politicking from his father, during his trade runs, and here in Amari. That experience allowed him to choose his words carefully.

"Probably more than you would like, Fulcrum."

The duchess' expression never changed. Neither did she flinch at his words or give away any hint of unease with her body. She was too old for that, he knew. Too well-mannered and too sharply honed to break in the face of such a statement. It made her reaction from earlier all the more telling.

"An accusation like that could be ruining for an Ashionen," the duchess finally said.

"As I'm not Ashionen, you must forgive me my missteps."

"Of course, Ambassador."

"I think after tonight, you may call me Honovi."

"In private, perhaps. I suppose you think I should offer you the same permission?"

Honovi shrugged. "I'll address you however you wish."

He waited her out, the seconds ticking down on the clock, before she nodded slightly. "You may call me Meleri in private if we are to work together."

"I'm not one of your cogs."

433

"Your husband is."

Honovi showed his teeth in a smile that wasn't friendly in the least. "My husband's duty is to the girl lying in that bed, not to you."

"They are one and the same."

"Are they?"

Meleri splayed her hand over the desk, veins standing out against thin skin. "You must understand what she will mean to those of us who remember the monarchy we had before the Inferno happened. She is everything we have prayed for."

"Does she know that?"

The duchess tapped a finger against the desk, gaze steady. "Caris keeps her secrets the same way we keep ours."

Honovi tipped his head to the side. "Her magic."

Meleri's mouth turned down at the corners in a dissatisfied moue. "Blaine really must watch his tongue."

"He is my husband. We don't keep secrets from each other."

"Perhaps you should think to."

"Don't presume to tell me how to walk my road with my husband."

Meleri lifted her hand. "Peace. I mean nothing ill by my words. Only that the Daijal court has eyes and ears everywhere."

"Apparently they have a Blade as well."

"More like Eimarille does. For all that Bernard wears the crown, he doesn't wield the power he thinks he does. The Twilight Star chose Eimarille for a reason, and that wasn't to give Bernard a place in history."

"You seem to know a lot about what happens in the Daijal court despite never leaving Ashion."

"An old woman like me is prone to gossip."

"I'm sure you'd like others to believe that." Honovi's gaze strayed around the room for a moment, lingering on the intricate artwork hanging above the credenza with its metal pieces, clockwork gears, and clarion crystal shards. "Blaine tells me you've uncovered what the death-defying machine does. What will you do about it?"

"Blueprints and memories aren't enough proof to accuse anyone of the misdeeds we know are happening. Proof would be finding the machine itself."

Honovi looked back at Meleri. "And have you?"

"We know of the quarry in the *vasilyet* governed by the House of Kimathi in Solaria through the inventor we rescued. Broaching such a subject with the Solarian emperor wouldn't get us anywhere. Besides, I don't have the clout to initiate such an overture."

"You used to."

Meleri smiled tiredly, gaze heavy with an old grief. "Once. When I had a queen to serve."

"Daijal would give you one."

"She may carry the Rourke name, but she is not Rourke. The North Star decreed it so and I have never been led wrong by my guiding star."

"But she can't lead you to the Daijal court."

"It is difficult to get spies into the higher social circles in that country's major cities. I have tried, and I know many cogs have died for my efforts. We still need to find a way. The death-defying machine proves we cannot stand by and let Eimarille continue on this path."

Honovi hummed thoughtfully, weighing his choices. "If you need a spy in the Daijal court, I could perhaps help with that. I would need the *Comhairle nan Cinnidhean*'s permission to do so, though. It is not an offer I can make on my own."

Meleri eyed him with a sharpness that made Honovi think she'd hoped for such a result from their conversation. "What are you suggesting?"

"That I get recalled back to E'ridia and have the *Comhairle nan Cinnidhean* send me to Daijal instead. I am not Ashionen, and it wouldn't be suspicious for my people to want to gauge the support and intention of both countries. I could walk where your spies can't."

"Your efforts would make you a spy."

"My efforts wouldn't make me anything but concerned for my country's continued peace."

"Ah, so we agree Daijal is a threat."

Honovi chose to ignore that statement. "Will you accept such a venture?"

"What would you and your country want in return?"

"I'll let you know when I speak with the *Comhairle nan Cinnidhean.*"

"I know you do this more for Blaine than for my country's future, but I'm not one to turn down such aid. If your *Comhairle nan Cinnidhean* approves your request, then I will take whatever information you can give me about this death-defying machine and what plans the Daijal court has for Maricol. I can't promise anything on behalf of Amari, but I can on behalf of the Clockwork Brigade."

"Curious that you don't limit the Daijal court's aspirations to Ashion."

Meleri's smile was flinty. "We both know you would not have offered such critical help if you truly believed Eimarille will not cross your border."

Honovi stood. "How shall I contact you when a decision has been made?"

"As loath as I was to agree to Blaine's continued contact with you out of the embassy, he hasn't been caught yet, and no one is the wiser. I will let him know to be on the lookout for your messages when he sends his reports to E'ridia."

"Very well. I'll send my request to the *Comhairle nan Cinnidhean* tonight. I may have an answer for you after sunrise if we are lucky. In which case, I'll come here."

Meleri tipped her head back, looking old and small in her grand leather chair, but there was a steeliness to her gaze that belied her age. "May the stars guide you well, Honovi."

"May your road be an easy one, Meleri."

He left Meleri's study and the Auclair estate without saying farewell to Lore or the girl sleeping off a bar fight, unaware of the world the people around her wanted her to build.

Twelve

EIMARILLE

"I'll kill them."

Eimarille spoke the promise with an icy fury that made her teeth ache. The anger hadn't left her since Terilyn had stumbled home, wounded and bringing with her such incendiary news.

Terilyn grimaced as Eimarille gently wiped at the edges of the burn on her arm with gauze soaked in a medicated tincture. She was naked from the waist up, clad only in the trousers she'd worn for her evening meetup.

"That is what I am for. I'm sorry I failed you," Terilyn said.

"No, my darling. You didn't fail me. You never could."

Terilyn's grimace smoothed out into something less fraught. She carried pain well; had learned to under the brutal hands of her teachers in the Star Order. Eimarille had never cared to see the woman she loved hurting, but she'd become an expert at tending to wounds over the years in the secrecy of the bedroom they'd shared before she married Wesley.

Here, in the palace in Amari, with staff willing to do anything to please her, Eimarille still worked beneath a set of rules the two had set down long ago. Which meant they were alone in the antechamber leading to her bedroom, curtains drawn over all the windows and a medical kit sitting open on the floor beside her.

She touched her fingertips to the unmarked skin just past the cruel redness of the burn. "We need a magician."

Terilyn shook her head. "They'll think you did this to me. I won't risk your reputation."

"Dearest—"

Eimarille was cut off by a kiss, fierce in its intensity and flavored from the acidic, clear *ika* liquor favored by Urovans. Terilyn had downed three shots before Eimarille had been allowed to tend to her burns.

When they broke apart, Terilyn sighed. "No. I won't have the public speak ill of you for something you didn't do."

Eimarille's gaze dropped from her lover's face to the burns on Terilyn's left arm. She'd shielded her face from the starfire cast in that pub, coming away with charred skin, singed hair, and ruined clothes. But she was alive, and Eimarille thanked the stars for that.

The kit had a burn tincture that Eimarille soaked a clean set of gauze in before placing it over the scorched skin. Then she carefully wrapped more gauze around Terilyn's forearm to keep it all in place.

"You should take something for the pain," Eimarille said quietly.

"You should tell me why you're so angry."

Eimarille rose to her feet from where she'd been kneeling in front of Terilyn, who wasn't inclined to leave the chaise she sat on. "Isn't it obvious?"

Terilyn tipped her head back and closed her eyes, the long fall of her black hair sliding over her shoulders. It put her bare breasts on display, along with the bruises she'd obtained in her pursuit of the cogs who'd worn veils. "The starfire, yes. That's clear enough. But you were angry before I arrived home. Why?"

Eimarille rubbed at her forehead before retreating to the wet bar tucked against the far wall. It was stocked with her husband's favorite whiskey and her own preference for oaky red wine. The bottle she'd opened when she received the coded telegram from Kote was more than half-empty. She poured herself another glass nearly to the brim and set the now empty bottle aside.

She swallowed several large gulps of wine in a way that would never be good manners, but which Terilyn had taught her was good fun on long winter nights. "I was informed by Kote that Bernard has requested a high-level meeting with his military advisors. The king apparently wishes to expand the Istal garrison into the Ashion side of the border."

Terilyn blinked slowly at her. "That wasn't in our plans this year."

"Not this year, no." Eimarille glared down into her wine before retreating back to Terilyn's side. She sat on the chaise and leaned down to pick up the bottle of *ika*, handing it to her lover. "We may need to change them if Innes doesn't hear my prayers."

Terilyn took a swig from the bottle, her bandaged arm resting on her lap. "Our lord always hears your prayers. Will we return to New Haven or remain in Amari?"

Eimarille had expected to stay the remainder of the summer in Amari, having tea with politicians, inviting specially picked nobles around for garden parties, and taking excursions to the smaller towns in western provinces. She was meant to be seen, to be *present*, and she couldn't do that if she returned to Daijal.

Neither could she let Bernard start a war with Ashion early when her personal army wasn't ready yet, but there was also the matter of the girl who could cast starfire. If Eimarille was to put out those rumors and find the people who had harmed Terilyn, she couldn't be in another country.

"We'll stay in Amari for now. This is my city, after all."

Terilyn listed to the side and rested her head on Eimarille's shoulder. Eimarille wrapped her arm around the other woman's waist, holding her close.

"It's your country," Terilyn said.

"And I'll not let someone else lay claim to it." She turned her head to press a kiss to Terilyn's hair. "We'll stay. I want those who harmed you found and executed, and I trust no one but you to lead that hunt.

I'll send Kote a telegram in the morning after our prayers, and you'll let my magician tend your arm before we leave for the day."

Terilyn raised her head to nip at Eimarille's bottom lip with careful teeth. "If you insist, my love."

They shared another kiss, finished their wine and *ika*, before Eimarille carefully stripped Terilyn of the remainder of her clothes in the privacy of their bedroom. They slid beneath the light summer sheets and gravitated toward each other like they always did. Eimarille held her lover close, careful of the wound on Terilyn's arm, and listened to her breathe.

"How will we find the girl?" Terilyn asked into the darkness.

Eimarille frowned, hiding her displeasure against her lover's hair. "You saw the face of the man with them, did you not?"

"Yes."

"Then we'll have a magician use mind magic to retrieve your memory of him and draw a portrait. We'll send the sketch to the Collector's Guild and have them issue a warrant. He'll be able to tell us who she is."

Innes had promised her that no one in Ashion with even a hint of the ability to command starfire had survived the Inferno. The girl could not be Ashionen. If she belonged to a member of the nobility or ruling class of another country, then Eimarille would take the foreign interference as the threat it was and act accordingly.

Thirteen

CARIS

Caris woke to a pounding headache and the familiar feel of her mother's hand on her forehead. She squeezed her eyes shut, swallowing back the taste of bile. The stabbing pain right behind her left eye pulsated at the exact rhythm she would keep when using a mallet in her workshop.

"I have your headache medicine with me," Portia said.

Caris' head was lifted off the pillow so she could swallow the pill with a few careful sips of water. Portia laid her back down, and Caris tried to breathe through the nausea. It took a few minutes for everything to settle before she risked cracking open her eyes.

The familiar ceiling of her bedroom in the Auclair estate met her blurry gaze. The curtains had been drawn over the window, dimming the sunlight. She blinked slowly, trying to kick-start her brain the way she would a machine whose components weren't working in sync.

"Oh," Caris said, eyes going wide as memory came back to her like a punch to the gut.

Her gaze cut to her mother, who looked more worried than relieved. "The duchess called me this morning to let me know you were unwell. Your father is filing some patents today, otherwise he would be here with you."

Caris licked her lips, gaze flicking back to her mother's face. "I'm all right."

"You used starfire. I recognize the signs."

Portia's voice was hardly louder than a whisper, her lips barely moving with the words. Caris heard her anyway. "I had to."

Portia set the water glass aside before wrapping both her hands around Caris', fingers cool and shaking just a little. "You know you shouldn't. You know you *can't*. What were you doing that you felt you had to?"

Caris opened her mouth, and then closed it, uncertain as to what she could say without revealing secrets that weren't hers to give.

"She was saving me when I should have been saving her."

Professor Arquette's voice cut between them, causing her mother's head to snap around. Caris followed her gaze to the doorway, finding him standing there, doorknob gripped tight in his hand.

"This is a private conversation," Portia said flatly.

Professor Arquette stepped inside anyway, closing the door behind him. "There is no privacy in a house full of spies."

Caris's tongue tripped over the words she wanted to speak, and the only thing that came out was a strangled sound that made her head hurt worse.

"I don't know what you mean." He came closer, and Portia let Caris' hand go, standing to her full height to face him. "Come no further."

"We haven't been properly introduced, Lady Dhemlan." He sketched a bow to her, even if his gaze remained on Caris. "I go by Tristan these days, but my name was once Blaine Westergard."

Portia went so still it was difficult to tell if she was breathing. "The Westergard bloodline is dead."

Professor Arquette—*Blaine*—didn't even blink. "As Lady Lore likes to remind me, I am very much alive. I have your daughter to thank for that after last night's run-in with a Blade."

"And before?"

Blaine's gaze shifted to Portia, an intensity to it that Caris didn't like. "The Dusk Star, in her infinite wisdom, asked that I bear witness when we fled Amari with Ashion's heart during the Inferno."

Her mother's face bled of color, washing out to a sickly hue. Caris got an elbow underneath herself, hating how the room tipped at the edges. "Mother?"

Portia reached behind her with a shaking hand until she could grip the back of the chair she'd been sitting in. She stared at Blaine with such raw emotion on her face that Caris didn't know what to *do*.

Caris breathed through her nose to keep the nausea at bay. "Mother, what does he mean?"

Portia cleared her throat, turning her head to look at Caris. "Nothing, my dear. He means nothing."

"It's *something* if you're so worried."

Portia shook off whatever malaise had settled on her and went to her knees before the bed. She grasped Caris' hand again, lifting the other to push back Caris' sweaty hair. It reminded Caris of when she was young and she'd come home furious that the latest invention she'd spent so much time on wasn't working right. Her mother was always one to soothe her hurts, and this was no different.

"You should rest," Portia said.

"I'd like to know what's going on," Caris retorted, grimacing at the way her voice echoed in the bones of her skull. She pushed through the pain anyway.

"Nathaniel is meeting with the duchess. Both of you should be present for it. There's some realignment going on with the cogs," Blaine said.

Caris' stomach swooped in a way that had little to do with nausea and everything to do with panic. "What?"

Portia shot Blaine a scathing look. "Now is not the time."

Blaine shrugged. "You and the duchess both seem to think keeping her in the dark will keep her safe. It won't, especially not after last night."

"I think you have said quite enough."

Blaine glanced between them before tipping his head in the direction of the door. "We'll be in the duchess' private parlor."

He left on quiet feet, closing the door softly behind him. Caris met her mother's eyes and searched her face. "You're a cog?"

"It's a trend that appears to run in the family." Portia sighed and got to her feet with a wince. "You should rest, my dear."

Caris pushed herself to a sitting position. "I think I should go with you to the parlor."

"Your father would want you to stay here."

"And you? What do you want?"

Portia slowly sat on the bed beside Caris, gazing at her with tired eyes. "I want you safe. I thought letting you come here as the duchess' ward would keep you that way."

"I was safe, Mother."

"You became a cog."

"Like you, apparently."

"Your father and I provide inventions when needed to the Clock-work Brigade. We had never received direct contact from Fulcrum, Mainspring, Locke, or Whisper until we came to Amari when you were sixteen. Our chain of contacts is short. Unlike yours, it seems."

Caris thought of all the names and information she'd been privy to beneath Meleri's watchful guidance over the last few years. "I wanted to help."

Portia's gaze softened, and she reached out to cradle Caris' face in both hands. "Of course you did. It's in your blood."

With a sigh, her mother stood once more, but this time, she helped Caris to her feet. Caris leaned on her mother's arm a little as they exited the bedroom. The light in the hallway made her wince, but the medicine she'd taken was specially prepared by a magician and was fast-acting.

Caris knew where Meleri's private parlor was. She led her mother there, and they came upon quite the gathering of people.

Meleri was present with Lore, Brielle, and Dureau, along with Blaine and Nathaniel. With them was the E'ridian ambassador, who stood quite close to Blaine near a bookcase. Nathaniel paced by the windows, the curtains drawn tightly shut like the ones in her bedroom. The moment Caris and Portia entered the parlor, Nathaniel stopped his pacing and went immediately to them.

"You should be resting," Nathaniel said, taking Caris' free hand in his. He brushed a kiss over the back of her knuckles before tucking it into the crook of his arm. She held on tight, leaning into him.

"You never told me you were a cog," Caris said.

Nathaniel grimaced. "It appears we both weren't forthcoming about such things. My apologies, but Fulcrum's orders are not to be disobeyed."

Caris nodded grudgingly at that point. Nathaniel and Portia guided her farther into the parlor. She sat gratefully on the chair that Dureau vacated. Portia took the spot off to her right on the sofa, while Nathaniel remained standing beside her chair. Caris adjusted the collar of the linen blouse she wore, the same one from last night's excursion to the Pemberry neighborhood. Belatedly, she realized she'd forgotten to put on shoes and curled her toes into the rug.

When Caris looked up, she found every eye in the room on her. "What?"

"How are you feeling?" Meleri asked her.

"Like I crashed a racing carriage, but I'll be all right. It's just a headache."

"And magical exhaustion, which isn't something to ignore," Blaine said.

Meleri shot him a sharp look that would've made anyone else clamp their lips together. Blaine stared her down in silence, and he wasn't the one who looked away first.

Lore cleared her throat, drawing everyone's attention. "Some of my cogs returned to the apothecary earlier this morning. The establishment is closed up, and everything inside is gone."

"Were you able to find anything?" Brielle asked.

"The workroom was situated over a cold storage room, though it's doubtful the space was used as such. My cogs said it looked more like an interrogation room, and there were spells for silence set in the earth." Lore paused and took a deep breath. "One found a bucket filled with rotting human hearts down there, but no bodies."

Meleri went a little green in the face, lifting one hand to press over her chest. "That sounds less like interrogation and more like torture."

"Do you think the shop was used by the Collector's Guild?" Dureau asked.

"There's no way to tell. The man I saw in the back room looked more like a warden, and they aren't supposed to have any interaction with the Collector's Guild," Lore said.

"One would think they'd have no interaction with a Blade."

"Speaking of Blades, Princess Eimarille's lady-in-waiting saw my face. I don't know what they'll do with that information, but my cover as a professor may be untenable now," Blaine said.

It was strange to think of him as someone other than the professor who had guided her through her engineering classes. Caris was beginning to realize she didn't know him at all and never would've known he kept secrets if they hadn't raided the train together.

The ambassador said something in E'ridian, to which Blaine responded in kind. Caris' eyebrows crept toward her hairline at that show of fluency. She'd known he'd gone to university in that country, but he seemed far more comfortable with the ambassador than a citizen of Ashion would normally be.

"If we crafted you a new identity, you wouldn't be able to stay in Amari," Lore said.

"I was hoping you could take over the manifest run, but that may not be possible now. There's enough focus on my family's company that my parents are becoming nervous. They've sent my sisters out of the city as a precaution," Nathaniel said.

Caris looked at him, squinting against the light. Her head still ached, but she had no intention of leaving. "Why is your company being targeted?"

Nathaniel blinked down at her before jerking his gaze to the duchess. "You didn't tell her?"

Caris scowled. "Tell me what?"

"She wasn't in your chain. She didn't need to know," Meleri said.

Nathaniel offered Caris an apologetic grimace. "My family was recruited by the Clockwork Brigade when I was a child. We move debt slaves out of Daijal by way of our trains. The raid has brought Daijalan oversight onto my family's company."

Caris' mind turned that information over and over, fitting all the bits she was being told into a picture that still missed so many pieces. But there was enough there to sketch out the whole of it. She realized, in that moment, how much she didn't truly know about the people around her, for all that they'd taken her in and made her feel like family when her own was back in Cosian.

"You could have told me," Caris said through clenched teeth, unable to keep the hurt out of her voice.

"No, he couldn't have. You were not in his chain. You were not a cog he was connected to," Meleri said.

"He called on me socially. You could have let us know the truth about each other."

Nathaniel reached for her but aborted the gesture when Caris stiffened in her seat. "Forgive me, Caris. I never meant to hurt you like this. I had no idea you were a cog until this morning when the duchess rang me and requested my presence."

Caris knew in her heart that her anger was misplaced when it came to the workings of the Clockwork Brigade. But she was twenty, and she cared for Nathaniel in a way she'd never learned to care for anyone else. That sense of betrayal burned like the starfire she'd called forth last night.

Her mind took an intuitive leap, the sort she was used to when holding a clarion crystal in one hand and a crystal-cutter in the other. The knowledge sang to her the way clarion crystal did, guiding her hand for the perfect cut.

"What did you all hope to do with me?" Caris asked into the heavy silence, staring at a far spot in the wall, though she wasn't seeing the intricate wallpaper there. No, in her mind's eye, she saw a park, with an old throne, and starfire that no wind or rain or wrongful bloodline could ever put out.

"Caris," Meleri said after a moment.

"*Don't* lie to me."

"The Inferno burned through every royal member and cadet

bloodline, eradicating whole families in an attempt to wipe out those magicians with the ability to cast starfire or the genetics to pass it on," Blaine said.

"Enough," Meleri said sharply.

Caris ignored her. "My parents weren't attacked."

Blaine's gaze flicked to where her mother sat. "They were newly added to the nobility genealogies with no record of magic in their history. The Blades overlooked them. And you."

She'd known as she'd grown older just how dangerous it would be if people knew what she could do. Ashion had magicians. Since the Inferno, the country had no one who could cast starfire.

No one except the Crown Princess Eimarille—and Caris.

She looked across the parlor at Meleri, seeing nothing close to guilt in the older woman's gaze. "Why did you ask me to be your ward while I went to university? Why did you want me to stay?"

Caris wondered if the duchess would lie to her, as she must have all these years. All the moments where she'd sat at the Auclair family table, been included in countless society calls and parties, tagged along on missions for the Clockwork Brigade until she grew old enough to run a few safe ones herself. All of it done with some ulterior motive Caris was only now seeing, here where all the cogs that truly mattered were finally turning together.

"I have never questioned where the North Star guides me, and Aaralyn guided me to you," Meleri said.

She knew what Meleri fought against. They all did, every last cog in the Clockwork Brigade. They fought against the Daijal court's encroachment in hope of putting someone other than Eimarille on a throne that had burned every single person who had tried to sit upon it.

Caris carefully pushed herself to her feet, jerking away from Nathaniel's efforts to aid her. She stood there, barefoot and in last night's clothes, hair a tangled mess and nowhere near presentable, filled with a sickening sense of hurt that made the pounding in her head laughable.

"I would like to go home, Mother," Caris said.

Lore's mouth twisted downward, a hint of guilt in her eyes that was absent in her mother's. "Caris, please understand—"

"I understand completely, Lady Lore. I understand you and your family think to use me for purposes you have refused to share with me for years. I won't allow it. I *won't*." Caris turned toward her mother, curling her hands into fists. "I wish to leave."

Portia rose to her feet, reaching for her, and Caris didn't flinch away from her family. "Of course, my dear. We'll depart."

Caris turned her back on the people in the room and the scope of the secrets all tangled around her, holding tight to her mother's hand. They left the parlor and were halfway down the hallway before the sound of footsteps reached her ears.

"Caris, please wait. Let me escort you home," Nathaniel said.

"I'm perfectly capable of driving my daughter home, Mr. Clementine," Portia told him sharply.

Nathaniel came around them in the hallway, holding up both hands in a pleading manner. Caris desperately wanted the concern in his brown eyes to be real. "I didn't know you were a cog until today, but it doesn't matter. It doesn't change how I feel about you. I don't know what I can say to make you believe me, and I know I don't have the right to press you on the matter, but please. Allow me to give you my sincerest apology for any wrong you feel I may have inflicted upon you."

Years ago, he'd promised her they would be friends above all else. They'd spent countless hours together discussing engineering and politics and business. Caris wanted to believe he'd meant it, all the attention and laughter and smiles he'd given her while she studied in Amari.

But she couldn't, and that hurt most of all.

"Please allow us to pass, Mr. Clementine," Caris said stiffly, falling back on the manners that her mother had drilled into her as a young girl and which the duchess had refined.

Nathaniel's expression fell, some hint of agony flashing across his face. He hesitated before taking the heavy gold signet ring off his right ring finger. His family wasn't nobility and had no crest, no peer granted land or title, but the Clementine Trading Company was one of the most successful and richest in the country.

The company's symbol was etched on the flat gold face of the signet ring. He took her hand and placed the ring in her palm, folding her fingers over it to hide it from view. Nathaniel's gaze searched hers, and she refused to blink. "All I ask is a moment of your time, however long you will grant me, when you are ready to receive me."

She stared at him, promising nothing, but she never let the ring go when Portia guided her past Nathaniel and down the hall. They went back to the bedroom that no longer felt like hers despite the years she'd lived in it. Portia found a pair of her shoes and slipped them onto Caris' feet like she was a little girl and not a twenty-year-old woman whose life was just upended.

Portia touched her fingers to Caris' cheek, offering up a tight, sad smile. "Let's go home."

Caris nodded, because she couldn't stay here. She was a Dhemlan, not an Auclair, and certainly not anything the duchess and everyone else wanted to believe she could be.

Hunted

936 A.O.P.

One

SOREN

Soren usually didn't pay attention to gossip, but it was impossible for him to ignore the pair of businessmen walking ahead of him on the Karnak train platform. A much younger man worked to keep pace with them while juggling an armful of folios. None of them seemed aware that Soren was behind them, pushing his velocycle toward the cargo carriage at the end of the train.

"Did you hear? Another delivery truck was lost between two towns in the House of Kimathi's *vasilyet*. I was told a warden went looking for the truck at the behest of the company and found it tipped over on a back road, all its inventory looted," the taller man said.

"What of the driver?" his companion asked.

"Dead, from what I understand. It was a revenant attack, and the warden had to hunt down the horde."

"That's the dozenth attack this season."

"The roads aren't safe heading into Bellingham. The only sure way to transport cargo into that city is via steam train or airship, but the cost is exorbitant. It's getting to the point we're thinking of closing up shop in Bellingham. The loss of inventory and hike in transportation costs isn't worth the risk or money."

Soren tightened his grip on the handlebars of his velocycle. He knew the number of revenants in the House of Kimathi's *vasilyet* had nearly doubled over the last few years. He also knew that the House of Kimathi's *vezir* had allowed hostility to fester in her *vasilyet* toward wardens. Getting accurate readings of the poison levels, or lack thereof, in the land around that major city wasn't easy these days.

Part of the problem was politics. The rest of it was revenants.

Mostly, it was a headache.

It wasn't just the House of Kimathi's *vasilyet* that had an influx of the dead. Ashion suffered from an uptick in revenants as well, both human and wild beasts, and the governor had been forced to allocate wardens accordingly to deal with the threat in both countries.

Which meant, when Soren wasn't keeping watch on the crypts below the Imperial palace, he ranged afield in the Southern Plains beyond Calhames, hunting down revenants. Vanya might have wished for Soren to stay within the palace grounds, at his beck and call, but Soren was a warden down to his bones. He knew his duty, and he kept it.

Duty was why Soren had returned to the Warden's Island to report on Solaria's compliance with the Poison Accords and the country's overall politics. The sanctions were stayed until the governor could be certain that issuing them wouldn't bring harm to every warden guarding that country's borders.

The Houses had played their murderous games in pursuit of power and the Imperial throne for centuries, but rarely had it spilled over onto the wardens. These days, with the tension brewing between countries, not just the Houses, the governor had to be careful.

Soren slowed to a stop, looking up at the departure board hanging over the platform. As he watched, the little numbers and letters flipped over to show the cities and departure times for other trains. His eyes locked on a train heading to Bellingham, a city he hadn't been allowed into for quite some time, that left in an hour from a different platform.

He knew Vanya and Raiah were in Oeiras for the duration of Eighth Month while Vanya hammered out a trade treaty with the

Tovan Isles representatives in that coastal city. Soren had a ticket for a train heading direct to Oeiras tucked into his back pocket, and that route didn't run through Bellingham.

He exchanged it for one that did.

The train rolled out of Karnak's train station an hour later with Soren sitting on a shared bench. He stretched out his legs, leaned his head against the window, and let the sound of the wheels chugging along the rails lull him to sleep.

Two days later, Soren disembarked at a way station situated down the road from a small town and a quarter day's ride from Bellingham. Soren squinted against the glare of the sun as he wheeled his velocycle out of the cargo carriage and down the ramp. He was the only one departing at this stop, and after two days sitting cramped on a bench, Soren was glad to be out on the open road alone.

Bellingham sat on cleansed land, but the surrounding area hadn't been logged in almost a year, according to the governor. Walking the border around that city wasn't Soren's current post, but the House of Kimathi had been a thorn in Vanya's side ever since Nicca's death.

Knowing the hostility he faced didn't stop Soren from crossing the railroad tracks after topping up his tank at the way station and taking time to eat a travel sausage roll. He rode west, parallel to the tracks but deeper into the prairie than most travelers went. His tires ate up ground as the sun moved across the cloudless summer sky.

Soren steered clear of the road that led to Bellingham, aiming for one of the smaller towns in the outskirts of the *vasilyet*. He stopped along the way when he reached the field markers, taking time to hurriedly log the records from the machines no warden had seemingly touched in months.

By the time he came within sight of the main road that stretched between Calhames and Bellingham, twilight had fallen. Soren would've switched on his velocycle's headlamp if not for the convoy of trucks rumbling down the road.

Trucks that turned off the road and into the prairie rather than continue south.

Soren frowned, staring at the taillights that became increasingly dimmer in the dark as the trucks drove farther away. "That's odd."

Any warden worth their pistols knew the maps of the areas they patrolled. Soren kept meticulous notes of the borders he guarded. He'd updated his working map of Solaria while at the Warden's Island from other wardens' records. He knew there wasn't any town in this area that would take delivery of anything past sundown.

But there *was* an area of land the wardens had been refused passage on.

Soren reached behind his seat for the storage compartment and withdrew the clip-on beveled lenses coated with an aether-magicked film that helped him see in the dark. He fitted those to his goggles, flipping them down. The blackness of the prairie lightened to something like predawn, which was better than nothing.

Soren eased his velocycle forward after a good ten minutes had passed, and the trucks had long since disappeared in the dark. He switched a toggle on the control panel in the frame between the handlebars. The pitch of his velocycle's engine became quieter, a mechanical trick wardens used to help hide their passage through poison fields or dangerous territory.

He kept driving, occasionally stopping so he could use his double-lensed spyglass to ascertain the best direction to take. The half-moon provided enough light to see by, and Soren was used to traveling in the dark over uneven terrain.

The pinprick of a stationary light on the horizon caught his attention maybe an hour later. Soren drove until the illumination coalesced into a scattering of work buildings in the distance, the trucks he'd been following parked nearby.

He braked to a halt and killed the engine before sliding off the velocycle and carefully laying it sideways on the ground. There wasn't any need for the thin, flexible tarp to hide it, but he did pocket the handheld device that would trigger the small flashing light which would enable him to locate the velocycle in case he became disoriented.

Soren's field uniform consisted of leather and fabrics. It was hell when riding beneath the summer sun, but it came in handy right then. He checked his ammunition, secured his holstered pistols, and rolled his shoulders against the weight of the poison short sword against his back.

He headed for the buildings that should be on a map but weren't. Soren made little noise as he traversed the prairie grass and crept closer to the perimeter of the place. He got as close as he dared before dropping to one knee and unhooking his spyglass from his belt to peer through it.

The wall around the buildings was little more than a metal fence, which wouldn't be much security against a revenant, human or otherwise. Bison roamed the plains in large herds, the massive four-legged animals having branched off from their domesticated cousins in an earlier Age. The metal fence wouldn't stand a chance against a heavily furred and horned revenant horde of bison or other wild beasts.

He supposed that was what the automatons roaming the perimeter were for. The boxy spiderlike machines outfitted with Zip guns were typical of the sort the Solarian Legion used. Only Soren didn't see anyone wearing a Legion uniform in the people moving about beneath bright gas lamps positioned on the warehouse roofs.

They looked to be a mix of Solarians and Daijalans, but the people standing near the trucks in chains were clearly debt slaves.

Soren pulled the spyglass away from his face and hooked it back to his belt. "What is going on?"

He stood and skulked forward, careful of every step. He wasn't sure who else might be patrolling the area, and Soren didn't fancy getting shot. But clearly something was happening here that the House of Kimathi *vezir* didn't want anyone to know about, *especially* wardens.

He took a path around the warehouses, steering clear of the automatons as he went. As Soren moved through the darkness, it became immediately clear that the warehouses were situated near the lip of a fissure dug into the earth—a quarry.

Soren moved as silently as he could, putting distance between himself and the group behind the iron fence. At one point, he went to his belly to crawl forward, bypassing an automaton that skittered past on patrol, its Zip gun swiveling about on its boxy frame.

Soren stayed in that position as he moved toward the edge of the quarry. The closer he got, the brighter the light was, and he finally had to flip the night lenses up. Blinking to settle his vision, he crawled to the edge of the quarry, far enough away from the warehouses that he hoped no one would spot him.

The gas lamps below him on the quarry floor illuminated a nightmare.

The day had been muggy, with little breeze blowing across the Southern Plains. Night was the same, and the weight of the air wasn't moving, which meant Soren didn't smell the dead until he was practically on top of them.

"Oh, fuck," Soren breathed out.

His gloved fingers dug into the dirt, heart beating fast as his eyes skimmed over the revenants packed into cages on the quarry floor. There were more revenants down there than would account from a bog or a fen. The numbers wouldn't be atypical for a town that succumbed to a poisoned mist, but there hadn't been anything like that near Bellingham in at least a generation.

Soren turned his head, staring back at the warehouses behind the fence. Whatever kind of partnership the Solarians here had made with Daijalans, Soren would bet their *vezir* was aware of what was transpiring, if not outright involved.

I need to warn Vanya, Soren thought. *And the governor.*

But first, he needed to know what was going on in the warehouse. He had a sinking suspicion that the debt slaves would end up at the bottom of the quarry, but Soren needed proof of some kind. He needed to see whatever was going on with his own eyes so a magician with mind magic could draw out the memories for him.

Getting any closer to the warehouses was risky, but Soren had no choice. He backed away from the edge of the quarry, not getting to his feet until he was well away from the hazy glow of gas lamps.

Rolling to his feet, Soren headed back the way he'd come, flipping his night lenses down over his goggles again to help him see in the dark. He steered clear of the automatons, moving slow so as to not draw attention. He was halfway to the other side of the warehouses when shouts and screams erupted from behind the fence.

Soren went to one knee, bringing out his spyglass again. Peering through it, he saw people panicking. The men and women in charge of the debt slaves had their pistols trained on them before shifting their stance and their aim to the threat staggering around the corner of a warehouse.

Newly risen revenants were slower, the spores still needing time to control the bodies. It took a few days, sometimes as long as a week, for a revenant to gain the speed that made them a threat.

The revenant racing toward the men keeping watch over the debt slaves looked like a newly risen revenant but moved with the speed and ferocity of one long dead. The men shot at the revenant, but the bullets only made it stagger, not stop. Behind the damned thing came another one.

Soren swore and got to his feet, flipped the night lenses up, and raced toward the fence. The automatons, alerted to the revenant threat, were scuttling back to the quarry, heading for the open gate. Soren didn't go that way but toward the area of the fence the debt slaves were pressed against and trying to climb. Behind them, the revenant had reached one of the men who'd been shooting at it.

The man threw his pistol at the revenant and made to run, but the revenant got its hands on his shoulders and proceeded to tear out the man's throat with its teeth.

Soren reached the fence and used his momentum to propel himself over it, feet and hands pushing against the metal bars. He flipped over the top, falling to the other side. The nearby debt slaves, chained together by a heavy chain running through ankle manacles, shouted in surprise, staring at him in wide-eyed shock.

Soren put himself between them and the oncoming revenants, pulling his pistol free. He aimed and fired, and unlike the dead man's bullets, Soren's put the revenants down. The dead fell to the ground, bodies twitching as the poison coating the bullets interfered with the spores.

He unsheathed his short sword and pressed a button beneath the cross guard with his thumb. Poison trickled out of the hilt and down the blade, just enough to ensure the revenants couldn't rise again after he cut off their heads.

Soren had separated the head from the second revenant on the ground when the shouting around him changed pitch. A blur of movement out of the corner of his eyes had Soren twisting around and bringing up his short sword.

The revenant ran itself through on the blade, fingers scraping down his leather vest as it lurched closer. It twisted its head, sinking its teeth into the meat of his upper right arm through his shirt, biting deep with inhuman strength in its jaws. The pain was excruciating, burning like acid, but nothing he hadn't felt before.

Soren put the barrel of his pistol beneath the revenant's jaw and blew its skull apart. He wrenched his arm away, needing to use the butt of his pistol to knock the damned thing's teeth out of his skin. Blood slid down his arm from the bite wound, staining his shirt, but he couldn't worry about cleaning it just then.

He ripped his poison sword free of the revenant, kicking the body aside. Twisting around, Soren raised his pistol despite the pain in his arm to fire it at the revenant that had got one of the debt slaves in his hands and was steadily pulling out the woman's intestines. The debt slaves on either side of the dying woman had nowhere to run, not with the chain connecting them.

Soren put two bullets in the revenant before striding over and cutting off its head. It shuddered, slumping over the bleeding-out woman with its hands still sunk deep in her abdomen.

She blinked up at Soren, blood trickling from her mouth and down her throat, sliding over the newly inked bank numbers that hadn't even lost their scabs. There was no saving her, and all Soren could do was line his pistol up with her heart and pull the trigger, granting her a mercy she would never find in this place.

It was a better death than the one she would've had if the spores got in her flesh.

"Where the hell did *you* come from?" someone barked behind him in Solarian.

Soren looked over his shoulder at two Solarians who stood with rifles in their hands, the barrels pointed directly at him. Soren's eyes flicked from the rifles to the men holding them, to the still-frantic scurrying of warehouse workers behind them. The thunderous sound of a Zip gun going off somewhere inside a warehouse echoed through the air, causing one of the men to glance over his shoulder.

"I go where the poison and dead take me," Soren said in the same language.

"Put your weapons on the ground."

Soren stared at him. "I'm a warden. The Poison Accords grant me passage anywhere."

The man barked out a laugh. "Not here they don't. Weapons on the ground. Now."

Soren calculated the odds of getting a shot off before the others could pull the trigger and decided against trying. Moving slow, he placed his pistol on the ground before driving the blade of his poison sword into the dirt as far as it would go. Soren reached for the second pistol holstered on his other hip and laid that down as well.

The man raised an eyebrow when Soren started to straighten up. "All of it."

He blinked slowly before deigning to remove his heavy belt with the extra ammunition, poison bombs, tiny vials of antidotes, and spyglass. He removed his goggles and the poison-tipped throwing knives attached to the strap that secured his leather pauldron and sword sheath in place. He removed his obvious dagger but left the stiletto one in his boot since the sheath was sewn in to not show the outline.

Soren stood with his hands above his head. The bite wound in his upper arm pulled with the motion, blood soaking his shirtsleeve. He really needed to tend to it.

The taller man jerked his head to the side a little. "Step back."

Soren did as ordered, hating leaving his weapons where they lay.

The younger Solarian stepped forward and knelt in front of everything Soren had divested himself of.

"I wouldn't touch any of that," Soren warned, watching the man freeze in place with his hand outstretched. "You're not immune to poison, and you're definitely not immune to revenant gore. It's as bad as a bite to someone who was never a tithe."

The man scowled before standing with an irritated huff, the trade tongue stilted on his lips. "And you think you're immune?"

Soren wriggled his fingers. "Warden."

"Yes, so it seems," a clear, female voice called out in the same language.

Soren looked past the men at the woman in a pair of coveralls who stalked their way. His gaze lingered on the mechanical prosthetic made of metal, clockwork gears, and chips of clarion crystal. His skin prickled at the presence of magic engraved in every line of her inorganic forearm and hand.

The woman was clearly Daijalan and the person in charge, judging by how the two Solarians deferred to her presence. She was older than Soren, pale in the way of someone who didn't get outside much, and the clinical way she stared at him made his skin crawl.

She stopped near the men, coming no closer to Soren, which was a pity. He'd have taken her hostage if she had, and she must have known that.

"You aren't the first warden to come crawling around where you shouldn't." Her gaze flicked from him to the downed revenants around them. "You proved more useful in a pinch than the last one, at least. That's not enough to spare your life."

Soren tensed at her words. "You've killed wardens?"

"A dead warden is still useful, and killing your kind keeps our secrets. Secure him."

The men holding their rifles on him stayed put. Several Daijalans obeyed her order, approaching him from the direction of the trucks. Soren took a step back, hands curling into fists as his eyes darted back and forth, looking for any way out of this mess.

"I wouldn't try it," the woman warned.

Behind her, a pair of automatons walked their way, Zip guns locked on Soren. He grimaced and didn't fight the Daijalan who grabbed him by his good arm and yanked him forward. The man's partner kept his pistol aimed at Soren's head, not willing to touch his bloodied arm. They hauled him before the woman, who looked at him like he was a specimen in a lab to be studied and not a living being.

It reminded him of his days as a tithe, locked inside the tiny room where the transmutation process occurred after every injection of alchemy concoction was given him.

She reached out with her mechanical hand, the metal cold against his throat as she slid the prosthetic fingers beneath the collar of his shirt. Soren froze when she pulled free the vow he wore, the gold medallion bright against the black metal of her hand.

"This is the crest of the House of Sa'Liandel," the woman said, tapping a metal finger against the roaring lion face on the medallion.

Soren met her gaze without blinking. "Is it? I wouldn't know."

"Doubtful. What's a warden doing with something like this?"

"I took it off a body in the bogs," Soren lied.

The woman stared at him for a long moment, some sort of recognition eventually seeping into her gaze. When she smiled, there was a shadow of cruelty to it that made Soren want to be anywhere else but within her reach. "Or it was given to you. Perhaps some years back as a thank-you for saving a particular prince's life?"

Soren shrugged, ignoring how the motion made his arm hurt. "I deal with the dead, and sometimes that means keeping what they no longer have any use for."

"You can keep it in your grave. I have orders to run all trespassers through the death-defying machine. No one can save you from that, not even a prince."

She let the medallion go, and it hung heavy from Soren's neck. He tried not to show his relief about keeping it. Losing Vanya's vow would have left him feeling unmoored. He'd not taken it off since the morning Vanya gave it to him, the promise a reminder that had gotten him through the long hours of border patrol.

Losing it like this would've been unacceptable.

The woman stepped back and made an imperious motion with her metal hand. "Bring him to the warehouse, along with the rest of the debt slaves. Put the bodies in the quarry."

The rifles still trained on him meant it would be foolhardy for Soren to attempt an escape. The Daijalans tightened their grip on his arms as they hauled him after the woman, heading to the nearest warehouse. The automatons took up guard position in the area, Zip guns swiveling around on their turrets as the machines kept watch.

Soren blinked to adjust his vision quicker as they came into the warehouse. He craned his head around, taking in the space with a quiet sort of horror that left him feeling sick to his stomach, the taste of bile in the back of his throat.

The cages that lined the walls of the warehouse were full of debt slaves, all of them alive and huddled together. Workers in fully enclosed suits were patching a hole in a holding area connected to a massive machine with a chamber at its center. The welding tools they used let off sparks that faded before hitting the floor.

A body in the holding pen was riddled with bullet holes, more raw meat than human-looking. Soren knew what a burst of Zip fire could do to a body, and it seemed whoever that person had been, they'd taken the brunt of such an attack.

"What is that?" Soren asked, heels skidding against the dirty floor as the Daijalan dragged him forward. A sharp tap from a pistol's barrel against his skull made Soren reluctantly pick up his feet.

The woman ignored him, calling out in Daijalan at the people around her. Soren wasn't fluent in that language, and he let the words wash over him, ignorant of their meaning. When the woman looked back at him, he didn't much care for the anticipatory gleam in her eyes.

"Put him in the chamber."

The barrel of a rifle dug into his spine as the man holding his uninjured arm dragged him forward. Soren didn't know what the machine did, but he knew he didn't want to find out. He dug in his heels and tried to twist out of the man's grip. The pressure of the rifle left only to return in the form of a blow from the stock to his lower back.

Pain from the brutal hit had Soren hunching over, a throbbing agony spreading across his back and down his left leg. Soren gritted his teeth against the pain and managed to slide free the stiletto in his boot. When he came up again with the thin blade in hand, he lodged it between the rifleman's ribs, piercing his heart.

He got one hand around the barrel of the rifle and yanked it free of the dying man's hand. Before he could use it, something slammed against his head with enough force to make the warehouse spin and melt along the edges.

"Should we kill him?" someone asked.

"Let the death-defying machine do the honors," the woman replied.

Soren went to his knees, breathing heavily through his mouth. Hands hooked under his arms and hauled him halfway to his feet before pitching him forward with brute strength. Soren landed on his hands and knees inside the wide chamber, the space large enough to house a dozen people, at least.

He stumbled to his feet, spitting out saliva and trying to breathe through the sudden nausea swirling in his gut. He staggered toward the opening, but before he could reach it, the door was slammed shut, locks sliding into place and sealing the only way out.

Soren banged his fist against the door as he peered through the thick glass window there. "Let me out!"

He could see people moving around in the warehouse, but he couldn't see where the woman had gone. He banged his fist against the metal door a few more times before giving up, flexing his fingers against the bruised feeling left behind.

Soren stumbled back, turning around to get eyes on the chamber he was in. Holes were cut into the metal siding high up near the curved ceiling, and there was a drain set in the center, heavily stained around the edges. Precisely cut, trapezoid pieces of clarion crystal surrounded a larger circular one in the center of the ceiling.

The clarion crystal was an opaque gray that looked wrong. It *felt* wrong, scratching at a sense Soren carried but which he'd spent nearly his entire life ignoring. But his head still spun, and it was impossible to ward off the heaviness blossoming behind his ribcage.

He tore his gaze away from the clarion crystal, staring at what looked like a viewing window above him. Through the thick glass, he could just make out the woman's face from her spot on a high platform overlooking the chamber. With the door shut, the rancid smell of old blood and body fluids hit his nose.

"Shit," Soren whispered, dragging one hand through his hair, wincing at the way his skull throbbed from the touch.

A sharp *click* echoed through the chamber, and then a staticky voice came through a speaker positioned above the viewing window. "Any last words, warden?"

"Fuck you!" Soren yelled, not sure if they could hear him.

A heavy thrum, like an engine, filled the air, vibrating through the ground and up his feet. Soren froze, gaze darting about as he tried to figure out what was happening. Then a hissing sound reached his ears, and he watched as sickening green gas poured into the chamber from the holes in the ceiling. The first whiff of the stinging, noxious scent made Soren drop lower to the floor where the air was cleaner, though it wouldn't be for much longer.

The changes the alchemists at the Warden's Island put every tithe through meant wardens could survive most poisons and even revenant attacks. But a sustained poisoning in an enclosed chamber like this would be enough to kill a warden given enough time.

Since he was locked in the damn thing, that woman would have all the time in the world to run her experiment.

No, he thought to himself, breathing in air that was steadily growing more poisonous by the second. *I'm not dying here.*

Whatever this death-defying machine was meant to do—and he had a horrifying idea what that was—Soren refused to be a victim. He refused to die in the poison fields like this and leave Vanya and Raiah wondering why he'd never returned.

Soren crawled toward the door, pressing his fingers against the seam in the metal, trying to see if air came through. But the seal was too tight, and he'd been forced to leave all his weapons behind.

That heat in his chest became a pressure that was nearly unbearable. Soren's breath came quicker than he could afford. The poisonous gas, heavier than air, drifted closer to the ground, already at head height in his kneeling position. Soren breathed it in, tasting it on his tongue, in the back of his throat. He drew it into his lungs because he had no choice—this was all he had to breathe.

He knew this poison, knew how it would numb his nerves until his lungs no longer worked and he suffocated for want of air. He could survive it if he got out.

He just needed to get out.

Panic cut through his ribs like how his poison sword sliced through rotting flesh. Something *broke* deep inside, the sound echoing in his middle ear like a ringing that would never go away. Soren became unmoored, drifting, the catalyst for a power he'd so carefully denied himself over the years at the behest of a star god.

The heat banked behind his ribs erupted like the volcano that had blown on the Tovan Isles some generations back. It exploded outward like a star gone nova, crashing against the chamber walls. Distantly, Soren heard crystal and glass shatter, metal squealing in the way it did when it twisted so painfully out of shape before shattering.

Starfire—uncontrolled, uncontained—slammed through the death-defying machine like a hungry beast. Through the crackling burn of pure aether, Soren heard the distant sound of screams that didn't last very long.

The chamber exploding set off a cascade effect in the machinery around him, though Soren was only vaguely aware of the destruction happening. He felt as if he were underwater, drowning in power he didn't know how to control and had no frame of reference for.

He might have, though, in some other life, some other time.

Soren collapsed to the ground, breathing in heated, untainted air. He coughed to clear his lungs, head and body aching. Pieces of the warehouse roof came down around him as starfire punched through the building. He blinked spots out of his vision, gritted his teeth against the pain, and forced himself to crawl out of the grave they'd attempted to put him in.

Somehow, Soren got his feet underneath him. Somehow, he stumbled his way out of a conflagration that was hot enough to melt metal but which he barely felt at all. He made it out of the warehouse in time to not die in its collapse.

Around him, everything had gone up in white-gold flames, starfire licking at the night all around him. The clatter of bullets popping in their magazines as starfire overtook the automatons was background noise. The Daijalans and Solarians who manned the warehouse couldn't outrun starfire and burned to ash wherever they were. The debt slaves were just as unlucky, and later, Soren would feel guilty for that, but he didn't have control over starfire the way Vanya did.

Presently, he was just trying not to immolate himself.

The world was too bright, making it difficult to see as he stumbled through starfire to where he'd been forcibly divested of his gear. He couldn't find his pistols, but he found his poison sword still where he'd left it, sticking in the dirt.

Soren collapsed to his knees, dizzy and weak-limbed. He wrapped one hand around the hilt of the sword, the other over the pommel, and leaned forward to rest his forehead against his knuckles. He closed his eyes, breathing shallowly, feeling as if he were being spun into nothing.

On your feet, warden.

The voice pierced through the roar of the starfire, loud enough that it startled him out of his daze. Soren jerked his head up, blinking at the flickering white-gold flames eating through the structures and fence all around him.

Striding through the starfire came a dark figure, dressed in Solarian robes, the gold Lion constellation tattoo wrapped around her throat shining like the sun. Soren was well acquainted with figments of the imagination in the poison fields, and this would have been no different save for the voice echoing through his mind like temple bells.

Let it die. Let it go.

Soren opened his mouth, cracked lips peeling apart, but he couldn't find his voice as Callisto came to a stop before him, staring down at where he knelt. Her dark skin was a shadow against the brightness of the starfire, though her eyes burned like one of those celestial bodies.

This isn't your road, child.

Soren tightened his grip on the hilt of his poison sword, breathing out words that hurt. "Isn't it? You put me here."

Callisto smiled, kind in the way only death could be. But he'd died for her once already, long ago, and woken in a nightmare, the silhouette of a life lost fading into the shadows. He didn't want to die for her again.

The Dawn Star reached for him, ghostly fingertips brushing against his forehead. Ice poured through Soren, freezing him like the snow he'd seen only in training exercises in the Eastern Spine as a tithe. When he breathed out, it felt like a blizzard left his body, whiting out his vision.

Walk the road I gave you.

The Dawn Star's words rang in his ears until the sound of her voice faded into the wind. He opened his eyes, finding himself lying on his back and staring up at a soft blue sky, the stars fleeing the sun breaking free of the horizon. Soren licked his dry lips, body aching fiercely, but he forced himself to move because a downed warden was a dead one in the poison fields.

Slowly, he sat up, swaying a little as he took in the charred devastation around him. Every building and vehicle was gone, burned to ash or melted down to misshapen slag. The land lining the quarry was nothing but blackened dirt, the scorch marks spreading down the far side of it.

If there'd been bodies left behind anywhere, they were nothing but ash.

Soren got to his feet, hissing at the throbbing in his arm with the bite wound and in his skull. He eyed the bloodstained shirt sticking to his skin and decided trying to clean it here was useless without his gear. He had a kit back with his velocycle, and he needed to get there.

He needed to get to Oeiras.

Soren carefully bent down to retrieve his poison sword, sliding the blade free of the earth. It was the only weapon of his that remained intact, the space around where he'd lain unmarked, and he carefully sheathed the poison sword on his back.

Taking a deep breath, Soren stumbled forward, leaving the ashes for the wind.

Two

JOELLE

Vezir Joelle was methodically going through the daily reports delivered from the *vasilyet*'s council when a heavy knock came to her office door. Considering the only people who had access to her this deep in her House's estate in Bellingham was family, she deigned to answer.

"Enter," Joelle called out.

She glanced up, watching as Artyom strode inside with a grim look on his face. One of her handmaidens who acted as her secretary rose from her seat at the side table where she'd been organizing files and left the office, closing the door behind her.

Artyom came to a stop before Joelle's desk and bowed. "Mother."

"Shouldn't you be at the council meeting?"

He'd taken over the duties as heir from Karima two years ago. Joelle's daughter hadn't taken the demotion well, the loss of power and influence within their House wounding her almost as surely as the loss of Nicca. Karima's erratic behavior merely proved to Joelle she'd made the right choice for her House's future by designating Artyom her heir.

Artyom drew a folded piece of paper from his robe's pocket along with a tintype photograph and set both on her desk. "A messenger came from the town by the quarry. It's gone."

Joelle frowned. "The town?"

"No. The quarry and the laboratory. A witness said it burned by starfire."

Joelle's gaze snapped to her son's face and the grim worry in his eyes. She picked up the photograph first, staring at the ravaged land it depicted. The ground was so black she'd have thought the printing process made a mistake if Artyom hadn't told her what she was looking at.

"The witness could have been mistaken," Joelle said.

Artyom shook his head. "I am inclined to believe the witness' report. The man was caught outside the walls by starfire and burned over seventy percent of his body before escaping the conflagration's boundaries. Someone from the town found him in the prairie. He spoke of what he saw before he died."

"A hallucination, perhaps."

"The revenants in the quarry holding pens were incinerated and the land scorched, but no wildfire raced across the prairie. It would have if it were a normal fire. This was starfire, and the witness said it was wielded by a warden Poppy had captured. There'd been a revenant breakout, and he'd helped cull them."

"Impossible. Wardens do not accept tithes that carry the ability to cast starfire. No royal of any country would give up a member of their blood to the wardens. The Poison Accords do not allow it."

"Then if not the warden, who would have cast starfire?"

Joelle set the photograph aside and picked up the letter and unfolded it. The hastily drafted message reported what Artyom had said, though with a little more detail in describing the devastation. She read it twice over before setting it aside. "My *rionetkas* have not reported back that any of the major Houses are traveling at this time save the thrice-damned emperor. He has been in Oeiras for weeks now, and could not have been at the quarry last night."

Artyom made a face before taking a seat in front of her desk. "Can those abominations even be trusted?"

"Nothing from Daijal can be trusted, but they can be useful. I know of every member of every House, major or minor, who has the ability to cast starfire. They are few, of varying strengths, and none were in our *vasilyet*."

Artyom raised an eyebrow. "You know every Solarian who can cast starfire, but what of those in other countries?"

Joelle stared down at the photograph, studying the blackened vista. Artyom was correct in that if it had been a wildfire, it would have raced across the prairie. They built walls around their cities using metal and stone as much to keep out revenants as to keep fire from ravaging their homes.

Of those from other countries who cast starfire, Joelle knew of some this generation. The numbers had dwindled after the eradication of the Rourke bloodline, with only Eimarille surviving.

That we know of.

The thought skittered across her mind, tilting the playing field before her with unknown possibilities. If one star god could favor a child, surely the other five could give their blessings to another?

"If the magician who cast starfire was truly a warden, then it begs the question of who gave them up. All children show the spark of magic young, and starfire burns hot in the blood. Giving a tithe with starfire to the wardens would have been done on purpose, perhaps to keep someone safe. The wardens would have broken the Poison Accords if that were the case," Joelle said slowly.

Artyom proved he was of her House and worthy of the title of heir as he put the pieces together. "You think this warden is from Ashion. You think he's Rourke."

Joelle tapped her finger against the photograph. "I think there are quite a lot of possibilities here."

Even if the warden wasn't Rourke, she could spin him as such. She could use the warden if they could find him.

"What will you tell Eimarille? The laboratory is destroyed, along with the death-defying machine they gave us, and we don't know who this warden is."

"I'll tell her the truth. That her laboratory was destroyed by starfire and we don't know by whom, but that they couldn't have been of the Houses." Joelle smiled, meeting her son's gaze. "We won't mention the warden. I want him found for our own uses."

Artyom stood and bowed. "As you will it, Mother."

He left the message and photograph on her desk and took his leave. Joelle retrieved both, hiding them away in one of the many secret compartments of her desk. Information was power, as much as a throne was. Leverage was what you made of it.

"Perhaps the broadsheets lied," she murmured to herself. "Perhaps Prince Alasandair lived after all."

One way or another, Joelle would use this to her House's advantage.

Three

VANYA

Oeiras was a coastal port city, situated near the mouth of the Tirsha River that fed the sprawling tropical rainforest that was the city's backdrop. The *vasilyet* overseen by the House of Dayal encompassed that dangerous greenery. The walls surrounding Oeiras were always manned against the revenant wild beasts that crawled out from beneath the canopy.

The Oeiras port was a bustling place of trade. Individual Tovanian ships, separated from their ship-cities, made anchor at many of the piers to offload cargo or let their crew enjoy time in the city. Daijalan ships, both merchant class and their navy, came and went, watched over by the Solarian navy. Urovan submersibles had specialized berths, though their presence this far south wasn't a large one.

Trade with the Tovan Isles was an important undertaking that Vanya approached like a war game. Solaria needed what clarion crystal the Tovan people were willing to part with from their island nation. Their clarion crystals were of a slightly different construction than the ones they got from E'ridia and were used in the more advanced machines the Legion's engineers invented.

The dignitary room used for trade talks with the Tovan Isles delegation in Oeiras' Imperial estate contained a deep pool filled with salt water. Anchored to the ledge was an elaborate floating cabana, decked out with all the luxury attributed to someone with an important rank in high society. The engines that kept it afloat were a soft thrum that was easy for Vanya to ignore from his seat near the edge of the pool. The low table he and his aides sat behind mirrored the one the Tovan Isles ambassador and her people were seated at.

Ambassador Akeheni, of the ship-city Matariki, had been a ship's captain for more than half her life, based on the thin tattooed lines that arced away from the outer corner of her hazel eyes and framed her chin and mouth. A six-pointed star tattooed between her eyes was the mark of a government official, and Akeheni took her role seriously.

She was, like most Tovanians, an extremely skilled bargainer.

The detritus of the midday meal had been taken away some time ago, and they were back to hammering out the thorny details of trade. It was tedious work, and Vanya was glad for an interruption after a week of politicking.

Alida entered the dignitary room, footsteps quiet as she approached, and bowed when she reached the table he sat at. "Your Imperial Majesty, please excuse the interruption, but an issue has come up within your household that requires your immediate attention."

Household was different than House, even if the distinction wasn't quite known by outsiders. Vanya looked back at Akeheni and nodded at her. "You must excuse me, Ambassador. Perhaps an afternoon break for everyone?"

Akeheni inclined her head at him, her thick gray curls tumbling over her shoulders. "A break is acceptable. Perhaps we reconvene in an hour if the situation isn't urgent?"

"An hour, then."

Vanya stood, careful to keep his expression neutral and showing no concern, though he felt it deeply. Alida never interrupted him unless it was truly necessary.

He left the dignitary meeting room, glancing over at Alida, who walked a step behind him. "What is it?"

"Soren finally arrived. The magician is tending to him," Alida said.

Vanya's eyes widened fractionally. "What happened?"

She grimaced. "You'll want to speak with him."

"Where is he?"

"The family wing."

Vanya needed no escort to that area, but Alida joined him anyway. Raiah was in the nursery at this hour, or perhaps out in the estate's garden. Summer at the coast usually entailed fine weather, and Raiah was more adventurous these days at four years old. She wanted to be out and about rather than stuck indoors learning her letters and numbers.

The estate had staff that cared for it year-round, but the servants in the family wing had come with him from Calhames, their loyalty assured. They bowed to him as he passed before continuing with their work.

Alida directed him to Vanya's private receiving room, the blue of the wallpaper evoking the waves lapping at the shore. It was a bright room, made brighter by the magic pouring out of the magician's clarion crystal–tipped wand.

"What happened?" Vanya said flatly as he took in Soren's appearance.

Soren had been stripped of his shirt and vest, along with his poison sword. The blade in its sheath lay on the low table between the chaise and a pair of armchairs. The shirt was a bloodied bundle on the floor, along with his vest. Vanya didn't see his pistols or belt anywhere. The medallion hung from his throat, still intact.

Soren was bruised, less so than he'd probably been due to healing magic. A thick, clean bandage was wrapped around his upper right arm, but Vanya could see flecks of dried blood still clinging to his skin.

Vanya stepped into the space between the chaise and table, reaching to grasp Soren's chin. He tilted the other man's head up, staring down into that face, noticing the faint unevenness of his pupils.

Vanya frowned. "You're concussed, and you have a fever."

Soren hummed. "It's been a few days. The headache is fading, and I took an antidote for the bite wound."

"Bite wound," Vanya echoed, eyes drawn to the bandage around Soren's upper arm.

"I cleaned it out. It's not infected."

Wardens were the only ones Vanya knew of who could survive a revenant's bite. He chalked that up to the alchemist interventions that gave them an edge in the poison fields.

Vanya had to consciously not tighten his grip. "You went to the Warden's Island and were supposed to take a train here. What sort of mayhem could have occurred on a trip like that?"

"Did you forget how we met?" Soren hissed suddenly, pulling free of Vanya's grip. "*Ow.*"

The magician wasn't impressed, still tracing the outline of a large bruise over Soren's kidney. "Don't move. Your organs took quite a beating."

Soren stayed still beneath the magician's ministrations. Whatever magical mending the magician was doing, it eased the pain lines on Soren's tired face. Vanya took a seat on the plush armchair opposite the chaise, never taking his eyes off Soren.

Alida left and came back with a tray of light bites and the seafood soup with noodles that was a local specialty, the broth tinged red from a popular chili paste. When the magician finished, he tucked his wand away before inclining his head in Vanya's direction.

"He needs rest, Your Imperial Majesty. The concussion will heal with time. The bite wound caused a low-grade fever, but he is correct in that it is no longer infected. He is lucky in that way. I'll leave some pills for the pain."

"Can I speak with you alone, Vanya?" Soren asked.

Vanya nodded, and Alida escorted the magician out of the receiving room, closing the door behind her. The windows over-looked a private inner courtyard that was empty for the moment. Vanya stood and joined Soren on the chaise, watching as he slumped low onto the throw cushions there.

"How were you attacked by revenants?" Vanya asked.

Soren let out a harsh-sounding laugh, lifting his arms so that he could press the heels of his palms to his eyes. "Does it matter? Dealing with them is part of the job."

"You wouldn't ask to speak with me alone over that. What happened?"

When Soren didn't immediately answer, Vanya reached for his hands, drawing them away from his face. Soren blinked tiredly at him, the shadows beneath his gray eyes from lack of sleep and pain.

"I was going to take a train from Karnak to Oeiras, but I went to Bellingham instead," Soren said after a moment.

Vanya tightened his grip on Soren's wrists. "Why?"

"Did you know your merchants are opting to ship their goods to that city by way of airships rather than trucks or trains, despite the cost? Too many revenants within the House of Kimathi's *vasilyet* are a threat they don't want to deal with."

"I'm aware of the issue."

He'd been aware for quite some time, but Houses were given legal latitude when it came to governing their *vasilyets*. Even the Senate wouldn't go against that lawful tradition without good reason. The House of Kimathi hadn't outright banned wardens from its *vasilyet*, but the hostility there had been brought up when the border reports were delivered.

"I went because the governor needs more information on the borders there. We've lost wardens who get assigned to the area over the last few years. I got off at a way station and drove the rest of the way to Bellingham. I was going to do a grid search, but ended up following a convoy of trucks off the trade road into the plains to a quarry. It wasn't on any map."

Vanya knew how the wardens prided themselves on their maps. They had many different types to reference, each kind updated yearly with the reports that wardens brought back. The placement of cities and towns, those still standing and those lost to poison and those rebuilt, were records the wardens religiously kept. "What was there?"

Soren's expression became stony, lips pressed into a hard white line, even as his eyes stared past Vanya at something only he could see.

"There was a laboratory run by a Daijalan engineer. Some other Daijalans were working there as well, along with Solarians. They had debt slaves in cages, and the quarry was filled with revenants."

Vanya went still, fingers pressed to the pulse point in Soren's wrists, counting out the rising beats there. "Debt bondage is illegal in Solaria."

Soren slanted him an unimpressed look. "Borders are lines on a map and legal designations in the courts. Atrocities still cross over."

Solaria did not interfere with the way other countries did business in their own lands. Solaria had never allowed the banks inside their borders to offer such poisonous, devastating loans to its citizens. Daijal had spent the past few hundred years espousing the merits of such loans and failing to find acceptance for the practice past its borders. Every emperor and empress that had sat on the Imperial throne had refused such business proposals, as had the Senate.

There was no peace to be found in debt bondage.

Vanya knew Solaria had taken in escaped debt slaves over the years, refusing to let the Collector's Guild operate within its borders. Oh, Vanya was certain they operated clandestinely within Solaria, but if they were ever caught, the bounty hunters were sent to prison. But for such an operation to be blatantly operating in a *vasilyet* spoke of tacit approval and support.

Just not from the Imperial throne.

"Tell me the quarry's location, and I'll order the Legion to secure it," Vanya said.

Soren's expression became shuttered. "There's nothing left."

"What do you mean?"

Soren sighed and tugged his wrists free of Vanya's grip. "The engineer was in charge of the death-defying machine."

Vanya blinked. "You found it?"

Soren wouldn't look at him. "They tried to put me into its chamber, but they didn't remove all my weapons. I blew it up with a bomb before they could shove me into it. Then I blew up the warehouse and set fire to the revenants in the quarry."

Vanya wanted to be angry about losing hard evidence of the assumed betrayal by the House of Kimathi, but the chilling knowledge he could have lost Soren was a heavy knot in his gut. He knew the poison fields weren't easy to tend, that the borders were dangerous even on cleansed land. One of these days, Soren would leave and never come back, and Vanya would live his life wondering where his lover's bones lay.

"What exactly did the machine do?" Vanya asked instead. He had an idea, but the thought was too horrific to be true.

He wanted it to be a lie.

Soren shifted on the chaise, letting his head fall back so he could stare up at the ceiling. "I think it turned the dead into revenants faster than spores can."

Vanya stood and began to pace, needing to burn off some of the adrenaline coursing through him. The sheer abhorrence of such a machine was a threat he couldn't ignore, especially coming from a witness he could trust.

"Joelle goes against the throne with this. She goes against Solaria," he spat out.

"She goes against the Star Order and the Poison Accords, but you can't prove it."

Vanya bared his teeth at that pointed remark. "I would if you'd left something behind for me to use."

Soren scowled as he levered himself up to a sitting position. "I wasn't about to leave a horde of revenants in that pit. There were easily a thousand in it. Burning them was the only answer."

"And the machine?"

"Would you rather I have died in it?"

"You know I'd never wish that."

"It was either leave it all intact or make sure no one else could use it again. I'm not going to apologize for doing my duty as a warden. I'm not yours to command, remember?"

I wish you were.

The traitorous thought was something Vanya could never give voice to. It would be easier to keep Soren safe if he could order the warden to *stay*. But even an emperor had no control over Maricol's wardens.

"Joelle will know by now of its destruction. If I were her, I'd have taken the last couple of days to eradicate any remaining evidence," Vanya said.

Soren closed his eyes. "I'm fairly certain I killed everyone with my bombs. They took my pistols. I need to get new ones."

"I'll have Alida retrieve a set from the Legion's weapons storage."

"You won't have the right kind. I need to go to a warden's resupply station."

"You need to rest."

Soren cracked open one eye and gestured at himself. "What do you think I'm doing?"

"Being stubborn." Vanya returned to the chaise, leaning down to brace himself against the back of it so he could kiss Soren with slow thoroughness. "I need to continue my trade talks with the Tovan Isles ambassador. That's not something I can walk away from, but I'll take a meeting with my military advisors tonight on this matter."

Soren's fingers tangled in the fabric of Vanya's richly embroidered robe, keeping him close. "Do you want me there for the meeting? It's technically a border report."

Enough rumors existed in the upper echelons of the government about Vanya's preference for Soren's presence that he'd rather not fuel that fire. "No. I'll handle it. You can keep Raiah company. She's missed you."

Soren cracked a smile at Raiah's name, expression softening. "All right."

Vanya straightened up and gestured at the food on the table. "Eat. I'll send Alida back in to tend to your needs."

He trailed his fingertips across Soren's forehead in a gentle goodbye before taking his leave, thoughts heavy with the knowledge of the threat clawing at his House and country.

Four

VANYA

Vanya cradled the telephone handset between his ear and shoulder as he flipped through the maps Alida had retrieved for him from the archive kept by the House of Dayal. The specific area he was looking at was the land outside Bellingham. The maps were copies of the ones updated yearly by their country's cartographers based on the border reports from wardens.

Soren had mapped the location for him during the evening meal before retreating to Vanya's bedroom to sleep. Raiah had been excited to see him, though Vanya hadn't let his daughter sit in Soren's lap how she preferred. Even with the magician's intervention, he could see that Soren was in pain and still recovering.

"Any House will protest the intercession of the Legion in their lands on your orders, Your Imperial Majesty. *Vezirs* command ranks on their own within their *vasilyets*. They'll demand those legionnaires be involved with any searches and not ones based out of Calhames," Imperial General Chu Hua said, her voice tinny through the wire. She was back in Calhames, the hour later there, but she'd answered the call regardless.

"Are you asking me if I care what they want? They lose whatever right they think they have for going against Solarian law when it comes to the dead," Vanya asked irritably.

"You called for advisement, which I am giving. Better not to tip your hand in a situation like this. Send a platoon of *praetoria* legionnaires to the area in question. We can say they're undergoing some field training while you are away to hide their true purpose. No one questions war game training."

Which was true, but that didn't ease Vanya's desire to eradicate a House down to its very foundations as his mother once had. Soren's explanation of what he thought the death-defying machine did was terrifying enough. Knowing that Joelle had allowed it all to happen, probably for years, spoke of a game Vanya was only just becoming aware of.

It spoke of betrayal to Solaria that no House could accept.

He'd risked the call to Imperial General Chu Hua only because her loyalty had never been in doubt, either by his mother or himself. Chu Hua belonged to no House, major or minor, but she'd risen through the ranks of the Legion and had spent the majority of her career within the *praetoria*, the personal guard of the Imperial throne. Their job was to guard Solaria. Their loyalty was to the country first, the Imperial family second, and the Legion after. She'd become the Imperial General during his mother's reign, and Vanya had supported her position ever since. Chu Hua would always fight for Solaria, even against a House.

"How fast can you deploy a platoon?" Vanya asked.

"We can muster up a training exercise within a day. I'll adjust assignments accordingly. We'll put them on a military train heading north to Bellingham but have them disembark at a way station."

Vanya straightened up, grasping the handset to hold it against his ear. "I wouldn't trust any communications station the House of Kimathi has control over. Send an ornithopter with the train, and have an aeronaut fly the report back to you."

"Very well."

Vanya glared down at the map and the grid area that Soren had circled. "Find me evidence, if you can."

He doubted there would be any left, but they needed to look regardless.

"As the throne wills it."

Vanya placed the handset on the base of the telephone, ending the call. He rubbed at his eyes, wishing he could rub away the headache that had grown in the wake of Soren's report. Sighing, Vanya set the maps aside in favor of reviewing the day's gains and concessions from the trade talks. They were close, he thought, to coming to an agreement. Perhaps another day or two, and he could leave Oeiras for Calhames.

He worked until the clock chimed the midnight hour. The grittiness in his dry eyes and the ache in his neck and shoulders from hunching over his desk for so long was what finally prompted him to go to bed.

The hallways leading to the private wing of the Imperial estate were dimly lit in deference to the late hour. Vanya passed a few legionnaires on guard duty on his way to his bedroom. A servant had left a light on in the antechamber, making it easy enough to navigate into the bedroom proper.

No light burned there, save what little filtered through the gauzy curtains hanging over the windows. The private courtyard used only by the Imperial family was lit by a single gas lamp throughout the night, providing faint illumination to see by through the windows.

Vanya didn't bother calling for his body servant at this hour. He removed his shoes and stripped out of his robe and trousers, leaving everything on the floor. In the summer heat, he wore no clothes to bed and crawled beneath the thin blanket and soft sheets that were all he cared for when the weather got warmer.

Soren had wrapped himself up in both without a care for Vanya's comfort. He had to smile at that as he tugged some of the blanket and sheets free.

"How'd the call go?" Soren asked, voice sleep-soft but clear.

Vanya wasn't surprised he'd woken up. Soren was a light sleeper even when recovering from wounds taken on the poison fields. "Well enough. I doubt we'll find any evidence we can use against the House of Kimathi, but the presence of *praetoria* legionnaires in the *vasilyet* will put Joelle on notice."

"Can you afford that scrutiny?"

"Every House is under scrutiny."

"What about Raiah?"

It was telling that Soren could cut right to the heart of Vanya's fears. Wardens were trained to see threats, though, so it should not have come as a surprise. While the political field was not usually their expertise, he supposed Soren had absorbed some insights from all the times Vanya had confided in him.

"I'll do whatever I must to keep her safe."

Soren slid closer, wrapping an arm around Vanya. "I know you will."

Vanya turned into Soren's warmth and closed his eyes, trying to set aside his worries in favor of much-needed sleep. Soren's breathing lulled him into a dreamless sleep he could have been cradled in until dawn.

He woke, instead, to the sound of a gun firing, ears ringing with it. He jerked to a sitting position and was promptly yanked back down again, Soren's grip like an iron vise on his shoulder. The warden leaned over him, newly gifted pistol in hand, still shooting at the shadowy figures in the room with them.

Vanya yanked a hand free of the sheets, starfire pooling in his hand, throwing the bedroom in high relief. Shock coursed through him as he realized the people who had tried to murder him in his sleep wore the uniforms of legionnaires with the patch indicating they belonged to the *praetoria*.

They'd been the ones on guard duty outside his bedroom when he'd retired for the night.

The sinking sense of betrayal didn't stop him from casting starfire in the direction of the wounded legionnaires bleeding all over his bedroom floor. Soren's instincts were to be commended, because Vanya doubted he would have survived what the traitors had planned.

"Leave some of them alive for questioning," Soren snapped, still leaning over Vanya, shielding him with his body.

Vanya's temper was such that he'd rather annihilate the threat in its entirety, but he managed to reel in the desire for murder. Starfire erupted around the arms of every legionnaire, the smell of burning flesh filling the air as Vanya seared through skin and muscle to bone, making it impossible for any of them to hold a weapon.

Their screams brought forth more legionnaires to the bedroom, shouts echoing in the hallway beyond, concern for Vanya in their voices, but he couldn't trust that.

Soren threw himself out of the bed, yanking his second pistol from its holster on the nightstand. No longer pressed to the bed, Vanya sat up, arm still extended, starfire curling around his fingers. Soren reached the door before anyone else, turning the lock and keeping one pistol aimed at it.

"Raiah," Vanya bit out around a painful knot in his throat.

Soren's expression twisted. "I can't leave you here alone."

"Then we'll leave together."

Someone pounded on the bedroom door, rattling it on its hinges. "Your Imperial Majesty!"

Vanya was in no position to believe the frantic worry in the voices beyond the door. Soren's pistol never wavered as Vanya hurriedly left the bed. They were both of them naked, but at least they were alive.

"Stay where you are. That's an order," Vanya called out.

Soren moved enough to switch on the gas lamp near the door. His attention shifted from Vanya to the writhing bodies on the floor, who were no longer a problem. None of them could hold a pistol or any other sort of weapon with no fingers. Soren's eyes widened in surprise, and Vanya followed his gaze.

Three of the legionnaires were dead, killed by Soren's bullets. The other two were still alive, though their arms were being eaten away by starfire. Their uniforms hadn't survived the attack, and charred fabric curled away from their shoulders and chest, revealing a line of ropy scar tissue Vanya distantly recognized.

"Vanya," Soren said sharply.

He ignored the warning in his lover's voice and knelt beside one of the bodies. He ripped the uniform jacket open and then the undershirt beneath, revealing vivisection scars on the legionnaire's chest.

Vanya touched his fingers to the dip in the sternum and the scars that bisected the skin over the bone there. "Do you think they are powered by a clockwork heart? Do you think it's a form of control after all?"

The wardens hadn't been able to completely decipher the spell-work in Soren's drawings and notes and the remains of the clockwork metal heart taken from the would-be assassin that had attacked during his coronation two years ago.

What the wardens had uncovered was that the device was meant to animate a person, but animating could mean many things. If they had been sent to kill him, the bigger question was who had given the order.

No proof meant no accusation, and rumors wouldn't hold up in a court of law.

It was a worry that had to be set aside for the moment. Vanya was stuck in his bedroom, not knowing if they were about to be under siege, and Raiah was alone in the nursery down the hall.

Raiah was all that could matter.

He stood, reaching for the clothes he'd discarded mere hours ago. "We'll need to check everyone in the *praetoria*."

Soren's pistol never moved from the door. "I remember a time you'd burn them all."

"Destroying my household will not solve our current problem."

He was and was not his mother in some ways. When she'd brought Rixham to ruin, she'd held more political clout than he currently had. He could not and would not bring starfire down on Oeiras the same way his mother had done to Rixham. The House of Dayal was not the rot he needed to excise from the country.

"Get dressed," Vanya ordered. "We're getting Raiah."

Soren nodded and dressed in his field leathers at a speed born from habit. The shouting on the other side of the bedroom door hadn't really subsided, and the tension only got worse when Vanya jerked open the door, filling the archway with an interlocking hexagonal aether shield.

Soren stepped in front of him, both pistols aimed at the crowd of legionnaires standing in their way. "Strip."

The lieutenant in charge scowled at him from behind her own raised pistol. "I don't take orders from you."

"But you take orders from your emperor. Do as the warden says. Remove your shirts," Vanya snapped.

Vanya desperately wanted to get to his daughter, but Soren's demand was one he followed, because it only made sense to make sure they didn't take a bullet to the back.

The *praetoria* legionnaires did as ordered, all of them undoing their uniform jackets and removing their shirts. Vanya peeled the shield apart so Soren could slip through and let his pistols lead him down the hall, getting eyes on every last legionnaire.

"They're clear," Soren called back from down the way before disappearing from sight.

Vanya pried the shield from the doorway, though he didn't let the starfire in his hand fade away. The lieutenant was already hauling her shirt and uniform jacket back on, staring beyond Vanya at the mess on his bedroom floor.

"Your Imperial Majesty," she said, some kind of horror and shame in her voice.

"Secure the bodies. The ones who tried to kill me tonight may not have been acting of their own free will."

She nodded, calling out orders to the legionnaires around her. Vanya pushed past them all, intent on getting to his daughter. The lieutenant overtook him in seconds, glaring at him. "Stay behind me."

The private wing of the Imperial estate had erupted in activity at the first sound of gunshots. Vanya knew it would be mere moments longer for the rest of the estate to wake. He couldn't trust anyone within these walls save the man he'd fallen asleep beside.

"Cordon off the wing. I want no one else around us until we have proof everyone is who they say they are," Vanya said.

The lieutenant relayed his order to the man marching at her left, and that legionnaire peeled off at a run. Vanya didn't watch him leave, heart beating faster as he heard gunshots go off. The lieutenant barked out an order that sent a trio of legionnaires racing ahead. Vanya would have joined them, except she forcibly shoved him back.

"We are nothing if you are dead, Your Imperial Majesty," she said sharply. "Do not get caught in the crossfire."

Vanya knew he should care about his own life, but the only one that mattered to him in that instant was Raiah's. More gunshots, and then his daughter's shrieking cry pierced the air. Vanya shoved past the lieutenant unthinkingly, only wanting to get to his daughter.

"Raiah!" he shouted.

"I have her," Soren called back.

The warden hurried around the corner just then, pistol in one hand and carrying Raiah in the other. Raiah had her small arms wrapped tight around Soren's neck, tears streaming down her face. Vanya's knees went a little weak as he realized his daughter was unharmed, even if he couldn't guarantee her safety.

"Papa," Raiah cried as Soren tipped her into Vanya's waiting arms.

"It's all right," Vanya said, smoothing his hand over her curly hair. "It's all right. I'm here now."

Soren took a step back, gaze flinty. "A couple of legionnaires had taken her from the nursery and were trying to leave. They're dead now."

Vanya tightened his arms around Raiah until she squirmed. "They didn't want her dead."

"No. I think they were sent to kidnap her."

"Lieutenant, I want everyone examined for the same scars the attackers have. If anyone has them, or if anyone refuses to bare their skin, do whatever is necessary to secure them alive. If anyone fights you, kill them."

The lieutenant snapped off a salute before stepping back and flagging down a couple more legionnaires. Vanya had faith in her ability to execute his order, but that still left him with far more questions than he liked.

Soren crossed his arms over his chest. "Two of them were still alive when we left your bedroom."

Vanya's lips curled. "Someone get me a magician with mind magic."

In the wake of yet another assassination attempt, this time from within, Vanya's full household was restricted from his presence. He couldn't trust the legionnaires despite their lack of vivisection scars. That insidious thread of doubt kept Raiah in his arms and Soren by his side.

Captain Javier Molina, in charge of the *praetoria* legionnaires that had come with Vanya to Oeiras, was a magician who had no compunctions about proving his loyalty by stripping completely out of his uniform and casting his weapons aside.

Vanya nodded at the man, glad to see no vivisection scars on his torso. "I need answers, Captain."

Javier gave him a grim salute in reply before getting dressed again, taking his pistol and wand in hand, and marching into Vanya's bedroom. Soren stood watch by the door, keeping an eye on what was happening with the dead and those that wanted access to the antechamber where Vanya paced. Vanya wanted to oversee the interrogation, but he didn't want Raiah to bear witness to that.

"Interesting coincidence this happens after your call with the general," Soren said.

Vanya grimaced, unable to know if Imperial General Chu Hua's loyalty had been compromised. "I need to return to Calhames to deal with this mess, but I can't leave the trade talks unfinished."

"Can someone else take your place?"

"I'm the only one who can sign off on the treaty."

"Your Imperial Majesty," Alida called out breathlessly as she darted into the antechamber, still shrugging into one sleeve of her robe. "Are you all right?"

The skin over the swell of her left breast and collarbone was unmarked. She appeared frazzled but within her own mind. Having his majordomo on hand would make passing orders along easier even if a dark little voice in the back of his mind wondered if he could trust her.

"We're fine," Vanya said.

Alida stumbled to a halt, staring at him before her attention was wrenched to whatever was happening in the bedroom. She paled before swallowing audibly and rallying to do her duty. "What would you have me do?"

It would be too much to hope the broadsheets wouldn't report on the attempted assassination, but Vanya well knew how quickly rumor spread. Vanya would have to show himself in public the moment the sun broke the horizon to prove he still wore the crown. At least they had some time to prepare to mitigate this fiasco.

"Send an envoy to the Tovan Isles ambassador residence to confirm they are safe. Has the House of Dayal sent a representative yet?"

"No, but we should prepare to receive one shortly."

"Prepare a statement of assurance that I do not blame their House for this."

Alida bowed at that and left to do his bidding. Soren pushed away from the doorway and approached Vanya on silent feet. He was armed now how he would be in the poison fields—guns, poison short sword, and a host of other weapons—and Vanya felt steadier for it.

"Give me Raiah. The captain needs you in the other room," Soren said.

Vanya handed his daughter over to the only person he trusted, and she went willingly enough, half-asleep and yawning. Vanya strode into the bedroom, seeing the dead had been wrapped up in the sheets from his bed and others from storage. The two legionnaires who had survived the attack were sprawled at Javier's feet, their arms burned off and barely alive.

Javier had the tip of his wand pressed to one of the men's burned forehead, the clarion crystal there glowing softly. His gaze was focused inward, but he came back to himself soon enough. He stood with a grimace, wand held tight in his hand.

"Their thoughts are not their own even if their personalities are," Javier said.

Vanya stared at the vivisection scars that he knew hid clockwork metal hearts. "So they *are* being controlled. Did they tell you who did this to them?"

Javier shook his head. "Those memories have been thoroughly erased in that area, as were the ones on who gave them orders. All they do know is that they are called *rionetkas*."

"Puppets," Vanya said, translating the Urovan word into Solarian. He wondered if these men and women once loyal to the throne had asked for a new heart or been forcibly given one. "And what were their orders?"

Javier looked him in the eye, voice a harsh growl. "To kill you and take the princess."

Nearly every House would've given an order to kill them both. He knew of only one who would target them so differently.

"These *rionetkas* will have clockwork hearts inside their chests. Remove the devices in all but one body and then prepare them for transport. We're taking them with us to Calhames when we return to the capital."

He'd keep the clockwork hearts this time, rather than give the remains to the wardens. He wanted Solaria's own aetherologists to examine the devices.

Javier gestured with his wand at the two charred figures on the floor. "And these two?"

"If they've given up what secrets they remember, I have no further use for them."

Vanya left Javier to handle the cleanup of the bedroom. He retreated to the antechamber, gesturing at Soren to follow him. The lieutenant and several others acted as an escort for them as he led Soren to his private office. No one followed them inside, and Vanya locked the door behind them. Raiah was sleeping in Soren's arms and he took a moment to drink them both in.

"They're called *rionetkas*," Vanya finally said.

Soren frowned. "There were rumors of the death-defying machine long before I stumbled over it. I haven't heard anything about people walking around with clockwork hearts since we first discovered the one device two years ago. We didn't hear any rumors before that either."

"They're being controlled, and no one knew."

The implications of that were horrifying. How many people were out there walking around with gears in their chest and magic whispering through their mind, ordering them about like marionettes? How many senators had been targeted? How many Houses? Was Solaria the only country being infiltrated in such a way?

Too many questions and no easy answers.

Vanya pinched the bridge of his nose. "The Senate will need to be informed."

"Okay."

"And I need to send Raiah away." He hated even speaking those words, but Vanya knew it was the only option right now.

Soren grimaced, gently patting Raiah's back. "Wouldn't she be safer with you?"

"Not if the House of Kimathi is behind all of this."

"You have no proof."

Vanya bared his teeth in a snarl. "Nothing but Joelle's refusal to grant wardens passage, whatever remnants we'll find in that quarry, and the knowledge she has wanted me dead since Nicca died."

"Their House wouldn't harm Raiah."

"No, they wouldn't, which is why the *rionetkas* sent to her nursery tonight had orders to flee with her, not kill her."

"That isn't *proof*, Vanya."

"Then I will find a way to prove it. That House would twist my daughter into someone who would never be seen as being of the House of Sa'Liandel. That's a type of death I will not allow Raiah to experience, and I will not let them use her to take the throne."

He wanted Raiah out of the line of fire right now, somewhere safe, but there were precious few corners of the country he could hide her in.

"Where will you send her?" Soren asked quietly.

"The House of Vikandir has been loyal. I could send her there."

"Can you be sure they wouldn't keep her as a hostage?"

Vanya smiled wanly. "My father was of that House, from a cadet branch off the main bloodline. Amir may wish to keep his House from taking the Imperial throne, but they still desire its power. They've found other avenues over the years to gain it."

"And if any of his people are walking around with clockwork metal hearts, what then? Do you trust them enough not to use Raiah the way Joelle would?"

Vanya said nothing in the face of that question, because to say yes was to give voice to a lie.

Soren studied him, gray eyes unblinking, pupils finally even after the healing done yesterday afternoon. "I'm not of your House, but I can keep Raiah safe if you send her away."

"You're a warden. You always say you're not supposed to involve yourself in matters of state."

Soren laughed, soft and bitter, before stepping close. "And what do you call the years I've known you? The nights I've slept in your bed? What would you call the vow hanging around my throat? I'm *involved*, princeling."

Vanya could only kiss him, hard and fierce, while Soren held Raiah safe in his arms. He'd wanted Soren to stay, and yet, their roads always diverged.

"I'll sign an Imperial writ. It will give you passage anywhere in Solaria," Vanya said roughly when they parted.

"I can get us through any border without that."

"You won't be welcomed into a House even if Raiah would be. The writ speaks as if I speak. It will get you where she needs to be."

Soren shifted Raiah in his arms so that he could lift a hand and run his fingers through Vanya's hair. "I'll take her to Karnak. I'll keep her safe until you can come get her."

Vanya had thought it had been difficult to bury his brother and parents over the years, but by far the most difficult decision to make was to let his daughter go. But keeping her on the move and sending her not where Joelle would expect him to would keep Raiah alive. He didn't want her in the crossfire he knew would happen when he accused another House of treason.

He caught Soren's hand in his, moving to press his lips against the pulse point of the other man's wrist. "Let's get you both ready to leave."

Within the hour, the writ was signed and tucked away in the inner pocket of Soren's vest. Alida had packed a small satchel of Raiah's clothes, as plain as she could find, and was off to sort out other provisions. Vanya said his goodbyes in the private courtyard of the Imperial estate, Raiah on his lap while he twisted her hair into two neat braids.

"But Papa, I don't want to go," she said sleepily, rubbing at her eyes.

He swallowed hard, but his fingers remained steady as he tied off the first braid. "You know how I always read you a story at night? Well, when I see you again, you can tell me all about the adventure you had with Soren."

"Why can't you come with us?"

"Because I must stay here. Your papa must work, and you'll get to play where you're going."

She yawned, head tilting back as he worked on the second braid. "No school?"

"No school."

"Will there be toys?"

He lied to her out of love, as any parent would. "Yes. Lots of them."

When the braid was finished, Vanya hugged her to him tightly, kissing the crown of her head, trying to memorize the way she felt in his arms—small and warm and oh so precious.

A soft clearing of a throat had Vanya looking up, meeting Soren's gaze from across the courtyard. "We're ready."

Vanya nodded, lifting Raiah in his arms. He carried her through the Imperial estate and to the garage, where Soren's velocycle had been outfitted with a ride-along seat meant for a child. Alida stood nearby, a child-sized helmet and goggles dangling from one hand, eyes wide and wet as she looked at them.

"If anyone asks, I'll tell them she's a tithe," Soren said as Vanya buckled Raiah into the ride-along seat.

Alida silently handed him the helmet, and Vanya carefully placed it over his daughter's head. He secured the tiny strap beneath her chin before placing the goggles over her eyes. Then he leaned down and kissed her firmly on the cheek.

"I love you," he said in a low, rough voice.

"Love you back, Papa," Raiah said with a sleepy smile.

Vanya straightened up and forced himself to let his daughter go. Soren slung a leg over his velocycle and started the engine. His own helmet and goggles were in place, the night lenses flipped down, because dawn was still two hours away.

He was leaving with no escort, weighed down with what weapons Soren could carry, a televox, an Imperial writ, and the heart of Vanya's House seated behind him.

Vanya desperately wanted to keep both of them by his side.

"I'll keep her safe, and I'll call when we've arrived at Karnak," Soren promised.

Vanya pressed his hand over Soren's chest, where he knew the vow rested beneath the leather vest. "I know you will."

Because Soren had kept him safe years ago, the same way he was doing now. Vanya would owe him more than he could possibly repay, and Soren had to know that.

Vanya didn't care about the legionnaires around them, about Alida, about anyone else watching. He leaned down and kissed Soren goodbye with a ferocity that he could never admit out loud was love, but it felt like that.

"Vanya," Soren whispered against his lips, quiet and aching in a way Vanya knew only too well. "I—"

"Don't," he said raggedly, pulling back. "Don't speak unless it's to ask me for what you want."

Soren's smile was a crooked, tight thing. "I'm not supposed to want."

But he did, and they both knew it, even if they never gave voice to what they shared between them in the nights Soren found his way to Vanya's bed.

And it felt like Vanya's world was breaking when Soren drove away, but Vanya was the one who let it shatter.

"What now?" Alida asked when the rumble of Soren's velocycle could no longer be heard.

Vanya tipped his head back and looked at the stars, finding the Lion constellation after searching the sky, the Dawn Star shining bright in the midst of celestial teeth.

"We bring a House to ruin."

Five

JOELLE

That morning's broadsheet arrived at the House of Kimathi late. It eventually found its way beside Joelle's breakfast plate, unfolded and placed within reach by a servant. The headline screaming from the top of the page put a frown on her face.

"He survived," Joelle said, making a moue of annoyance.

Artyom looked up from the fresh flatbread he was dipping into the spiced tomato and poached egg dish that was their morning meal. "That's a pity. And Raiah?"

"Not mentioned in the article."

If Raiah had been injured or worse, the broadsheets would have led with that story rather than Vanya's latest survival in the face of another assassination attempt.

"The *rionetkas* failed, then. Which means Vanya may be aware of them," Artyom said.

Joelle set the broadsheet aside and picked up her cup of chai, taking a sip. "That was always a risk."

"Can we continue to afford to take them?"

She set her chai down. "No one has ever attained the Imperial throne by not taking risks."

"We should not put Raiah in danger."

"She was never in danger. All *rionetkas* have their orders to take Raiah if they can and bring her here. They will die before seeing any harm come to my great-granddaughter."

It was an order Joelle had demanded be bound in the *rionetkas'* making before accepting any of them into her service. The *Klovod* had provided what she needed, and despite this setback, Joelle had no plans to stop using them.

A servant hurried into the parlor, out of breath, and bowed. "*Vezir*, there is an urgent call for you from Oeiras."

Joelle set aside her piece of flatbread and stood, hiding her wince of pain from the motion. She hadn't yet had her medicine draught that morning, and her joints ached. "Have the switchboard send it to my office."

Artyom offered his arm to her, and Joelle gratefully took it. He escorted her to her office and didn't leave once she was ensconced behind her desk. One of her handmaidens oversaw the transfer of the call to the telephone on her desk. When it rang, Joelle answered.

"Yes?" she demanded.

The sound of rapid breathing filled the wire before the voice of the only spy she'd ever been successful at getting into the Sa'Liandel household came through. "He sent the girl away."

Joelle tightened her grip on the handset. "Where?"

"I don't know, but she went with the warden as her guard."

"A warden." Artyom straightened in his chair as Joelle spoke, eyeing her with focused intent at that word. "Which one?"

"The one who always brings the border reports. He goes by Soren."

It might have been years, but Joelle still remembered the name of the warden who had been feted after saving Vanya's life. It seemed the rumor of Vanya's favor was indeed true.

"He knows about the *rionetkas*. He kept the bodies," her spy said.

"You've done well, and you will be rewarded for your loyalty. Continue your duty." Joelle placed the handset back on the base, ending the call. "Send a messenger to the press archives. I want a copy of the broadsheets from six years ago, around the time of the train wreck that nearly killed Vanya. They will have a picture of the warden that saved his life."

"What has he got to do with anything?"

"Vanya gave Raiah into his safekeeping, and if Soren is the one rumored to be Vanya's lover, so much the better."

"We should take him alive, if that is the case. Perhaps he could tell us which warden wields starfire."

"It will be in the orders that go out. I want it today. We'll be leaving for Calhames tonight via airship."

Artyom blinked in surprise. "Our House hasn't been to the capital in years."

"Vanya will not stay in Oeiras. He will not let this attack lie how he has others, not with the failed retrieval of my great-granddaughter. He kept the bodies of the *rionetkas*, and if I were him, I'd show them to the Houses and the Senate. We must counter his argument. To do that, we must be present."

She and her House had not set foot in Calhames since Nicca's death. They hadn't even sent an honor guard to retrieve her body, forcing the House of Sa'Liandel to escort Nicca home for a final good-bye. Joelle had kept her distance out of pride, but now need required she appear at the capital.

Artyom nodded and stood, bowing to her. "I'll brief the messenger on their task and prepare the House for the journey to Calhames."

Joelle nodded. "See that it is done."

Artyom left her office, closing the door behind him. Joelle didn't much care for long trips these days, not with the way her bones ached. Still, her body would not keep her from chasing after what she desired for her House.

Six

HONOVI

The invitation to a dinner honoring Maricol's ambassadors wasn't one Honovi could decline. He wished he could have.

The palace was decorated differently from the ball he'd attended nearly a week ago. The crowd was smaller this time, chatter a changing tune of accents and languages that buzzed in his ears. The E'ridian delegation was decked out in kilts and plaid, braids twisted through with clan beads and ranking hair adornments. He'd brought along several consular officers as well as a few aides to help facilitate communications between other countries.

He was surprised to see a delegation from the Tovan Isles present, believing Amari too far inland for that country to send its people for a long period of time. Honovi gripped his glass of whiskey and made his way to the Tovan Isles ambassador, pausing here and there to have a quick conversation with a few other people.

"Well met, Ambassador," the older Tovanian said in the trade tongue with a smile and a salute of his drinking glass in Honovi's direction.

The man's face was tanned and weathered, the facial tattoos blurred a little from years beneath the sun. The lines on his chin, around his eyes, dotting his forehead, and pricking his cheeks spoke of a long life of command. His light brown hair was tied back in a queue, hazel eyes ringed in dark lashes.

"Honovi, of Clan Storm," Honovi said, inclining his head. "It's nice to see another who appreciates the sway of a ship."

The Tovanian ambassador laughed. "I miss it, but my government asked me to leave our beloved waves behind. Who am I to tell them no?"

"How fares your health?"

Honovi well knew the land sickness Tovanians suffered from if they spent too long off their ship-cities. Port Avi was their country's capital for trade and political reasons, but the majority of its people called the open waters of Maricol's seas and oceans home. Some bloodlines called the island home on a more permanent basis, but they rarely left it.

"Our magicians have created better potions over the years to counteract the land sickness. Tastes awful, but it does its job for a while." The man offered his hand in greeting. "Tipene Kahale."

Honovi grasped his hand and shook it. "Well met."

They chatted for a bit about their experiences in Amari, keeping their answers polite and positive because of the company they kept. They only stopped when the Crown Princess Eimarille Rourke was announced to the guests at large.

Honovi watched her sweep into the room in a deep blue gown, escorted once again by the prime minister. His attention strayed to the Blade who shadowed her every step, fingers tightening on his glass as he worked to keep his expression calm while Blaine's attacker smiled at the room at large.

"I'm so pleased to honor all of you this evening," Eimarille announced before launching into a speech.

She was a great speaker, engaging and personable, and Honovi could see how she'd swayed public opinion in her favor over the years. Her heritage played a big part in it, he was certain, but fondness for the past couldn't make a future. He simply didn't trust the future she was looking to build for two countries.

When it was his delegation's turn to greet the princess, Honovi bowed to the precise degree, no more and no less, before straightening up. "Your Royal Highness."

"Ambassador Honovi, I'm happy you could join us tonight," Eimarille said, smiling.

He kept his attention on Eimarille and not Terilyn. "Your invitation was gladly accepted."

Eimarille's gaze went to his throat. "I have not seen your wife in attendance lately. I hope she is well."

"Husband," Honovi corrected her. "And he resides in Glencoe at the moment handling clan affairs in my absence."

"You must miss him."

Like an ache in his bones that never went away, but he didn't say that. "Always."

Honovi spared a few moments to introduce those with him by rank and clan, their riot of plaid a visual representation of their unity. Eimarille focused on each person, her warm attention making everyone feel as if they were the only person in the room.

Politics is personality, Honovi thought, sipping at his whiskey.

And Eimarille was exceedingly personable.

She proved that throughout the dinner, where she presided over the long table in the grand dining hall of the palace. Dinner was an exquisite, multi-course meal that Honovi didn't walk away from hungry even if he was wary of every bite he took. It was one thing to sit at a table with royalty, quite another to sit with an assassin.

He was careful to not let his opinion show, even when Terilyn smiled at him with a kindness he knew was a lie as Eimarille said her farewells.

"I do hope E'ridia will find what Daijal wants for trade acceptable," Eimarille said.

"You would have to speak with the ambassador assigned to that country, Your Royal Highness. I'm here for Ashion," Honovi said.

She kept her smile and gave no indication of her opinion on that distinction. "Of course, Ambassador. But you are aware our countries are critically intertwined. Tonight was about ensuring we're all on the same road."

Memory came to him, a flash of Blaine's pale, young face blurred from time as he walked away from the airship that had ferried him away from a broken country. Honovi was certain Eimarille's road would never cross theirs in a helpful way.

"We are all children of Maricol," Honovi said, the rote line of scripture from the Star Order coming easily to his lips.

Eimarille's smile never wavered. "And all children need guidance."

Honovi heard the warning clear as temple bells. He kept his expression easy and neutral as he bowed to her. "Thank you for the dinner and conversation. It was most illuminating."

"I'm sure. Have a good evening, Ambassador."

Honovi's retinue escaped the palace for their motor carriages on the driveway. Siv sighed once they were in the vehicle, muttering under her breath, "I'm glad that's over with."

"Not a fan of the company or the food?" Honovi asked dryly.

"Bit of both."

He hummed a wordless agreement and got settled. Leaving the palace for the city streets was easy enough. The drive west across the river over Hollows Bridge took less time than earlier now that the evening traffic had thinned out some.

"Take me to the embassy," Honovi told the driver.

Siv glanced up from the diary she'd been scribbling in since they left the palace, jotting down her observations of the dinner guests. "Burning the midnight oil, Ambassador?"

"Work for the clans never stops. My driver can drop you off at the residences after we go to the embassy."

"That's very kind of you."

The motor carriage continued down the Promenade on the west side of the Serpentine River. Honovi was let out at the front gate of the embassy, one of the guards already pushing it open for him.

"Ambassador," the woman said with a respectful nod.

The motor carriage drove away at a slow speed, with Siv waving farewell from the back seat. Honovi walked onto the embassy grounds and headed inside the building. The hour was late, but he was used to being present when the bustle of work was gone. Honovi made his way to the telegraph room, surprised at the person waiting for him amidst the machines.

"Who are you?" Honovi demanded, staring at the dark-haired Ashionen.

The face was unknown but not his voice, and Blaine's familiar accent reached his ears. "It's me, Honovi."

His husband reached up to undo the clasp at his throat, features shimmering as the veil was removed. Blond hair and hazel eyes were revealed, a tiredness to Blaine's expression that concerned him. A pistol was holstered to his belt, something Honovi wasn't used to seeing.

"What's wrong?" Honovi asked as he approached, cupping Blaine's jaw to tilt his head up for a kiss.

Blaine smiled wanly when they broke apart. "How was the dinner?"

"I can see how Eimarille makes a sympathetic figure. Why are you wearing a veil?"

Blaine grimaced, balling up the veil in one hand before pulling a folded-up piece of paper from his back pocket with the other. Honovi took it and unfolded it. He nearly ripped a hole in it with his fingers, stomach clenching in a bad way as he read the warrant issued by the Collector's Guild.

"Fulcrum's cog embedded in the Collector's Guild saw it come off the printers. Terilyn must have had a magician skilled in mind magic retrieve her memories and draw the portrait," Blaine said quietly.

Honovi stared down at the remarkable likeness of his husband's face, bracketed by charges, and a reward sum that could buy someone's way into the nobility genealogies and still have aurons leftover to pass on to heirs.

"You need to leave Ashion. I can get you on an airship heading back to E'ridia tonight. No one would know," Honovi said hoarsely.

Blaine shook his head, a pained expression crossing his face. "I can't. You know why."

Honovi clenched his hand into a fist, crushing the warrant. "I won't see you dead for your duty, Blaine."

"Those of the Westergard bloodline have died for Rourkes before this."

"You aren't a Westergard. You're clan. You're my *husband*," Honovi said fiercely.

Blaine reached up and framed Honovi's face with both hands, fingers cool against his skin. "I'm bound by the Dusk Star's decree until my duty is done. You know that."

That decree had kept them separated the last few years, clandestine meetings here in the E'ridian embassy their only true moments of togetherness. The separation wasn't one Honovi wanted to continue.

He resented Caris and knew it was foolish to do so. The girl didn't know who or what she was, that had been apparent during the meeting in Meleri's parlor. Her lack of knowledge meant Blaine couldn't leave her side. Honovi didn't know how his husband could keep her safe when his face was now on a warrant and every debt collector worth their pistols would be hunting him from here on out.

"You put her at risk if you stay. You have to know that."

Blaine's expression twisted, mouth opening to argue, but his words died in his throat as the door to the telegraph room opened. Honovi looked over his shoulder, frowning at who stood there.

"Siv? What are you doing here? I thought you went back to the residences?" Honovi asked as he turned to face her.

Siv's answer didn't come in the form of words but a bullet that ripped across his right side with a brutalness that stole the breath from his lungs. His ears rang with the sound of the discharge, Blaine's furious shout echoing from a distance as Honovi staggered from the hit, one hand pressed to the bleeding wound.

Another gunshot echoed in the air as he crashed to his knees, and he flinched but didn't take another bullet. Then his nerves caught up with his brain, and the agonizing pain of being *shot* slammed through his body, making him groan.

He lifted his head in time to see Siv on the floor, her head turned toward him, fingers twitching against wood as blood pooled beneath her. The pistol she'd carried was now in Blaine's hands, his husband stumbling away from where she lay.

"Honovi!" Blaine cried out.

The pistols clattered to the floor beside him as Blaine hurriedly stripped off his jacket, balling it up to press it to the wound in Honovi's side. Honovi cried out from the pressure, black spots eating away at the edge of his vision.

Thunder pounded through his head, coalescing into a handful of guards who ran into the telegraph room, nearly tripping over Siv's body.

"Ambassador!" someone shouted.

"Someone get me a magician! Honovi's been shot," Blaine snapped, gaze never leaving Honovi's face.

"Who are you?" one demanded.

"His husband."

Hands helped Honovi lie down, and the pressure on the wound made him clench his teeth so hard he nearly chipped a tooth. "Blaine?"

Fingers touched his cheek, his husband blocking out the sudden brightness overhead as the lights were turned on in the telegraph room.

"I'm here. I'm right here," Blaine said, voice cracking. "We need to check if the bullet is still in you."

Honovi hissed as he was rolled half onto his side, fingers pulling at his clothes. He cried out when fingers touched the searing pain in his back, barely hearing Blaine's shaky sigh over the ringing in his ears.

"Looks like it's a through and through, but a doctor will need to assess it further. I need another cloth to stop the bleeding," Blaine said.

"You're all right?" Honovi ground out, blinking tears out of his eyes.

Blaine laughed hoarsely, no mirth in the sound. "Better than you."

Fingers curled around his own, and Honovi gripped his husband's hand tight enough to bruise. Someone leaned what felt like their entire weight on the bullet wound, causing Honovi to nearly black out. Breathing hurt, or maybe it was the overriding pain in his body.

He swallowed hard, mouth strangely dry. "Siv was clan."

"Siv was a traitor."

Honovi tried to breathe through the pain, aware of the dampness seeping into his shirt and kilt. The noise in the room had only gotten louder, but everything felt foggy and removed. "Why would she try to kill me?"

His question went unanswered, their conversation interrupted by a relieved shout from a guard. "Karla is here."

The diplomatic officer in charge of the consulate's day-to-day needs rushed into the telegraph room, graying braid falling over one shoulder. Her office was a few floors down, and Honovi wasn't surprised she was working late, as she saw the midnight hour more than most of them.

"Ambassador," Karla said, going to her knees beside him. Her dark eyes were wide, lips trembling, but her hand was steady when she raised her wand. She'd been a priestess before she left the Star Order for the diplomatic corps but would always be a magician.

"Can you stop the bleeding?" Blaine demanded.

"Hush, let me concentrate."

The warmth of magic wasn't unknown to Honovi, having grown up beneath his mother's gentle ministrations and prayer. He hissed against the sensation of the aether crawling across his skin, dizzy even while lying prone. The pain didn't lessen, and neither did the pressure on the entrance and exit wounds.

"He needs to go to the hospital. I can keep him stable, but the wounds need to be tended to by a doctor," Karla said.

Blaine's expression twisted as he looked down at Honovi, a particular sort of agony in his eyes. "I can't go with you."

Honovi blinked slowly, frayed thoughts finally remembering the warrant he'd dropped after being shot. "I know."

Blaine looked over his shoulder at something Honovi couldn't see from his position on the floor. He closed his eyes but opened them again at the frantic tapping of fingers on his cheek. "Stay awake. We're going to move you."

He sucked air through his teeth and nodded jerkily. "All right."

The flurry around him didn't abate, not until someone cried out in surprise and said, "The ambassador needs to see this."

"The ambassador is on the way to the damn hospital," Blaine snapped.

A voice, strained and thready, let out a cry. Siv sounded as if she was dying, but he couldn't see her, not with Blaine blocking his view. Blaine swore under his breath before reluctantly leaving Honovi's side to act in his stead and deal with the woman who had laughed with Honovi during dinner and shot him, unprovoked, afterward.

"Oh," Blaine said some moments later, sounding horrified and panicked in a way that made Honovi try to sit up.

Karla pressed his shoulder to the floor, keeping him in place. "Stay still until we're ready to move you."

"I need to see," Honovi protested.

He couldn't leave here without knowing what had caused Siv to shoot. She'd been working in the diplomatic corps since before he arrived in Ashion, and her actions made no sense.

The bundles of clothes pressed against the wound on Honovi's side were kept in place by willing hands. Blaine returned and curled a hand over the nape of Honovi's neck, helping to sit him up. Pain radiated out from the wound, and he breathed rapidly against it, teeth clenched against the light-headedness that came with being mostly vertical. Blaine looked over his shoulder at the ever-growing crowd of people who had joined them in the telegraph room.

"Bring her here," Blaine said.

Honovi blinked, and when he opened his eyes again, Siv was on her knees in front of him, arms held tight by two guards. Her blouse was undone, the white fabric stained red from the wound that had torn through her shoulder. Blood flowed from it in a steady trickle that told him an artery might have been nicked. She was white from blood loss, eyes glassy, but it was the vivid vivisection scars crossing her chest beneath her torn bodice that drew Honovi's eye.

"I don't know how she stayed alive after wounds like that," Blaine said, voice tight.

"Revenant?" Karla asked in a strained whisper. "Should we find a warden?"

She held her wand at the ready, clarion crystal tip pointed at Siv.

Honovi swallowed, wanting to hunch over, but the hands holding him up and keeping pressure on his wound wouldn't let him.

"Why did you try to kill me?" Honovi asked.

Siv didn't answer, too far gone to give up any secrets, but she wasn't looking at him in that moment. Her fading attention was on Blaine, and Honovi didn't like that at all.

Honovi breathed through the nausea, looking up at the guards who held Siv in custody. "Grant her a kindness after Karla is done with her mind."

"Aye," one of the guards said quietly.

He'd given such orders before, rare though they were. Sometimes accidents happened out on the trade winds, sometimes the dead caught the living, and offering a quick death over a painfully long one was the kinder option. Whatever was done to Siv, he wanted to believe she hadn't asked for it.

"The body should be examined," Blaine said.

"We need to take Honovi to the hospital first," Karla snapped.

Honovi turned his head, catching Blaine's eye. "The *Comhairle nan Cinnidhean* needs to be informed of what happened."

Blaine nodded jerkily. "I'll make sure they know. Karla, I need you here."

"I need to see Honovi safely to the hospital," she said.

"And we need Siv's memories."

"Stay," Honovi ordered, his rough voice cutting through their argument.

Karla shook her head hard before sighing harshly. "Very well."

Blaine leaned over Honovi and pressed their foreheads together, their breath mingling. "I'll see you when I can. Whatever is happening, I need to warn the others."

"Take a televox from the diplomatic stores and anything else you want. If you need a way out, ring me. I won't leave you behind," Honovi said.

He didn't want Blaine to be without a way for Honovi to reach him. Whatever was going on, it felt as if their roads were diverging, and he'd be damned if he let Blaine walk away from him without a way back.

Honovi gripped Blaine's jacket, keeping him close, staring into hazel eyes he'd woken up to countless times over the years and wanted to again. "Be careful."

Blaine smiled, a quick, fragile thing, and kissed him with all the careful tenderness that came with loving someone, no matter what. Then Honovi was hauled carefully to his feet, pain whiting out everything, the throbbing ache in his side all he could focus on as his people saw to it he got the medical care he needed while under guard.

Honovi looked back to catch one last glimpse of his husband, finding Blaine staring right at him, Siv at his feet, duty pulling both of them in opposite directions.

Seven

CARIS

Caris carefully maneuvered the cutting tool in her hand, gently carving out the shape of a decagon from the piece of clarion crystal held in the clamp. The buzz of the rotary tool at the head of the mechanized handset gently ground away at the pale blue crystal. Even with her goggles on, she could see the glow suffusing the crystal, a soft light she knew few others in the clarion crystal industry were capable of seeing.

She felt the hum it produced more in her bones than her ears, a quiet song whose notes warned her if the shape she intended was wrong. This piece was meant to channel the aether as part of a set to power a filtration machine. The order was so large and intricate that her father had brought part of it with him to Amari for him and Caris to work on.

Crystal cutting for more delicate jobs was routinely relegated to them. They should have already been back in Cosian, but the patents her father had intended to file had been repeatedly rejected. None of them could figure out why, and he was back at Ashion's Bureau of Patents today to try and get them accepted once again.

It was left to Caris to finish some of their company's work, and she didn't mind the hours spent in their makeshift lab in their small home at Sixteen Rose Court Garden. Concentrating on cutting clarion crystal helped take her mind off things.

Things like people she had considered friends, and maybe more, lying to her for reasons she couldn't understand.

She huffed out a sigh, attention on the clarion crystal as she carefully adjusted her wrist to sharpen the point between two sides. She hummed along with the melody coming from the crystal, the tune solid and happy, not discordant notes indicating cracks in the crystal.

Someone cleared their throat behind her. "Caris."

She pulled the cutting tool away from the edge of the clarion crystal, switching it off. The buzz of it faded to nothing as she set the handheld vise down on the worktable along with the tool so she could turn and face her mother.

"I'm almost finished," Caris said.

Portia nodded. "I can see that. You have a caller. They're in the parlor, waiting to see you. I'll bring them to you if you are agreeable."

Caris groaned and flexed her fingers, easing some of the tight muscles there. She'd been working for hours, and while a break would be nice, she wasn't in the mood to chat with anyone. "I decline."

"Nathaniel made a compelling argument for the right to apologize. I thought you might wish to hear him out."

Caris stiffened at Nathaniel's name, that swoop in her stomach not entirely tied to anger. Her hand drifted toward her pocket where she carried his ring before she aborted the motion. "He's here? And you let him stay?"

Portia's gaze softened. "Hear what he has to say. For all that you're angry, we can't excise our knowing of the Clockwork Brigade, and they cannot let us go."

She spoke openly because the laboratory was heavily spelled to keep the clarion crystals stable. No one would think it odd that magic existed in their laboratory or that they would have spells to block eavesdroppers due to their company's proprietary information. Still, Caris knew, from her years under the duchess' tutelage, how much of a risk it could be.

She also knew driving someone away completely simply because she was angry was never good business.

Caris fiddled with the hem of her work blouse, cognizant of the drab clothing she wore, her dirty hands, and messy hair. But Nathaniel had seen her in such a state before and never minded. "Very well."

Portia nodded slightly before leaving the laboratory. "I'll bring him."

Caris used those precious few seconds to clean herself up a bit. Not that Nathaniel had ever minded her appearance after lab work when she was in university.

Portia returned a few minutes later, Nathaniel at her back, hat in hand and an anxious expression on his face. She waved him inside before pinning Caris with a stern look. "I'll return in twenty minutes."

She left them alone, closing the door behind her and leaving them without a chaperone. Nathaniel cleared his throat but didn't move from his spot by the door. "After the other day, I suppose I see now why your mother wasn't as strict with chaperone duty the last year."

"What makes you say that?" Caris asked sharply.

He gestured at nothing, eyes on her. "Your innate gift."

It was a tactful, roundabout way of speaking, but Caris was done with secrets for the moment. "You mean my magic?"

Nathaniel appeared pained. "You shouldn't—"

"Our laboratory is spelled. We can speak plainly here."

"It's never wise to speak openly when the crown princess is within the city limits."

"Then how do you wish to have this conversation?"

"With honesty." Nathaniel stepped forward. "I came to apologize for what hurt I may have caused you, but I can't apologize for keeping secrets to keep others safe. As a fellow cog, you must understand that duty."

Caris tipped her head to the side, blinking slowly. "I know what duty means, and I know what it asks of me for the Clockwork Brigade and my family's company."

"Please believe me when I say I had no knowledge of your position, that you were a cog."

"Would it have changed things if you had?"

Nathaniel shook his head, something like fondness seeping into his gaze. "No. You've always been exactly what you are."

"And what's that?"

"Someone who cares. You wouldn't have stayed by Fulcrum's side if you didn't."

Favor was coveted by those within high society. Caris had learned the steps of that dance because she'd had to. Meleri wouldn't let her shirk her lessons on navigating amongst the nobility in lieu of staying in her room, fiddling with her latest invention. Machines still made more sense to her, but she'd gotten better with people because of the Auclairs.

Caris stood, smoothing down her wrinkled blouse. Nathaniel's eyes followed the motion of her hands before snapping back up to her face. Caris had no dearth of dance partners these days, unlike her first visit to Amari. But the one she danced with more than all the rest on those evenings stood before her with his hand outstretched, asking for a forgiveness she could only in good conscience give.

There was no point in being angry with him. Nathaniel had been kept in the dark as much as she had when it came to their positions. He was right in that they were both cogs, spinning in place amongst all the rest, working to keep the Clockwork Brigade from falling apart. If she were to be angry at his secrets, she'd have to be angry at her own.

"Do you know I've never looked at another since I saw you scribbling in your notebook in Tristan's class that day?" Nathaniel said.

"His name is Blaine."

Nathaniel smiled wanly. "Old habit."

"My mother doesn't care for him."

"He's as dedicated as they come. Like you." Nathaniel closed the distance between them and reached for her hand, lifting it so he could brush a kiss over her knuckles. She let him. "My deepest apologies for making you think I didn't care about you. I do, Caris. Truly."

She tightened her fingers over his, staring up at him. "We all keep secrets. I'd rather you and I didn't."

Nathaniel straightened up, though he didn't release her hand. "What would you have me know? What would you have me tell you?"

He was a cog, one who took orders from Meleri herself. He'd called on her as a friend, waiting until her studies were done, until she was old enough for something more. Despite what had been revealed in the duchess' parlor, she couldn't stop trusting him.

She didn't want to.

Caris raised her other hand and folded her fingers down over her palm. When she lifted them again, starfire burned against her palm, molten hot and incapable of hurting her. The tiny flame licked at the air, its glow reflecting in Nathaniel's wide hazel eyes.

"Caris," he got out in a strangled voice, nearly bruising her fingers as he tightened his grip on her.

Perhaps it was reckless, what she did, but Caris wouldn't regret it. She'd kept secrets all her life, and others had kept them about her as well, it seemed. But for all her mother's desperate, hushed requests, Caris knew this one couldn't be kept forever. And it was *hers*, this magic, this gods-given power. She had the right to share it with those she cared about.

"Do you know what this means?" she asked softly, staring at the starfire.

The starfire burned softly against her palm for a few seconds until she made a fist, snuffing it out, the heat of it disappearing. Nathaniel's touch was warm, though, and she lifted her gaze to his. The wonder she saw in his eyes didn't unnerve her quite like she thought it would.

"You're an impossible dream, aren't you?" he said slowly.

"I won't be anyone's dream."

Nathaniel stepped close, ducking his head until she could feel his breath ghost over her lips. "If I said I'd like you to be mine?"

Caris swallowed, the sound loud in her ears. "I'd hate to disappoint you."

"You never could."

He kissed her gently, lips pressed against hers in a way she'd never

517

quite wanted until just this moment. She could feel the warmth of him through the scant inches that separated them, though he pressed no closer, even if Caris thought she might like it if he did. She breathed in sharply, lips parting, and held his hand tighter as the kiss deepened enough to something like a promise.

Then the door to the laboratory was slammed open, and Caris jerked back from that moment of giddy impropriety, face flushed as she peered around Nathaniel. Blaine stood in the doorway, a veil clenched in one hand and a grim expression on his face. He was armed with a flare gun holstered to his belt. She thought it an odd choice.

Portia ducked under his arm and entered the laboratory. She didn't say anything about Caris' kiss-stung appearance, and that's how she knew it was bad.

"We need to speak with Fulcrum. Store your tools, and let's be off," Portia said.

"What's going on?" Caris asked.

"Have you read the broadsheets?" Blaine asked tightly.

"Do you mean the terrible attack on the E'ridian ambassador last night? I'm aware of it," Nathaniel said.

Blaine nodded tightly. "The updated edition just came out. The press is blaming the Clockwork Brigade for the attack."

Caris paled. "I've been working in the laboratory all morning. Is Ambassador Honovi all right?"

The worried expression on Blaine's face made her heartsick. "He was shot. He's supposedly been in the hospital since the attack. That's all I know."

"I'm sure Fulcrum knows about the attack. There's no need to rush over there," Nathaniel said.

Blaine's eyes flashed with anger. "She doesn't know about the *rionetka* that was behind it."

"Pardon me? The what?" Caris asked.

Blaine jerked his thumb over his shoulder and stepped out of the laboratory. "I'll explain on the way, but we need to *go*. My motor carriage is out front."

He pulled the veil back over his face, and Caris made a questioning sound. "You don't need your veil here."

"The Collector's Guild has a warrant out for me. My identity as Tristan Arquette is no longer viable. I have no doubt someone from the university will report me for the sum of money they're offering. Which means any of my acquaintances may be questioned, including both of you. I need to know you're safe."

A chill coursed through Caris at that news. She shared a wide-eyed look with her mother before she turned toward her worktable. She hastily powered down cutting tools because her parents were sticklers about safety. She didn't have time to put everything back to rights and so left the moderate mess behind.

Nathaniel caught her hand on the way out, giving it a squeeze. "I'm sure Fulcrum will have a plan."

Caris swallowed, tongue dry against the roof of her mouth. "One hopes."

Once outside, they climbed into the motor carriage, a sleek black one whose motor hummed under the hood once the ignition was turned. At any other time, Caris would have asked questions about the make, but she was too keyed up. She sat in the back seat with her mother, while Nathaniel took the front passenger seat.

They were blocks away, Blaine white-knuckling the steering wheel, when Caris finally asked the question tumbling through her thoughts. "What is the *rionetka* you mentioned?"

In the rearview mirror, she could see Blaine's mouth twist. "Siv was a diplomatic officer who worked at the E'ridian embassy for years. She was clan, and she was loyal. She still shot Honovi and nearly killed him. I shot her, and she ultimately died from the wounds, but not before a magician examined her memories. A medical examiner performed an autopsy in secret under diplomatic immunity afterward."

"How would you receive diplomatic immunity?" Portia asked.

Blaine glanced back at her in the rearview mirror before his gaze cut to Caris briefly. "Because I've been a member of Clan Storm for longer than I was ever Ashionen. Honovi is my husband."

Caris blinked in surprise. "You don't have a marriage torc."

"I couldn't wear it here." Blaine flicked the indicator and turned left at the intersection that would take them onto the boulevard leading to the civic heart of the city. They needed to cut through that area before reaching the Auclair estate. "We needed diplomatic immunity to keep quiet what we found, and I acted in Honovi's stead."

"The *rionetka*, I assume?" Nathaniel asked.

Blaine nodded. "Siv had vivisection scars on her chest, though she lived and breathed like any one of us for who knows how long. When the doctor cut her open, he found a metal clockwork heart inside her. The magician who examined her memories found blank spots in her mind. We don't know how this process came about, but we know she knew herself as a *rionetka* and could not disobey the magic that animated her."

"Was she even alive?" Portia asked tightly.

"Living under duress isn't living. I sent the magician back to E'ridia this morning via airship. The *Comhairle nan Cinnidhean* must be told, and so does Fulcrum. I have an airship on standby in case we need it."

"This is high-level information. Should you even be telling us this?"

Blaine's gaze caught Caris' in the rearview mirror once again. "Probably not, but I'm telling you anyway."

Portia went quiet, her hand finding Caris' without her even needing to look. The drive down the boulevard was made in fraught silence. As they drew closer to the civic heart of the city, traffic slowed to a crawl. More people were on the street than usual for that time of day. Caris looked out the window, seeing more than one passing group of people holding signs nailed to sticks.

"It's a protest," she said.

"Must be about the latest banking law. Part of why Eimarille came here was to push that through the summer session," Nathaniel said.

"Emmitt is going to be at the Bureau of Patents. The peacekeepers aren't fond of protests," Portia fretted.

"Probably not the best place for him to be if he doesn't want to get caught in the crowd."

"Can you go any faster?"

Blaine lifted one hand off the steering wheel and pointed at the stalled traffic in front of them. "We aren't moving anywhere, and this is the only way to get to the Auclair estate."

"At this rate, we won't get there until supper," Caris said.

Portia made an aggravated sound. "Stop the motor carriage."

"Not a good idea," Blaine warned.

"We'll move faster on foot in this crowd. Find a place to park." Portia spoke with the demanding tone of a woman who had spent years presiding over a company. Some might say it was noble arrogance, but running a company took far more work than presiding over a landless title.

"Do as she says," Nathaniel said.

Blaine swore, but he still turned off the boulevard once they made it to the next intersection. The cross street was less crowded, but only just. Other people seemed to have the same idea, peeling out of the traffic to bypass the large group of people marching to the protest near the palace. Two more turns and Blaine managed to find a parking spot on the street.

"It's probably a good thing I don't own this motor carriage," Blaine said after he turned the engine off.

"You don't?" Caris asked.

"No. I borrowed it."

Nathaniel got a pained look on his face. "And by borrowed, please say you don't mean stolen."

Blaine shrugged before getting out. "All right, I don't mean that."

They started walking down the street, away from the traffic and the crowd. Caris knew better than to ask all the questions sitting on the tip of her tongue, though she wanted to know more about the *rionetka* Blaine had fought. She was deep in her thoughts, keeping pace by her mother's side, and so was badly startled when a paddy wagon screeched to a halt next to them on the street and four men exited the vehicle to surround them.

Caris bit back a shriek, jerking close to her mother as they became boxed in. The men paid them no attention; they only had eyes for Nathaniel.

"Nathaniel Clementine?" one of the men asked.

"What's this about?" Nathaniel demanded.

One of the men held up a metal badge that made Caris draw in a sharp breath. The six-pointed badge with a set of numbers crossing the center was only held by debt collectors. "We have a warrant for your arrest."

Portia drew herself up to her full height. "On what grounds?"

"This doesn't concern you, ma'am."

"That's *Baroness* Dhemlan to the likes of you."

The man smiled smarmily, but his attention never left Nathaniel. "It's still not your business."

Two of the men moved toward Nathaniel while the last kept his focus on Blaine, hand resting on his pistol. Caris spared Blaine a frantic glance, glad to see his veil was still in place. She knew that might not remain the case if he got caught up in another fight.

Without thinking about the risk, Caris flung herself between Nathaniel and the two debt collectors, arms outstretched, trying her best to look helpless. "Please don't take him! There must be some misunderstanding!"

"Miss, move out of the way," the first man ordered. "We're collecting him on a warrant for treason."

"For—*what?*" Portia choked out, one hand going to her mouth.

Caris didn't move. "Treason? That's preposterous."

"Warrants don't lie."

That she knew was a lie.

"Caris, come here," Blaine said in a tight voice.

She raised her chin, staying put and staring down the debt collector. "You can't collect him. Nathaniel has always been loyal to Ashion."

The debt collector gripped the butt of his pistol. "It's not Ashion he committed treason against. His family forfeited their loans when they aligned themselves with the Clockwork Brigade to allow their trains to be used to smuggle debt slaves out of Daijal. Now, step away if you don't want to be considered collateral, miss. I won't ask again."

Caris was too shocked to say anything, staring uncomprehend-ingly at the debt collectors surrounding them. A rushing sound filled her ears, and she didn't know how shaky she was until Nathaniel's hand settled on her shoulder, steadying her.

"It's all right, Caris," Nathaniel said in a voice leached of all emotion. She turned to face him, searching his pale face, watching how he rallied enough to give her a smile. "I'm sure this is merely a mistake."

They both knew it couldn't be, but the fear coursing through Caris left her wanting to cry. Whatever had brought the attention of the Collector's Guild down on the Clementine family was a threat Fulcrum needed to know about.

But she didn't want to leave Nathaniel behind.

"Nathaniel..."

He smiled gently at her, gaze never leaving her face as he neatly guided her around as if they were at a dance and this was a waltz. She memorized how he looked in that moment, dappled with sunlight streaming through the tree branches above. She licked her lips, wishing she had the courage to kiss him once more, but it was too late.

He was already being taken into custody.

Hands settled on her shoulder, holding her still when she would've stepped forward as Nathaniel's arms were pulled behind his back.

"You can't help him," Blaine said quietly into her ear "Don't put yourself in danger trying to."

Caris remembered her lessons from Meleri well and stayed put when all she wanted to do was rail at the injustice happening before her. But getting caught up in a collateral charge would help no one.

"I'll find you, Caris," Nathaniel promised as he was escorted away by two debt collectors.

He hadn't fought, and he hadn't run. Caris would always wonder if things could have been different if he had, if she'd used starfire to keep him safe.

If she'd done anything in that moment to forge a different road.

But there was no taking back his decision as Nathaniel went

quietly to ensure they weren't targeted. Caris covered her mouth with one hand, blinking back tears as she watched him get pulled into the paddy wagon. The doors shut seconds later, and the vehicle drove off, muffler popping.

"How did they find him?" Portia asked.

"They must have followed him to your home. It's a good thing they didn't follow us to the Auclair estate," Blaine said.

Caris couldn't help the faint sob that escaped her, and she suddenly found herself wrapped up in the comforting familiarity of her mother's arms. Caris squeezed her eyes shut, but that didn't stop the tears.

"How do we get him back?" Caris asked.

"We'll figure something out," Portia murmured. "Right now, I need to find your father."

Caris sniffed a little, trying to get herself under control. "I left my televox at home."

"I have mine. I'll meet up with him, but I want you to go with Blaine."

"Mother—"

"Listen to me." Portia put her at arm's length and framed Caris' face with both hands, offering her a smile with trembling lips. "I love you very much, but I want you safe. Blaine will keep you safe."

Caris wiped the back of her hand over her cheeks, trying to dry her tears. "I want to go with you."

"No, darling. Not this time."

"I'll guard her," Blaine said in a quiet voice filled with a sort of conviction Caris didn't know what to make of.

Portia stared at him with an indecipherable expression on her face. "I know you will. Your duty was always to her."

"Mother?" Caris asked.

Portia shook her head and kissed Caris on the cheek. "I love you. I always have and always will. Remember that."

It was a farewell, but it felt heavier than that. Blaine stayed by Caris' side, matching his stride to hers, and guided her forward while she kept looking back at what she was leaving behind.

Eight

BLAINE

For the first time in all the years that Blaine had lived in Amari, he entered the Auclair estate through the front door.

The only reason he wasn't thrown out immediately while wearing a veil was due to Caris' presence.

"Is Her Grace available?" Caris demanded of the servant who answered the door.

"She's in her study and asked not to be disturbed, miss," the maid said with a quick curtsy as they entered the mansion.

"She'll want to see me."

Caris swept forward with the assuredness of someone who knew her place. Blaine overtook her on the stairs and led the way to Meleri's private study. He knocked loudly on the door to give a warning before testing the knob. Finding it unlocked, he pushed the door open.

"We have an emergency, Your Grace," Blaine said in greeting as he removed the veil.

Caris ducked past him into the office, nodding at Lore and Meleri. Both women looked tired but focused, and Blaine wondered how long they'd been awake. Lore sat in a chair in front of her mother's desk, but she stood at their arrival. Blaine kicked the door shut but didn't bother locking it.

"We've read the broadsheets. We know the Clockwork Brigade is being blamed for last night's attack," Meleri said, setting her teacup aside.

"The attack on the ambassador is the least of our concerns," Blaine said.

Lore crossed her arms over her chest. "I would think the attack would be your top priority."

Blaine glared at her as he shoved the veil into his pocket. "My husband will always be important, but he knows I have a duty to Caris."

"Blaine," Meleri warned sharply as she rose from her seat.

Caris turned to face him, hands clenching into fists at her side. "No, I want to hear why. You've hinted as much to my mother, and no one has told me *anything*."

"He's a cog. We all have a duty to each other."

"That's not an answer."

Blaine stepped closer and squared his shoulders before bowing to Caris to a degree reserved only for heirs to a throne, causing her to suck in a breath. "Emmitt and Portia Dhemlan are your parents, but they are not your bloodline. I carried you out of Amari after you were born on an airship captained by the Dusk Star."

"Now is not the time," Meleri said, sounding desperate.

Blaine straightened up, never taking his eyes off Caris' pale face. "When will it be time, Your Grace? When you crown her after using her to gain the throne you're after? I warned you keeping her in the dark would not serve you well."

"Caris needs to be kept *safe*."

"And the North Star wants her to fight. If you wish to go against a star god's decree, then so be it, but my orders come from the Dusk Star. They always have."

"You called yourself Westergard after I woke up from the pub fight," Caris said quietly.

Blaine nodded. "My father died to keep you safe. I was taken as witness."

"Why?"

"For you. My father took you from Queen Ophelia's arms and handed you to me. I carried you out of the palace and to the airship. We almost didn't make it, and my father died to keep the enemy at bay while we launched into the sky. I was with you on the flight to Cosian, and that was the last I saw of you until you came to my class a few years ago."

Caris' lips trembled. "You took me from the palace?"

"You were born Princess Caris Rourke despite your name never being written in the royal genealogies. But I stand as witness, and I can attest to those memories." Blaine smiled crookedly at her. "The Westergard bloodline has always guarded the Rourkes. You are my duty, Caris."

She'd gone pale in the face, trembling, but didn't appear as if she'd faint. Those who called the Eastern Basin home were forged strong at the borders. In that moment, Caris proved the star gods' choice to see her grow up far from her birthplace was the right one.

"Do my parents know?" she asked quietly with a hitch in her breath, blinking wide eyes at him.

"I was not privy to what the Dusk Star told them, but everything they've done for you, it was done to keep you safe. If the Daijal court knew you lived, the king would have done anything to see you dead."

Caris pressed her lips into a hard line before shaking her head and spinning around. "You knew, didn't you?"

The accusation leveled at Meleri wasn't enough to make the duchess flinch. "I've known who you truly were since Blaine told me four years ago, but none of us knew you could cast starfire until the train raid."

"And *none* of you thought to tell me the truth?"

"What good would it have done you if you'd known?" Lore asked sharply. "You came to Amari to go to university. You came to learn."

"And you taught me all the things you thought a future queen should know, isn't that right?" Caris asked bitterly. "All the parties and teas, all the visits to far-flung bloodlines, the lessons on politics, all of it done to introduce me to people I'd have known in some other life, but not this one."

"I won't apologize for guiding you down this road," Meleri said.

Caris made a cutting gesture with her hand. "My road isn't yours to walk. I *had* a road. I had a future. I'm a Dhemlan."

"You're a Rourke," Lore pushed back, eyes bright in her face as she stood. "And you are needed."

"I won't walk the road you'd have me stay on."

Blaine grimaced at the viciousness of Caris' tone. He moved so he could see her face, catching her eye. "The Dusk Star left me in E'ridia. I spent years in that country, and I learned to call it home. I gained a clan and a husband, but my road was never going to end there. Yours was never going to end in Cosian, but that doesn't mean you can't find a new path forward."

Caris looked at him, all righteous fury and grief, twenty years old and shaped by too many hands into a country's possible savior. But the core of her was sharp like clarion crystal—he'd seen it in the years he'd taught her, watching her grow into a well-educated engineer. Caris wouldn't break, but that strength didn't come from Meleri's teachings or his own. That was all Caris and the teachings of the family who had raised her in the wilds of the Eastern Basin.

Blaine looked away from Caris to meet Meleri's gaze. "I'm taking Caris out of Amari."

"She shouldn't leave," Meleri protested.

"She'll be safer away from Eimarille. You know that."

"Caris—"

"Is standing right here and can decide for herself," Caris shouted, cutting them both off. "I'm not going anywhere without my parents."

"You shouldn't go anywhere without an escort," Lore said.

"She'll have me," Blaine replied.

"In which case, I'll be going with you."

"Mainspring is needed here."

"On the contrary. I'm needed wherever Caris resides. You are not the only one who serves the Rourke bloodline."

"I'm not Rourke," Caris bit out.

Lore eyed her pityingly but for once didn't press the subject. Blaine cleared his throat, drawing everyone's attention. "Debt collectors took Nathaniel on the way here. His chain is compromised, as is his family and their company. The trains are no longer safe to use to transport debt slaves out of Daijal."

All the blood drained out of Meleri's face. "No."

Lore swore in a very unladylike way. "You couldn't have led with that report?"

Blaine glared at her. "Does that make you want to stay?"

"Absolutely not. You'll need my help while on the run," she shot back.

"Tell them about the *rionetka* who attacked the ambassador last night," Caris said.

Meleri's gaze darted from Blaine to Caris, then back again. "The press is reporting it was a diplomatic aide who harmed your husband."

"Siv shot Honovi, but she wasn't in control of her actions." Blaine dipped his fingers into the inner pocket of his day jacket and withdrew several tintype photographs. He approached Meleri's desk to hand them to her. "You'll see by these photographs that her heart was replaced by a clockwork machine. The magician who took her memories before she died said Siv referred to herself as a *rionetka*."

Meleri peered at the photographs. "A puppet?"

The images were macabre, taken when Siv's chest had been broken open to reveal the metal clockwork heart nestled in the cavity there. One or two other photographs showed a close-up of the spellwork on the framework before the self-destruct spell had slagged it all.

Lore touched her finger to the photograph depicting Siv's body. "Our cogs found a bucket of hearts in the apothecary."

The horror in her voice was echoed in Meleri's eyes. Blaine nodded in the face of the duchess' questioning gaze. "Siv was Siv right up until she shot Honovi. Whatever she was before that, it was a lie. Someone else pulled the strings of her life, making her obey their orders to further their own needs. No one at the embassy was the wiser."

Lore's expression became bleak. "The bucket had so many hearts. She can't be the only *rionetka*."

"I think it's a safe assumption that these *rionetkas* could be anyone, anywhere, no matter the country."

"There was an article the other day about an attempted assassination on the Solarian emperor. The assassin was never identified. We can't ignore the possibility such an attempt was done by one of these *rionetkas*. Not with the death-defying machine operating in the House of Kimathi *vasilyet*."

"We'll need to break some chains to ensure the Clockwork Brigade isn't compromised any more than it already has been. The news you bring of Nathaniel and the *rionetkas* is news that must be shared," Meleri said.

"Brielle can spread it amongst the nobility. Dureau can send notice off in code to those cogs who must be told."

"I take it you are still coming with us?" Blaine asked.

Lore bared her teeth at him. "Try and stop me, Westergard."

The dig at his bloodline didn't bother him nearly as much as it used to. "I have an airship waiting for us in the airfield. We'll retrieve Caris' parents first from the Bureau of Patents and then leave Amari."

"And go where?" Caris demanded.

"Home," Lore said before heading to the door. "Allow me a few minutes to change and retrieve some supplies."

"We don't have time," Blaine replied.

"Then *make* time. I want to be armed, and you'll need more than a flare gun."

Lore swept out of the office, closing the door behind her with a steady hand. Blaine sighed and gestured at the tintype photographs. "Keep them. I've sent copies to the *Comhairle nan Cinnidhean* in E'ridia."

"I'd like a moment alone with Caris," Meleri said quietly.

Blaine glanced at Caris but made no move toward the door until she nodded. "Very well. I'll ring the captain of the airship and put them on notice we'll be departing soon."

Blaine left the office and made his way to the parlor down the hall.

No servants were about when he pulled from his pocket the televox Honovi had given him and used the dial to enter the aeronaut captain's number. Karla had organized their flights out of Amari. She'd left first, and his airship was waiting for his call.

He put the televox to his ear, the hum of clarion crystal a sharp sound that abruptly disappeared when a familiar voice came through.

"Where are you?" Honovi asked.

Blaine opened and closed his mouth, but nothing came out for a few seconds. When he finally found his voice, he had to remind himself not to shout. "*What* the bloody fuck do you think you are doing? You should be in the hospital!"

"I was. I left."

"*Clearly.*"

"I wasn't going to stay behind while you ran off again."

"You were *shot*. You shouldn't be running anywhere, much less captaining an airship."

"The *Comhairle nan Cinnidhean* recalled me after the attack was reported back to them. I'm not staying in Amari."

"We aren't going to E'ridia."

"Blaine." He snapped his mouth shut, wincing at the tired but firm tone in his husband's voice. "I have a magician with me and a doctor. They're seeing to my wound so I can see to you. Where are you?"

"We need to pick up two more people in the city's civic center before we can make our way to the airfield."

"I'll start our engines and ready for launch."

"It might take some time. There's a protest happening around the palace and parliament that we need to maneuver through."

"All the more reason to be ready. Do you have the flare gun with you?"

Blaine fingered the tool in question holstered to his belt. Karla had given it to him before leaving for her own flight. "Yes."

"Fire it if you need to. I'll come to you if I see the marker in the air."

"Is the airship you're on even cleared for diplomatic use?"

"It doesn't matter."

The harshness of his words had Blaine closing his eyes. "I don't want to put our country at risk any more than I already have."

"You weren't the one who harmed Siv or shot me. I've little concern for Ashionen or Daijalan laws after what we've uncovered." Honovi's voice softened some, but Blaine could still hear the burr of pain in it. "I won't leave you behind. Not again."

Blaine swallowed tightly. "Keep the engines running, then. I'll get us there as soon as I can."

He ended the call, tucking the televox away in the small case secured to his belt. The door to the parlor opened, admitting a red-eyed Caris, followed by Lore, who had exchanged her dress for nondescript trousers and a day jacket, a veil wrapped around her face.

"We're ready. We'll take one of the motor carriages in the garage," Lore said.

"I rang my mother. She and my father are waiting at the Bureau of Patents," Caris said.

Blaine nodded. "Then let's be off."

They left the parlor, heading for the stairs, and Blaine wasn't at all surprised to see Meleri waiting for them at the landing. The duchess stood tall beneath the weight of everything she'd carried over the decades. Whatever she and Caris had spoken about in private, they didn't reiterate the argument.

Meleri still reached for her. Caris stiffened beneath her touch but didn't jerk away. "I only ever wanted to keep you safe."

"I don't want your excuses. Find Nathaniel and get him back. That's all I want from you right now," Caris said.

She stepped forward, forcing Meleri's hand to drop away. Lore pulled her mother into a quick hug, whispering something into her ear that Blaine couldn't hear. Then she started down the stairs after Caris, leaving Blaine and Meleri on the landing.

"Caris will be queen if she lives," Meleri whispered into the silence between them. "Make sure she lives."

"I know my duty," Blaine said.

He bowed to the duchess, then started down the stairs, leaving her behind to mend the Clockwork Brigade's broken cogs and chains.

Nine

CARIS

Caris slammed her foot on the brake, lurching forward against the lap belt as the motor carriage came to an abrupt stop. She narrowly missed hitting the group of protestors who'd darted in front of her vehicle. One shouted rudely at her before smacking the hood of the motor carriage with their wooden sign.

"Hey now!" Caris shouted back.

"I don't think we'll be able to get through this crowd," Lore said from the back seat.

Caris tightened her grip on the steering wheel and drove the motor carriage forward. She didn't get very far. "We're three blocks from the Bureau of Patents. I'm not leaving without my parents."

She'd already lost Nathaniel today. She absolutely refused to lose her parents. Any other day she'd be right there in the thick of the protest, but today she wished it were happening anywhere else but here.

"We could get out and make a run for it," Blaine said.

"How do you expect us to make it to the airfield if we leave the vehicle behind?"

"I think between you and I we could hot-wire a motor carriage."

Caris drummed her fingers against the steering wheel, contemplating that option. Lore leaned forward to hiss in her ear. "That will bring attention you don't want. The press is everywhere around here. Look."

Caris followed where she pointed, squinting through the windshield at the reporter set up on the corner and taking photographs of the protesting crowd. Behind him was a cluster of peacekeepers. They had their batons out and gripped in both hands as they marched alongside the protestors, most likely to meet up with their fellow peacekeepers down the street.

"Oh, hell." Caris yanked up the emergency brake and shifted the motor carriage into park. "Let's go. It'll take us hours to get through this crowd if we stay."

Lore swore under her breath but didn't try to change Caris' mind. Caris undid her lap belt and shoved open the door. The summer heat was a heavy weight in the air, what breeze blowing through the air slow and almost stagnant. The leaves on the trees lining the sidewalks barely moved.

Lore linked her arm with Caris, pulling her forward. Blaine was at their back as they slipped into the crowd, the sound around them almost deafening. Someone somewhere in the crowd had drums, and the occasional sound of a handheld horn ripped through the air. Protests against banking laws weren't new, but this was the largest Caris remembered one being in recent memory.

She assumed it was because Eimarille was in residence at the palace. The protest was marching that way, and they got caught up in the flow of it. Caris stayed steady on her feet as Lore pushed their way forward and dragged her along.

They were a block away from the intersection that would take them down a side avenue where the Bureau of Patents was located when the roar of the crowd picked up. The steady beat of the chanting took on an edge of fierceness that made Caris glance nervously around her.

"What's going on?" she asked.

Blaine's hand gripped her shoulder, and he pushed her at an angle through the crowd. "Peacekeepers are lining the sidewalks on both sides. I can't see up front, but I'd bet they're blocking the street in front of the palace. It's going to turn into a kettling situation."

"We can't afford to get arrested. We need to get out of here," Lore said.

"What do you think I'm trying to do?"

The crowd surged around them, the chanting taking on a defiant pitch. Caris nearly lost her balance, but Blaine kept her upright. He stayed close, a steady source of strength she knew—irrationally—would never leave her.

Westergards were always loyal. She knew *that* from the history Meleri had taught her.

Someone let off another handheld horn from somewhere in the crowd up ahead, the noise a piercing sound that didn't fade away. It grew louder, deeper, and it took Caris a few precious moments to realize it wasn't a horn but a warning siren.

The crowd's shouting faded in the wake of the sound, the fearful uncertainty an almost palpable thing in the air. The crackle of a speaker reached her ears, followed by a voice that sounded far too calm in that moment.

"Revenants in the civic center. All citizens to clear the area and shelter in place. All wardens within the city limits to lend aid."

Blaine's grip on her became bruising, and Lore's was no better. Caris had no time to wonder what was happening as the two shoved their way to the edge of the crowd with a brutality that couldn't stop the crushing surge of panic that ran through everyone around them. The chanting of the crowd turned into screams. The vaguely orderly march turned into a maelstrom of bodies all looking for a way out—one which the peacekeepers refused to allow.

Lore slammed against the side of a motor carriage and yanked Caris closer. The crowd made it difficult to breathe, but Caris climbed for the roof of the vehicle without needing to be told. Blaine had already made it on top of the hood, crouched there as he kept an eye on the people racing past them in the street.

Beyond them, at the intersection, Caris saw the peacekeepers had parked the paddy wagons close together to act as a barricade against the crowd. Flashes of magic from wands held by a few peacekeepers kept protesters from fleeing down the side streets.

As she watched, peacekeepers clambered on top of the paddy wagons, with one thrusting his fist into the air. "This is for the Clockwork Brigade!"

Lore cursed, eyes widening in horror. "We never sanctioned this."

Caris knew they hadn't, because the Clockwork Brigade was built on secrecy, not the horror the peacekeepers—if they really were peacekeepers—let loose. The backs of the paddy wagons all faced the boulevard with the protestors. The peacekeepers on the roof yanked the long metal rods up out of the locking mechanisms.

For a moment, the doors stayed shut.

Then they slammed open with a crack that sounded like a drum. Revenants burst free of the paddy wagons and ran into the crowd of protestors. Caris bit back a scream, unconsciously jerking backward at the sight of revenants.

Blaine yanked free his flare gun, pointed it at the sky, and set it off. The sound of it discharging echoed in her ears. Caris followed the path of the projectile into the sky. When it burst, purple-colored smoke erupted into the air, marking their location.

Blaine glanced back at them, a grimly determined look in his eyes as he reached for the pistol he'd taken from the Auclair estate. "We need to hold our ground here. Honovi will come for us."

"Are you *mad*?" Lore shouted, pulling free a pistol holstered to the small of her back. "We're about to be overrun by revenants!"

"What about my parents?" Caris asked, heart in her throat. "I can't lose them, too."

"We can't get to them from here," Blaine said.

She knew he was right, but that didn't make it any easier not to throw herself off the motor carriage and try to make her way to them.

Blaine thumbed off the pistol's safety and took aim at the closest revenant in the crowd. He managed a headshot, but the bullets weren't spelled or poisoned, and the revenant's body still staggered forward, lacking one eye and part of its skull. None of them had a machete or sword or studded baton to hack off heads or bludgeon them to nothing to keep the revenants down. A physical weapon was long-lasting where bullets were limited in use.

Caris remained crouched beside Lore, who held her pistol with both hands, grip steady despite the frantic look in her strange-colored eyes. Lore looked nothing like herself except for how she comported herself in the face of danger—ruthlessly determined to survive.

"Drop your weapons or we'll shoot!"

The shouted order made Caris look over her shoulder at the pair of peacekeepers standing on top of the brick wall surrounding a nearby building. Rifles were pointed at Caris' group while Blaine's and Lore's pistols were pointed at the revenants. Lowering their guard against the dead would ensure they'd be killed, but not doing so risked them being shot.

Caris raised her hand in the direction of the peacekeepers, ignoring Blaine's warning shout. She wasn't reaching out in entreaty but in protest, and the starfire that exploded from her hand was a cascade of power that engulfed the weapons the peacekeepers held. She didn't think about her actions. Perhaps she should have, but the peacekeepers weren't there to help the citizens of Amari. They'd proven that when they let revenants loose in the city streets.

The rifles melted into liquid, and the peacekeepers fell back screaming, their hands blackened down to bone. Caris exhaled shakily, skin feeling too tight and dry, as if she were about to burst. Starfire danced at her fingertips, its heat something she barely felt.

Blaine caught her wrist, dragging her off the roof and down to the hood. She cried out, more because of the hail of bullets that passed through where she'd been than because of his rough handling.

Lore had dived off the vehicle, landing on the sidewalk rather than the street. Neither position was safe. Caris wrenched her hand free and sent another burst of starfire in the direction of the shooters.

"What happened to *don't use your magic?*" Blaine shouted as he took aim at a revenant in the process of biting through a protestor's arm two vehicles away.

"I'm sorry, would you like to become a pincushion of bullets?" Caris snapped.

The nerves behind both her eyes pulsed painfully, but she ignored the building headache in favor of opening herself to the aether in a way she'd rarely done before. Her control was better than it had been at sixteen, but she still lacked finesse.

But one didn't need finesse in the midst of a riot.

One just needed fury—which Caris had plenty of.

She called forth starfire in a wave that burned through the revenants staggering their way over downed bodies. The dead went up in flames, screaming until they lost their voice and became nothing but ash drifting through the air.

Caris was dimly aware of people in the crowd staring at her, of the distant flash of a camera's lightbulb going off. All she could focus on was the way her chest burned, cracked open like the tintype photograph of the dead girl Blaine had left behind with the duchess, exposed for the entire world to see.

Shouts reached her ears, and she turned her head, the world moving as if she were in water as the aether poured through her veins. She watched as peacekeepers ran down the sidewalk toward them, separated from the riot and revenants by parked motor carriages. Lore shouted something Caris couldn't make out as she spread her fingers through the starfire.

She wasn't sure if she could have killed them. That day, she didn't have to find out what it felt like to take a life.

The sun was eclipsed by a shadow that spread all around them. The heavy sound of a Zip gun going off sent bullets ripping through the peacekeepers, tearing through them like paper.

Caris jerked her head up, taking in the sight of the airship descending fast above them, the roar of its engine nearly deafening. Crew leaned over its side, taking aim at the revenants below in the crowd with crack shot precision. The Zip gun on its aft side shifted its aim at the remainder of the peacekeepers by the paddy wagons, all of whom scattered.

A rope ladder was tossed overboard, its ends dragging on the sidewalk. Lore lunged for it, pistol forgotten behind her in favor of escape. Lore climbed with an ease Caris only hoped to emulate as

Blaine yanked her off the hood of the motor carriage and toward their only way out of this mess.

"Climb!" Blaine yelled.

Caris gripped the rope rungs with both hands and started to climb. As soon as there was space below her, Blaine followed after her. He shouted something in E'ridian she couldn't understand, voice carrying to the crew above. The rope ladder swung wildly as the engines changed pitch, the airship rising over the crowd. Caris peered down at the rapidly diminishing ground, watching as a revenant just missed the trailing knots of the rope ladder, falling back amidst the mass of bodies.

Bullets pinged off the thin metal plates shielding the balloon, ricocheting wildly. She wanted to close her eyes as the airship gained altitude, but clinging to the rope ladder wasn't any way to stay safe. With the wind whistling through her ears as they flew over rooftops, Ashion growing smaller and smaller below, Caris put one hand over the other and climbed.

Lore reached the decking first and immediately leaned over the railing to offer Caris her hand. She was hauled to the relative safety of the airship, knees giving out on her once she was no longer dangling over open air.

Blaine needed no help in hauling himself over the railing. A crew member immediately pulled up the rope ladder behind him. Blaine knelt beside Caris, giving her a frantic once-over.

"Are you all right?" he asked.

Caris could only nod numbly, warm despite the chill air blowing against her skin as the airship flew east. Her head hurt, but not as much as her heart, for she knew what she'd left behind.

"My parents," she said, unable to stop the tears welling up in her eyes.

Blaine's mouth twisted, but he didn't try to placate her with false comfort. "I'm sorry, Caris. We can't go back."

She watched him stand and go to where Honovi leaned heavily against the flight deck's doorframe. Blaine touched a hand to Honovi's hip before kissing him with a fierceness she'd wanted to experience with Nathaniel. But she wouldn't get that now, for he was as lost to her in that moment as the road she'd thought she'd been born to walk.

Caris pulled the ring Nathaniel had given her out of her pocket with trembling fingers, staring at the company crest engraved on it. Not a bloodline, but close enough. "I'll find you. I swear it."

Caris undid the clasp of the simple gold necklace she wore and slipped the ring onto it before hooking it around her throat once more. Then she pushed herself to her feet and walked across the deck on shaky legs, determined to find the answers to all her questions from someone who knew more about herself than she did.

In the city they left behind, in the wake of a riot and a revenant incursion, the broadsheets would blame the Clockwork Brigade for the terror perpetuated that day. The blame would be meaningless in the face of the front-page picture that would change the course of a future no longer locked in orbit like a comet—that of a dark-haired young woman wielding starfire in defiance of a purge that had not completely taken root two decades ago.

Some things, after all, could not be burned away.

Ten

NATHANIEL

Nathaniel lifted his head as the door to his holding cell in the Collector's Guild company building in Amari was opened. He'd known they'd operated openly in Amari since their expansion was approved by the Daijal court. He just hadn't realized how many cells they'd hidden inside the building until he'd been dragged through its halls.

"Time to go," the man said.

Nathaniel warily eyed the wand in the magician's hand as he struggled to his feet, fingers curling around the chains threaded through the manacles locked around his wrists. The ones connecting his ankles clattered against the floor. He had burn marks beneath his clothes from being prodded with wands while in custody. Some of the debt collectors had inflicted pain simply for their own terrible enjoyment.

He'd known they could be cruel, but experiencing it firsthand was nauseating. If this was what he had to look forward to for the rest of his life, he'd do everything in his power to escape, with or without help from the Clockwork Brigade.

"Where are you taking me?" Nathaniel asked.

The backhanded slap wasn't expected, though really, it should have been. Nathaniel staggered, the edge of his lip tearing on the magician's ring. Blood filled his mouth, coppery and hot. He spat it out, breathing harshly against the hot pain throbbing across half his face.

"Debt slaves don't ask questions."

He didn't have a bank number tattooed over his throat—yet. Nathaniel wondered if that was where he was being taken to. Somewhere amidst this hell was a bank accountant with a tattoo gun. Nathaniel had seen men and women taken from their cells and returned with ink embedded in their skin.

He'd tried not to listen to them cry, but it'd been impossible to ignore their sobs. Pain echoed off the walls in this place.

Nathaniel kept his fear for his family to himself. He'd been collected on a treason charge, which meant his family must have been as well, but he had no idea where they were or if they were even alive. His parents and himself were the only cogs. His younger sister and extended family weren't involved, but a collateral charge meant that wouldn't matter.

He only hoped the Clockwork Brigade would come for him.

The magician dragged him up from the basement cell he'd been kept in. The change in brightness from the gas lamps made his eyes water, and he blinked the wetness away. The receiving room was mostly empty save for a clerk manning the night desk and a Blade waiting for them by the front door.

Nathaniel didn't think his stomach could twist any tighter, but it did in that moment.

Terilyn wore a light summer cloak over black velvet trousers and a black silk blouse. Nathaniel thought she was dressed in that color to hide whatever blood she'd cut from a person.

"Is this Clementine?" Terilyn asked.

"One of them," the magician said. Nathaniel bit back the instinctive urge to ask after his family, knowing he wouldn't get an answer.

Terilyn stepped forward, her cloak shifting around her body enough that Nathaniel could see the sleek pistol holstered to her belt. He doubted that was her only weapon. She was a Blade, after all. "Put him in the motor carriage."

The magician grabbed Nathaniel by the arm and dragged him outside. He didn't fight the manhandling, only wincing when his head was banged against the side of the motor carriage as he was shoved into the back seat.

The chain linking his manacles together was connected to one bolted to the floor of the motor carriage. It drew his arms tightly down and forward, providing little give. Terilyn slid into the seat behind him, a stiletto held in slim fingers as a warning to him.

"Drive," Terilyn said.

The driver nodded and started the engine. Nathaniel didn't ask where he was being taken but knew it wasn't anywhere good. He didn't know what he could have possibly done to put himself within Eimarille's sphere of interest. That was the only reason Terilyn had to be involved, and the thought kept his heart thudding fast against his ribs.

Nathaniel stared out the window, watching the streets pass them by. That Terilyn wasn't hiding the route from him was disconcerting in so many ways. He recognized some of the buildings they passed even in the dimly lit streets.

They eventually pulled up in front of a pillared, red-bricked building tucked away behind an iron fence. The gas lamp on the porch was cold in its sconce, but the guards on duty didn't seem to mind. Light shone through a few of the windows of the Daijalan embassy, that country's flag flying high from the roof.

Terilyn reached down and unlocked Nathaniel's chains from the floorboard, keeping her stiletto aimed at his throat. The silent threat was more than enough to keep him from doing anything stupid. Nathaniel had been in his fair share of fights over the years, but he'd not last long against a Blade.

"Inside," Terilyn ordered.

She pressed the stiletto against his back, guiding him into a nightmare. The person who greeted him in the embassy's foyer wasn't the ambassador but the woman every Daijalan bowed to.

Crown Princess Eimarille Rourke stood beneath the light of the chandelier, a serene expression on her face as she studied him. Like Terilyn, she was dressed all in black, the color washing her out.

"Nathaniel Clementine," Eimarille said, her gaze holding his with an intensity that burned. "What do you know of Caris Dhemlan?"

Ice slid down his spine at the question, fingers spasming around the chain he held. He wanted to lie but knew it would be pointless. So he said nothing at all, and Eimarille only smiled at his silence. "Your secrets won't be kept past dawn."

She turned on her heel, and the pressure against his back from Terilyn's blade had Nathaniel walking forward. The chain connecting the manacles around his ankles scraped against the wooden floor as Eimarille led him deeper into the embassy.

No servants attended them, the place quiet to his ears. That changed when she led them into a library and went to a bookcase. She spun the rings of a miniature astrolabe, and the quiet sound of gears moving filled the room.

One of the bookcases opened outward, revealing a hidden space behind it, with stone steps leading down in a spiral staircase. Eimarille didn't look back as she gathered the skirt of her gown in both hands and stepped into that hidden space. Terilyn shoved him forward, and Nathaniel could only stumble toward a fate he couldn't escape.

The descent was slow, but Terilyn let him take his time so he didn't fall and break his neck. Though perhaps that would've been the better option.

Because down below, in the catacombs, was a horror worse than death.

When they reached the bottom of the staircase, a short corridor led to a door marked with spellwork that Nathaniel couldn't read. He thought it had something to do with silence, for it was quiet in that corridor, but his ears filled with someone's agonized scream the second he shuffled through the door Eimarille had pushed open.

He couldn't comprehend what he saw in that moment. Not right away.

The laboratory was brightly lit by gas lamps that spotlighted a worktable where a woman lay. She was naked, body covered in blood and other fluids. Her arms were outstretched and strapped down by metal restraints, as were her legs. Tubing ran from ports in her veins to machinery around her.

A man dressed in a warden's uniform had his hands buried in her chest, her ribs cracked open like grotesque butterfly wings.

Nathaniel thought she was dead, that the scream had come from one of the other two people he could see huddled in a cage at the far end of the laboratory.

But then her head turned toward him, eyes staring at him unseeingly, as the warden pushed something into place in her chest cavity. When the warden removed his hands, they were covered in blood.

"*Klovod,*" Eimarille said. "I have a task for you."

Nathaniel's mind tripped over the name, staring at the puppet master and finally understanding what he was seeing.

"You make the *rionetkas,*" he croaked out.

Terilyn shoved him forward, and he had no choice but to approach the woman's deathbed, for all that she was still alive. The stench of rotten flesh lingered in the air, even if she looked nothing like a revenant.

Set against the pulsating beat of her lungs, nestled amidst the gore of vivisection, was a clockwork metal heart. In the center of that intricate framework was the glimmer of magic, the aether beating like the heart it had replaced.

Bile crept up his throat, acid searing his tongue, as Nathaniel hunched over and got sick.

"I need to finish with this one," the *Klovod* said.

"Make it quick. This man is to be your priority." Eimarille stepped aside, her gown swirling around her ankles. The hem dragged through the blood on the floor, but the black color would hide the stains. Nathaniel averted his face from the torture happening before him, but he was unable to block out the sounds of the woman's screams and the crack of bone breaking.

Eventually the screaming cut off, and the quiet was almost worse. He chanced a glance only once, sick at the sight of the *Klovod* sewing up the woman's chest. The docile expression on her face reminded him of a child's doll—empty and mindless.

When the *Klovod* finished, he undid the metal straps, disengaged the tubing with its chemicals, and tapped a brass wand against a newly scarred chest. "Sit up."

The *rionetka* sat up, revealing no pain in the aftermath of the horrifying operation she'd undergone. The blankness in her gaze never left, and she only obeyed her master as the *Klovod* sent her to stand in a different cage from the other prisoners.

Then he turned his hideous attention on Nathaniel.

"He's a merchant. Useless for your politics," the *Klovod* said.

"He's a cog, and I want answers," Eimarille replied.

The *Klovod* grunted and came around the worktable, tapping the wand against his leg. Nathaniel jerked back, right into the point of Terilyn's stiletto. It cut through his ruined day jacket and into his skin, making him hiss.

Terilyn tipped her head back, catching his eye. "Don't move."

The *Klovod* stood in front of Nathaniel, reaching up to remove the blood-spattered goggles he wore. The scar on his cheek pulled at his lips oddly. This close, Nathaniel could see the impression of teeth in the scar tissue.

"Why are you doing this?" Nathaniel asked.

The *Klovod* raised his wand, lips twisting into a mirthless smile. "Because a star god asked it of me."

No remorse could be found in the warden's voice or his magic. Aether poured out of the clarion crystal–tipped wand and Nathaniel breathed it in unwillingly. It tasted sickly sweet in the back of his throat, seeping into him.

Foreign magic clawed through his mind, picking apart his memories without care. The pressure from the *Klovod*'s intrusion became heavier and heavier until all he could do was spit it out in the shape of words.

"Stop," Nathaniel pleaded. "*Stop.*"

The years spun away from him, unraveling like a skein of thread.

Bit by bit, memory by memory, Nathaniel lost himself to the threads the *Klovod* used to stitch him up, all anew.

"He's in love with the girl you're after. The one who casts starfire," the *Klovod* said.

"What else does the cog know?" Eimarille asked.

All the secrets Nathaniel had spent his life keeping came undone beneath the *Klovod*'s mind magic. He gave them up because it was the only way to stop the pain of the aether eating away at his mind.

When Nathaniel finally came back to himself, he was on his knees, bleeding from his nose, with Eimarille's fingers curled over his chin. At some point, someone had removed the manacles around his wrists and ankles, but freedom was a lie, there in that underground horror.

His skin didn't feel like his own, pulled tight over his bones, ready to split. His head ached, the room spinning around him, and it felt like someone else was looking up at Eimarille through his eyes.

"Do you know that every heart is meant to break?" Eimarille asked in a falsely gentle voice. "But we'll mend yours into something useful. Something that will carve Caris' into pieces and ruin the duchess' dreams."

Nathaniel's breath rattled in his lungs, and the words were slow to come, but they made it past his lips somehow. "I'll never hurt her."

"You won't have a say in the matter."

Eimarille let him go, and the *Klovod* flicked his wand at Nathaniel in a lazy, dismissive manner. "On your feet. Get undressed."

His body jerked itself to its feet, and Nathaniel swore he was screaming, but it was only in his mind. His hands stripped off his clothes with wooden motions, leaving everything on the floor as his body walked toward the worktable. He tried to stop himself, tried to dig in his heels, but his body didn't listen.

It sat on the cold metal slab, smearing someone else's blood around as he lay down beneath the gaslights. The machinery clanked and whirred when it moved around him as the *Klovod* worked to secure Nathaniel to the worktable and slide needles into his veins.

His body was docile beneath the disinterested touch, mind wrapped up in someone else's control. Nathaniel stared past the gas lamps and the chemicals favored by alchemists, screaming in the cavern of his mind where no one could hear.

But at the first touch of the scalpel against his skin, cutting deep enough to nick bone, Nathaniel found his voice again. Or the *Klovod* let him have it back.

Either way, Nathaniel screamed as if he were dying, but that was a blessing denied to him, even when the *Klovod* took his heart.

Eleven

EIMARILLE

Eimarille's arrival back in New Haven at the end of Eighth Month after the revenant attack in Amari was unexpected, to be sure.

She preferred it that way.

Her motor carriage came to a stop in front of the palace entrance within the inner courtyard. A servant immediately opened the door, offering his hand to help her out. Eimarille accepted the help and adjusted the fall of her gown's skirt once she stood on the cobblestone.

She glanced back, watching as Lisandro was helped out by Terilyn. The Blade used her right arm as if no wound existed beneath the long sleeve of her suit jacket. Eimarille knew otherwise. The burn had been healed to the point that it looked months old rather than days, courtesy of a magician.

Terilyn took Lisandro by the hand and looked at Eimarille, nodding firmly. "I have him."

"I know you do," Eimarille said before sweeping up the stairs to greet the star god who waited for her.

Innes was dressed in a fine suit that day, of a fashion that would not be out of place amongst courtiers. His lips curved in a smile that Eimarille returned with a deep curtsy.

"My lord," she said.

Innes offered her his hand, and she settled her fingers into his grip as she straightened up. "How fares Amari?"

"I've made it so the Clockwork Brigade will have much to answer for." She frowned prettily at him as they stepped inside the palace, leaving the heat of summer behind for a more moderate temperature. "But there is a girl."

Innes' expression never wavered. "I am aware of what the broadsheets are reporting."

"You promised me I would be the last Rourke and the only remaining magician in Ashion who could cast starfire."

"I hear doubt in your words, princess."

"I don't question your methods, my lord. I question the efforts of your brethren. The North Star set her decree, after all. Would it not be amiss for her to have a pawn in this game as well?"

"Would you rather walk the road Aaralyn could have given you over mine?"

"Never."

"I promised you a throne, Eimarille. You will have it."

She nodded at that pronouncement, relieved to know she still had his blessing. "I've sent a *rionetka* after the girl. She'll not see the threat."

"You hope."

"Love makes people blind."

"And what of yourself?"

"I have never let my heart blind me. I've proven that to you before, and I will prove it again today."

Innes tipped his head in her direction, pride in his eyes when he looked at her. "I must say, you are dressed better for this coup than the last one you were part of."

She'd changed clothes on the flight over, opting for a floor-length lilac-colored gown cinched in by a metal belt made out of silver. The long flowing sleeves opened at the elbow on the outside and tapered down to a length that ended past her fingertips. The high neck of the collar was tied in place with a silken bow at the back of her neck. Fitted over her shoulders, with points ending near her shoulder blades and curved around her breasts, was a filigreed metal adornment that mimicked armor.

She'd twisted her hair up into a bun secured at the back of her head, low enough that it didn't interfere with the tiara she'd chosen to wear. It wasn't one from the Iverson bloodline's collection but one which the prime minister had gifted her at the behest of a historical society in Amari.

The tiara was silver, lined with diamonds and opals, a royal headpiece her great-grandmother had apparently favored. Eimarille thought it only fitting she wore it for the meeting she steadfastly marched to.

The soldiers assigned to the palace guard nodded respectfully as Eimarille and Innes passed them in the hallways on their way to the wing of the palace Bernard worked out of.

Kote had kept her apprised of Bernard's interference with the military. Upon reflection, after everything that had occurred in Amari, Eimarille wasn't averse to the border breach he wanted. He just wouldn't be the one overseeing the incursion into Ashion.

If anyone was to break the armistice, it would be Eimarille.

"Where is the king?" Eimarille asked a passing servant as they left the public area of the palace for the private one.

The young woman dipped into a deep curtsy, looking a bit startled at Eimarille's sudden appearance. "Meeting with the prime minister in the Cobalt Room, Your Royal Highness."

Their small group moved on, following a familiar path to the room where Eimarille had observed many a meeting over the years. The guards on either side of the door leading to the Cobalt Room were too high-ranking for the job of standing watch. She eyed their uniforms and allowed herself a smile.

"Is High General Kote inside?" she asked.

The captain to her right nodded sharply. "He is, Your Royal Highness."

"Excellent." She looked over her shoulder at where Terilyn stood, holding Lisandro in her arms. "Give me a moment to get this sorted."

Innes lifted Eimarille's hand to his mouth and kissed her knuckles softly. "I await your coronation, my dear."

"I'll crown myself, thank you very much."

"Of that, I have no doubt."

Eimarille left them behind and pushed open the doors to the Cobalt Room, her sudden appearance putting a momentary halt to the argument currently being held at the long table. Eimarille let the door fall shut behind her, taking in everyone who was there.

Bernard sat at the head of the long table with Wesley to his right. Ranged down the right were men in dark suits, seated in terms of rank, with the prime minister in the chair next to Wesley. On the other side of the table sat Kote with several high-ranking military officers, all of them in uniform.

Kote stood at her arrival, as did the officers with him, while everyone else remained seated. They bowed to her, and she inclined her head at their show of manners.

"Welcome home, Your Royal Highness," Kote said before retaking his seat.

"Gentlemen," Eimarille said calmly. "It is my understanding you wish to cross the eastern border."

"What are you doing here, Eimarille? You're supposed to be managing the mess in Amari," Wesley said, appearing startled by her presence.

"I would assume you'd be absent from such a meeting as well, husband. You tend to prefer getting drunk with your contemporaries rather than participating in politics."

Wesley flushed, half rising from his seat. "You've no business here."

"On the contrary. The ruling of Ashion *is* my business, and I have every right to be here. Or have you forgotten what name I carry? Because it certainly isn't yours."

A tense pause followed her words, and Eimarille let her attention settle on Bernard. The king stared back at her through narrowed eyes, jaw clenched in a way she knew meant he was displeased.

"What I decide to do for the good of Daijal will not be waylaid by your hysterical argument, Eimarille," Bernard said into the tense silence.

She raised an eyebrow. "Do I sound hysterical?"

"Your actions speak for you. You have no say here, and my word is law. The high general will implement my orders and expand our military presence into Ashion."

"Quite so. You just will not be the one in charge."

"Eimarille, you are making a fool of yourself," Wesley snapped.

Bernard pointed a finger at her, gaze snapping with anger. "You forget your place."

"My place?" She raised her chin slightly, staring him down. "Perhaps you should remind me. Are you speaking of the one I had in Ashion when I was a child or the one you were ordered to give me here in Daijal when the Twilight Star brought me to your court after you sent Blades to murder my family?"

Someone sucked in a harsh breath on the politicians' side of the table, but no one spoke. She could feel Kote's gaze on her, warm and heavy. Eimarille knew if she asked it of him, he and his officers would hold everyone at this table at gunpoint.

"Reunification has always been our family's goal," Bernard bit out.

"Your idea of reunification is not mine."

Bernard laughed, the sound holding no humor in it. "I will not permit you to entertain this fallacy of power you seem to think belongs to you."

"*Permit?* I will be *queen*, and you will be nothing but ash."

Bernard stood, planting both hands on the table before him, leaning forward. "Get out."

Eimarille raised one hand, fingers splayed, and let the aether flow through her until it took the shape of starfire burning against her palm. "Your bloodline started the first civil war, and now you wish for a second. I will make it happen, if only to undo what your ancestors wrought, but you won't live to see it. You lost the right to starfire generations ago and had to steal *my* road in an attempt to remake yours. But you never could see the pitfalls I built you."

Bernard jerked back, face going as white as the heart of the starfire

Eimarille held in her hand. His mouth opened, but whatever he was going to say got lost in a scream when Eimarille thrust her arm forward and set him ablaze with her magic.

Starfire was the purest form of the aether, raw energy that burned white gold. The heat of its passage over the table had the politicians and Wesley pitching out of their seats with panicked shouts. Kote and his officers moved with far more precision. They stood quickly, pistols already in hand, and aimed the weapons at the men across the table from them.

"Don't move," Kote barked out.

"*Eimarille*," Wesley forced out, hunched over as he watched the burning column of starfire that used to be his father stumble backward.

She rotated her wrist until her palm faced outward and her fingers pointed at the ceiling. Magic coalesced around her arm, glittering motes of power that could never be contained by a clarion crystal–tipped wand.

Eimarille used her magic to send the burning body that was Bernard crashing through the window. The force of her magical push cracked the heavy table right down the center, breaking it in two. She made a fist, letting the starfire flicker around her curled fingers. The door behind her opened, and Eimarille didn't have to look to know that Terilyn had arrived.

"Mama?" Lisandro said in his sweet voice, sounding curious rather than scared.

Terilyn stepped up beside her, carrying Lisandro in her arms, a steady presence that soothed her in the face of Wesley's horror. Eimarille glanced over at them. "It's all right, my love. Terilyn will take you to your rooms."

"High General Kote," Terilyn said in that low, quiet voice of hers. "Do not let the queen leave your sight."

"Never, my lady," Kote promised with a crisp salute.

Terilyn stepped close enough that she could brush her lips over Eimarille's cheek before leaving, Lisandro safe in her arms. Eimarille didn't watch her go, more interested in the storm of emotions twisting across her husband's face.

"Why?" Wesley asked, voice breaking on the word.

"The Iverson bloodline was never meant to rule. I'll tell my son he has your eyes, and that you loved him, but not as much as you loved what you hoped to become, and which you will never attain," Eimarille said.

She would have killed him—for her son, for her country, for the world she wanted to shape.

The high general did it for her.

Kote's gun went off in quick succession, two neat bullet holes appearing in the center of Wesley's forehead and right over his heart. Eimarille didn't flinch at the splatter of blood that erupted on the wall behind him. Nor did she flinch at the volley of bullets that tore into the prime minister and the handful of other politicians whose loyalty could never be trusted if she let them live.

The air in the meeting rooms smelled of fire and charred flesh, tickling at the memories she had of the Inferno from so long ago. Eimarille drew in a deep breath and let the starfire she held in her hand fade to nothing. It left behind a warmth that spread through her body, centering in her chest as a feeling of rightness after all these years.

Kote holstered his pistol and turned to face her, then went to one knee. "Your Majesty."

The other officers followed his lead, some vicious sort of pride shining in their eyes as they looked at her. Eimarille dipped her head slightly in acknowledgment of their loyalty. "We have our work cut out for us, High General."

Kote got to his feet, his officers half a second behind him. "We'll follow wherever you lead."

Eimarille smiled and turned on her heels, leaving the bodies behind. She had a government to take control of and a border to cross.

But first, there was the matter of a crown.

Twelve

SOREN

Raiah tugged on Soren's shirtsleeve, peering up at him with big eyes from where she sat next to him on the train bench. "I'm hungry."

"Did you finish your fruit and nut paste bar?" Soren asked.

She wrinkled her nose at him, pouting. "It had a yucky taste."

Soren was used to travel food, but apparently the little princess' taste buds were more refined than his. He'd thought the treat he'd bought for her at the train station they'd left behind in some small trade town that morning would be enough to satisfy her. Apparently, he'd been wrong.

Soren reached for the rucksack between his feet and rifled through one of the pockets there. He wasn't used to feeding children and hadn't thought much about supplies other than buying what she could easily and safely eat. Taste had been secondary, but perhaps he should've thought about it.

They were a day's ride from Karnak, and Soren hadn't slept much since leaving Oeiras. He'd resorted to taking a stimulant to stay awake and aware of their surroundings. Soren hadn't wanted to risk riding through the back roads with Raiah for very long and had made the decision to travel the last leg of their journey by steam train.

It put them in the public eye, but it was a risk Soren had weighed and reluctantly found acceptable. It let Raiah sleep, let her stretch her little body rather than be strapped in the ride-along seat behind him for hours on end.

Raiah wasn't as recognizable beneath the little helmet and her child-sized goggles, but he knew it was odd for a warden to be traveling with anyone, much less a child. Despite Alida picking out the plainest set of clothes in Raiah's closet, they were of a make and style that clearly marked her as well-off.

Raiah's accent—refined, even for a four-year-old—stood out amidst the working-class folks they traveled with. Soren had noticed more than one odd glance thrown his way in the train carriage, but Raiah's happy demeanor was enough so far to keep anyone from enquiring about why she was with him.

Except now she was pouting because he didn't have the right snacks, and she turned her nose up at the misshapen bits of wrapped toffee he found at the bottom of his rucksack's pocket.

"I want fruit," she said.

Soren sighed and tipped the toffee back into his rucksack. "The dining carriage might have some."

Raiah perked up at that, nearly bouncing in her seat. "Let's go."

Her imperious little command reminded him of Vanya, and Soren couldn't quite hide his smile. "All right."

He'd have preferred they stay in their train carriage, but he'd learned once they'd boarded that Raiah's curiosity and inquisitive nature wasn't easily corralled. Soren stood, hefting the rucksack onto one shoulder before lifting Raiah into his arms. She wrapped her skinny arms around his neck and didn't reach for the hilt of his poison short sword. She'd taken his warning not to touch any of his weapons seriously and had so far adhered to his firm instructions.

Soren carried her down the aisle to the door that led to the narrow covered bridge that rose over the couplings, linking the two train carriages. The roar of the engine farther down the train and the rhythmic sound of the wheels spinning along the tracks drowned out almost everything as they passed into the next carriage, and then the next.

The dining carriage was meant for first-class ticket holders who could afford a sit-down meal. Everyone else on the steam train packed their own food in travel bags or ate at food stalls at one of the many stops along the railroads.

Wardens were given more leeway than most people. He didn't need to buy a first-class ticket in order to access food in the dining car, but Soren rarely took advantage of that hospitality clause from the Poison Accords. Wardens were supposed to be welcomed anywhere, but he'd found over the years that was a pretty little lie.

Raiah's presence eased the way enough that when they made it to the dining carriage, the servant on host duties didn't sneer at him. She did look down her nose at him, which was a feat in and of itself seeing as how she was half a head shorter than he was.

"Ticket, please," she demanded.

Soren hefted Raiah higher in his arms and reached for the belt pouch that held his wallet rather than his ticket. "We're not here for a table. I just need some fruit for the tithe in my care."

The servant sniffed disdainfully. "You should've brought your own food or purchased some at the last stop."

Soren smiled thinly even as he maneuvered his wallet open to snag an auron bill while keeping hold of Raiah. "We've been traveling for quite some time. I'll take whatever fresh fruit you have available."

The servant took his offered money and retreated down the narrow aisle between the rows of tables to the galley at the other end. It was between mealtimes at the moment, so the only ones sitting in the dining carriage were those taking tea or alcohol. Soren ignored the stares and waited patiently while Raiah squirmed in his arms, taking everything in.

The servant came back, holding a small paper bag in her hand, which she passed over to Soren. He shook it open, studying the green plum, purple fig, and two small apricots that sat at the bottom. She'd shirked him on fruit, but Soren wasn't in the mood to call her out on the markup.

"Thanks," he said.

Raiah reached for the paper bag as he turned back the way they'd come. He let her have it, keeping her balanced in his arms as he walked back to their seats three train carriages away. He ignored the whispers that trailed behind them but didn't much care for the piercing stares of a few passengers on the train carriage ahead of theirs.

Soren was glad for the goggles and helmet that hid Raiah's hair and half her face. She was too busy biting into the fig to chatter at him, which he was thankful for. They made it back to their bench, and Soren got Raiah settled in her seat by the window before dropping his rucksack on the floor.

He took the aisle seat again, boxing her in protectively, and kept his eye on the train carriage door they'd just come through. The prickle of unease skittering over his skin wasn't something he was willing to ignore. He hated thinking that anyone on the train could be a *rionetka*, but that distrust wouldn't easily fade.

His uneasiness was justified three stops and several hours later.

Raiah was napping with her head resting against the window when they pulled into a train station attached to a walled-off farming town in the distance. A small way station meant for travelers driving between Karnak and Bellingham sat adjacent to the tiny train station itself. The fuel pumps weren't out of place, but the ornithopter and racing carriages definitely were.

Soren's gaze lingered on the two-seat flying machine where it sat on the grass, blades rotating lazily above its round body. There was nothing out here but farmland, and its presence made Soren tense.

The platform was shorter than the train they rode, and Soren had to lean across Raiah's sleeping form to get eyes on it as the train braked to a halt. The platform was unexpectedly crowded for such an out-of-the-way stop in the prairie. Half a dozen men and women stood on it, with fitted robes that didn't quite hide the pistols holstered to their hips.

They could have been guards or gunslingers, but after everything that had occurred in the past few days, Soren wasn't leaving anything up to chance. He'd risked a fast retreat to Karnack by train for the second leg rather than the dangers of the back roads with Raiah. If he were a gambling man, this would be the worst hand of cards he'd ever held.

Soren picked up his rucksack and slung it over his shoulder before reaching for Raiah. She didn't wake when he picked her up and held her close, head tucked against his shoulder.

He made his way swiftly toward the rear of the train carriage and hit the stop request button that would notify the attendant that a rider needed to get off and retrieve luggage from a cargo carriage. That done, he slipped through the door and onto the narrow landing. No bridge connected to the cargo carriage. Soren's boots hit softly against the metal steps that led off the train, and he paused on the last step.

"Riders off!" a train attendant called out.

A uniformed woman jogged past seconds later, sleeves marked with the stripes of a baggage attendant. Soren peered around the edge of the train carriage, noted the momentarily empty platform down the way, and then jumped lightly down to the gravel.

"Are you the one who wants off?" the baggage handler asked.

"I need my velocycle," Soren said, standing so he could see the train carriages and platform behind him.

"Right, the warden. I'll need to winch down the ramp. That'll take a couple of minutes."

"Make it quick."

She scowled at him but set about doing her job. The loud clank of the cargo doors sliding open roused Raiah from her nap. She lifted her head, raising a hand to rub at her eyes before she remembered the goggles were in the way. With a pout, she shoved them up to her forehead and rubbed sleep out of her eyes.

"Are we there yet?" she asked, yawning through the question.

"Not yet," Soren said.

He could hear the baggage attendant's muffled swearing from within the cargo carriage as she clattered about. Someone stuck their head out of a window down the train, and Soren turned his back on them in favor of lifting Raiah into the cargo carriage. He hopped up after her, ignoring the affronted shout from the train attendant.

"You aren't allowed up here!"

Soren ignored her, lifting Raiah once more into his arms and hurrying to where his velocycle was locked upright in the travel rack, wheels secured in clamps. He set Raiah in the ride-along seat, buckled her in, then dragged her goggles back over her eyes.

"I want a fig," she demanded.

"Later," he said, knowing it was a lie. He'd left the paper bag with the remainder of her fruit on the seat bench. "For now, close your eyes."

"Why?"

"We're going to play a game, but you need to close your eyes first. And no peeking."

Raiah pouted at him but then squeezed her eyes shut.

He kicked at the storage lock to undo the latch, listening as the clamps clanked open. He rolled the velocycle forward, already reaching for the ignition, when someone else clambered into the cargo carriage.

Soren changed the motion of his hand without thinking, freeing his pistol with a quickness the mercenary clearly didn't expect, aimed, and pulled the trigger. The mercenary fell back into open air with a cry, the pistol in his hand going flying, red dotting the air in a wet arc.

Raiah shrieked at the noise and covered her ears while the train attendant screamed. Soren slung his leg over the seat, turned the ignition, and kicked the stand up. He gripped the handlebars and revved the engine, driving toward the open cargo carriage door so fast he left rubber burn marks on the metal floor.

Soren drove the velocycle out of the cargo carriage, front wheel angled up, and landed on grassy dirt, back wheel first. Raiah screamed behind him, high-pitched from fear, and he desperately wanted to comfort her, but now wasn't the time.

"Keep your eyes shut!" Soren shouted. "Pretend we're in a race!"

She was too young to understand how and why he was trying to protect her. But he'd promised Vanya he'd see Raiah safely to Karnack, and he'd be damned if he didn't keep that promise.

Bullets slammed into the dirt around him, aiming for his tires, but

Soren drove in a zigzag pattern at a speed that had the wind whistling past his ears. In a moment like this, he hated having Raiah behind him.

"He has the princess! Don't shoot her!" someone shouted behind them.

Soren didn't doubt for a moment they'd still come after him and Raiah. Swearing, he sped up, squinting against the wind and wishing he'd had time to put on his own helmet and goggles.

He had half a tank of fuel according to the gauge. He couldn't be sure it'd be enough to outride the racing carriages coming after them.

The ornithopter was a different problem entirely.

The steady *whup whup* sound of the ornithopter's spinning blades got louder as it drew closer. The pilot flew after them at a low angle, wind making the prairie grass around them flatten out. Soren sped up, teeth clacking together, listening to poor Raiah crying behind him in her ride-along seat.

Outrunning a flying machine wasn't viable.

Giving up Raiah wasn't an option.

Soren pressed hard on the foot brake at the same time he pulled back the brake lever on the handlebar. The velocycle's forward motion abruptly decreased. Soren modified his pressure on the rear brake as the velocycle skidded over dirt at an angle that put him perpendicular to the oncoming racing carriages.

The train had left the station in the distance, the conductor clearly not one to stick around when they had other passengers to think of. Soren couldn't even blame them, not with the threat barreling toward him and Raiah.

She hiccuped on a sob, voice coming out on a scared little wail. "Papa!"

Dust floated in the air from behind the wheels of the racing carriages. Soren couldn't hear the pounding of his heart over the ornithopter's approach. He watched as one of the racing carriages spun out, skidding to a halt, a dark-clad woman tumbling out of it. She rolled with the motion, coming to her feet with a pistol in her grip, the barrel pointed at him.

"Move away from her!" the woman shouted.

"No," Soren said through gritted teeth, knowing they couldn't hear him.

He'd never know if they were *rionetkas*, dancing to the steps of a master Soren couldn't see. His instinct said yes, but instinct wasn't proof. Vanya would want proof of some sort—bodies with vivisection scars and clockwork metal hearts beating in place of real ones.

Except Vanya wasn't here, and Soren knew of only one way he could return to the man who haunted his memories during every lonely night spent in the poison fields.

This was his road, and maybe it was always meant to be walked this way.

Soren raised his hands, taking in the threats surrounding them. "Close your eyes, Raiah. Everything's going to be all right."

Soren tapped into that well of power he'd tried to ruthlessly carve out of his awareness for most of his life, the aether like a dream once lost coming back to bleed through him. He felt the spark in his veins, heat cracking through his chest, searing through his fingers.

It washed through him like a long-ago inferno—and he let the starfire burn.

The Emperor's Bone Palace (Infernal War Saga II) will release on April 10, 2023 .

If you like urban fantasy and mythology, check out Hailey Turner's Soulbound series, starting with *A Ferry of Bones & Gold*.

Join Hailey Turner's newsletter for future updates.

Glossary

Short descriptions of words, acronyms, and phrases used in the story that weren't readily explained in text. Included as well are character names.

A.O.C.: Age of Constellations. A past Age on Maricol that occurred after A.O.S. and before A.O.P.

A.O.P.: Age of Progress. The current Age on Maricol, beginning in 0 A.O.P.

A.O.S.: Age of Starfall. The first Age on Maricol that encompassed landing and initial colonization of Maricol. This Age held the Dying Times and the Great Separation.

Aaralyn: Star god. Also known as the North Star, patron goddess of life. Apex star god of the Star Order. Her constellation is the Wolf, and her tattoo is located on her right arm.

Aeronaut: One who captains or crews on an airship.

Aether: The fifth element that powers magic and clarion crystals, located in an otherworldly plane.

Age: Denotations of historical and current eras.

Airfield: A landing field located outside major cities and large towns for the anchorage of airships.

Airship: A lighter-than-air craft powered by steam engines and commercial flight balloons.

Akina, Kote: Daijalan. High General of the Daijal army.

Alida: Solarian. Majordomo to Vanya's household.

Alrickson: E'ridian. Listed in the royal genealogies. Current *ceann-cinnidh* of Clan Storm.

Amari: City. Capital of Ashion.

Ashion: Country. Debt bondage is outlawed within its borders. Its capital city is Amari. The country's patron guiding star is Aaralyn, the North Star. The country's affirmed constellation is the Wolf.

Ashionen: Denoting ties to or nationality of Ashion. Language descriptor.

Astrolabe: Astronomical instrument used for navigation.

Auclair, Brielle: Ashionen. Listed in the nobility genealogies. Named Whisper in the Clockwork Brigade. Oldest child of Meleri.

Auclair, Dureau: Ashionen. Listed in the nobility genealogies. Named Locke in the Clockwork Brigade. Youngest child of Meleri.

Auclair, Lore: Ashionen. Listed in the nobility genealogies. Named Mainspring in the Clockwork Brigade. Middle child of Meleri.

Auclair, Meleri: Ashionen. Listed in the nobility genealogies. Spymaster. Named Fulcrum in the Clockwork Brigade. Head of the Auclair bloodline.

Auron: Currency. Used in every country on Maricol.

Automaton: A clockwork machine that varies in size, shape, and use. Generally powered by steam engines but can also be powered by clarion crystals and the aether.

Bellingham: City. Located in Solaria.

Blade: Secretive Daijalan Star Order sect of assassins.

Blaine: E'ridian. Listed in the nobility genealogies. Clan Storm. Married to Honovi. Last surviving member of the Westergard bloodline.

Bloodline: Those of noble and royal families who can trace their lineage back thousands of years through genealogies to prove genetics not damaged by poison.

Broadsheets: Daily printed publication containing news.

Caelum: Solarian. Chief Minister to the Imperial throne.

Calhames: City. Capital of Solaria.

Callisto: Star god. Also known as the Dawn Star, patron goddess of death. Her constellation is the Lion, and her tattoo is located on neck and throat.

Catacombs: Ancient tunnels and passageways built beneath Amari with lost technology.

Ceann-Cinnidh: (pl. *cinn-chinnidh*) Ruling rank in E'ridia. Position in the *Comhairle nan Cinnidhean.*

Civil War: The first war between bloodlines that ultimately cleaved Ashion into two countries, forming Daijal in the west and leaving Ashion in the east.

Clans: Distinctive groups within E'ridia. Currently number six in total.

Clarion crystal: Crystal mined from the earth that can transmute the aether into magic or energy, depending on the cut.

Clementine, Nathaniel: Ashionen. Merchant and heir to the Clementine Trading Company. Cog in the Clockwork Brigade.

Clockwork Brigade: Underground rebellion originating in Ashion that exists to free debt slaves in Daijal and smuggle them to freedom in other countries, as well as work against the Daijal court.

Cog: A rebel belonging to the Clockwork Brigade.

Collector's Guild: A powerful association formed in Daijal that helps companies and individuals find and retrieve escaped debt slaves.

Comhairle nan Cinnidhean: Ruling body of E'ridia.

Constellation: Stars in the sky that represent a star god in a celestial map.

Cosian: City. Located in Ashion.

Daijal: Country. Debt bondage is sanctioned within its borders and an integral part of its economy. Its capital city is New Haven. The country's patron guiding star is Innes, the Twilight Star. The country's affirmed constellation is the Viper.

Daijalan: Denoting ties to or nationality of Daijal. Language descriptor.

Death-defying machine: Machine that can turn the dead into revenants on a mass scale.

Debt bondage: Legalized slavery that results from citizens in Daijal putting up their lives as collateral on bank loans and being forced to pay it off with work when they cannot afford monetary payment. Bank loans with life collateral come with astronomically high interest rates, ensuring the people who are collected for bondage never escape it. The debt can be applied to families and rolled into generations.

Debt collector: A bounty hunter working for the Collector's Guild who hunts down and retrieves escaped debt slaves.

Debt slave: Someone who has sold themselves as collateral to a bank to pay off a loan. Their status is denoted by bank numbers tattooed onto their necks.

Delani: Current wardens' governor.

Dhemlan, Caris: Ashionen. Listed in the nobility genealogies. Magician. Engineer and heir to the Six Point Mechanics Company. Undocumented member of the Rourke bloodline and youngest child of Queen Ophelia.

Dhemlan, Emmitt: Ashionen. Listed in the nobility genealogies. Engineer and owner of the Six Point Mechanics Company. Caris' adoptive father.

Dhemlan, Portia: Ashionen. Listed in the nobility genealogies. Engineer and owner of the Six Point Mechanics Company. Caris' adoptive mother.

Dying Times, the: A period of time during A.O.S. when the planet's ancient colonists struggled to adapt to Maricol's poison and deal with the threat of revenants.

E'ridia: Country. Debt bondage is outlawed within its borders. Its capital city is Glencoe. The country's patron guiding star is Nilsine, the Dusk Star. The country's affirmed constellation is the Eagle.

E'ridian: Denoting ties to or nationality of E'ridia. Language descriptor.

Emperor/Empress: Ruler of Solaria who has claim to the Imperial throne.

Emporium: A seller's market bridging the space between two inner defensive walls of Istal.

Farren: Star god. Also known as the Eclipse Star, dual patron god and goddess of the sea. Their constellation is the Leviathan, and their tattoo is located on their back.

Fletcher, Samuel: Daijalan. Listed in the nobility genealogies. Engineer and inventor. Creator of the death-defying machine.

Foxborough: City. Located in Ashion.

Garnier, Sabine: Daijalan. Listed in the nobility genealogies. Magician. Cog in the Clockwork Brigade.

Genealogies: Identification records that track families from the earliest Age on Maricol. Created in the past to weed out genetic mutations caused by poison. Currently used as class markers.

Glencoe: City. Capital of E'ridia.

Great Separation, the: A period of time during A.O.S. when the people of Maricol split into different countries under the guidance of the star gods.

Haighmoor: City. Located in Ashion.

Helia: City. Located in Daijal.

Honovi: E'ridian. Listed in the royal genealogies. Clan Storm. Aeronaut captain, *jarl* to a *ceann-cinnidh*, and ambassador for his country.

Houses: Noble bloodlines in Solaria.

Imperial throne: Seat of power in Solaria.

Inferno: A coup by Daijal against Ashionen, perpetuated by a star god, that resulted in the Rourke bloodline and all cadet branches being annihilated.

Innes: Star god. Also known as the Twilight Star, patron god of fire. His constellation is the Viper, and his tattoo is located on both shoulders and his pectorals.

Inventor's Guild: An engineering association with chapters in every country that helps members find mentors, jobs, teaching positions, and other work. It also provides networking opportunities to fund projects.

Istal: City. Located in Daijal.

Iverson, Aleesia: Daijalan. Listed in the royal genealogies. Queen of Daijal.

Iverson, Bernard: Daijalan. Listed in the royal genealogies. King of Daijal.

Iverson, Wesley: Daijalan. Listed in the royal genealogies. Prince of Daijal.

Jarl: Title of an heir to a *ceann-cinnidh* in E'ridia.

Karnak: City. Located in Solaria.

Khaur, Ezra: Daijalan. Listed in the nobility genealogies. Cog in the Clockwork Brigade.

Khaur, Melvin: Daijalan. Listed in the nobility genealogies. Magician. Named Marshal in the Clockwork Brigade, providing him with an officer-level position to guide cogs.

Kimathi, Artyom: Solarian. Listed in the nobility genealogies. Son of Joelle and Heir to the House of Kimathi.

Kimathi, Joelle: Solarian. Listed in the nobility genealogies. *Vezir* to the House of Kimathi. Head of her House.

Kimathi, Karima: Solarian. Listed in the nobility genealogies. Daughter of Joelle and mother to Nicca.

Kimathi, Nicca: Solarian. Listed in the nobility genealogies. Granddaughter to Joelle Kimathi. Wife to Vanya Sa'Liandel. Deceased.

Klovod, the: Urovan word for *puppet master*. Ex-warden who is a magician and the creator of *rionetkas*.

Legion: Standing army of Solaria.

Legionnaire: Soldier in the Legion.

Lehan, Wyatt: Daijalan. Engineer and inventor.

Magic: The transmuted form of aether.

Magician: A person gifted with the ability to control the aether and transmute it into magic and control it with a wand.

Maricol: World. Named from a linguistic shift of the word *miracle*. The planet refugees from a galactic war drifted to after their generation ships were thrown off course. Its high levels of alkaline, alkaloids, spores, poisons, and toxins requires continuous alchemist intervention for people to survive.

Matriskav: City. Capital of Urova.

Mind magic: A type of magic some magicians are skilled with that can interfere with a person's thoughts and memories. Can also be used to control people.

Month: Part of the Fourteen Month calendar Maricol runs on.

Motor carriage: Four-wheel ground vehicle.

New Haven: City. Capital of Daijal.

Nilsine: Star god. Also known as the Dusk Star, patron goddess of wind. Her constellation is the Eagle, and her tattoo is located on her right thigh.

Northern Plains: Geographical area spanning much of Ashion and part of Daijal.

Oeiras: City. Located in Solaria.

Ornithopter: Flight machine with spinning blades powered by a steam engine.

Poison Accords: Binding agreement between all countries to tithe citizens to the wardens to ensure continued cleansing of the poison fields inside their borders and removal of revenants.

Port Avi: City. Capital of the Tovan Isles.

***Praetoria* legionnaire:** A soldier in a specialized unit who guards the Imperial throne and the House that controls it.

Provence: An administrative district in Ashion and Daijal. Generally overseen by a noble bloodline.

Revenant: (pl. revenants) Dead infected by spores that rise to walk again.

Rionetka: (pl. *rionetkas*) Urovan word for *puppet*. People controlled through mechanical means, the aether, and mind magic.

Rixham: City. Located in Solaria. Permanently walled off and inhabited by revenants.

Rourke, Alasandair: Ashionen. Listed in the royal genealogies. Deceased prince of Ashion.

Rourke, Eimarille: Ashionen and Daijalan. Listed in the royal genealogies. Princess and heir to the Ashionen throne through blood as well as the Daijalan throne through marriage.

Rourke, Lisandro: Ashionen and Daijalan. Listed in the royal genealogies. Prince and son of Eimarille and Wesley.

Rourke, Ophelia: Ashionen. Listed in the royal genealogies. Deceased queen of Ashion.

Sa'Liandel, Raiah: Solarian. Listed in the royal genealogies. Daughter of Vanya and Nicca. Heir to the Imperial throne and member of the House of Sa'Liandel.

Sa'Liandel, Taye: Solarian. Listed in the royal genealogies. Emperor Consort of Solaria and member of the House of Sa'Liandel. Deceased.

Sa'Liandel, Vanya: Solarian. Listed in the royal genealogies. Prince then Emperor of Solaria. Member of the House of Sa'Liandel.

Sa'Liandel, Zakariya: Solarian. Listed in the royal genealogies. Empress of Solaria and member of the House of Sa'Liandel. Deceased.

Scarlette: Daijalan. Cog in the Clockwork Brigade and freed debt slave.

Seaville: City. Located in Solaria.

Sextant: Double reflecting mirrored instrument used for navigation.

Ship-city: Mechanized Tovanian ships that traverse Maricol's oceans and seas.

Solaria: Country. Debt bondage is outlawed within its borders. Its capital city is Calhames. The country's patron guiding star is Callisto, the Dawn Star. The country's affirmed constellation is the Lion.

Solarian: Denoting ties to or nationality of Solaria. Language descriptor.

Spores: The reproductive unit of a plant and fungus that reanimates the dead to ensure future continuous propagation.

Star god: One of six immortals who are the guiding stars for the citizens and countries of Maricol. Each star god was a refugee during the Age of Comets. Upon landing on Maricol thousands of years ago, they were poisoned by the planet and the aether to such a degree that they cannot die and became revered as gods.

Star Order: Continent-wide religion that worships the six star gods.

Starfire: The most powerful application of transmuting aether into magic and an extremely rare ability. Considered a mark of royalty or someone with connection to a royal bloodline.

Submersible: Underwater vehicle.

Telegraph: Point-to-point text messaging machine.

Televox: Handheld communication device. A newer invention.

Terilyn: Urovan. Blade.

Tithe: Citizen of any country given as payment under the Poison Accords to the wardens. Tithes are trained at the Warden's Island and turned into wardens through alchemy. Not all tithes survive the process.

Tovan Isles: Country. Debt bondage is outlawed within its borders. Its capital city is Port Avi. The country's patron guiding star is Farren, the Eclipse Star. The country's affirmed constellation is the Leviathan.

Tovanian: Denoting ties to or nationality of the Tovan Isles. Language descriptor.

Trade tongue: Language drawn from all others on Maricol into a pidgin form spoken for trade.

Urova: Country. Debt bondage is outlawed within its borders. Its capital city is Matriskav. The country's patron guiding star is Xaxis, the Midnight Star. The country's affirmed constellation is the Bear.

Urovan: Denoting ties to or nationality of Urova. Language descriptor.

Vasilyet: An administrative district in Solaria governed by a major House and overseen by a *vezir*.

Veil: A woven device created with thread magic that can alter a person's facial appearance.

Velocycle: Shortened from velocity cycle. Two-wheel ground vehicle.

Vezir: Governing official of a *vasilyet*. Typically head of a major House.

Wand: A device used by magicians to focus the aether into magic, usually with the help of clarion crystal.

Warden: A person who is tithed from a country by order of the Poison Accords into the ranks of wardens. They become stateless and neutral. Alchemy is used to make them immune to most poisons and toxins found in the poison fields. Their sole job is to patrol the borders between countries and the ones between the living and dead, as well as map the poison fields for later alchemy intervention to cleanse the land.

Warden's Island, the: Island located in the middle of the Celestine Lake, where wardens are trained and report back to. Considered a neutral administrative city under the Poison Accords.

Wastelands: Desert. Located in Solaria and rife with revenants and spores.

Xaxis: Star god. Also known as the Midnight Star, patron god of earth. His constellation is the Bear, and his tattoo is located on his hands and forearms.

Zip gun: A rapid-fire, multibarrel firearm.

Author's Notes

Creating a new world is always intimidating, but it never stops being fun. I love getting to tell stories, and sharing them never fails to bring me joy, even when I want to scream at the characters.

Special thanks goes out to May Archer, Lily Morton, Lucy Lennox, Aimee Nicole Walker, Jex Lane, and Sheena Jolie, who listened to me swear about this book over the course of nine months as I tried to finish it around a crazy trial schedule at my firm. Leslie Copeland will always be the last bastion of sanity for when I question my words. Bear never fails to make my words look pretty on the page.

I would be thrilled and grateful if you would consider reviewing *The Prince's Poisoned Vow*. I appreciate all honest reviews, positive or negative. Reviews definitely help my books get seen, so thank you!

Connect with Hailey

Keep up with book news by joining Hailey Turner's newsletter and get several free short stories.

Join the reader group on Facebook: Hailey's Hellions.
Follow Hailey on Instagram.
Follow Hailey's author page on Facebook.
Follow Hailey on Facebook.
Follow Hailey on Goodreads.
Follow Hailey on Pinterest.
Follow Hailey on BookBub.
Visit Hailey's website.

Other Works By Hailey Turner

M/M Science Fiction Military Romance:

Captain Jamie Callahan, son of a wealthy senator and socialite mother, is a survivor.
Staff Sergeant Kyle Brannigan, a Special Forces operative, is a man with secrets.
Alpha Team, the Metahuman Defense Force's top-ranked field team, is where the two collide and their lives will never be the same.

Metahuman Files
In the Wreckage
In the Ruins
In the Shadows
In The Blood
In The Requiem
In the Solace

A Metahuman Files: Classified Novella

Out of the Ashes
New Horizons
Fire In The Heart

M/M Urban Fantasy:

Patrick Collins is a broken mage running from his past.
Jonothon de Vere is a god pack alpha werewolf searching for a home.
In a world where magic is real, myths and legends exist, and gods
walk the earth, Patrick and Jono are thrown together by the Fates
themselves to fight against an enemy that threatens to consume the
world. For if the gods fall and demons from every hell rise up,
humanity won't stand a chance.

Soulbound
A Ferry of Bones & Gold
All Souls Near & Nigh
A Crown of Iron & Silver
A Vigil in the Mourning
On the Wings of War
An Echo in the Sorrow
A Veiled & Hallowed Eve

Soulbound Universe Standalones
Resurrection Reprise

LGBTQ+ Epic steampunk-inspired fantasy:

Welcome to Maricol, where the land will kill you, kinship turns the
gears of war, and burning the dead lest they come back to life is the
only way to survive.

Infernal War Saga

The Prince's Poisoned Vow

The Emperor's Bone Palace

Infernal War Saga Novella

An Emporium of Hearts

Contemporary gay romance

Short stories previously published in the Heart2Heart Charity Anthologies.

From the Heart: A Short Story Collection

Audible

All of Hailey Turner's books are available in audiobooks. Visit Audible to discover your next favorite listen.

Hailey Turner Audiobooks

Thanks for reading!

CPSIA information can be obtained
at www.ICGtesting.com
Printed in the USA
LVHW041513170523
747246LV00001B/23